An
Uncompromising
Place

An Uncompromising Place

Keith Weaver

IGUANA

Publisher: Greg Ioannou
Editor: Holly Warren
Front cover image: Courtesy of iStock by Getty Images
Front cover design: Victoria Feistner
Publicity and Branding: Emily Niedoba

Library and Archives Canada Cataloguing in Publication

Weaver, Keith, 1947-, author
        An uncompromising place / Keith Weaver.

Issued in print and electronic formats.
ISBN 978-1-77180-125-6 (paperback).--ISBN 978-1-77180-126-3 (epub).--
ISBN 978-1-77180-127-0 (kindle).--ISBN 978-1-77180-128-7 (pdf)

        I. Title.

PS8645.E2175U53 2015   C813'.6   C2015-903920-7
                                               C2015-903921-5

This is the original print edition of *An Uncompromising Place*.

For Maggie,

who creates a large bright world

The past is never dead. It's not even past.

The distinction between past, present, and future is only a stubbornly persistent illusion.

Le passé n'éclairant plus l'avenir, l'esprit marche dans les ténèbres.

(When the past no longer illuminates the future, the spirit walks in darkness.)

One

So that's it? I asked myself rhetorically, standing there clutching my envelope, like a lost soul. It was a bright afternoon in early July. Smiling cumulus clouds drifted, like fat cherubs in cerulean bathwater. Looking up and down University Avenue, my gaze was met by brightly but minimally clad bodies and sunglassed faces. It seemed an incongruous setting against which to have just chucked my job. Somewhere inside, a whiny little worm squeaked, "Go back! It's not too late! Tell them you've changed your mind!" But there was no going back, and even the worm knew it.

The walk home took twenty-five minutes—longer than usual because this time I followed an unaccustomed route: behind hospitals, through small internal courtyards, under a row of trees next to a church. A light, warm breeze plucked sensuously at everything, and the metallic chirping of sparrows in the green canopy above was a hallmark of summer. I opened the door of my condo to see my suitcase and bag of books next to the coat closet where I had placed them that morning, reminding me that this whole affair actually did have a plan behind it. I called my real estate agent and booked a meeting with her for five days later. Grabbing my cellphone charger, the suitcase, and the bag of books, I headed back down to the parking garage. Within ten minutes I was on the Parkway driving north. Looking in the mirror, I expected to see a snarling mass of work-drugged, road-raged commuters, trying to beat the outbound jams (it was, of course, the attempt to beat the jams that caused them), steaming home toward domestic dystopia, grass that grew too fast, and a mower that had bit the dust again. But it was too early, and the rush wouldn't begin in earnest for another half-hour.

Reflections on my life usually follow one of two courses. Either I lean back smugly thinking that I have done not too badly at all. A life full of interest. Good professional career. Well known among my peer group. Lots of published work. A man at the top of his form. Or, I hunker down, depressed, reflecting on what a botch I have made of things. A life that veered hither and yon out of control. A career adrift, buffeted continuously by fate into its present doldrum—then a stricken feeling that there is no such thing as a single doldrum—unknown outside a ragtag bunch of querulous and argumentative eggheads. Author of a collection of obscure papers now consigned to that great Sargasso archive of technical literature. A man scarcely knowing which way is up.

That day I had been leaning toward the brighter image, but the minor earthquake of occupational disconnection was turning that into a struggle.

I was now on the freeway, and the miles sped past, the kilometres even faster. Obsessively replaying the exit interview in my head, reliving the mild feeling of amputation as I had shoved my access cards across the desk, I almost missed the exit at

Highway 62 and the road to Greenvale. Here, the traffic was even lighter. Rich farmland. Corn six feet high or more. Three villages, well spaced out. Then the row of hills came into view, the first distant cohort of moraines. The road began to wander more, moving around and through a densely packed herd of drumlins.

And then I crossed what had become an emotional boundary: I was approaching home. I was into the extraordinary little Green Vale, home to the eponymous village. Friendly glacial giants crowded in on both sides, forming a whimsical topography through which the Muir River danced and giggled.

As on catching sight of a disrobed beloved, my mood shot through the roof as my house came into view, a rock-solid stone structure, set to the left of the road just past the first of the two S-bends in the village, and sheltering among scattered deciduous trees. The window boxes of geraniums danced and applauded my arrival; the rock garden managed a chiselled smile; and the weeping willows on low-lying land to the south, near the edge of my property, wept openly for joy.

There had also been a plan behind my acquisition of the house. Having a condo in Toronto, I really didn't need a house, but I had decided to bring it back to its original condition over three or four years and then sell it. However, having a condo equipped for one person reflected a deeper personal situation that I resisted facing: the fact that I had never come to terms with the loss of my wife Alice, now, incredibly, almost twenty years in the past, the fact that I was in the grip of a variation on the Peter Pan syndrome despite my denials, my irrational fear of becoming bland statistical wallpaper paste—a house in the suburbs, a station wagon, a wife who was 3.2 inches shorter than me, 1.9 children, and three-quarters of a dog. Studiously ignoring all this, I stuck to my blinkered buy-renovate-sell plan. But, as both mice and men will testify...

The renovation was back-breaking work, but secretly I loved it. There were the standard tasks associated with renewing any old building, but then there were the items that gave me greatest pleasure: a lovely rock garden at the front of the house, terraced on the model of a small irregular amphitheatre, in a rough semicircle enclosing a stone patio; an outside living space patio at the rear, covered in large paving slabs, and including an inviting open wooden arbour, trellised on two sides and covered by vines; and then my large vegetable garden. Almost every weekend I was at it, from late April to the end of November, plus several high-intensity weeks each summer when work crews needed to be supervised. It was all a managed project, very like the sort that I oversaw every year at work, but without the irrational clients—if I discounted myself, that is—and I developed a particular fondness for tracking things on my charts and budget sheets. When it was all finished, I tore up my original plan for selling. I had put a great deal of myself into the place by then and loved it far too much.

I unloaded the suitcase and books from the car, unlocked the house, threw open all the doors and windows, pulled on some shorts, and then went out to the front patio.

The afternoon sun was a few cubits short of the yardarm, and there was time to relax and begin coming to terms with my new life situation.

A mental picture of Ms. Anderson came into view. The exit interview had intruded again.

"Are you sure about your decision? At," and here she consulted a file prominently labelled Richard Gould, Principal Consultant, "at fifty-four you're very young to retire." I told her I was sure.

"The separation package you've opted for wasn't really directed at people of your calibre. Are you sure that the package hasn't influenced your decision?" Of course it had influenced my decision. If someone stepped up to you with that much cash, would you brush it off as a bagatelle? And isn't that the purpose of a separation package?

"I just want to make sure that you've considered all the angles of this. Let's face it, it's a big decision." This was becoming tedious. It was a big decision, but rest assured that I wasn't going to wake up the next morning at four a.m. in a muck sweat and a blind panic wondering what the hell I had done. But I had to allow her genuine concern and that she meant well.

But then, there was the view from my front patio, the scene around me, which I found hugely elevating. It had been a year of good rainfall, and the large muscular shoulders of the hills protecting the valley from all harm were green and lush. The air had that "Big Mama" overripeness of high summer, when the Earth has delivered on its promise of bounty, and the fruit trees are bent low by their own fecundity. The late afternoon sun cast a shifting dappled gold over my glorious property, and I responded to the first stirrings of hunger, realizing that I had not eaten anything since toast and jam that morning.

There were three restaurants in the village, plus the excellent dining room at the Pavilion, but on such a beautiful day the obvious choice had to be the patio at The Fox and Esker, behind and above the old railway station, and looking down the valley. Even as I thought of the change I had embarked upon, there was a clear sense of my life resetting itself. There was no doubt that I would miss my work—the technical and project challenges, the research in support of new projects, the satisfying application of my expertise, and the daily company of a handful of very solid colleagues—but already it felt like all that was slipping away, becoming dreamlike, yesterday's relevance. Tomorrow would be the first day of my new life, and although undoubtedly there would be one or two false steps initially, already my new projects were settling in as the current reality. What I was looking forward to was the challenge and potential reward that lay ahead in my major project, although I couldn't have guessed just how high that was going to soar. Nor could I have known how far-reaching would be the personal devastation I was going to face.

Two

First respondent: "What?! You restored some old house?" Second respondent: "And you're going to live in it most of the time?" Third respondent: "And it's out in the sticks?"

This all happened a few months before I retired. The respondents were colleagues at work with whom I had shared my plans for a prospective new life. The same questions kept surfacing:

1. How do you just move into a new life?
2. Won't the slow pace of the country get to you?
3. How will you fill your time?

As answer to the second of these questions, I pointed out that I had been raised in the country so I knew what I was getting into. The third question I fielded rhetorically by noting that surely they all knew me well enough by now and were aware that I had many interests. It was my rejoinder to the first question that stopped them cold: "Gentlemen," I began sonorously, "you must know that a large fraction of people are led through life by the nose. They don't know where they're going or why, and they don't even know who has hold of their nose. But their main comfort is that they don't need to ask questions or do a lot of thinking for themselves." The great poster called *The Lure of the Underground* flashed across my mind, but it would have been too difficult to put across in a few words.

Instead, I looked around at them theatrically.

"But there's a difference between cities and villages. In cities, nobody wants to know anything about anyone else, so you find most people trying to avoid any sort of eye contact. In cities, personal isolation is not only possible, it's easy, it's the default, in fact it can be very difficult to avoid. In villages, most people want to know everything about everybody else, and there's not much some of them will stop at to find out what they're burning to know. So, in a village, it's best just to play the game, and the easiest way to do that is to find the three important gatekeepers, and get to know them as soon as you can." This was almost turning into a technical presentation, and I glanced encouragingly from face to face to see who could suggest the identities of these gatekeepers. They returned my gaze in silence, as would cows at dusk, waiting their turn to be milked.

"So, when one is new to a village, there are three people to look for immediately. They are the village librarian, the owner of the hardware store, and the owner of the best pub. If the village doesn't have all three of these, it's apt to have a wizened social life, and it's time to get out of Dodge. The librarian has to be interested in books and people, but not be bossy or prying. The hardware store owner should 'hold court' in his establishment, where he's the chief jester and raconteur. The publican has to be the ultimate chameleon, capable of switching from deep philosophy to ribald humour across the span of a conjunction."

I was able to report to them that Greenvale possessed all these characters and that they all passed the requirements with generous flourishes. "So, you see gentlemen, the eagle has landed."

A little later, I asked around. They had all queried each other on what I had been talking about, and two expressed the view that obviously I was retiring none too soon.

But in fact I *had* found all three of these people in Greenvale.

I knew as soon as I bought the house that the locals would want all the details and would seek them out displaying an intensity and dedication at least equal to that applied by Michael Ventris and John Chadwick in the decipherment of Linear B.

A trip to the library led me to Mrs. Williamson. She had been an accountant at a local firm, and on leaving that firm she went into business for herself, but she also pursued a long-term interest. She presented to the village council a business plan for a library that had knocked them all flat. The village community centre had long wanted to start a small library, and the village council had put up $1500 for books to get it started, but that was just a lick and a promise, waving limply in the breeze without benefit of plan, strategy, or enthusiasm. Mrs. Williamson had matched that sum on a four-to-one basis by drumming up donations from individuals and businesses. She had generated a full business plan, whereas the two other aspirants, both retired teachers, had only flimsy milquetoast suggestions to camouflage their hopes for a comfortable sinecure. Mrs. Williamson swept them away, set about her new role with fierce energy, and within two years had built up a respectable 16 000-book collection using donations, purchases of castoffs at fire sale rates, and extracting good will from anyone who came into her crosshairs.

Despite her reputation, she was friendly and relaxed. The day I met her, although she was all business, she radiated calmness and an air of professional curiosity. Her pleasant attire—olive slacks, white blouse, and a short grey jacket—matched a well-kept figure, and complemented her high forehead and grey eyes which formed part of a sober expression (neither fierce nor vacant). It all added up to an alluring combination of knock-out young woman looks overlain by maturity and depth.

"You're new here." It wasn't a question.

"Yes, I purchased the old Adams house and I'm going to fix it up."

"Very admirable," she allowed, "but it's in pretty bad shape, isn't it?"

"That's the skin-deep assessment. It will take lots of time, effort, and money, but it's basically solid."

We chatted a bit more, and she collected some personal information about me.

"But what I really would like is a library card. How do I get one?"

She looked at me doubtfully. "Do you think that there could be anything here you would be interested in? What I mean is, I'm proud of our collection, but it's only a village library after all."

5

"One never knows," I said, "but since I plan to be here, I want to support local institutions, and there are not many things more important to a community than its library. After all," I said, modifying an Italian proverb, "a village without a library is like a body without a soul."

This fell well short of moving her to maudlin tears of joy, but in a few minutes I had my card.

"So now," I said, "how could I make a $2000 donation to the library?"

She came as close to doing a double take as Mrs. Williamson would permit herself, but recovered nicely. I filled out and passed her a cheque, and offered to bring cast-off books from Toronto whenever I could, an offer that was received with both alacrity and grace. We said goodbye for now, and I left knowing that, from then on, Mrs. Williamson would hunt down and destroy without mercy any unfavourable gossip about me.

In terms of size, Greenvale is at one of those cusps. It is too small to attract an assault by the usual grotesque settlement of big boxes at the edge of town, but big enough to worry about the possibility. Entering the village from the south, one encounters, in order, a pharmacy, two service stations, a bakery, a general store, a hardware store, the railway station, two pub/restaurants, a seasonal arts and crafts gallery, a tiny cellphone shop, an Internet café, the post office, the liquor store, and the municipal offices. There was once a hotel, but it had been converted to a tasteful set of condos some years earlier. The bakery struggled on valiantly. The pharmacy, general store, and hardware store had managed to expand sufficiently that the capital cost for entry of potential big box competitors seemed to be too great, but it was a nervous standoff rather than any decisive Wellingtonian defeat.

Jimmy Napier owns the hardware store. He is small and wiry, has short, steel-grey curly hair, a twinkle, and laughter lines that crowd the corners of his eyes. He had adopted the trading name of one of the larger chains, but he kept the place as a traditional rural hardware store. The wooden floor squeaks eloquently. His cash register sits atop an authoritative bar he had salvaged from the hotel when it was converted. Two large barrels in front of the bar provide welcome rests for tired forearms. On the wall just inside the door hang four or five old style brooms, none of which, I was to discover, had sold in over fifteen years. I half-expected to see a parrot that would shout "Billy Macaw!" "It be Miss Purity!" or just whistle lewdly.

Jimmy actually went by the name of "Lonny", and it was his quiet private joke until I rumbled him in a discussion about logarithms and the cognate link to his surname.

"That's the trouble with you educated people", he complained in some heat. "You know too much."

"Don't worry, Lonny", I reassured him conspiratorially. "Instead of a little secret for one, it can now be a little secret for two."

"Get away!" he said when I told him about renovating the Adams place. "It's a fecking ruin!"

"You might think that", I agreed, "if you just looked casually through any of the broken windows. It won't be a quick fix, but the bones are good."

He looked at me closely. "By God, you're serious about this, aren't you?"

"Yes, and I expect to be wanting from you quite a few supplies as the work moves on. Sometime when you have a spare half-hour, perhaps you could go over the place with me, I can show you what I have in mind, and we can get a better idea what I might need from your emporium here."

His look of doubt mellowed to one of speculation. "Well, me schedule is never wide open, but I dare say we can carve a decent niche. When do you plan to start?" I could see him juggling schedules for bingo, pub nights, bird watching, drag racing.

"This weekend I'll begin to work on drainage. And I want to have a new roof on the place by the end of the autumn."

We arranged a date for a tour without fuss or bother.

One can find characters in cities, but they tend, in my experience, to be more odd than interesting. In villages, things are a bit different.

Jasper Armadale is a massive block of rough-hewn manhood. His sandy hair is buzzed, his face is a set of intersecting planes looking as though they were cut using an adze, his legs are like tree trunks, and in an average day he might utter ten words. His pub, The Fox and Esker, has no need of a bouncer.

I had come directly from Lonny's place; it was late afternoon. The Fox and Esker had been a railway warehouse in a previous existence. The high ceilings and large beams blended well with the bare brick interior walls. A large fireplace had been fitted on the east side of the room and included an inset alcove that looked as though it could store six or eight cords of firewood, large windows had been installed in the south-facing wall giving a spectacular view over the exterior patio and down the valley, the warehouse offices had been converted into a kitchen, and a large peninsular bar extended from the kitchen to halfway down the room. Walking up to the bar I nodded to Jasper and asked for a pint of a good local ale brewed about fifteen kilometres to the south. For a large man, Jasper moves with economy and surprising grace. He placed my drink in front of me with a nod, and said, "New?"

I offered my name, indicated that I was new to the village, then went silent waiting to see if he had something more to add or ask. But Jasper had gone silent as well, and appeared to be rooting around to find another word.

"I've bought the old Adams place. I'm going to fix it up."

His blue eyes flickered but gave away nothing. "Big job", he said finally. He had now used up 30% of his day's allocation of speech, and two regulars looked around, surprised by this burst of loquacity.

I gave him something like the same rundown I had offered Lonny, he nodded once or twice, and I ended by asking him if he knew anybody who was good at general building because I would need some help. Wordlessly, he reached for a pad and pen and jotted down three names and telephone numbers. "Good men", he summarized as he passed me the sheet. I assumed they were all locals, and I folded and pocketed the paper. Looking around the room appraisingly, I offered the view that the renovations had been done very well.

"Did you do them yourself?"

He gave a single nod of the head, and then idly wiped a small puddle of water from the bar.

"If you care to drop by the Adams place sometime, I can show you around."

He cracked a faint, attractive smile and offered me his hand.

This was all six years in the past now. But even back then it had been evident that my early groundwork had been well worth it. In very short order after making the acquaintance of these three gatekeepers, I was introduced to a dozen or so people who seemed already to have been briefed on who I was, where I came from, what I was up to, but most importantly that I was all right, and that if word got back to the original three about anyone passing on nasty gossip, retribution would be as brutal as it was swift.

Within a week, I had contracted two of the labourers whose names had been given to me by Jasper, we had grubbed out the junk on both floors of the house, I had set up a camp space at the back of the ground floor where I could sleep and make scratch meals during the first phase of the renovations, and about a dozen locals had toured the place. Things were humming along.

Three

During the renovations, The Fox and Esker was one of my homes away from home. I had become a fixture there, and after only a few weeks there was always lively interest in how the work was coming along. The work proceeded as separate projects: water courses, new roof, basement and flooring, windows, and interior work. I detected after the second year a feeling that quite a few of the locals were impressed at how the work progressed in nice, orderly, well-defined stages. The work on the house itself had taken four years. Another year was spent on building the carport, stabilizing the hillside, levelling and gravelling the driveway, and putting in the main elements of the back patio. In the sixth year, I had done all the finishing touches: the berm and red currant hedge around the back patio, a final extension to the vegetable garden, and my real labour of love—the front patio. Now it was all done, and being retired I could enjoy the job of "maintenance".

A familiar panorama stretched out before me once again. From where I sat now, on the patio of The Fox and Esker, I could look out over the old railway station, twenty metres below, where I had left my car in the car park. Beyond the station, my gaze was drawn down the graceful hillside to the river below, which in turn followed the sweep of the valley itself to the south, the valley sides caressing the eye as does a well-designed garment. The whole scene was one of space and volume, and of Nature's mastery of form, at once asexual and seductive. Rain from a few days before, and the heat of the day, breathed humidity into the air giving it a blue haze–hint of volume and solidity, and a nectar sweetness that was irresistible. From the station below, I had crossed the tracks and climbed a set of steps leading to a lane that hugged the contour of the hill but rose slightly toward the pub, which sits on a promontory a hundred and fifty metres along the lane from where the steps join it. Contemplating the large glass of beer in front of me, contemplating my new retired status, not yet a day old, I thought of the mill, my next project. It had been ten days since I was last in Greenvale, and we were falling behind on the project, something I planned to remedy starting first thing in the morning.

"Bunch of unemployed layabouts", said a loud voice, brushing aside my musings. "Don't know what the place is coming to." The voice's owner sat down heavily opposite me, uninvited, and cast a doubtful eye at my beer. "Suppose you'll be asking for handouts soon." He was tall, wore his dark wavy hair short, and squinted into the sun.

"No", I said, languidly rotating the beer on its mat. "I'm gainfully employed, doing a job that everybody sees as necessary: I murder politicians by night, and I've started on mayors. So how are you doing, Mr. Mayor?"

I had known Greg Blackett since I had bought the house. In fact, he was the first person who called on me as I got started on the drainage work. He had been elected mayor of Greenvale for the first time that year. We had chatted easily on that first occasion. I showed him around the place and explained what I had in mind for it, leaving out the bit about intending to sell once I had finished the renovations. He was very interested, and said that he had never seen the inside of the house but knew a bit of its history. I had probed about the history angle, but it was soon clear that he knew no more than I did. He remarked on how much work would be needed to bring the house up to snuff; I agreed, but said that the house and the property as a whole had appealed to me very much.

"Expensive impulse purchase", he ventured, evidently trying to provoke a response.

"Some might look at it that way", I replied neutrally. "But it's not a consumable, and I expect that at the very least it will retain its value. I don't lie awake nights."

He just nodded in agreement, and we carried on in our tour. We looked at the fireplace, the authentic but ornamental indoor pump, and the second floor where everything needed to be ripped out back to the studs. I recounted the main points of the inspection I had commissioned prior to buying. Solid basic structure. Large floor joists on twelve-inch centres, and in very good condition. A small amount of wet rot due to a localized leak in one corner of the roof, but this was limited to a restricted area of the second floor north wall. All other wood in very good condition, apart from the roof which had kept out the weather thus far but basically was not recoverable. Piping needs replacing. House not insurable given the present wiring. No insulation to speak of, apart from a rough homebrew job that had slapped a covering over the heating tape on the water pipes. All drains, and the stack from the squalid little loo on the second floor in poor condition. Windows and window frames in poor condition.

"Well, I don't need to tell you that you've taken on a big job", he said, and I thought I detected a hint of scrutiny.

"Yes," I agreed, "but I need a big project outside my regular work. And spread over about four years, recovering this place is something I can manage financially and as a time commitment."

He looked at me a bit more closely. "Ah, so you have at least a scope and schedule?"

It was my turn now to give him a sceptical look. "I had a first version of that in place before I signed the purchase agreement."

"Thanks for the tour. I appreciate it." Glancing at his watch, he said, "I'm off for a quick bite of lunch. Care to join me? There's a reasonable spot just down the street."

I agreed. One of my prime concerns about making the purchase in Greenvale had been the possibility of encountering a small-town mentality. My encounter with the librarian, hardware store owner, and publican had eased that concern. But I hadn't counted on meeting someone of Greg's calibre. Here was a man who was clearly intelligent, open to the outside world, sophisticated, and worth getting to know better. The "reasonable spot" had been The Fox and Esker where we were sitting now again, six years later.

Looking across at Greg, I recognized someone who had become a good friend and a business partner. He had been intriguing right from the beginning, and early on, after it became obvious that we were going to get along, I had asked him point-blank: "Apart from being mayor, what do you actually do for a living?"

His answer ("A bit of this, a bit of that") sounded like a dodge, but in fact it turned out to be accurate. Tackling his reasons for wanting to be mayor, I was eventually able to get a fairly surprising answer out of him.

"Villages, communities, are similar to individuals. They need a plan. Without a plan, an individual drifts, and chances are that he or she will drift into something drab and deeply unsatisfying. The same is true of a village. Without a plan, the most likely outcome is that it will drift into a depressing state of mediocrity unless somebody takes the reins. I didn't want to see Greenvale drift into the condition of rural mediocrity that affects far too many Ontario communities. That sounds insultingly elitist, but I think it's what could happen. This place is so appealing, so beautiful, that it was crying out for a vision. And things happen when people try." He stopped short of saying that he had supplied the vision, but that is what he had done.

And during the first two years I knew Greg, I came to realize just how expansive and ambitious his vision was. He was local, although not from Greenvale proper, and he had excelled in the liberal arts programme at Trent University, walking off with the English Prize and making the Dean's Honour Roll every year. A year after finishing, he surfaced as manager of a hardware store, and then went through a series of commercial positions over the following three years, ending up in a firm specializing in high-end renovations. There he thrived and demonstrated true ability as an entrepreneur. He was soon taking on his own projects and making very substantial profits, and eventually branched out on his own. His first big project brought him to Greenvale, where, along with three partners, he bought the old dance hall at a receivership sale, and within 18 months had turned it into something he called the Pavilion. There were three parts to the Pavilion: a set of four units that he quickly rented out to individuals running small businesses, a Community Centre that started off as nothing more than a meeting room, still lacking paint and wallpaper and equipped with only card tables, cheap metal chairs, and a rudimentary bar, and a Corporate Centre that entered the world as a well-fashioned set of two small conference rooms. Cash flow went from a trickle to a steady and healthy stream, and within five years, the Community Centre had a curling rink and a bingo hall, and the Corporate Centre sported a full range of conference facilities and a catering service. As mayor of Greenvale, a position that took relatively little of his time, he had sold his share of the Pavilion, but retained a partnership in a firm that buys, renovates, and sells properties.

Greg had and continues to develop a natural flair for effective advertising and marketing. He convinced the village to make use of the website he established for the

Pavilion, and he then designed and populated it with news, information, and interest stories about the village. At the time he bought the old dance hall, the village's fortunes were clearly sagging. The feed mill, a small farm-implements dealership, and an auto repair service were all shuttered in quick succession. Although Greenvale continued as the geographic centre of a thriving farming area, little of the money generated flowed into the village. The turning point in the village's decline coincided with three things Greg did. He bought a completely run-down Victorian farmhouse across the valley from the station, and set about the long process of recovering it to a flagship residence. During and after the renovation, he milked, mercilessly, the photogenic aspects of the place, both external and internal, as a way of demonstrating to anyone who would look or listen the kind of high-end residence that could be developed in Greenvale. He formed something he called the Greenvale Social Circle, had a local historian help him compile a sourcebook on local history, local prominent families over the past two centuries, intriguing bits of local industrial archaeology, and the geology of the area, and he used this material to provide a running commentary as spice for walks up and down the railway line through the village, walks that he organized and led. Interest in the Social Circle picked up only slowly at first—during the first year there were days when his biweekly walks brought out only one or two people. That changed when he induced a reporter from the *Kingston Whig-Standard* to take the walk with him, which resulted in a very nice human interest story. That story was quickly pinned up on the bulletin board in the post office, presented with panache on the village website, and made available as a handout at the Community Centre. Invitations started coming in for Greg to speak at service clubs, chambers of commerce, and local meetings on economic development (and he made sure that a solid flow of publicity was generated by these events). At that point, the village really turned a corner.

But the third item, the wild hare-brained scheme that had everyone chuckling, initially, in either sceptical or cynical disbelief, was The Bus. He found two old front-wheel drive Bluebird buses, cut the back half off each of them, and joined the two front halves together, so he had a vehicle with a cab and an engine at each end. He then had the whole thing mounted on bogies so that it could drive on the railway line. There was quite a bit of backroom jockeying to win over the railway enthusiasts from their outrage and consternation, but the promise of a substantial annual contribution to their society quickly brought the realization that this was actually just the thing they had wanted all along. As one would expect, there was a lot of fuss about safety and licensing, but this was sorted out over a period of ten weeks or so, and the vehicle was governed so that it couldn't travel any faster than 40 km/h. They tried it out early one Saturday morning. Not a hitch. Greg had planned to use The Bus for his Social Circle "walks", to attract those who might want the outing but not the walk, or to carry on even if the weather was iffy.

A week after the initial trial, the machine had its formal baptism. It sat next to the station, a two-headed oddity sporting a fresh coat of black paint made exciting by two bright yellow stripes down each side. Each side also bore a plaque, newly bolted in place and covered by a discreet little curtain. The local railway enthusiasts and some other curious folks turned out for the unveiling, but the biggest contingent was the village's children. They all wanted a ride. There was an initiation ceremony, and of course a photographer. The little curtains were removed with a flourish to reveal the vehicle's name—Scylla and Charybdis. Everyone piled aboard, Greg climbed into the cab, and off the thing lumbered to the north end of town. Greg then switched off the engine, walked to the other end of S&C, started up the second engine, and they all trundled to the south end of town. The squeals of delight brought smiles and laughter to the faces of the adults lining the trackside and left no doubt that S&C was here to stay.

Greg did use it for the Social Circle "walks", but it was also soon in service as the village bus, carrying children to and from the primary school and eventually taking adults to the Pavilion at the north end of the village, or to the Saturday farmer's market at the south end. This all worked fine, since the narrow, steep-sided valley means that nothing is very far from the railway line that runs along the eastern bank of the river. Not surprisingly, S&C featured in all the local newspapers, and there was increasing talk of the "Greenvale spirit". Naturally, Greg pumped this for every ounce of publicity, and a contest was held to choose a full-time driver, a job that eventually went to Sam Daniels, a retired dentist. The final changes to S&C came a few months later when Greg had two mock nineteenth-century locomotive smokestacks built and mounted on The Bus's roof, one at each end. A train whistle operated by compressed air completed the picture.

Behind the scenes, Greg was quietly working to bring three small businesses into the village, and to tout it as an ideal spot for retirees. Eventually, he was successful in both these initiatives. As a result of all this, the mood within the village changed sharply over a period of just a few years, from one of irrelevance and aimless drift to something much more upbeat.

"I guess it's better than watching paint dry."

"Taking inspiration from a glass of beer?" I said, half musing but tuning in to the present again. "I was just thinking of my part-time residence in Greenvale over the past six years, and now another big change."

"But you have a plan", he said, making it sound half-statement and half-question. "So what's next?"

"What's next, Greg, is for me to move into my new life. There's some stress involved in letting go something I've lived and breathed for thirty years, and that will take a bit of time, but work is the answer. I've finished all the drawings for the mill now, I've done most of the research we need, and tomorrow I'll complete the model wheel."

The model wheel was a quarter-scale water wheel that I would be using for tests to get operating information for the real thing. And the actual wheel was indeed a water wheel for the mill I had bought three months earlier. Well, actually, to call it a mill is something of a stretch, since it was really a ruin. But the history of the place, once I had sussed it out, was fascinating, its location couldn't have been better, and its potential seemed almost unlimited. The only thing was the cost.

I had hired a building inspector, and we spent a day scrambling over the ruin. I took dozens of photos and made hundreds of laser measurements. He scribbled pages and pages of notes which he turned into a concise report. The bottom line was that there was no basic reason why the place couldn't be refurbished. For a price.

It took less than a day to enter the measurements I had made into Mathcad and produce a good set of drawings for the mill in its present state. I obtained figures from the local authorities on the river flows, by season, for the past twenty years, and it took less than another day to produce an initial plan for refurbishment, concentrating on making assessments detailed enough to produce a reliable initial cost estimate. Visits to some local builders and building supply merchants, without giving away what I was doing, filled in the blanks. The cost estimates made me swallow hard, but they were nicely offset by rough first guesses at revenues. All this allowed a preliminary estimate on cash flow, which was anaemic but positive. My initial estimates had been quite conservative, so as far as I was concerned, we were on the road.

Greg waved at the waiter and asked for a glass of beer. "When you first suggested the mill as a project," he said with a smile, "I really did wonder about you, but when I saw your figures, that clinched it." Within two minutes, he was off on another blue-sky trip, talking at increasing speed and excitement about options, possibilities, publicity, and before-during-after photos. I let him swan around, because although the ideas he was exploring were only half-formed, none of them was rubbish by any means and it was a delight to see him exhilarated and at his extroverted best.

He stopped so suddenly that I raised my head quickly to look at him. He was regarding me intently. "But what about you? You're right in the middle of a big change." (Translation: Is this all going to settle down to something stable for you?)

I smiled at him comfortably. "I guess we'll just have to see, Greg." Although this came out with what I hoped was confidence, arriving at a net sum from all the pluses and minuses was far from easy. I had loved my career. I liked many of my work colleagues; a few of them were good friends. Some clients were pains in the ass, but those situations almost always turned into positive challenges. My pension and investment income meant that now I was financially independent, and the thought of learning new things was exciting. But for anything I took on now, the burden was entirely on my own shoulders. No corporate backup. No colleagues as sounding boards.

I guessed that Greg read my thoughts, because his smile was hesitant, and I cocked my head at him in query.

"You're a city boy", he said. "Aren't you going to lose interest in all this fairly quickly?" The sweep of his arm indicated the village, valley, and all around us.

I took a sip of beer and leaned back in my seat. "I guess we'll just have to see." But once again, I hoped that the confidence I projected was more convincing than my doubt-ridden inner state. The life change I was making was immense, and although I had no immediate plans to relinquish my Toronto condo (in doing this, was I just secretly hedging my bets?), a brutally frank interpretation of my situation was that of an urbanite pretending to be a local but on a hobby farm basis. On the other hand, I felt that I really did like the place, and that it could be home.

I looked around, and confirmation of that thought was at hand. A thousand water nymphs playing invisibly in the river caught the sunlight and tossed it back to us. The line of willows some distance down the riverbank, next to a small picnic area, swayed languidly. Petunias in waist-high boxes along the side of the patio danced in the same puffs of breeze that tugged at our hair. Cloud shadows chased each other up the side of the valley.

I put my empty glass down decisively and announced, "I'm going to check on things at the mill."

Four

We were at the mill in less than five minutes. Each time I went to the place, I became excited all over again. Here was a real project that I was running myself, but had only myself to account to. Once I got started, it had taken a day to clear the site of junk, another three days to remove the safety barriers the village had erected, a further day to take a slew of photographs, and another week to erect construction-site fencing around the property. As Greg and I let ourselves in through the access door in the fencing, I followed in my mind once again the path that had brought us to this point.

It had taken some time for my interest in the mill to kindle. The ruin itself was evident from the time of my first visit to Greenvale, of course. It was impossible to miss, a rather imposing mass sitting next to the river, covered in dust, mud, weeds, vines, and abandonment. When I asked around out of idle curiosity how long it had been in that state, the answer that came back was "years", meaning in effect "forever" in terms of anyone's memory.

Some digging in local libraries revealed a sketchy history, that it had been a grist mill in the nineteenth century, that it had been used to generate some electricity early in the twentieth century, and that there had been a fire in the 1930s. It had apparently been abandoned after the fire, and the last known owner had been a Mr. Ambrose. After a child had broken a leg while playing in the ruin, the village, on legal advice, had expropriated the property and erected barriers around it to prevent any other injuries. That had been 25 years ago.

The information on electricity generation had caught my eye right away. I located a few old pictures of the mill. I spent time looking at the site from different perspectives, including from the hills on the opposite side of the river. I did some calculations. Then I thought about it for a month.

After some discussion with a local, but not too local, real estate agent, I made my move. There was the usual minuet with the village, which owned the mill ruin. We danced for weeks, but my agent played the game well, and eventually there were strong hints that a price of about half what the village had asked originally would probably fly. Up to this point, nobody knew who the agent was representing. We submitted a formal offer.

I knew that I was in a ticklish situation. Over a meal, but some time before the deal had been inked, I had told Greg that it had been me all along. As I expected, he became quite angry.

"Why didn't you tell me? Do you realize the position you've put me in?"

"Greg, I haven't put you in any position. You had no information about this until now. What would have been different had you known it was me making the inquiries? Would you have tried to get more money out of me?"

"Richard, that's not the point, and I'm sure you know it. This whole thing could look as though I've helped keep a friend's identity secret while he negotiated with a body where I play a prominent role. There's not a lot of love lost among small-town politicians, and I wouldn't put it past them to have tried to jack up the price if they had known it was you. So they might very well look at me now and say that it's my fault the village got less for the property than it might have done."

I shook my head in disagreement. "If that had been the case, what kind of discussion would we be having now? Wouldn't you be in just as bad or a worse situation if you had to decide to support your colleagues' attempt to screw more money out of me, resist them, or just duck the whole thing and recuse yourself? I'm pretty sure that situations like this have arisen before." I couldn't say it, but I knew that Greg had made some similar moves when he had purchased the old property that became the Pavilion, and I was relying on him suspecting that I was a good enough researcher to have uncovered this. "Besides, there's no way I would have played that game. You and I both know that the intrinsic worth of the property, as it stands, is zero, and that its net present value is negative. I would have just walked away from the whole thing, and the village would be right back where it all started. Except that in that situation, the local politicos would have pissed off somebody who has chosen their village as a place to live, and has put quite a bit of cash into the local economy as well. Have you or they thought of that?"

He fixed me in a steady gaze for some time, and it was clear that his anger was dissolving. A slow smile spread across his face. "What do you really have in mind?"

"The short answer is refurbishment", I replied, after a considered delay. Looking at him directly, I said "I want you fully in on this Greg, and the first step in that is to give you a comprehensive briefing, but I'm not ready to do that yet. You'll have questions, and I just don't have all the information I'll need to answer them. Give me a month."

On an afternoon in early August, when Greg's wife, Jill, was off at a conference, I invited him around to my house for dinner. We started on the patio with olives, chilled Prince Edward County white wine, and French bread homemade that afternoon. The main course was thick steaks, green salad and tomatoes from my garden, and potato salad with potatoes, green onions, red peppers, chives, and beets all from my garden as well. By seven o'clock, we had moved inside for cheese and I led him to my desk where I had laid out a few drawings, an artist's sketch, notes, lists, and a few outline calculations. So then I let him in on the whole plan.

Within ten minutes, his enthusiasm had reached white heat. I explained about the grant available for recovering a heritage property. I told him how much power was available from the water flow and the distance it could fall through. I laid out for him the contract that was available for supplying small-scale hydroelectric power to the local grid. But the icing on the cake was recovering the site as a significant historic feature in the village and as a working flour mill. I explained what other small operations had done in terms of having local bakeries use locally made flour, and my initial queries at bakeries within a thirty kilometre radius. I discussed schedules, capital costs, expected cash flows, and what had to be done to minimize financial risk.

He was off like a greyhound after a rabbit. "Shit, man, you've really got this thing nailed, haven't you?"

I started mouthing some words of caution, but he waved it all off impatiently. "Good God! Within a few years, the property taxes on this place alone would swamp whatever trivial amounts the village might have been able to get as a sale price, even at the most optimistic." Within two minutes he was painting vistas of before and after, breathless progress reports, accounts in local newspapers.

He stopped gushing so suddenly that I had to look up from the drawing we had been reviewing. "I want in", he said in all seriousness.

I shook my head. "Not yet. I want to get this project fully on the rails, and then make it known generally that I'm looking for investors. It will be then that I definitely want you in. By that time, any initial scrabbling for cheap political points will have stopped and the whole thing will be just a business venture."

He was nodding, but almost immediately asked, "But can you carry this? How much will it cost to get the place operating?"

"There'll be grant money up front. It will take, all in all, about $450 000 if I do a lot of the work myself, but I can't front all that out of my own resources and the keys here will be leveraging and staging, so that I use as much grant money as possible up front and so that cash starts flowing in as early as possible, and ramps up as quickly as possible in stages. The first of the cash flow will be from selling electricity and soon after that from selling flour. And I'm hoping that I can have some good discussions with the local politicians helping them to get the word out that Greenvale is a go-getting place and is open for business. That means I'll be looking for some slack on taxes, I'll be looking for shoulder-to-shoulder solidarity to show to the outside world, and I'll be looking for a greased runway for permits. There is a slew of permits and permissions to get, and I need to get them in the right order and within the right time windows."

"What do the bottom-line finances look like?"

"I haven't finished the detailed planning yet, and some of the numbers I have are still estimates," I cautioned, "but even being somewhat pessimistic about possible problems, and allowing what I think is a generous contingency, the place should be making a profit and paying down its debt by the end of the first season."

"Season?"

"Yes. The mill will generate its own power from the water wheel, but that will have to be shut down when serious freezing starts, sometime in December, and won't be able to start up again until April."

He looked somewhere between puzzled and disappointed. "But you won't just lock up for the winter, will you?"

"God, no! This place will be selling tangible and intangible products, and it has to be available all year."

"But where will the power come from in winter?"

"It will be bought." I could see the bigger picture was missing. "Let's back up a bit. First, this is one of the most picturesque mill sites I have ever seen. The building is large, but its dimensions, and the size of the water wheel relative to the profile of the building, and set against the hills on both sides of the village, will make it hugely attractive and tremendously elegant, in that rough pioneer way. That's definitely something to capitalize on, and I want it to become a local icon. Second, the power from the water wheel will all be converted to electricity, and a small part of that will be used to drive the two sets of milling wheels: the stone wheels that visitors can Oooh and Aaah at, and the steel wheels that will grind the great bulk of the flour. The rest of the electricity will be sold to the grid. The electricity route is dictated entirely by reliability and efficiency considerations. Third, at some point, and sooner rather than later, I want to have a high-end rustic coffee shop and restaurant in the mill. There's more than enough space to do all that. Fourth, there'll be a small bakery on site to serve the restaurant and coffee shop. Imagine the attraction of eating bread at the mill where the flour that it was made from was ground."

Greg was shaking his head, almost in disbelief. "Man, you really have got this thing nailed!"

"No I haven't", I said with some emphasis. "Nowhere close yet. There are dozens of ducks to line up. The number of permits to get and the amount of paperwork is unbelievable. Plus, I have to design and build a water wheel. The reliability model needs to be finished and the calculations done, verified, and stamped. There's a lot of equipment that needs to be sourced. I have outline plans for new internal floors and the roof, but they need to be checked and stamped by somebody who has experience in old buildings like this. I have a financial model in place but it needs to be refined and kept up to date as the rest of the design details emerge. And I have to have all the right things in place so that I can get a roof on the building by the end of August at the very latest, and get some temporary heating in place in case it takes longer than I expect for the interior to be done, the equipment installed and tested, and the whole thing ready to go. At the most pessimistic, we need to be ready to run on purchased power by mid-December, and be ready to have the water wheel deliver power at the earliest possible date next year. We're in August now, so the deadlines will start coming thick and fast. It's all possible, but the planning, scheduling, and procurement effort will be brutal, not to mention the actual site work. On the pessimistic view, the bottom line is that the place has to be ready for full operation the moment it's warm enough next spring to get the water wheel turning. But there's an optimistic picture as well, and that's what I want to aim at. It says that the water wheel will be installed and operating this year. No point in deliberately aiming low."

"Working water wheels have always intrigued me, but I have no idea how you would go about putting a new one in place."

I nodded understanding. "There are quite a few aspects to the wheel. One of them is aesthetic. But the big one is practical. I don't have any pictures good enough to show what the original wheel looked like, and there might have been more than one wheel over the years. The main problem I'm wrestling with is reliability. The place needs to be operating at capacity every possible second, but there can be only one water wheel, so it has to be a nearly perfect piece of equipment."

"But designing a water wheel from scratch?" he asked dubiously.

"I've designed lots of pieces of equipment in the past, some of them original, and many of them far more complicated than this, and over the past few months I've done quite a lot of research on water wheels. Pretty exciting, I have to say, looking at descriptions of old mills and at recent engineering work." I couldn't suppress the impish grin of a kid with a new toy. "I've also built a scale model to get some data and make sure I know all the important design features and what needs to be optimized."

He wanted to see the model right away, so I took him to the basement where I had the thing set up. I tried explaining it all, but Greg was evidently off in the future somewhere, so I opted for a live demonstration.

I showed him how I was taking all the measurements I wanted, and the small used computer I had connected to the model to do this. When I switched it on and the wheel began turning, with a bit of splashing at first, his eyes lit up and a huge smile split his face.

Back at my desk upstairs, Greg looked at the artist's sketch of the refurbished mill through new eyes.

"So what can I do?" he asked.

"Publicly, nothing. Not yet. But privately you can be my sounding board."

As old pictures of the mill indicated, you enter on the land side at the southern end through a wide but not too high wooden door. That door was of oak, and although it had decayed badly it was clearly at one time almost a rustic work of art. But several pieces were missing from it, the hinges, lock fittings, and frame were all badly rotted, it would no longer have been able to keep out intruders or the elements, and would need to be replaced.

When Greg and I entered the mill, we could get a good initial view of things because the absence of a roof, apart from the few skeletal roof spars remaining in place, allowed lots of sunlight to flood in. Part of the floor at the level of the door was still in place, but the general scene was chaos. There had been three floors in the mill. The floor immediately above had almost completely collapsed. A few beams clung crookedly to the stone wall. Looking down, we could see just a jumble of broken beams, broken floor boards, and patches of charred wood in the upstream half of the mill basement, presumably an indication of where the worst fire damage had occurred eighty years earlier. The stone blocks in the wall were large and all appeared to be in good shape.

"Wow", said Greg softly. "I've seen some ruins in my time, but…"

"Yes. The first thing is to clear out all the rubble so that I can do a close inspection of all the stonework and foundations, and then put a roof on that will allow us to work in here full time regardless of the weather."

"How will you get all this stuff out?" he asked.

"We'll have to winch it out in a large bucket. There's no other practical way."

"So, let me guess", Greg said as he scanned the space to the right and below us. "The generator will be over there next to the wall, the other electrical machinery will all be in the basement, the milling equipment will all be on this level at the back, and the public area will be all this space where we're standing now. Am I right?"

I gave him an appraising look. "Not bad", I said. "For a municipal functionary."

He mouthed an expletive at me.

We talked about the business plan, and he asked me some pointed questions about what would have been called "critical success factors" during my quickly fading consulting days. I explained that revenue from grain milling would likely be ten times greater than that from selling electricity, so maintaining a steady production of flour would be crucial. So, by extension, a high reliability of all equipment associated with flour production would be key. I said that I thought there would be other reasons why the water wheel itself would be important, aesthetic reasons, and a general fascination for a working artifact from the past. This was where the whole package of a working historic mill came into view. I walked back outside with Greg, and we climbed down the slope to the corner of the mill. Looking around the corner, we could see the two large stone supports for the wheel, and the small strip of grass between the waterside wall of the mill and the water.

"My calculations indicate that the wheel will be turning fairly slowly, about ten revolutions per minute, or about once every six seconds or so. It won't squeak or groan, but there will be some splashing of water, so the sound coming from it will be close to white noise."

I indicated the slope we were standing on. "Here's my plan for this area. I want to level this piece of ground, cover it in stone flagging, and put some tables and chairs here, enough for up to thirty people. They can sit here and have a glass of wine while they watch the wheel turn. There's enough space for a path between the inner wheel support and the wall of the mill, and this can form part of the tour route. In fact, there's enough space to have a path for a tour route all the way around the outside of the mill."

"Tour route?"

"Indeed. An inside tour is essential. But think of an outside tour loop that allows you to walk within a few feet of a large working water wheel." Pointing to the water downstream of the stone wheel supports, I said, "I also want to have a low stone retaining wall form a lagoon around this area here, closing off a pool where the water falls out of the wheel buckets, leaving a small passage for outflow just beyond the outside patio. And I want to have underwater lights just inside the retaining wall and trained on the wheel and on the side of the mill. The ripples in the lagoon should have a very nice effect on the wall of the mill. But we can test all that long before the wheel has been installed."

"Not bad", he said. "A lagoon would be classy."

"Well it has a more important practical purpose, and that's to prevent branches and other debris floating in and snagging or damaging the wheel."

We walked the rest of the way around the outside of the mill. Climbing back to where the car was parked, I went back in, closed and locked the door to the mill and then closed and locked the access door through the protective fencing. We stood for a moment looking up at the mill structure. It was huge, forlorn, and helpless, like a large tortoise on its back that had grown tired of waving stubby legs pointlessly in the air.

I was going to right this tortoise.

Five

After saying goodbye to Greg at the mill, I had gone home, spent three hours working on the design for the mill's electrical system, looked again at alternatives for the floor layouts I had provisionally determined, called several building supply companies, called my accountant, called two generator manufacturers, and at seven o'clock, called it a day. There was half a small pan of pastitsio that I covered in foil and shoved into the oven to warm up, and in the meantime I quickly put together a Greek salad. As background, I put on Elgar's *Enigma Variations*, and turned up the volume. Unimpressed, the cat gave me a lugubrious look and slunk away.

The cat is Maxwell, otherwise just Max. I had found him as a kitten, left in a small cardboard box outside my door. He was asleep and weak. After two days in the vet's kennels, he had been revived, inoculated, and transformed into a black and white bundle of pure energy. Some weeks later he was neutered. I noticed early on that he was an ace fly catcher, but that he caught only the slower moving flies, which reminded me of Maxwell's demon. Hence the name. Max is now fully grown, and we get along fine, as long as I do what I'm told.

In the newspaper, there was the usual insipid diet of political posturing, so I strolled from the kitchen into the den, and began scanning the bookshelves for something of interest. I hesitated over John Williams's *Augustus*, and then quickly determined that I would make another assault on *Foucault's Pendulum*. Carrying it back to the kitchen, I managed a chapter before the pastitsio was heated, then set the book aside. A decent merlot washed down my meal nicely and brightened my mood at the same time. After finishing dinner, I decided to take a walk before full dusk settled.

Huge folds of magenta cloud swirled to the north and west. It was a very mild and windless evening, and I decided on a leisurely round trip to the mill. My house is between the two sets of S-bends in the village, and although it is separated from the mill by about only 300 metres, there isn't an unobstructed view of either from the other. Trees to the south and the east shield my house, and it rests next to the hill on the west. The mill sits within the southern S-bend. As I walked toward it, the structure sat there as if modelling itself in silhouette. Indirect pink light from the western clouds wreathed the building, giving the stone a soft glow, and making the broken and blackened roof spars look less apocalyptic. The sheer mass of the building spoke of permanence, determination, indomitability. The *Mary Ellen Carter*. The Once and Future Mill. Having now done enough work to produce the first rough drawings, it was only during the past week that, upon entering the mill, I could picture the piping and cable runs, could see where the ventilation ducting would be placed, could anticipate the scents of fresh beams and planking, could imagine the sharp metallic smell of new electrical equipment. I was making that first step from ownership of an inanimate thing to collaboration with another being. The mill was starting to take up residence in my life.

Contrary to the common notion that engineers are unemotional, and go about their days in a cloud of expletives punctuated by a convulsive waving of socket wrenches, dog-eared and smudged field drawings, all the while displaying dirt-clogged fingernails like badges of honour, any engineer who doesn't have some sense of connection, some feeling of visceral understanding of the equipment or structures he or she designs, builds, operates, or maintains, isn't very good.

A shift of the clouds bathed the western side of the mill in a sudden slow pulse of pink light. The walk back home brought more spring to my step, a response that acknowledged the mill's smile back at me just now, and sod any tutting over the pathetic fallacy.

By the time I walked in the door, things had changed. Dusk had arrived with a thud, and the late majestic integration of engineering vision and aesthetic vibrancy, accompanied and encouraged by the strings and woodwinds of crepuscular zephyrs, of colour-splashed cloud sculptures, and of affirming river chatter, had been transformed into a cat fight instigated by an aroused and grumpy unconscious. Questions reared up as challenges: *What are you doing talking to a ruin, for Chrissake? You sound like a sentimental schoolgirl, or like Prince Charles!* The rational doubts were not far behind. I had already spent over $8000 on this project. The uncertainties were still legion. What I stood to gain from it all as a guaranteed return was still nothing more than a flirtatious giggle lurking somewhere in the bushes.

In a flare of vehemence that surprised me, I swept all this aside impatiently and went back to my notes. As I had done for all my past projects, in this work I kept a detailed and strictly monitored plan. The rule was, the greater the level and the more sources of uncertainty, the more detailed the plan should be and the more frequently it should be monitored. I had a risk log, had updated it just two days previously, and there was nothing alarming there. A major risk that had just been removed was possible lack of funding for the restoration of a heritage building. I had just been given the green light on that one, the only proviso being that drawings for the restoration had to be approved before the work began. That was all in hand and the funding was promised to appear in stages starting in two weeks. This was all good news, because that funding would be a major fraction of the total cost of the mill rehabilitation.

A lot of the work was just lining things up in the right order, and finding people and companies who could do what was needed. Three days previously, I had located the old stone grinding wheels in the rubble within the mill's basement, their grinding surfaces undamaged during the descent from an upper floor during the fire. I had begun my own milling education by setting up tours for myself at the five other craft flour mills that were within fifty kilometres of Greenvale. I had also followed up seriously on my initial queries at local bakeries, and begun putting out the word that a new local source of flour would soon be on the scene. This led to first guesses on potential demand. The next day, I was to meet a possible helper suggested by Greg.

"His name is Buck Filmore", Greg had said. He'd paused, not quite pregnantly, then added, "Don't be too quick to judge. He's good at most things, he works hard, he's trustworthy, and he takes instruction."

The first job in the morning was to meet Buck at the mill at eight thirty, determine whether I wanted to use him, and if so, go through the mill with him and outline the jobs that needed doing in the next three days.

I was asleep before my head hit the pillow.

Six

Buck was already at the mill when I arrived there just after eight o'clock. He was in his mid-twenties, well over six feet tall, had blond curly hair and brilliant blue eyes, was built like Hercules, moved like Frederick Ashton, and gave every impression of being as thick as a post. But I kept Greg's request in mind, introduced myself, and noticing that he was wearing safety shoes and carried a hard hat, we entered the mill and I showed him around. I explained about the partial floors where I had erected temporary safety railings, the removal of the broken roof timbers still in place, the rubble from the floors and roof lying in the basement that had to be hoisted out, the process for constructing the roof truss in segments and raising and installing them, the initial work of inspecting and possibly dredging the river bottom around the water wheel location in preparation for constructing the lagoon wall, and how I planned to build and install the new water wheel.

Buck scanned the open roof slowly. "Where will we build the roof segments?" he asked in his slow but pleasant drawl.

"In the basement", I replied, "once we've pulled down the remaining roof spars and then cleared all the rubble."

"How many people needed to do that?"

Not being sure where the question was coming from, I said "I think you and I should be able to do it. We'll build all the roof truss segments in the basement, and then crane them into place. That craning should take two days."

He nodded slowly. "Never seen a roof built like that", he noted, as if for the record, all the while gazing upward somewhat blankly and for slightly too long.

"It's not that uncommon", I said, probably with a slight hint of impatience in my voice. "You don't sound too sure about it."

He looked at me in some surprise. "Oh, no. I just haven't done it this way before. Looks interesting. When do you plan to start?"

"How about right now?"

His face brightened suddenly, and I realized that he was pleased to receive a signal that he had passed and was accepted. "Do I need tools? I have mine in the truck", he offered, waving vaguely at the door.

"No", I replied. "I think I have everything we need. So, come over here and I'll show you what we'll do over the next few days." I led him to a rough bench I had built next to the wall where I had a schedule and some hand drawings. I walked him through the safety drill, indicated that we should be able to pull down the remaining roof spars before the end of the day, and get ready to winch out the rubble from the basement. "We should be able to do all that in two days, but I've allowed three just in case. The timber for the new roof arrives tomorrow, so when we've finished winching rubble out we can start winching new timber in. Then we start building the new roof segments. Do you mind working on Saturday if we need to?"

He looked at me quizzically. "No", he said but was clearly looking for an explanation.

"It's going to take two days to have the roof segments all put in place temporarily, and another day to bolt them all down permanently. There'll be five of us for that job: you, me, a crane operator, and two others. The thing that I want to be in a position to do as soon as possible is to put a temporary cover on the roof truss so that we have protection from the weather in here for the time being. A separate crew of roofers will come in when I call them."

Buck gazed in puzzlement at the three-pulley crane I had rigged up for the winching.

"Ah! I see", I said. "No, we can't use that crane to lift the truss sections, obviously. It won't reach. I have a commercial crane coming in on Friday, and we need to be ready for him to start as soon as he sets up."

I looked at Buck speculatively, and he soon became nervous that no comment or question was forthcoming. "You haven't asked about working times", I said. "I expect fairly long days, at least until we have the roof in place. Will that be a problem for you?"

Buck's expression cleared immediately. "You mean eight in the morning till eight at night?"

"Yeah, something like that."

"Hell no", he said with a laugh, and a disarming and completely ingenuous smile cratered a large dimple in his left cheek.

There were twenty-eight complete and partial roof spars to be taken down, and although they were big pieces of timber, the wood was old and rotten and the work went faster than I anticipated. By late morning we were able to start bringing the rubble out from the basement. Buck worked like a horse, but loading the rubble onto the pallet and winching it out was punishing, and we took a short break after each load was outside and in the container. The loading, winching, and unloading was tedious, since we had to climb down the ladder into the basement, load the pallet, and then climb back up, winch the loaded pallet up, manoeuvre it out of the mill through what used to be the shipping door, unload it into the container, lower the empty pallet back into the basement, then climb down to begin the next cycle. But the work went quickly, and by four o'clock that afternoon it was clear that we would be finished while there were at least four hours of useful daylight remaining. So I decided that when the rubble removal was done we would begin the river bottom inspection as a prelude to scoping out any dredging work that might be needed.

The second-last load of rubble was heavy, probably because we were getting near the bottom of the pile in the basement and the wood was partly saturated by water. Our process had me operating the crane to raise the pallet slowly until it was clear of the ground-level floor, Buck would then grab a long rope fastened to one side of the pallet, back out through the shipping doorway, and pull the pallet sideways through the doorway while I slowly released the brake on the crane. All went as usual for this load, until two things happened. Buck temporarily lost his footing, but recovered quickly, and I saw the line he was holding become suddenly taut as he overcompensated. At the same time, however, I eased off too much on the brake, causing the pallet to swing sideways suddenly, and strike the edge of the doorway. The shock reverberated through the empty building. I quickly reapplied the brake, locked the hoisting spool in place as insurance, and within a few seconds was outside to check on Buck.

"You okay?" I asked in some alarm. "I'm sorry about that. It was my fault."

"No", he said quickly. "No harm done."

"Well, let's finish removing this load and leave the rest until tomorrow. We're both getting tired." I went back to the crane, we eased the pallet of rubble out the doorway, and loaded it into the container. I walked back into the mill through the shipping doorway and looked at where the pallet had impacted the corner.

"Gave it quite a thump", Buck said, looking at the crushed timber and slightly dislodged stonework.

"Certainly did, but I think this mill has seen worse." I decided to give it a closer examination later. Something didn't look right at all.

I grabbed one of my hand drawings and Buck and I walked around the edge of the mill and down the bank toward the water's edge. The shoreline below the location for the water wheel was clogged by branches, dead wood, plastic bottles, and a variety of other refuse. The two large stone supports for the water wheel rose out of the water like an Epstein nightmare, or a sudden embodiment of Thor's Twins. The mill itself towered over everything.

"What I want to do first of all", I explained to Buck, "is to remove all this junk along the shore. We can load it into the boat", and here I indicated a largish rowing boat tied to a stake driven into the shore to our right, "and then haul it up to the waste container. I'm sorry that it's going to be just more grunt work, but I can't think of an easier way to do it. At least we can work from the water. It isn't deep here, and I have a couple of pairs of hip waders for us to use."

"I've done this sort of stuff before", Buck said in a matter-of-fact way. "Should be not too hard."

I also outlined for Buck what we had to do later. "There will eventually be a stone retaining wall going from the bank just upstream of the water wheel and coming around in a long arc to just about here, where we're standing. The main purpose of this will be to prevent more floating debris drifting in and interfering with the operation of the water wheel. So, just about there", I indicated, pointing to a spot a couple of metres from shore, "there will be a narrow outfall channel for the water operating the wheel to flow out of this enclosed area."

"What about ice?" Buck asked, and I cast him a reappraising glance, impressed by his pragmatism.

"Good observation", I commented. "The only reason I can even think of doing this is because it appears some previous owner of the mill had placed large pieces of rock and broken concrete in the water in an arc similar to what I just described but a bit further out. I presume they did that for the reason you mentioned, to prevent damage from ice being pushed in from further out in the river. Without that, any retaining wall could be taken out in short order during a bad winter."

We climbed into the hip waders and some old sandals I had brought, pulled the rowboat along the shore, and started loading trash into it. The work went quickly and in two hours we had all the large items piled high in the boat. We dragged the boat back to its mooring, and off-loaded everything onto a flat portion of the bank just up from the shore. Loading it into the waste container would be a task for the morning. There was something more I wanted to do before the day was out.

Wading out from shore, I confirmed my earlier guess that the water was not more than mid-thigh depth, and this was the case right out to the point where I encountered the first large pieces of rock and concrete.

"What's that?" Buck asked.

"It's an underwater viewing scope, so that I can get a good idea of how rough or uneven the bottom is. Go ahead. Take a look."

Buck pushed the end of the scope below the surface, peered in the top, and his eyes lit up like a kid's at Christmas. "Cool!"

Starting from about where the retaining wall would come back to shore downstream, I quickly walked along the edge of the rubble bank scanning the bottom. It was fairly smooth, and had a depth that was constant at a bit more than a metre. But the act of walking around stirred up silt to the point where the bottom soon became invisible. The exercise was enough to convince me that the bottom was relatively smooth, that dredging would likely not be needed, and that my plan to take still photos through the scope, about every half metre along the arc where the retaining wall would sit, was viable. But that was a job for later. It was well after seven in the evening, and time to call it a day.

"Let's go back to shore", I said. "It's time to pack it in. Buck, you've done a tremendous day's work. I'm impressed." He looked at me with the delight of a Mickey Mouse fan who had just been awarded a trip to Disney World. "Come along behind me, if you don't mind." Retracing my steps along the rubble bank, I glanced down occasionally through the scope. The silt was settling faster than I had expected.

Then I stopped suddenly. It took a second and a third look to convince me I wasn't seeing things. Three large letters stared back at me through the scope: P-O-L.

Seven

P-O-L from the previous day stood out as an intriguing puzzle amid the dozens of more pedestrian tasks all clamouring to be organized. In order to get the big tasks at the mill done, there were a lot of small tasks to finish first. Equipment had to be brought into the mill and put in place; rubble and demolition waste had to be taken out. I had to spend time planning all this.

But I also wanted to look at the corner where the pallet had struck the edge of the doorway. The old wood was splintered and crushed, but one of the stone blocks had also moved through about 30 degrees. This seemed odd, since the pallet could hardly have delivered enough impact for that. Applying a crowbar, I found that I could move this block further with surprisingly little effort, and it soon became evident what had happened. This section of the wall was apparently part of an old and rather large mailbox, drop box, or something similar, whose use had been discontinued, and some stone facing was added so that the wall looked continuous. It wasn't a good job, and my impression, increasingly, was that whoever had owned the mill during its last years of operation had kept it going using a string-and-chewing gum approach. This section of wall would need to be rebuilt properly. I was about to move the stone back into place when the crowbar slid further into the space behind and struck something that was not wall. Pulling out my flashlight, I peered in and could make out a black, flat, rectangular shape. After manoeuvring the stone a bit more, I was able to lift out this object. It was quite heavy, between five and ten kilos, was completely covered in tar, and when tapped it sounded slightly hollow. Given the day's work that lay before us, I brushed aside my curiosity, carried the black box out to my car, and placed it in the trunk.

When Buck arrived about half an hour later, we winched shovels and two large heavy plastic bins into the basement where we began the floor-levelling work. Two hours later, we had raised four bin loads of mixed soil and rubble out and transferred it to the container. By noon we began building the roof truss sections.

We were making good time.

At one o'clock, we broke off and stepped outside. The sun roared its pleasure from a crystalline blue sky. I said, "Buck, let's go have some lunch."

"I brought my lunch", he said, giving a leathery Marlborough man squint, and brushing back a blond lock stuck down by sweat.

"Well, if it will keep until tomorrow, you've earned a sit-down lunch and a decent break. On me."

"Can't very well object then, can I?" he drawled, a composite picture of youth, laughter lines, and dimples.

There seemed to be a lot of small construction jobs in progress in Greenvale, and The Fox and Esker was about two-thirds full of men exuding a metaphorical cloud of testosterone, and a literal olfactory haze that was essence of recent male exertion. Buck and I found a table near the wall, and a server dropped two menus on our table along with a promise—"Back in a minute"—then moved on, carrying her tray, apparently not bothered by either the virtual cloud or the real haze.

"Have yourself a beer, Buck", I offered. Gazing around the room, I recognized several faces I could put names to, and a few that were familiar but nameless.

The server returned, we ordered, our mugs of beer arrived as though by auto-reply email, followed just a few minutes later by our meals. Half of Buck's beer vanished immediately without even touching the sides. Continuing my sweep of the room, I acknowledged nods of recognition, and then I noticed one Alexander Philip Montgomery. Monty, as everyone knew him, was hard to miss. His eyes sparkled like fountains of youth, and his expression was always backlit by intense mental activity. Ideas and stray thoughts tumbled from him in barely controlled volatility, and he recycled snippets of information with ease, whether he had read them in the paper that morning or come across them decades ago in a dusty journal article on Eocene coprolites. He looked over and spotted me, and I could see him making excuse-me noises to his companion.

"Richard!" he chirped, in genuine delight, as he approached our table in his signature pizzicato gate. "Hello, Buck."

Buck looked up, but before his facial recognition machinery had ground out the needed identity, Monty was already a couple of conversational leagues downwind. Following hard on the heels of "Mind if I join you?" and "How are things?", leaving precious little gap for the socially acceptable "By all means" and "Fine", Monty noted that I had started work on the mill, reminded me that he had been promised a tour, wanted to know if we had turned up anything interesting, and asked if I had taken any pictures. This represented more conversational gambits than Buck would be comfortable with in an average half-hour, and he returned to his meal as though retreating from an oncoming tornado.

During the short interval while Monty stopped to draw breath, I interjected, "Yes, we've started working on the inside, we have a tight schedule to put on a new roof, nobody will be doing any tour until that roof is in place, and I've taken about 1200 photos to date."

"Great stuff!" Monty exclaimed, his hands massaging the air vigorously.

"We did see something odd but likely of no interest", I noted. The wattage in Monty's face doubled instantly. "I was taking a first look to see whether any dredging work might be needed in the lagoon, and there's something there in the mud that has the letters P-O-L on it."

"P-O-L. P-O-L." Monty tapped the table in delicious impatience and stared into space for a few seconds. "How large are the letters?"

"About six inches, maybe eight. So it wasn't anything like a licence plate, or some small object like that. Hard to say just how big the letters were because I was looking through an underwater scope."

"P-O-L. P-O-L..." The inner effort drove a cat's paw of mixed excitement and frustration across his face.

"Tell you what, Monty. Buck and I have to eat and get back to work. If you have time, why don't you come by my place tonight about eight thirty? I'll show you some pictures and we can talk about things."

"Great! I'll be there!" he agreed swiftly, as though he had just been offered a seat on the Nobel committee. Glancing at his watch, he leapt to his feet exclaiming, "Got to run! Late", and dashed off.

There was a longish silence, as though Buck were waiting for the aftershocks to play out. "I've seen him around, but don't know much about him."

"He's not everyone's cup of tea", I began, "but I find him fascinating. He was a professor of mechanical engineering, but then developed an interest in eighteenth and nineteenth century technologies, and managed to talk his way into a chair of history of technology. Probably wore them down to the point where they begged to know where they should sign."

"What does he do now?" Buck asked.

"A little bit of everything. He maintains his link to the university, but he's on practically every committee of local history in the district. Plus he still writes articles, papers, letters. He's on several advisory committees, but he spends a lot of his time doing what he did just now—talking to everybody, keeping up on the work being done on any old building, structure, or archaeological site."

"He seems to be quite interested in our mill. I mean in your mill."

I nodded. "He looked me up when I was just starting to renovate the house six years ago. Said he had had a running battle with the village about the building, over the lack of any maintenance on the place, how it was slowly falling into ruin. When he learned that I was going to renovate the mill, he looked me up again, and brought a huge folder of old records, newspaper clippings, and notes that he wanted to discuss with me. He helped me put together the application for the refurbishment grant from the government. What he doesn't know about anything historical in this area either hasn't been uncovered yet or isn't worth knowing."

There were things about Monty that I didn't mention. The fact that his parents brushed close to divorce court because of Monty's name, which had been selected unilaterally by his father, a military history buff, and rammed through over his mother's objections. His personal 5000 volume library that he mines systematically. The fact that he had become highly expert at using the Internet, and could find things even skilled librarians and information researchers could miss. His enormous list of correspondents and network of colleagues. His complete devotion to historical integrity, and his unfailing generosity in giving his time and sharing his knowledge.

Buck munched his way through his meal, and I took the opportunity to ask him about himself. His parents still lived in Belleville, and he visited once a month. Buck had made it through Grade 10, but then gave up because it was too difficult, he didn't see any point in going further, and he wanted to get out into the workforce. He said it had become evident by the age of fifteen that he had natural aptitude with his hands, and he was now a respectably accomplished carpenter, plumber, electrician, and general mechanic. He had built himself a small bungalow on the edge of Greenvale over a space of about three years, and he had now settled into a predictable life, during the winter, of odd jobs as they became available and curling for diversion, and construction work and baseball for fun in the summer. His one extra activity, something that was part hobby and part job, was fretwork, at which he had become sufficiently competent that he had begun taking contract jobs from two companies that supplied the construction trade.

"Not that much", Buck said in response to my question about how much time he spent on his fretwork, but a couple of further questions revealed that in fact he was now spending an average of about six hours a week on it, all of it in the evenings. I quickly accepted his offer to come round some time and look at examples of his work and his workshop. It seemed evident that he was bringing in more than enough money to meet his needs, which were few, and his luxuries, which were even fewer.

Back at the mill, the afternoon flew by, but the construction of roof segments also advanced quickly. I marked the timber for cutting, working through my drawings in sequence, while Buck did the cutting and stacked the pieces along the wall by numbered roof segment. After all the timber cuts were marked, I switched over to help Buck with the cutting, and by four o'clock we had begun assembling the roof segments. By seven o'clock we were more than two-thirds done, and I told Buck to call it a day. We could easily finish the remaining segments in the morning well in advance of when the craning would need to begin.

We tidied our tools away, switched off the lights, cleaned up, and then locked the main door to the mill and the gate in the chain-link construction fencing. As we walked toward our vehicles, Buck looked sideways at me and said, "I'm really enjoying this." I was somewhat flattered and taken aback, but recognized what a statement like that meant coming from a shy man.

"Well, Buck, I'd say we work well together. This job is going smoothly."

He gave a self-effacing smile and a nod, and picked up his pace toward his truck. "See you tomorrow morning", he sang out over his shoulder. I watched him climb into his blue F150, start it up, and drive off to the south.

I had taken about forty-five more pictures during the day, so after laying out the ingredients for a quick dinner of pasta with ham pieces, broccoli, snow peas, and tomatoes in a white sauce, I downloaded the pictures. Noting that Monty would be arriving exactly (of course!) at the agreed eight thirty, I threw the meal together, ate, cleaned up, then lined up a selection of photos for display on the large Mac computer screen, and got out my logbook for the project.

I had just about polished off another chapter of *Foucault's Pendulum* when the doorbell sounded precisely at eight thirty. Monty swept through the door even before it had fully opened, he wished me good evening, waved a thick file consisting of "notes I thought we might need", and somehow managed to arrive exactly in front of my desk despite his erratic bird-like skipping path.

"So, tell me more about this P-O-L", he began without preamble, struggling against invisible restraints, as eager as a beagle puppy.

"Slow down Monty", I said through a laugh. "Let's start from the beginning."

"I am", he said. "This P-O-L stuff might just be very significant, so that's where we should start. Look at this", he said, opening his file. "Here's a picture taken presumably not too long after the fire. You can see the protruding remains of roof timbers." He gave me fifteen seconds, practically an eternity, to absorb the photo. "Here's another picture", he said, flopping a second large print onto the desk, "probably taken about ten years later." He let me look at the two photos, clearly expecting me to notice something significant, and giving me ample time, about five seconds, to do so.

"In the time between the two photos, the water wheel disappeared."

"Y-e-es", he said, in partial confirmation, as though I had not quite got the full answer.

"The wood decayed during that time to the extent that the wheel just collapsed into the lagoon."

"Yes", he affirmed again, in the same tone. "That's one possible explanation."

Our eyes met, mine reflecting puzzlement, his radiating that impatient and expectant encouragement of a teacher to a pupil he feels can do much better. "Look again at the first picture", he said.

Both pictures were hazy and grainy, shot by amateur photographers using cheap cameras, and blown up a bit more than made sense. Then I saw it.

"It's hard to be sure, but it looks like there's something odd about the way the wheel spokes meet the axle."

"Bingo. Or at least half bingo."

I stared at the first photo more intently. "Aha!" I said, as my moment arrived. "And… the number of spokes! There are only six spokes, far too few for a weak material like wood."

Monty did a little skip, sang out "Yes!" and I half-expected him to toss me a peanut in reward.

By then it was close to nine o'clock, and after a long day I was becoming hazy. Monty and I spent about another forty-five minutes looking at pictures on the Mac, and the ideas and suggestions continued to bubble irrepressibly from Monty's chronically overheated imagination. Just then the phone rang. It was Greg.

"Richard. Hi. Sorry to call this late. Just got in from a long council meeting."

"It's not fair", I said, "how come you get all the excitement?"

The earpiece delivered two half-strangled expletives. "You have no idea", he muttered as if through gritted teeth, then in more normal speech after a short delay Greg commented, "I saw Monty today." I knew Greg was looking for an update, but given both our energy levels, the most we could expect to do was to make some tentative arrangement to meet.

"Tomorrow will be quite busy, Greg, but I've decided to take Saturday off completely. Could we get together for lunch?"

"Agreed", he said, sounding almost as tired as me. "The Fox at eleven thirty?"

"I'll be there", I replied, before we both hung up.

Monty and I worked through another dozen or so photos, but when my head nodded involuntarily, Monty stopped speaking.

"I'm sorry, Richard. You are obviously beat, and I've stayed too long. Would you mind if I called you first thing Saturday morning, say about nine thirty?"

"Yes. That's fine Monty. I should be the one apologizing. I can't work these long days then sit up into the night the way I could in my twenties."

We shook hands and made satisfied departing noises at the door. The wall clock read nine fifty-five. I switched off the computer, reordered the pile of drawings, and flopped into an easy chair for a moment. A few seconds later, at one forty-five, I awoke with a start, and dragged myself to the bedroom.

Eight

Friday morning. I awoke without benefit of the alarm at five twenty-five, rested but stiff of leg and back. To my ears, an improbable number of birds, parked in the trees outside, were singing merrily, but in reality were likely posting arch avian blogs of ownership and dominance, and threatening death and disfigurement to any winged being who ignored them. The decibel level birds can produce relative to their size has always struck me as incredible, and makes me ponder how much more stentorian and unpleasant a world it would be if each of us could hear clearly anybody who was within three hundred body lengths.

The water from a scalding shower gurgled down the drain, and carried with it a lot of my stiffness and the twenty years of additional age that seemed to have settled over me during the night. A large glass of orange juice and a thick piece of toasted walnut bread got the rest of the cylinders firing, and I sat at the kitchen table with my project logbook noting the tasks to be completed over the next few days. Their number seemed endless and I plodded through the list of them. One stood out: assemble the water wheel. In principle it was simple, but despite this, and despite all my thinking and planning, the whole operation made me nervous. This was my first experience with a water wheel, and certainly would be my first experience in assembling one at full scale as part of an operation that had to work.

Brushing aside these ongoing concerns, I finished my notes and checked the time. Six thirty. Buck and the other two labourers were due to arrive at the mill by eight, and the crane would be there between nine and ten. Sliding the drawings I needed and the logbook into my large leather carrying case, I locked the house, walked to the car, and was reminded of the day before when I went to deposit the case in the trunk. There lay the black box I had pulled from the wall of the mill. The flutter of curiosity from the day before settled on me again. I decided that I had fifteen minutes to spare for a quick look. Unlocking the house again, I took the box into my workshop, and carefully began chipping away the heavy tar covering. Although it chipped away readily, it evidently still provided a good seal, both airtight and watertight. The surface of a well-made wooden box began to appear. The wood had dried and cracked a little but still had its colour and looked like oak. Fortunately, I had started on the correct large side, and within five minutes had exposed the top face of the box. There were no fastenings. Wedging the box securely in my large vise, I grabbed a mallet and a piece of two-by-two and began tapping upwards on the slight lip around three sides of the top of the box. It was on fairly securely, but began to lift after a dozen or so taps, and the shims that had given it a tight fit started to become visible. This was the work of a master cabinetmaker.

In another minute, I was able to lift the edges of the lid, and it came free with a faint squeak. Looking back at me from inside the box was a large book that was set into a custom depression in the bottom of the box. Its leather binding was grey from age. Raising the box carefully so that the covers of the book were vertical, I eased the book out delicately and placed it flat on the bench. Lifting the top cover of the book slightly to avoid any possible cracking, I peered in and saw a page of Gothic script, and at the bottom of the page was printed

Germantown
Gedruckt von Christoph Sauer

This really had my attention, and I could only stare at it in a mixture of wonder and excitement. But I had to sweep all this aside. If I did not get a move on, I would soon be late arriving at the mill, and that would be a terrible impression to give. Carefully sliding the book back into its box, I tapped the lid down lightly, carried it to my desk, and locked it into a large empty bottom drawer. This was a puzzle that needed a systematic approach and specialized help.

By the time Buck and the other two labourers arrived, I had spread out my drawings and had the morning clearly planned in my head. There were handshakes all around. I had already met the other two briefly at The Fox, since they were two of the names given to me by Jasper Armadale. I asked Buck to carry on assembling the roof truss segments, and I took the other two up the scaffolding, showed them how the segments would be craned up, where they would be placed temporarily, and how we would begin putting the full roof truss together. Then all three of us descended to the basement to help Buck in assembling the roof truss segments. When it appeared that this work was in hand and flowing smoothly, I climbed back up from the basement just in time to see the crane pull into the mill.

Just as I finished briefing the crane operator on what had to be done, I was surprised to see Greg's car pull up, and he and another person emerge from it. I was to learn that the second person was Jeremy Aitken, a videographer Greg had come across several years ago, and had used on a number of occasions. They were here to record the crane set up, and the lifting of the roof segments to the top of the mill. Jeremy proved to be a very pleasant person, but almost without conversation. On the one occasion I did try to engage him, he just smiled, nodded, then went back to adjusting his equipment, which seemed to be his only real companions.

Once the craning work began, it moved swiftly. Buck and I were in the basement with the assembled truss segments; the crane assistant and my two labourers were at the top of the mill on the scaffolding. We soon found that it took about twenty minutes to raise each roof segment. By five o'clock we were finished. By five thirty the crane operator and

I had done all the paperwork. By six o'clock we had draped the stacked roof segments in protective cover in case of bad weather over the weekend. By six thirty, Buck, the two labourers, and I had reviewed what needed to be done to start putting the segments in place, beginning Monday morning. At seven o'clock, I locked up the site, said goodbye to Buck and the two others, drove to the post office, emptied my mailbox, then drove home.

The first priority was to update the project logbook. A close second was to shower and put on fresh clothes. And I had decided that a third priority was to go out for dinner. The end-of-week release from pressure and tight schedules had dropped my life into the luxury of whim, so I called Monty without giving the decision to do so any deep thought.

"Ah, Richard!" he said, his typical enthusiasm bubbling from the telephone. "How are you?"

His question was genuine. He could have made a dig about the previous evening's abrupt end, but it would have simply been out of character.

"I'm fine Monty, thanks. I was just going to The Fox for something to eat, and wondered if you would like to join me."

There was a short pause. "Yes, Richard, I would love to do that. Should I bring anything?"

The question puzzled me briefly, but then I realized that Monty would probably be quite happy to pick up where we had stopped the day before. "No, no need to bring anything. I know we're getting together tomorrow, and I assume that is still on"—affirming noises from Monty said it was—"but I have come across something else that I wanted to talk to you about."

"Nothing to do with P-O-L, I assume."

"No, Monty, this might be far more interesting and is as different as it is unexpected."

I could almost hear the flutters of mental impatience and excitement. "See you at The Fox in twenty minutes", he said, and the line went dead.

Nine

It was about eight fifteen when I arrived at The Fox, a few minutes before Monty. The crowd was thin for a Friday, and I took a table next to the large windows looking out on the patio and down the valley. The day had been one of delightful fair-weather clouds, but they had now cleared to a serene blue sky, and the westward listing sun bathed the east side of the valley in a brilliant golden light that made a pleasing contrast to the deep shade clinging to the hills opposite. The moment I looked at the menu, I realized how famished I was, after another long and stressful day.

I quickly settled on pork tenderloin medallions, something The Fox kitchen does particularly well, and then realized that I didn't really have a clear plan on what I wanted to tell Monty or what I expected from him. Any rumination and dithering on that score were left stranded as I saw Monty sweep into the room, carrying once again a fairly thick file under his arm.

It's hard to be in Monty's company and not be in a buoyant mood. His entire person crackles with life and an intense optimistic curiosity. He approached the table at his usual rapid and sprightly pace, sat down quickly, thumped the file down beside him, and rubbed his hands together.

Before he could say anything, I jumped in, "Just so there won't be any arguing, Monty, this is on me."

"Nonsense, Richard", he said waving his hand dismissively, "but let's not waste time on this social pirouetting. What have you found?"

After a moment's hesitation, I came straight out with it. "A bible. A bible in German from 1743."

A horde of expressions swept in sequence across Monty's face: confusion, disappointment, awakening curiosity, and then faint illumination as an interior light came on.

"1743? In German? Could it really be a Sauer bible? What condition is it in?"

"It appears to be in mint condition. And it *is* a Sauer bible. I just peeked carefully at the first page. It was printed in Germantown by Christoph Sauer."

"But what does this have to do with the mill?" Monty asked, failing to hide disappointment that he was not going to be present at the unveiling of an invaluable technological artifact.

"That's the curious thing, Monty. It seems to have nothing at all to do with the mill. Even finding it was simply sheer accident." I looked steadily at Monty. "You seem to know a bit about historic bibles."

"Let's just say it comes from a fondness for intellectual byways, but we need to stay on topic. Was there anything else in the box apart from the bible?"

"Nothing that I could see", I replied, "but bibles often have letters, notes, and other stuff hidden away at favourite chapters and verses. I haven't had time to look through it, and I might need some help there because I don't want to damage it."

"Well", Monty continued, "I've had some experience with old documents. I should be able to tell right away whether we need the help of an experienced conservator. When can we look at it?"

"We can look at it tonight, if you have time, but not until I've had my first real meal of the day."

My meal arrived. Monty had ordered a salad and wolfed it down, not because he was hungry but because he does everything at top speed. Twenty minutes later, I paid and we left.

Dusk was upon us as we pulled into my driveway. Two pinpoints of light flashed at us, and then I saw Max, sitting on the stone wall by the patio, looking bored and gazing at us disdainfully. I let us in, switched on some lights, and retrieved the box from my desk drawer. Monty's interest leapt a couple of orders of magnitude. "Have you kept all the tar bits that you chipped off?" he asked pointedly.

"Well, I haven't thrown them out."

"Good", he replied. "One never knows."

I pulled out a pair of white cotton gloves and handed them to Monty, who gave me an approving nod. He looked closely at the box without touching it. After thirty seconds or so, he indicated that I could open it, and I lifted the lid off gently. He gazed at the dry leather cover, then slid the book out of the box much as I had done earlier, and laid it carefully on a clean piece of newsprint I had placed on the desk. He looked closely at all sides of the book, then slowly began lifting the cover, revealing the frontispiece as I had seen it earlier. After turning several more pages carefully, Monty let out a long, barely audible sigh.

"This is magnificent!" he whispered. "It looks almost as though it's never been opened. Look, there are no signs of any wear or deposits of sweat or soiling from fingers where you might expect them, here along the top corners of the right-hand pages. The binding seems to have dried out somewhat, but is still very much like it must have been the day it left the printer. And it wasn't produced in signatures. Looks like each page was printed individually. And look at the typeface! Must have come from Germany."

Monty carefully turned a few more pages. The book relaxed slightly on the desk, revealing a location where one section of the pages eased away from those below it. Monty then, again very carefully, lifted the pages at that point. A sheet of heavy paper had been folded and inserted into the bible. I looked at the location. I nodded at Monty, since he was wearing the gloves. As he unfolded the sheet, some poetry sat before us, and I quickly glanced at the first line:

Lange lieb' ich dich schon, möchte dich, mir bei Lust

Monty looked at me hopefully, and said, "My German is non-existent."

"I've seen this poem before", I murmured. "I think it's by Hölderlin."

This brought a sharp, inquiring look from Monty. "Early in my career", I explained, "I spent six months at Karlsruhe. I had studied German for three years in high school, but by the time the Karlsruhe opportunity arrived, my German had become a non-functioning mass of half-remembered parts of speech."

Monty's inner impatience began to manifest itself externally. "Okay, Richard, but the poem…"

"I then took courses—"

Monty interrupted again, "The poem, Richard, the poem…"

Finally I got the message.

"Okay Monty. I'll tell you my life story another time. The short answer is that I spent several weeks in Heidelberg in my late twenties, and that's where I first came across Hölderlin."

Monty nodded in satisfaction, and he had the appearance of wanting to say "That wasn't so difficult, was it?"

He then closed the bible carefully. "This is fantastic Richard, but there is something here and now that's more important. Why was this walled up in the mill?" He paused, waiting for me to provide some reply, and when I didn't he asked, "What do you know about the history of the mill? And to satisfy my own curiosity, what *really* prompted you to buy it?"

"I have no idea why this was walled up in the mill, Monty." Short pause. "Why did I buy the mill? This is going to sound stupid, and the reasons are complicated and a bit fuzzy, but the simple statement is that I have a soft spot for things linked physically to history, and the mill seemed to me to exude history. I also wanted a big project to work on, and I could see that if it was handled properly, the mill would have a good deal of inherent dollar value. But without that feeling of history, I think I probably wouldn't have touched the place. Does that make any sense?"

Monty gave a short bark. "You're asking a historian if it makes sense to respond seriously to a feeling for history?"

"Coming back to why it was in the mill", I said, "I found the box only yesterday, and I've known what was in it only since this morning, so there hasn't been a lot of time for reflection. But as far as I can see, there are four possible candidates for who did the walling up: Joseph Adams, William Adams, Robert Harrison, and Gus Ambrose. Of those four, my money is tentatively on Ambrose for one very hazy reason. There is an unpublished history of Greenvale that was written in the early 1950s by Harold Simpson, and in that history he states some things about the mill and refers to its owner Ambrose as someone whose spoken English was faintly accented by German. It's all pretty tenuous, and I have no idea where his 'facts' come from since he doesn't reference anything. I surmise that Ambrose must have been a casual acquaintance of this chap Simpson."

Monty had been nodding as I twisted my way through this explanation. "That's a reasonable inference, Richard, given the information available, but I agree it's all tenuous. We need to try to find out more about this Ambrose."

We sat there, both of us temporarily floating in thought. My gaze drifted across the bible to its box, and was caught by something. Picking up the box, I looked at it end on, then tapped the bottom on the inside, which was a cruciform pattern of inlaid marquetry. Grabbing my ornamental letter opener, I carefully worked the tip into one of the joins of the inlaid cross. One of the pieces of inlay moved relatively easily, and after only a bit of manoeuvring I was able to lift it out completely. The remaining pieces of inlay then came out readily, and as I laid them down on a sheet of paper on the desk in the pattern they had made in the box, Monty marked on the sheet next to each piece the numerical order of their removal. Beneath them in the box was a smooth flat sheet of thick paper, grey-brown and looking brittle from age. Monty, still wearing the cotton gloves, lifted this sheet of paper out carefully. Beneath the paper was another compartment within the box, sized by closely fitting pieces of wood, which created a space in the bottom of the box. Within this space rested another, smaller and thinner, book. Monty and I looked at each other in excitement, and I nodded to him to lift the book out. He did so with great care, and laid it on a separate sheet of newsprint I had placed on the desk to the left of the box. Slowly, Monty lifted the hard cover of the book and we peered inside. At the bottom of the page was a date: 1563. Monty lifted the cover a bit more, wincing when it made a faint crackling noise. We both stared at the first word on the page: *Catechifmus*.

With great reverence, Monty lowered the cover of the book. "This changes everything", he said softly. "This book is a hundred and eighty years older than the Sauer bible, and I think I know what it is." He gave me a long look. "I'm definitely no expert, but I think this might be an original version of the Heidelberg Catechism."

We sat in silence for a moment. "Okay, Monty. Here's what I'm going to do. We will put all this back as we found it and close the box. On Monday morning, I will rent a safety deposit box at the bank and place this box in it. As a cultural artifact, this could be stunning, but as a potential collector's item it is likely to have a dangerously high value. Nobody but you and I is to know about this. Agreed?" Monty nodded emphatically. "Tomorrow, when we get together at the mill, I'll take several dozen photos of where I found this box. Right now, I'll take photos of what we have here. Next week, the research priority will be to troll for every scrap of information we can find about the mill and its owners over the past hundred and forty years. Agreed?" Monty nodded again.

I set up my camera and photographed both books from various angles as they lay on their sheets of newsprint. I also photographed the empty box and both sides of the box lid. We carefully placed the small book back in its false-bottom compartment, laid the sheet of paper back over it, refitted the marquetry pieces, placed the bible back in the box, then closed the box by tapping down its lid, taking photographs of each step. Then I locked the box back in my desk drawer.

Moving to the cabinet at the side of the room, I pulled out a bottle of eighteen-year-old Macallan. I poured a large measure for each of us, we clinked glasses wordlessly, and sipped. Monty gazed into his glass, and nodded in approval at the smoothness of its contents. He then looked at me and asked, "What were the dates for this chap Hölderlin?"

I opened my mouth to answer him, and then froze.

After several seconds delay, I said, "I'm very glad you asked that question, Monty, obviously the experienced historian coming through."

"Why?" Monty asked, somewhat puzzled. "It was just a question." But then his antennae twitched, and he said in a different tone of voice, "Richard? "What is it?"

"Unless I'm mistaken, that poem is entitled 'Heidelberg,' and Hölderlin wrote it sometime in the first five years of the nineteenth century, no later. My suspicion is that this bible has lain in its box for a very long time. It's in mint condition, and that means that it most likely had only one careful owner since it was printed in 1743. Even if that owner was twenty years old when he obtained it new from the printer, that means the owner would have been about eighty at the time Hölderlin wrote 'Heidelberg.' If you allow a few more years for a copy of the poem to reach North America, that would mean that the owner would have to have been at the very least near the end of his life then, and more than likely dead."

"Where are you going with this Richard?" Monty asked, his question laden by intrigue and intense curiosity.

"We've been thinking so far of previous mill owners in connection with this bible. But that would mean that it had to have two, three, or more owners, and I very much doubt that it would survive that and remain in the shape it is in now. So, I think it was boxed and tarred long before even Adams was on the scene. The story of this bible likely goes back much further, and it was stored in this box somewhere else long before the mill was built. There's another person involved here."

From the look on Monty's face, it was clear that we were both peering back into the gloom of history, and wondering just what was going on.

Ten

After Monty left, Google and I teamed up for a bit of research, one result of which was to track down a copy of the book by Bierma. This brief and superficial research on my part into the Heidelberg Catechism revealed that it is one of the basis documents for all modern strains of Protestantism, but it also indicated the subject has an extensive literature. While the size of this literature was not a real surprise, the variety and length of Protestantism's pedigree was. My own curiosity about almost everything remains one of my greatest weaknesses, and I was resisting it now. Specifically, I was resisting the urge to dig into the academic literature on the subject, something I knew would consume hours of time and open several equally enticing avenues. A few good encyclopaedia articles would have to suffice. I switched off my computer, was enfolded by my big leather chair, and sipped another generous glass of Macallan.

I thought that I would have great difficulty dropping off to sleep that night, but I went out like a light and awoke refreshed, as a cherry-red dawn lit the sky and pumped the arterial life of a new day into my room. It reminded me suddenly of long ago, of Alice, but I turned off that thought and locked it back inside its cubicle.

Breakfast was eggs on toast, a peeled grapefruit, and two cups of strong black coffee, all prepared and consumed as the strains of Beethoven's *Fifth Piano Concerto* reminded the house, its contents, and its occupant that life's drama was ever renewed.

A craven text to Greg asked to cry off our lunch appointment and said could he please contact me. He texted back almost immediately saying that something had come up for him as well and that he would call me during the day.

By seven thirty I was at the mill, well in advance of my eight o'clock appointment with Monty. I then dragged the rowing boat from beneath its protective tarpaulin and slid it into the lagoon. I had brought the underwater scope and the hip waders, since I expected that Monty would want to get down and dirty with whatever would turn out to be the explanation for P-O-L. The waterproof bag I used for my camera was big enough to carry the project logbook as well. It was a gorgeous morning, and I expected our efforts to be really nothing more than some juvenile splashing about in water as an activity for its own sake, and yielding nothing apart from a diverting frolic and some worthless artifact resting on the riverbed. I was sitting on the grassy bank making some notes in the log when Monty arrived, fifteen minutes early.

"Richard! Good morning! Great day for treasure hunting! After last night, I can't help but feel that Clio is smiling on us."

"Good morning Monty. As for the treasure hunting, well…the trouble with Clio and the rest of them is that we never know what their real agenda is."

Monty waved this off as weakness of the faint of heart. "I presume you have a plan for how to go about this. What do you want to achieve today?" Monty asked briskly.

"Yes, I have a plan. When Buck and I were here last time, I made some detailed notes based on marks on the mill wall and the opposite shore that we can line up to find the spot again. I thought we would go out in the boat first, and locate our target without kicking up a lot of mud from the bottom. You can have a look at what we saw. Maybe we can work out from the boat what we were looking at. If not, then we can put on the hip waders and do more detailed peeking. What I would really like to achieve this morning is to determine just what we were looking at so that we can decide either that it's nothing noteworthy or that we need to do something more and just what that something might be."

"Sounds excellent", Monty trilled enthusiastically. "Let's get started."

We cast off and I manoeuvred the boat to the point where our position and the two marks lined up. "What I suggest, Monty, is that you take the oars and hold the boat steady while I locate the spot through the scope." After a couple of minutes of awkward seat changing, I was peering over the side. It took some searching, but eventually I recognized the letters. They were a bit blurrier than I remembered, probably because some of the silt Buck and I had stirred up had settled back onto them. Monty was a picture of impatience, scrambling as quickly as stability would allow, to get into position to look through the scope.

"Ah! Yes! I can see it!"

I gave him a few minutes. "Any guesses, Monty?"

"Not really. The letters are well formed. They aren't an illusion. But there just isn't enough to make anything other than completely wild guesses."

"Okay", I said. "Back to the shore we go and into the hip waders." But before we set off, I pulled out a fishing float and a sinker connected by a couple of metres of fishing line. "Just so we have as little trouble as possible locating the spot again, because when we wade out there we'll be stirring up a lot of silt unavoidably."

We rowed to shore, pulled on the waders, and then started back out. I suggested to Monty that we approach the spot from the south, because there was likely to be a slow drift from the north induced by the natural flow of the river.

"What's that for?" Monty asked, pointing to the scuba fin that was now dangling from a hook on my sleeveless Tilley jacket.

"I expect we'll want to fan the bottom, to see if we can uncover more details. I really should have a small pump and suction line, but I think this will do nicely."

Because of the fishing bob, we had no trouble locating the spot again, but almost immediately the view was obscured by the silt our feet had stirred up. I unhooked the fin, lowered it into the water, and began fanning the area. An underwater volcano of silt rose before us and was driven to the south by my fanning action. I continued the fanning for two or three minutes working on all sides of the tantalizing P-O-L. I clipped the fin back

45

onto my jacket, and scanned the bottom using the scope. Standing up, I handed the scope to Monty. "Take a look", I said in my best deadpan.

Monty bent to the task, but after just a few seconds his small adjusting movements stopped and he froze in place. He rose suddenly and demanded, "Give me the fin."

He fanned like a madman, so much so that I had to suppress a snigger, since he reminded me of Max working up to a really good dump after long abstinence. Monty rose, his face bearing that faint smile of victory, and he handed me the scope saying, "Now you take a look."

The bottom revealed two ribs, between which were the words POLSON FOUND. "Monty, what am I..." I began, but then stopped as I scanned further along the direction indicated by the ribs. "Oh my God! It's part of the water wheel!"

"Yes!" Monty couldn't have been more radiant if he had just found the Koh-i-noor. "Do you have any idea what this means, Richard? What we see down there is POLSON FOUNDRY. They were active in the nineteenth century and did a huge amount of work making components for power equipment, entire steam engines, structural members, all sorts. They must have made the structural element of the water wheel for this mill. What we have here is a hulking great chunk of cast iron! Now, please God, let it be still in one piece."

The next half-hour was something of a blur, in more ways than one. We took turns fanning like idiots until our arms were on fire. Eventually, we were able to see that the entire structural element for the wheel lay there on the bottom, as far as we could tell still in one piece. The six spokes were consistent with the grainy photo Monty had shown me two days earlier. We took at least fifty photos through the scope. During all this time, Monty was in almost continuous monologue. He said we had to take a full set of detailed close-up photos using a good underwater camera and a tripod. He needed to be able to examine photos like that to look for cracks. He recounted everything he knew about the Polson Foundry, and cursed the gaps in the historical record. He railed against a succession of long dead Toronto mayors. He characterized every historical society he could think of in terms that would have made a trooper faint. He outlined at least three papers that he insisted he and I would begin working on immediately. He apparently had the salvage operation already sketched out in his head.

While I agreed that this was an exciting find, inwardly I groaned. It would mean almost certainly that there would be pressure to raise and mount the wheel on the mill. At the very least, it would need to be brought ashore for permanent display in some museum. While I wasn't against any of this, I knew it would mean extra effort, a diversion bound to impact my tight schedule for getting the mill into production. But I suppressed gloom-and-doom thinking, since first Monty and I needed to assess what we had in a level-headed way, and this could be done only after the adrenalin surge of discovery had faded.

We waddled ashore, climbed out of the waders, covered the rowboat again, and stowed the gear in my car. Time had flown; it was now almost eleven o'clock. At my suggestion, we went back to my place, put the gear in my workshop, and then downloaded the pictures from the camera. I gave Monty a copy of them on a memory stick, and transferred another set to my tablet.

"I suggest", I said to Monty, "that we spend a bit of time thinking about this. If you have time, that is." He nodded in a way that indicated not even wild horses…"Let's sit out on the front patio and enjoy the day while we're at it." More nodding.

Grabbing a tray, I loaded onto it a collection of soft drinks, a couple of glasses, a scratch pad, some pencils, my tablet, and a damp cloth, and I led Monty out to the patio. After brushing leaves and dust from the patio table, I pulled up two chairs, laid out our material and we sat. Neither of us said anything until the soft drinks were selected and poured. Taking a big swig, I leaned back in my chair, gave silent thanks to whoever might be responsible for such a beautiful day, and watched the shifting sun and shade through closed eyelids. Cicadas were singing the promise of a warm afternoon, and large cumulus clouds were building to the south. My efforts at pruning last autumn had delivered results; the trees all around my property were healthy and profusely leafy.

I took another sip of my drink and gazed at Monty. He was looking down at his hands in intense thought and nodding slightly to himself every few seconds.

"A penny for them", I started, "but first let me say, Monty, that I hope I can rely on your expertise in both these ventures."

He looked up in surprise, almost in shock. "Richard! I would be deeply disappointed if I could not go the full way on both these extraordinary discoveries. The water wheel is squarely in my area of expertise, but I suspect that the books are far more significant, although well beyond my professional competence. But I do know people. Could I suggest that we first explore what we might do on the water wheel? The books will require thinking of a different order, but I can get my teeth into the water wheel business pretty much right away."

"My thoughts exactly. So, let me outline what I see as the constraints on moving forward on the water wheel business. Assuming that this will raise some professional historical interest, I'd like to see things move ahead as soon as possible. But, my priority is still getting the mill running, and although I assume that you feel it important eventually to have the Polson wheel at work on the mill, if possible"—vigorous nods here from Monty—"I can't see how it will be possible to do that this year. I hope we'll be able to raise the wheel from the riverbed by the end of autumn so that we can give it a close examination, and so that I can see whether, and if so how and at what cost, it can be put to use in the mill. I'd much prefer to see it functioning the way it was intended, rather than being locked away in some musty display as just another historical orphan. Putting it to use in the mill might not be possible, of course, if the wheel is damaged, cracked, weakened. Speaking perhaps a bit crassly, some good academic interest in the wheel as a living artifact wouldn't do any harm at all to the mill as a historical renovation nor as a commercial operation. But, it needs to be clear that the initial priority is on retrieving the wheel, understanding its condition, and getting all the facts on it straight."

The faint shadow that had begun to cloud Monty's features suddenly cleared. "I'm pleased to hear you say that, Richard. Not only do I have no bias against commercial interests; the more that artifacts can be incorporated into the fabric of the present, providing suitable protections against them being degraded, the more their history becomes a living thing. But let's set philosophy aside for a moment."

Monty took the pad and a pencil and started making point form notes.

"Here are my thoughts. Our first priority is to clear more silt away from the wheel, and get a set of good high-resolution pictures of it. Second, I would like to announce our discovery to the historical world, and a large set of high-quality pictures would certainly grease that nicely. Third, we need to get as much grant money as possible to support raising the wheel and evaluating its condition. But before we will be able to get any grant money, we need to show that we have a competent plan for raising and inspecting the wheel. I know people who can help us do these things, so I suggest that I start talking to them almost immediately. Do you agree with all this?"

"Well", I said, "looks like you have a pretty good handle on things already. Yes, I agree, but with two further comments. First, I will produce an outline plan on what needs to be done to get the wheel mounted and operating as part of the mill. When I have that in place, we can compare our two plans and fit them together. Second, Greg will want to have his own publicity campaign, so I can suggest to him that he put together a statement of what he would like to do and when he wants to do it, and we can compare your notes and his. Otherwise, we're absolutely on the same page, Monty."

We hashed through the thing for another half-hour, and the ideas were flowing freely, but when it had become an armchair problem-solving exercise in the absence of infor-mation, we both called it quits. Monty tore off the two pages of notes he had made; mine were already entered in my tablet.

"So, Richard, I propose that we get together again tomorrow and compare outline plans. I want to head off home and flesh out what I've jotted down here. Any chance that we could get some good-quality photos tomorrow? Some of the ones we took today are not bad at all, but they can be a lot sharper if we use a tripod."

"That works perfectly because Monday will be a busy day and apart from tomorrow I can't see me having time to go back to the lagoon before about Thursday. I have a tripod and an underwater camera housing. Would another eight o'clock start be okay for you?"

"See you then", Monty said, already rising from his chair. We shook hands, and he skipped to his car and sped off. As I watched his car recede, I was a bit surprised to find myself looking forward to collaborating with him on the papers he had proposed. I had to admit that as much as I was enjoying the hands-on aspects of the mill refurbishment, I was missing the more austere and disconnected cerebral aspects of my old employment, and felt a brief wave of nostalgia wash over me.

The remainder of the day passed like a river in flood. Greg called to say that his day was something of a train wreck, but that he had freed up some time and wanted me to see the footage from the craning work. I told him about what Monty and I had found, and after a couple of excited barks he said he would be right over. When he arrived, we did almost a repeat of the discussion Monty and I had. We walked through the pictures on my tablet, I told him about the constraints I had related to Monty, and what we were doing in terms of trying to establish a timeline for the next few weeks, and it was clear that Greg's normally high-speed mental processes were running now well into the red zone. I told him as well about the plans Monty and I had for the morning, and Greg said he would be there as well.

"What? And miss church?"

For that comment, I got a good dose of the bent eye.

After an hour or so, Greg left saying that he wanted to make notes and think about this find more carefully. I worked the notes in my tablet into a draft plan that soon stretched to four pages and raised more questions. At three o'clock, I cleared everything off the patio, put my notes and tablet in the den, and spent four hours working on the parts of the wooden water wheel. At seven thirty, I got out some frozen garlic bread to thaw, sliced some mushrooms, and went out to the back patio to prepare myself a steak dinner. It would be the perfect night to put a large dent in a bottle of good Vino Nobile.

By nine o'clock I had cleaned up and cracked open *Foucault's Pendulum* again, but by nine thirty, Umberto Eco's prose lost the battle against my drooping eyelids, and at ten o'clock, I slid between the sheets.

Eleven

Taking high-resolution photos of the wheel at the bottom of the lagoon was a long and tedious business, but a clear, sunny, windless Sunday was a perfect day to do it. The comfortable chatter of the three of us engaged in focused but undemanding work echoed around the lagoon. Greg agreed to operate the boat as a floating equipment platform, while Monty and I stood thigh-deep with camera and tripod, taking the photos. A review of the first several pictures convinced us that we were getting good-quality, high-resolution images.

The entire effort took a little more than five hours, but by then we had 170 pictures, and even the demanding and fastidious Monty reckoned that that should be enough. We dragged everything ashore, stowed the rowboat, and stopped to watch Scylla and Charybdis rumble past on the other side of the river. Sam Daniels sounded a toot of recognition on the horn, and the happy chatter of youngsters drifted over to us. We then went off to my place to jettison equipment and to download and copy the pictures.

"We'll rely on Monty", I said, "to cast the expert's eye over these to see whether we're likely to face any obvious problem in raising the wheel, but we should all study them", as I handed thumb drives to Greg and Monty.

"Isn't raising the wheel going to be tricky no matter what?" Greg asked.

I had had an idea that morning in the shower for raising the wheel, and I sketched it out quickly. Monty looked at it and said, "Well, you clever dick! I think that just might work." He chuckled and did a little anticipatory victory dance.

By the time Greg and Monty had departed, it was after three o'clock. I spent an hour looking at the pictures, printed out a dozen or so, and convinced myself that we could produce a respectable collage of about a quarter of the wheel, which would make a good reference when the time came to display the individual pictures to others.

Shortly after four o'clock, I let myself into the mill and climbed to the roof. I wanted to make sure that everything was in place for the morning, when we would start early on putting the roof truss segments permanently in place. There would be four of us—Buck, my two labourers, and me—and I could see no reason why we could not finish the job tomorrow, even though it would likely be a long day. But already the roof was fading as a concern, while other priorities rose to take its place.

The intruder alarm system would be installed and tested the next day. The first of the deliveries of electrical equipment and cables were due to arrive on Wednesday. Some temporary utility lighting would be installed the next day as well, since having the roof truss in place and covered in translucent plastic would make everywhere inside the mill gloomier. Once the craning work for the roof was complete, we could begin putting in place the floor joists for the top level in the mill. The roofers would start installing the rust-coloured steel roofing panels in another week, and as soon as that was done, the scaffolding contractor would take down the interior scaffold that now ran the full height of the mill, so that the concrete for the basement floor could be poured. The pour would take only a few hours, but would need an overnight to dry and harden sufficiently. At that point, the scaffolding contractor would erect enough scaffolding on the new concrete basement floor to allow the existing partial main floor to be removed and new joists to be installed. At the same time, the scaffolding contractor would erect scaffolding around the water wheel supports, so that the job of assembling the wheel in situ could begin. Along the way, I knew that there would be dozens of little problems to solve and wrinkles to iron out, and the next ten days would be anything but dull.

I was back home by six, had a light dinner, then spent another three hours working on the last of the water wheel components. Just as I was finishing up, a half-hearted thunderstorm passed over Greenvale.

Monday dawned clear and fresh, and we were at the mill and at work by seven o'clock. We quickly settled into a routine, and the sound of Buck whistling softly to himself made me smile. Despite our different backgrounds and makeups, there were a number of things that brought Buck and me together, and I realized, with something of a start, what two of these things were. First, how much I had come to respect Buck's mechanical skills, and second, that he had an intuitive sympathetic feel for the mill, and would be perfect as a miller. I pondered that last one at some length. The more I thought about it, the better it seemed, and I decided that when we were finished the heavy construction work I would sound him out on the possibility. Thinking that far ahead felt good; it was some sort of confirmation that there was a clear road forward, although we were by no means in the home stretch.

There was good-natured kibitzing as we broke for lunch; the morning's work had gone well, and the roof assembly was almost half complete. We were on the main floor, having descended to collect lunch bags; I sat to one side, eating a sandwich, and noticed Buck looking up at the partly completed roof, and around at the stone walls. He caught me looking at him, glanced upwards quickly, looked back toward me, gave a decisive nod, and smiled. My guess is that the mill was casting a spell over him as well. The idea of Buck as miller returned with greater force. I finished my lunch quickly, drove home to retrieve the oak box and its books, drove into the village, rented a safety deposit box at the bank, and stowed the oak box in it.

By the time I had returned to the mill, the three men were back at it. They had the finish line in their sight, and they worked like demons through the afternoon. By five o'clock, the last of the truss segments was fastened in place. By five thirty, I had given the entire structure a close inspection, and everything was as it should be. By seven o'clock, we had put the plastic cover in place over the roof, pulled the ropes tight to stretch it firmly over the roof form, and tied off the ropes to anchor the covering against wind gusts.

I complimented the three of them on a job well done, and thanked them for their effort on a long day. "There'll be free beer for you all this weekend at my place. My treat. Just let me know what kinds you'd like." This brought nods of enthusiastic approval, and another round of kibitzing. But they were clearly tired, and the two labourers headed for their trucks and their homes. Buck hesitated. He turned back toward the mill and looked at it for a long time. I stopped, wondering what he was thinking, but then realized, with a start, that if things had worked out the way Alice and I had hoped, we could well have had a son who would now be just about Buck's age.

"Could I talk to you sometime…Richard?" he asked in his slightly self-deprecating way, clearly still having trouble addressing me by my first name but doing so at my insistence.

"Sorry, Buck? I was daydreaming."

He hesitated again and fiddled with his hard hat.

"When you have a moment, I'd really like to talk to you about something."

"Sure, Buck. Anytime."

We gathered our things. The days were closing in now. I set the new intruder alarm system, locked the door to the mill and the gate in the security fence, and we walked out into the evening. I headed for my car, waved once more to Buck as he was climbing into his truck, and drove into the village to collect my mail.

My mailbox was stuffed with the usual disappointing junk. But as I was leaving the post office, Greg waved from the opposite side of the street and loped across to me. He was still charged up about the wheel in the lagoon, and we passed about ten minutes going over things again, until I suppressed a yawn, at which point Greg apologized for detaining me, wished me a good evening, and went off to his car. By the time I got home it was dusk, night was falling, and I was really beat.

As usual, I pulled in to my driveway intending to swing directly into the carport, but was surprised to see Buck's truck parked next to the front patio. Suddenly I felt silly that I hadn't realized that when Buck said he would like to speak to me he meant right away, and now I had kept him waiting for half an hour. I stopped behind his truck, got out, and noticed Buck flopped, in his signature casual grace, in one of the chairs on the patio. A smile creased my face; he appeared, as always, completely relaxed, and despite my tiredness, I found myself looking forward to sharing a beer with him and spending some time discussing whatever he had in mind, hoping that somehow he had guessed that I wanted him to be working with me in the mill when it began operation.

There was a spring in my step as I approached him, and I was about to reach out and poke him playfully on the shoulder when I realized, from his staring sightless eyes, that Buck was dead.

Twelve

Confused. Dazed. Disoriented.

Images flashed before me, in the manner of the anecdotal moments of drowning, as I struggled to separate nightmare from reality.

At the time, it seemed that I was in this wild state for hours—How?—Why?—Who?—gyrating madly on the lip of a black maelstrom, but it couldn't have been more than a minute or two. Clawing my way out of the inky confusion, I grabbed my cellphone with shaking hands and called 9-1-1, asking for both police and EMS. Then I called Greg. He answered on the second ring, and gasped audibly as I blurted out the news to him without any softening preamble. I confirmed that I was at my place, and he said he'd be right over. I disconnected again and waited.

Looking around, but trying to keep my gaze from returning compulsively to Buck, I thought closely about what I had done here. Had I moved anything? *No.* What had I touched? *Don't be stupid, Gould. It's your place. Your fingerprints will be everywhere.* Where had I walked? *Straight from my car to within four feet of Buck, where I was still standing.* Had I gone in the house? *No.* Was the house locked? *Should be.* Had anyone broken in? *Don't know.*

A siren whooped briefly in the distance.

Lucidity began to return, but it was absurdly afloat on what seemed a bottomless pit of irrationality and contradiction. Odd thoughts rose out of the murk. I worried briefly whether Buck was comfortable. The question "What did Buck want to talk to me about?" went round and round in my head. What would I do with any tools that Buck might have left in the mill? While trying to quiet these troubled waters, I was walking toward the entrance to my property, thinking that I needed to intercept Greg, prevent him from entering what might soon be determined to be a crime scene.

Greg and the EMS vehicle arrived at the same moment. The EMS attendant asked where "the body" was. I pointed, trying not to look where I was pointing. He asked whether the police had arrived. Not yet, I said. The attendant moved over, checked Buck, and shook his head negatively. Just then a cruiser drew up, and a uniformed officer stepped out.

He nodded at Greg. "Mayor Blackett," he said flatly, and then turning to me he asked abruptly, "are you Gould?"

"Yes", I said, still in a daze.

"And where is the subject?"

My heart sank at the thought that we had here someone of limited capability but who was eager to recite the jargon he had learned at the academy, something that I knew would raise my hackles.

"Over there in the chair", I said, pointing again.

"And is the scene just as you found it?"

"Yes", I replied.

"Have you moved anything?"

"No."

Turning to Greg, he asked, "And why are you here, sir?"

"Mr. Gould phoned me when he found Buck, and I came straight over."

"Found who?"

"Buck Filmore", Greg said. "The man in the chair."

"And how did he get in the chair?"

"I don't know", I replied. "What you see here is what I found when I returned home."

"Whose vehicles are these?" he asked.

"The truck belongs to Buck. The car is mine."

"And you just pulled in directly behind the truck?"

"Yes. I didn't know it was there until I saw it in my headlights."

"Why did the subject come here?"

"I don't know...I won't ever know."

"Remain here please", he said, and he pulled out a powerful flashlight, a small camera, and a roll of police tape. He walked carefully toward the truck, shining his flashlight on the ground in front of him. He then walked to the chair, shone the light over Buck, and then all around on the ground near the chair. I watched him take a dozen or so pictures. He then walked slowly toward the carport, and did a long circuit around Buck's truck, going as far as the trees at the edge of my driveway. He shone his flashlight on the ground, and took another six or seven pictures. He then walked back toward us.

"The gravel over there near the trees is disturbed. Looks like somebody accelerated away quickly. Did you do that any time today or yesterday, sir?"

"No", I said, and made involuntarily to go and have a look. A uniformed arm suddenly barred my way.

Just then another car pulled up, and a man in jeans and a light jacket stepped out. He walked to the constable. "Harrison", he said in curt greeting. Turning to me, he said "Inspector Raymond. And you are?"

"I am Richard Gould. This is my house. And this is a friend, Greg Blackett." Greg and Raymond nodded to each other in recognition.

"Good evening, Mayor Blackett", Raymond said neutrally. Turning to the constable, Raymond said, "What have you done so far, Harrison?"

"I have quartered the scene, checked the subject, identified what might be the scene of a struggle, and found some disturbed gravel over there where a vehicle appears to have left in a hurry. And I have taken fifteen or twenty pictures." All delivered in a ponderous monotone.

"Have you checked for tire impressions?" Raymond asked, again neutrally.

"This is all gravel here—" Harrison began confidently, but Raymond interrupted him.

"There's soil near the entrance from the highway. Did you check there?"

"No. I considered the probability—"

"Please check now", Raymond said interrupting Harrison again, this time more forcefully. Harrison moved off, not trying to hide his ill grace.

Harrison rejoined us and said, slightly defensively, "There appears to be a tire impression over there", pointing to the edge of the driveway just before it joined the shoulder of the highway. A fleeting look of impatience clouded Raymond's face, and he nodded non-committally. "Please stay here", he said to me and Greg. Turning to Harrison, he said, "Walk me through what you've found."

They both moved off, spending at least five minutes near the chair where Buck sat, and examining the ground nearby. Raymond turned to look at us, and asked "Mr. Gould, did you enter your house this evening?"

"No", I replied.

"Is it locked?"

"Yes. I locked it this morning."

Raymond had pulled on latex gloves, and he moved toward the front door, tried the handle, and checked the windows on either side of the door. Raymond said something to Harrison, who then walked around the house, came back to where Raymond was standing, and shook his head. He and Harrison then continued their inspection. Raymond was now making notes in his notebook. They moved to the location where Harrison had reported disturbed gravel, and we could hear murmurs as they discussed something at length. Raymond produced a measuring tape and measured the distance between the wheel marks in the disturbed gravel. He then moved to Buck's truck and to my car and used his tape again to check the distances between the rear wheels. He then went into conference with Harrison again, pointed to several locations and swept his arm across part of the front patio. Harrison went off and shot another couple dozen photos, including quite a few of Buck from different angles. He then cordoned off the front patio, and ran another length of police tape across the entrance to the driveway. Raymond went to his car, took out a sheet of heavy black plastic and what looked like four bricks, and covered the spot where Harrison indicated there were tire impressions.

Raymond turned to me. "How do you know Mr. Filmore, Mr. Gould?"

"He's working for me on the mill restoration."

"Was he working with you today?"

"Yes."

"All day?"

"Yes."

"Was there anybody else working with you?"

"Yes. Two other labourers." I gave him their names in response to a further request.

"And when did they leave?"

"The other two left together, in separate trucks. I left about a minute after them, and Buck was climbing into his truck as I drove off."

"And where did you go then?"

"I drove into the village to collect my mail."

"Do you know where Mr. Filmore went when he left the mill?"

"No."

"What time did you leave the mill?"

"It was about seven forty-five."

Raymond was taking continuous notes as I answered.

"How long were you in the village? And when you left the village, did you come straight here?"

"It took me about five minutes to get to the village and collect my mail. As I was coming out of the post office, I met Greg and we stood out front talking for about ten minutes. Then we separated and I drove straight here."

"And what time did you arrive here?"

"It must have been shortly after eight", I said. The long day, unrecognized hunger, and shock, were making my thinking woolly.

"So you pulled into your driveway, found Mr. Filmore, and then what?"

"I called 9-1-1. There will be a record of the time for that call. Then I called Greg right away." Greg already had his cellphone out.

"And that was at eight minutes past eight", he said, looking at the record of my call to him.

Raymond made a note of all this, but offered no comment. He flipped through the several pages of notes he had made, then closed his notebook.

"Is there anywhere you can stay tonight, Mr. Gould? I'm afraid I can't let you into your house until the crime scene group has finished, and I can't say for certain when that will be. And I'll need the keys to your house and to your car. You will need to leave your car here."

"Yes", said Greg. "He can stay with me." I passed my sets of keys to Raymond.

"Good. Can you both give me your phone numbers? Here is mine", Raymond said, handing one of his cards to each of us. "I expect to be in touch with you again tomorrow morning, Mr. Gould. I'm afraid there will be many more things I will need to ask you, just so you are aware. Do you have any questions?"

"Yes", I said. "How did he die? And are you considering that there was foul play?"

"In answer to your first question, I don't know and I won't speculate. That's a matter for the medical examiner to determine. In answer to your second question, that's something either to be confirmed or ruled out."

He looked from one of us to the other, to determine whether we had more questions. "Very well", he said. "I'll be in touch tomorrow morning, Mr. Gould."

Raymond turned away from us, and indicated to the EMS attendant that he would need to wait until the medical examiner arrived. Greg gripped my arm gently and turned me toward his car.

When we parked in the driveway to Greg's picture-postcard nineteenth-century house, all the lights were on inside. Even before I reached the door, it opened, and Jill came to me and unashamedly gave me a very tight hug. I could feel her tears on my neck. She pulled away, brushed her wet cheeks, and said, "Come in, come in", in a wavery voice. Inside, she blew her nose loudly, regained control, and all three of us went into the sitting room. Coffee had been made and was sitting to the side. Greg looked around and assumed control; without asking, he poured three cups and carried them across to the table on a tray, on which there were also two glasses containing generous measures of brandy. Without thinking, and without any finesse whatever, I picked up one of the glasses and took a large chug, remembering as I tasted it that Greg didn't drink cheap crap.

"You've just had a hell of a shock after a long day, Richard", Greg said in a matter-of-fact voice. "You should take a shower and borrow a change of clothes. That will make you feel at least a little better."

"And after that, you must eat something", Jill pronounced. "I bet you've had nothing since lunch."

I had drunk half my cup of coffee by then. "Come with me", Greg said, and led me to what he referred to as the guest suite at the back of the house on the ground floor. The "guest suite" was a large bedroom and an adjoining bathroom. "You get into the shower, Richard. I'll be back with a change of clothes in two minutes."

Even in my half-numbed state, the shower felt good, and I cranked up the hot water as high as I could bear. When I stepped out of the shower, there was a neat pile of clothes on the vanity next to the towel rail. I towelled myself viciously, changed into Greg's clothes, combed my hair, and then rejoined Jill and Greg in the sitting room. Jill had made a plate of ham sandwiches on thick-cut whole wheat bread, and she passed me a napkin and shoved the plate toward me. I took a sandwich and bit into it without enthusiasm, but as the flavours of ham, mustard, and mayonnaise filled my mouth, my hunger awakened with a vengeance.

We sat and talked of various things. Jill tried to draw me into a discussion of the water wheel at the bottom of the lagoon, and I answered her politely but without really engaging. I finished the rest of Greg's excellent brandy, and three minutes later was surprised when my head nodded.

"Okay, Richard. Off to bed with you", Jill said in a soft motherly tone.

I remember pulling the sheet up to my neck. And I remember weeping hot bitter tears of fatigue, grief, and anger just before the blackness flooded in.

Thirteen

The bedsheets somehow had a different smell, and I lay in a fog for a few seconds. As the world came into focus, I was puzzled at not being in my own bed. Then the pain of remembrance rushed back in and I groaned.

But it was seven forty-five, and despite the circumstances, or perhaps because of them, I had to be a good guest. I slid out of bed and staggered into the bathroom, where I found that an airline emergency toiletry kit had been placed conspicuously beside the sink. Comb, disposable razor, toothbrush, toothpaste, deodorant. I washed, shaved, and dressed quickly, and went out to the large kitchen. Jill and Greg were sitting at the table in front of mugs of coffee and opened newspapers. They both rose as I entered. Jill came directly over and gave me a long hug; Greg found a cup and poured me a high-octane coffee.

"Sleep okay?" Greg asked.

"Yes, fine thanks", I said, while managing a weak smile, and biting back the further comment *and woke to the same shitty world.* "Did Raymond phone?"

"No, not yet."

I was just about to take my first swig of coffee when my cellphone vibrated. Pulling it from my pocket, I checked the display. "Raymond", I said, and answered. He was polite, asked how I was, and requested that I come to the detachment office within the next half-hour. I promised to be there, then I called my two labourers, apologized for the late notice, and said that we would not be working for the next day or two, that I would let them know when to turn up again. I looked at Greg.

"Of course, I'll drive you", he said, and we both headed for the door. Jill hugged me once again before we left, and in my state of loss and need I clung to this sheer animal comfort.

The interview at the detachment office was more formal. Raymond covered all the same ground as the previous day, and some aspects of it he went over three or four times. He asked me many more questions about Buck, and nodded without comment at my responses. I suspected that he had checked on quite a few of my statements from the previous night earlier that morning.

And then it was over.

"You're free to go Mr. Gould. I do understand what a shock it must have been to find your friend like that, and I hope you accept my sympathies. I'm sorry that we had to put you through the wringer, but we're reasonably convinced now that you had nothing to do with this."

But he wouldn't answer any further questions. How did you reach your conclusion about me? What did you find? Where is the inquiry going now?

"Sorry. Can't comment."

Raymond returned my keys, and I got a lift in a squad car back to my house. Max was outraged by my absence, even though he has been chipped and can come and go through his own exclusive entrance to the house. But, then, cats are a lot like people—they hate to be in the dark and not in control.

The first thing I did was throw open all the doors and windows. (Not true, actually. First I cuddled and fed Max.) Then I went outside, in great trepidation. The patio furniture had all been moved around, presumably by the police. The chair Buck had been in, and I realized with a shudder that he probably had been placed in it, was still there, and there was dried blood down the webbing on the back and on the seat. There was also a small pool of blood on the patio. Walking over to where the gravel had been disturbed by a car accelerating away, I noticed there was a small depression where a patch of gravel and some soil apparently had been removed, probably also by the police. I reached two decisions immediately, and went back into the house to act on the first of these.

The phone at the other end was answered after the second ring.

"McLachlan."

"Stuart! Hi. It's Richard."

"Hey, Richard! How the hell are you? What's up?"

"I need to talk to you, Stuart. Do you have any time free this afternoon?"

"Well, yes I do. But judging by the display, you're calling me from somewhere north of the treeline."

"I can come into town. There are things I need to do there anyway. I can be there by three thirty. Does that work for you?"

"That's fine. Are you going to your condo?"

"Yes. That's where I'll park."

"Okay. Let's meet at Bellagio at about four. I'll try to grab a corner table on the patio."

"Perfect. Thanks, Stuart."

"See you soon, Richard. It's been too long."

The second decision involved a bucket, a scrubbing brush, soap, and some bleach. My plan was to remove—no, to scrub into oblivion—the stains from the stone flagging on the front patio, to clean up the chair, then to disassemble the table and stack table and chairs in the carport, ready to be carted off the next day to the second-hand shop. But at the last minute, I thought better of it, and put the cleaning stuff back in the utility room.

It was midday on a Tuesday, traffic was light, and by three fifteen my car was in its parking spot in the basement of my condo building. I made several calls from the condo, then went to the unit next door to see Ms. Cameron, who had agreed to collect my mail from the mailbox downstairs, although most of it was being forwarded by now. She invited me in, we had a cup of tea and a chat, I collected my mail, commiserated on the state of the world and the noise in the city these days, and then left.

From my condo building to Ristorante Bellagio is a five-minute walk at most. From the name, you might think that the place can't decide whether it's snotty or Clooney, but in fact it's a very nice, slightly expensive spot that has a strong and steady clientele, maintains a superb northern Italian cuisine, and presents a wine list that manages to combine the sensible and the exotic. Its patio is in an enclosed courtyard, where tables are sufficiently separated that your neighbours aren't jotting down the details of your conversation. And, as promised and expected, there was Stuart sitting at a table in the only corner of the patio that was in sunshine. He rose immediately, waved, and his boyish smile flashed across the patio.

We exchanged the insults that are standard between close friends, the usual trivialities that get one past the first three minutes, and Stuart asked about the mill.

"I'm here because of something related to the mill."

Stuart's inclined head gesture invited me to continue. I spent fifteen seconds talking about the construction programme, then got right into the matter of Buck's death. I needed to go on for only about a minute; Stuart was always incredibly quick at picking up the outline of a "case" and homing in on the right questions.

"How much blood was there?" he asked. I knew enough not to worry about tracing the reason for his questions. Best just to answer since we would get to the nub of the matter faster that way.

"Very little. Probably less than a quarter of a cup altogether."

"Was your house broken into?"

"No."

"Was anything stolen from outside the house?"

"No."

"What did the police tell you?"

"About their investigation? Nothing."

"Did they take anything away? Any tools? Any objects of any sort?"

"No tools. My tools are all locked in the house. Nothing from the front patio. No chairs. I think they did take a scoop of gravel and the sand underneath it from near the car tire marks."

It was my turn to ask Stuart. "Do you think whoever did Buck in was waiting for me? Do you think it was a burglary gone wrong?"

Stuart shook his head. "No to both. If he had been waiting for you, I think he would have taken more trouble to avoid the possibility of somebody else showing up. I doubt that it was a burglary gone wrong. If he had planned to break in, he would have made sure he knew where you would be for a decent length of time. If he'd been watching you that evening, he would have known that you had finished work, that you drove off into the village and would be gone for some unknown and possibly short length of time, but then would likely be coming home. No, I think he went there for another purpose."

"What purpose?"

"Not sure. Maybe he wanted to case your house. Maybe he wanted to do something else. I need to take a look. But I think that whatever he came to do would take only a short time to complete. Your friend Buck was just very unlucky."

"Do you think this was a professional job?"

"Professional in the sense he was used to operating in at least a minor way on the shady side of the law. I doubt that he was a professional thief. He would have planned it better. I doubt very much that he was a professional murderer, for the same reason, but also because of the evidence of panic as he sped away, if it was his car that made those marks. I think he was probably alone. But, look Richard, these are just my best guesses."

"You say you need to take a look. When could you do that? When would you be able to come to Greenvale?"

"How about right now?" Stuart said without hesitation. "If we leave now, we can be there well before dark. I can stay overnight, and be back here by seven tomorrow morning."

And so it was decided. We finished our glasses of frascati over five minutes' more small talk and catching up, paid, and left. Stuart knew the way to Greenvale, so we travelled separately, since he would need his car for an insanely early start the next morning. On the way home, I took a detour to Heinrich's Surf and Turf, a quirky, old world, one-man country vendor that has the best beef and fish for miles around, and picked up two large rib-eye steaks and some rainbow trout, so that I could cover Stuart's favourite meals that night. We got there within fifteen minutes of each other (me first), while there was still more than an hour of light in the sky.

"I assume this is the chair", Stuart said, looking at the dark streaks on the back webbing. "And I suppose the chair was about here", he indicated, "and that this patch of blood was where your friend bled after he was placed in the chair."

"You think he was placed there?"

"Yes. One could suppose that he was struck from behind while he was sitting here, but it would be hard to sneak up on someone like that." Stuart stopped and listened. "It's quiet here. It would probably be quieter still in another half-hour when it would be full dusk. No. I think that whoever was here heard your friend drive in and had time to pick a place to lie in wait."

"Couldn't he have just waited until Buck left?"

"He could have, but what about his car? It seems that it was there and fully visible. What if Buck had been suspicious and got on his cellphone to report a possible prowler? And what if Buck had a key and let himself in to wait? What if you two had an appointment to meet here? No. I think that whatever this guy was trying to do, it wouldn't take that long to complete and either he hadn't started yet, he was in the middle of it, or he had just finished and wanted to get away. In any event, it looks as though his plan was to turn up, do what he wanted to, and leave without there being anybody to know he was here."

"So, you think he didn't really intend to kill Buck?"

"No. I don't think he did. I think he panicked and hit him way too hard. I think he wanted Buck to be unconscious for a few minutes—you would find him or he would report the incident to you, there would be a short police investigation, they would conclude that it was a ham-fisted burglary attempt that was thwarted, and that would have been it."

"So what would the guy have been trying to do?"

"Let's take a look", Stuart said.

I just stood back and watched. Stuart walked to the middle of the driveway, where he could see the highway, the land sloping away to the willows on the south, the entire front of the house, and the carport. He then walked to the tire marks, stooped and examined them for almost a minute, drew a measuring tape from his pocket and measured the distance between them, and followed their projected path out to the highway. He stopped for about thirty seconds to examine the edge of the highway. He then walked back and looked at the house. After a moment, he walked up to the window to the left of the door, looked in, and then examined closely the edges of the window. Next, he walked back down to the gravel driveway, across it to where the grass verge began, and continued down the slope where the grass fell away from the edge of the driveway and led down to the row of willows, which stood about twenty metres away from the edge of the driveway. He walked around each willow tree, carried on through some shrubs at the edge of my property out to the highway, and then beckoned me to join him over there.

"Whoever came in here was planting bugs", he said, as I neared him.

"Bugs?"

"Listening devices. Follow me, but don't say anything."

We walked back to the house, and up to the window he had examined and he pointed to the top left corner of the window. I looked where he was pointing and shrugged, puzzled. He indicated to follow him, and now we retraced his path down to the willows. He went to the third tree from the highway, the largest one, and the one having the most luxuriant weeping branches. We parted the hanging willow fronds and made our way in under the tree's canopy. Stuart walked to the back of the tree and pointed to an area of disturbed soil that had been covered, apparently hurriedly, by the few bits of leaf and bark that had been lying around. My raking last autumn had left lean pickings. But then Stuart pointed to a thin wire that rose out of the ground and was stuck to the tree bark using duct tape.

Stuart beckoned me to follow him again, he led me to his car, and gestured for me to get in. We both climbed in and closed the doors.

"What's going on?" I asked.

"Somebody is listening to what's happening in your house. They're using fairly cheap and dirty tools, but those tools are reasonably effective. There's a small bug in the corner of the window, and it transmits a signal to the box buried next to the tree, and that box transmits it on to wherever they're listening."

"Is there any way to find out where they are?"

"Not easily, but they can't be all that far away. Those devices have a limited range."

"What would they be listening for?"

"No idea. But they've gone to a fair amount of trouble, so it's something they have a serious desire to know."

"Well, let's just rip the listening device off the window."

Stuart shook his head. "No, they could just come back and replace it. For now we have a slight advantage in that we know they are listening, but they can't be sure that we know that. Buck's death will have cast a shadow over their efforts, but they can have some confidence that you don't know they're listening. Because the signal would have stopped if you had removed the device. But the somewhat darker side of all this, potentially, is that they're still listening. They haven't cut their losses, even though the police have become involved. That means that there's something they want to know pretty badly."

"What do you suggest?" I asked.

"Well, we have to inform the police of what we know fairly soon. Not to do that would leave us open to a charge of interfering with a police investigation, and neither of us wants that. But first, we need to do a bit of homework. Is there a hotel in town?"

"No."

"Okay. There must be one or two motels within about five kilometres of here."

"Yes, there's one, the Greenvale Motel, about two kilometres south of the village. The next one is at least fifteen kilometres south of here."

"Good. Fifteen kilometres is too far. What I want you to do now, Richard, is go into the house, mutter to yourself a bit, moan about a long day or something, and then pretend to take a phone call. Make the caller completely imaginary, not anybody that you or anyone else here would recognize. Talk about anything. Have a one-sided conversation for about two minutes, then say goodbye and hang up. In the back of the car here, I have a device that will tell me whether that box is relaying what you're saying. So, I'll go down to the tree now and wave to you when I've set up. You then go into the house, count to five, and start your mumbling."

We carried out Stuart's plan. After I had finished, I slipped outside again and climbed into Stuart's car.

"It's working", he said, "so someone is probably still listening. Now we need to go have a look at the motel." We drove south, past the motel, and stopped about four hundred metres away, in a lane leading to a farmer's field. Stuart reached across and took a small pair of binoculars and a notepad and pencil from the glove compartment. He handed me the notepad, and focused the binoculars on the motel.

"Could you note this down, Richard? Grey late model Altima, plate AXMH 337, red Volvo, looks like an XC60, plate BBFR 019, dark blue Ford Focus, plate BAST 955. There's another car around the side, but I can't see the plate."

"Is it a brown Subaru?" I asked.

"Yes. Does it belong to the owner?"

"Yes", I confirmed.

Stuart pocketed the notebook and put away the binoculars. "All right", he announced, "let's go and see the police."

Fourteen

Raymond came through the security door into the public area of the police station, smiled wanly, and extended his hand. He looked tired. One eye was badly bloodshot, and there were damp patches at both armpits of his shirt. "Mr. Gould. I didn't expect to see you again this soon. Please come through to my office."

Raymond punched in the code, the door clicked, and we passed into a dismal corridor flanked by offices whose walls and doors were last cleaned during the Flood, and whose interiors would surely be even more dismal. Raymond opened the door to his office, and gestured to us to enter. From a round wooden guest table, generously marked by years of less-than-gentle use, he pulled out two utilitarian chrome and fabric chairs that were well past their best-by date. "Please have a seat. What can I do for you?"

I looked at Stuart, then jumped straight in. "It's related to Buck's death. Let me introduce a friend, Stuart McLachlan." Stuart had his private investigator's ID ready and passed it over to Raymond. The temperature in the room immediately plummeted by 20 degrees.

Raymond looked at Stuart without enthusiasm, then turned to me. "I am disappointed, Mr. Gould, that you should have felt the need to bring in a—" and he paused here as though stepping around something unsavoury on the sidewalk, "a private investigator. I don't need to warn you, Mr. McLachlan, but I will anyway, that if you interfere with or hinder our investigation in any way, there will be consequences."

Before I could continue, Stuart began speaking in a neutral, even conciliatory voice. "Let me assure you, Inspector, that the last thing we want to do is interfere or get in the way. Richard understands that there is little, if any, information about your ongoing investigation that he can be made aware of. In fact, we've come here today, because there's new information that we want to pass on to you that might be useful."

Raymond's face was the picture of scepticism. "Perhaps I wasn't clear enough, Mr. McLachlan. I don't want either you or Mr. Gould meddling in the matter."

"And I have already said, Inspector, that that is the last thing we want to do. Please just let me outline—" but he was not able to finish.

"I see that I will need to be blunt, McLachlan. I'm telling you both to keep out", and as he said this, Raymond rose from his chair to match the hardened crescendo of his voice, and to indicate that the interview was over.

I recognized later that this was the moment my stubbornness and determination finally began dictating my role in the entire affair. And in retrospect, I was surprised at the strong tone I used.

"Inspector Raymond, please sit down and listen! Somebody has planted at least one listening device at my house. It is operating as we speak. That's what Stuart discovered just this afternoon, and we've come here to make you aware of that situation. You can try to brush this off if you like, but there's an ongoing invasion of my personal privacy occurring, and if you are prepared either to ignore it or to do nothing about it, then I assure you that I will go public with this information. So can we please have a rational discussion about this!"

Raymond stared at me coldly. "Mr. Gould, I do not respond to threats, and I suggest strongly—"

"Inspector Raymond. I do not make threats. But I do promise you that I will go public if that's the only course left to me."

Raymond ran his hand through thinning grey hair, turned, and walked to his desk. From a drawer, he pulled out a plastic bottle of water. Holding it up, he said, "Would either of you like one?" Stuart signalled no, and I yes. Raymond moved slowly and ponderously back to the table, set the two bottles down gently, then retook his seat. It was clear that he was making a considerable effort to reset his approach, and at that moment I felt sympathy for him.

He looked at me, then at Stuart, and then began speaking to Stuart. "Very well", he began. "First, Mr. McLachlan, can you give me some idea of your background? Then please outline what you found, how you found it, and what prompted you to look for it."

Stuart spoke at length, stating first that he and I had known each other for more than twenty-five years, and that he had spent eighteen years with a national security agency ("and that's as much as I can tell you about that part of my background"). He recounted my telephone call to him that morning, how I had come to Toronto and he and I had talked, and that we had then both driven to Greenvale. He gave times for all these events. He described his suspicions about the entire situation leading up to the attack on Buck, he indicated why he thought it was neither a burglary gone wrong nor an attempted attack on me that had gone off the rails, and how he was led to the conclusion that somebody was at the very least sussing out my house, and possibly going further. "So", he concluded, "although I had no specific reason for suspecting that somebody wanted to spy on Richard, it seemed a good possibility. Once I started looking for a bug, it wasn't hard to find it." He went on to describe the bug itself, and the relay transmitter hidden next to a willow tree, that we had not disturbed them and that they were still functioning.

By this time, Raymond had begun listening closely, and was making notes.

"Why would somebody be eavesdropping on Mr. Gould? What would they be listening for? What would they want to learn?"

"We have no idea", Stuart said.

Raymond thought for a second. "Just knowing about a listening device indicates that the situation could be much more involved than we have suspected up to now, but it doesn't on its own get us much further forward." He tapped his pen against the desk, indicating that he detected a blind alley.

"On its own, no, it doesn't", Stuart agreed, "but we might be able to move ahead by making some assumptions."

Raymond looked at Stuart speculatively. "Go on, then", he prompted.

"First", Stuart began, "assuming that this isn't being orchestrated by someone in the village, then somebody from outside has set it up. The transmitter they're using doesn't have a long range, so they must be listening somewhere nearby. They wouldn't just sit for hours in a street or at the side of the road; it would invite too much suspicion." Stuart reached into his pocket and pulled out the notes I had made of cars and plate numbers at the motel. Stuart explained what we had done and passed the sheet over to Raymond. "If one of these cars belongs to our eavesdropper, and if he's at the motel listening, then he would be likely to react in a predictable way to what he might see either as good news or bad news coming to him from the bug. Good news could be that he hears what he's looking for, but we don't know what that might be. Bad news would be if he became aware that his identity and location had become known, or if he were to detect that the bug suddenly went dead, indicating that somebody had found it. In either of those cases, I suspect that he would be spooked. But there's also another way around this."

"I hope what I'm about to hear is legal", Raymond said with considerable misgiving.

"It involves trickery", Stuart replied, "but it's entirely legal. There's one thing, though, that I would like to do first, as a precaution. It's probably me being paranoid, but all the same I think we", and here Stuart was addressing me, "should do it."

"What's that?" I asked.

"We need to look for other bugs", Stuart said to me. "But that's something you and I can do separately."

"Hang on a second", Raymond said ominously. "This is a police matter, and I stress again that I will not have you interfering in it as you see fit."

"Sorry, Inspector. I didn't mean it that way. We would do this only with your agreement in advance. And anything we find would be reported to you right away. I'm happy to let you and your people take the lead, but, and without intending any disrespect whatever, I've had a great deal of experience in this. On that basis, do you agree?"

There was a pause here. "Yes, okay, but one of my men will accompany you."

Stuart and I looked at each other doubtfully at that point.

Raymond sighed. "No, it won't be Harrison."

Stuart spent the next five minutes outlining what he had in mind. Raymond shook his head and suggested a somewhat different approach. There was a to-and-fro discussion, and further questions from Raymond, who still seemed quite uncomfortable with the whole thing. Then Stuart and I left. When we arrived at my place, a constable was already there waiting. I had to hand it to Raymond; he could move quickly, although perhaps he was just distrustful. Constable Brierley introduced himself, and we waved him to my car where we sat and planned how we would search for other bugs.

We left the car, and then worked in silence as we quartered the outside of the house. It didn't take long; we found a bug by the kitchen window at the back of the house. Stuart looked at it closely, made a rough drawing of it in a notebook, and scratched a few lines of notes. We went around the house twice, but didn't find a third bug. Stuart then waved us back to my car. We climbed in and shut the doors.

"It's a more sophisticated bug than the one we found earlier today. It works through cellphone signals, so you dial in to listen."

Brierley demonstrated that he was awake. "Why would they install a second bug, and why have it different from the first?"

"I'm not entirely sure", Stuart said, "but it might just have been insurance, in case the first one should fail. Also, it's a different design altogether, so both would be very unlikely to fail in the same way." Stuart changed gears at that point. "Well, Constable, I think we're finished here. What I propose to do now is send a text message to Inspector Raymond saying that we've met you here, we've done the search, we found a second bug, and that I will send him further details in a more formal report. Thanks for your help."

We left my car and shook hands with Brierley, who climbed into his cruiser and drove off. Stuart then spent a few minutes composing and sending the promised text message. "Okay", he said. "Now I have to rearrange tomorrow. Our little plan with Raymond means no early start in the morning, and that's a bit of a relief, actually." Stuart worked on his cellphone, sending a number of text messages, then closed it and put it away. "Done. What's next?"

"I think next is dinner", I announced, and told him what I had picked up on the way to Greenvale.

"Ah! That's my man! I vote for the steaks!" Stuart said with enthusiasm through a broad smile, and we headed for the front door. After only a few steps, Stuart's hand on my arm caused me to turn and look at him questioningly. The smile was still there. "I suggest", he began, "that we keep up the interest of chummy at the other end of the bug. Let's go inside and have a short provocative conversation where we don't actually say anything but give him something to chew on all the same." And he outlined what he meant.

Having delivered our non-message to the listener and delivered several bottles of wine from the clutches of the wine cooler, we headed out to the back patio, which Stuart judged to be well outside the range of either bug. I immediately put Stuart in charge of getting the barbecue fired up and being wine steward, while I prepared potatoes for baking, laid out condiments, some bismarck herring for starters and baklava for dessert. It was a mixed bag gastronomically, but I heard no complaints from the gallery.

While the potatoes were baking, initial glasses of Negroamaro slid down silkily, and we watched the first stars switch on. Under the effects of the wine and the deepening night sky, things went quiet, and as he had been able to do in the past, Stuart surprised me, "Anything wrong?" he asked.

I took a long look at my glass, and failing to find an answer there, said, "Oh, not much. Just everything. Buck's death. Not being entirely sure why someone wants to spy on me, or who that someone is. And I don't really buy your rationale for the second bug."

Stuart waved a hand dismissively. "Well, that wasn't a rationale at all, just something for the constable's consumption."

"Something else is concerning me", I said, and then continued when Stuart inclined his head questioningly. "Monty and I discussed both the books freely in my living room. If the bug was in place then, whoever is listening will know about them, and in particular will know that I have them."

Stuart thought for a moment. "If it really is the books they're after, I would have expected them to bring a professional thief in right away to take them from the house before you had a chance to place them somewhere more secure. The guy who was interrupted here was nowhere near that level, so I assume that he was here to install the bug. He probably planned to arrive at dusk, when visibility is poor and before you got home, plant the bug, in and out."

I felt some relief at this, then went on to another topic.

"What made you want to look for a second bug?" I asked.

Here there was an uncharacteristic pause. "Just call it a funny feeling."

"Did you expect to find a second bug?"

"I don't know. But when we found it, there was another funny feeling."

I looked at Stuart directly. "Do you think that the two bugs are independent, that they were planted by different people?"

"It's possible", he said, "but if so, it's quite bizarre."

When I said, "Maybe not that bizarre", Stuart looked up sharply. But then I shook my head, waved an empty wine glass in the air, and said, "Where's the damn wine steward when you need him?" Stuart moved to get the bottle. "Come to think of it", I continued, "where's the damn chef?"

We both smiled in the twilight, I got the steaks ready to slap on the grill, wine glasses were refilled in a spirit of Mediterranean abandon—spilling a little just to show what's really important—and we dug into large delicious portions of bismarck herring. Having broken the gloom barrier that had quietly piled up around us, I spent the next fifteen minutes bringing Stuart up to date on my new life in Greenvale, while fielding the jibes and relaxed insults that had always made everything work for us. For the rest of the evening, we pushed aside all thoughts of bugs and got on with the simple job of being friends.

Fifteen

Stuart was already up and had coffee on the go when I emerged and came down to the kitchen. The previous evening's activities had capped off a long day, and we had both turned in fairly early, despite a shared desire to talk ourselves further into the night. Even accounting for a sound sleep, I noticed a spring in my own step that I didn't find an explanation for until later. This was despite the matter of bugs and spying gnawing away at a deeper level.

It was another cloudless and windless morning, so we took all the breakfast clobber out to the grill on the back patio, and lashed up bacon, eggs, and toast. It was a simple setting, but it captured a sensuous moment: the tangy smoke coming off the bacon, the hiss and sputter of bacon fat falling into the fire, the campground smell of toast prepared over hot coals, the rich, sweet, fatty scent of eggs cooking in butter, something that always reminded me of a French kitchen, and the whole primeval response evoked by the sight of smoke ascending through slanting sun into the morning air, as though to appease the gods. Over coffee, which was consumed at a languid pace, I caught Stuart gazing almost wistfully at the sun burning off the high morning mist, at the grass on the hills behind us, heavily laden by dew and winking prismatically, and at the blanket of fog that had been tucked, as by a loving parent, over the slight dip in the highway just to the north of us. I knew what Stuart was thinking: *A beautiful and sublime moment, to be sure, but I would be stark, raving, foaming-at-the-mouth bonkers here in less than two weeks.*

Constable Brierley called in at eight thirty to work out the details of the sting we had agreed on in rough form the previous afternoon in Raymond's office. After Brierley had left, I noted to Stuart that we (or at least I) had to be at the mill by nine o'clock because the delivery of electrical components and cabling had been promised between nine o'clock and noon. I suggested that he might like a tour of the mill while we waited for the delivery, an offer he agreed to without hesitation. So we cleaned up the breakfast things, locked the house, and walked the short distance to the mill.

As we approached the mill from the road, Stuart looked up at it. "It's a big bugger, isn't it? Why was it made so large?"

"When we get to the other side of the mill", I said, "you'll see part of the reason, and I'll explain the rest as we go along." I unlocked the security fence gate and the big door to the mill itself, disabled the intruder alarm, and switched on the temporary lights. I wasn't ready for the feelings that washed over me. Although it lasted only a few seconds, the series of images was powerful: the painful recollection of Buck having worked in here and how he took to it so quickly and so strongly; then the oddly anthropomorphic aura that covered every part of the mill structure—of something proud, abandoned in its prime, and now slumped in despair—that I felt when I first saw the mill as a discarded ruin; the initial sight of the solid interior walls which spoke of strength, longevity, defiance, and determination; the day when the afternoon sun suddenly waxed brilliant, and the mill reflected back to me a hopeful and encouraging smile; the surge of optimism at seeing the roof truss finally in place, the scent of the fresh timber transfusing the air in the mill and promising new life; and over the past few days, a feeling almost of partnership with the old building. That day, the usual hit of happiness and enthusiasm was there, but it was more subdued, almost as though some new bit of reality had entered the picture, or a minor but still unwelcome disadvantage had suddenly become obvious. But much worse was the sense of almost being able to hear Buck's carefree whistle echoing throughout the empty structure. I knew at once what had triggered my smile earlier (was it really just two days ago?) when I had stopped to listen to Buck working and whistling. It had been the sound of someone belonging, of being at home, of expressing a proprietary interest, and that, I now knew, was what had brought to my mind the idea of Buck as miller. As I reflected on that moment, I knew, now, that another mental shift had just occurred.

Stuart was standing there, looking at me quizzically while I ruminated, and I came back to the present with a thud. It was clear that seeing the mill up close had moved Stuart from a position of mere polite interest to a state of much greater curiosity and engagement. So I gave him the full tour. We clambered up and down ladders. I indicated where the new equipment would be placed.

We then went outside, around the south side of the mill, and walked down to the water's edge. I pointed to the twin supports for the original water wheel, which rose from the lagoon like a giant split conning tower. "The original wheel rested just there, on those two supports. The bottom of the wheel would have cleared the surface of the water, so you can see how large the wheel would have been. That explains part of the reason for the size of the mill—to accommodate the large wheel. If you look out over the river", I explained, "you can see that the mill was located at just the right spot. The river is at its narrowest just upstream of us and the obvious place to put a dam, the gradient of the river bottom is greatest just in this stretch, and it was easy to conduct water around the dam and along the raised channel over there and supply it to the top of the wheel."

"But even so", Stuart commented, "the spindle for the wheel would be about six feet above the water level, and the top of the wheel would be about twelve feet, definitely not more than fifteen feet, up the side of the mill, but the mill has to be at least forty feet high. That's a lot of internal space. What did they use it all for?"

"Old Adams, the guy who built the mill in the first place and really got it working, was apparently something of an empire builder. Ever thought of the logistics of milling flour? People eat bread and cake all year, but all the grain is harvested in just a few weeks at the end of the summer. Today, there are companies whose existence is dedicated to storing grain until it's needed for milling. In the nineteenth century, and particularly before the railway came through, virtually every little settlement had to take care of this logistical problem on its own, and keeping harvested grain free of pests, moulds, moisture, and whatnot, isn't that simple. And when you depend on your granary for sustenance until the next harvest, it all becomes suddenly quite important. Old Adams wanted to be a one-stop service. He wanted to buy the grain, store it under his control and for a price, of course, and have it available immediately when he needed it for milling."

"So he used the extra space to store grain?"

I nodded. "But also to store the milled flour, and the bags to put it in, and it became a sort of living space for times when milling might go on day and night. It was probably also a storage space for spare millstones, and a workspace, since he would need to have a stonemason sharpen the stone grinding wheels every once in a while, and he would have to maintain a rather long powertrain of shafts and wooden gears. I expect that you're right though, that the mill is a lot bigger than it really needed to be. But it would have been a hell of a symbol of his wealth and standing."

"Can you make all this pay for itself?" Stuart asked directly.

I smiled in a way that I hoped was suitably sphinx-like. "The answer to that I shall deliver in two parts, or maybe more than two. The first part is that there's always some risk involved in a venture like this, but at one level I have a who-gives-a-shit attitude", and I noted with satisfaction his mild double take.

"I've always been amazed at how people try to diminish the role of emotions in their decisions. My first attraction to Greenvale, and later, to this mill, was a visceral one. I didn't logic my way to it, at least not initially, and I have no real idea how anyone would do that. So, I'm doing what I'm doing because that's what I really want to do. The second part has several subparts, but I won't bore you with the details. Can I make it pay? I have a plan going out five years to do just that, and it looks feasible, and I'm certainly going to give it one hell of a try."

Stuart took all this in, while gazing at the walls, roof truss, the stonework around the windows, and he seemed, at the same time, to be imagining new floors, the sound of a working flour operation, the splashing of the water wheel. I thought I heard him mutter "You lucky bastard."

At that point I had to break off since the truck delivering the electrical equipment had arrived, and I needed to show them where to put it. When I returned to where I had left Stuart, he then turned to me and said, "Show me where you found the books."

We went to the shipping door, and I opened it to give more light. I showed him the block of facing stone, which I had now slid back into place, explained the hoisting operation that had originally led to this block being dislodged, and how I had come back later that same day, on my own, and found the tar-covered box.

"How long had it been there?" he asked.

"I've thought a lot about that in the past few days. The last owner of the mill was a man called Ambrose. He apparently abandoned the place in the 1930s, and that was either just before or just after the fire that ate through the interior floors and took off most of the roof. Did he hide the box here before he vanished? I don't know why he would do that, especially since it seems he didn't come back for it. After he vanished, did he come back surreptitiously and hide it? That seems even more problematic. Did somebody else hide it? If so, who, when, and why? Monty is trying to make an estimate of when the box was placed there, but I don't know on what basis he's doing that. I've had another idea that I haven't had time to follow through on yet. So, I just don't know, Stuart."

"Do you know where this Ambrose went, what happened to him?"

"No, not a clue."

"Do you have much information on him?"

"A little. Why?"

"If he hid the stuff here, he might not have been able to come back for it."

"Because something happened to him?"

"Could be any of a number of reasons."

"So, I don't see…"

"Well, I have a decent track record at finding people. And I've always liked a puzzle. I could give it a try."

This was something I hadn't thought of at all, and I accepted Stuart's offer immediately. "I'll get you the details I have as soon as we go back to the house. And we need to get back there soon", I said, looking at my watch.

We talked as we walked back to the house. "We have to remember", Stuart began, "that we can't be certain what exactly the listeners are interested in; it could be something having intrinsic value, it could be something that might be damaging to someone, we don't know. So we have to keep our conversation general. For the benefit of our listeners, I'm visiting you to make an archaeological assessment of some aspect or feature of the mill that we don't need to be specific about, but the main purpose is to give the listeners information that nobody will be in your house for a good three hours." We batted around some lines, but then went silent as we turned up the driveway toward my house. I unlocked the door, and we went in.

"So, just to finish what I was telling you in the car", I said, as we walked into the living room, "I have no idea what happened after that. Have a seat. Can I get you anything? And I must say, Mr. Kraus, I am indeed grateful to you for coming all this way to see me and to make this assessment."

"Not at all", Stuart (Mr. Kraus) said. "A bottle of water would be fine, if you have one."

Taking two bottles of water from the fridge and two glasses from the cupboard, I also grabbed a file from my desk and walked over to the sitting area. "Here you are", I said.

"Ah, thank you."

"And here are the papers I was telling you about in the car." I passed to Stuart a few photocopied pages relating what little was known about Ambrose.

After we had poured out our water into the glasses, I broached the main part of the discussion, "Going back to what we were saying earlier, what would one of these items be worth?"

There was a short delay, then Mr. Kraus said pensively, "Well, just for its rarity as an artifact, perhaps a couple of thousand dollars. It's hard to imagine anyone wanting to add it to a personal collection, but people do collect the oddest things. A serious collector, who had already an extensive collection, might put a fairly high value on it, and we could be talking about quite a few tens of thousands of dollars. But something like that is hard to move around. And I really must state again, Mr. Gould, that the item in question has considerable historical value, and information about it is bound to leak out, sooner or later."

I laughed comfortably. "It will be just fine. This is Greenvale, for Heaven's sake. We aren't bothered by vandals and thieves here. In any case, now that we know about this amateurish snooping operation, I'll be getting rid of it soon."

"Well, I would feel better if you took my advice, Mr. Gould, but I won't press it further."

There was a short gap here while we sipped our water. "So", I began enthusiastically, "would you like to meet Professor Montgomery?"

"Ah, yes! Very much so! I've heard a great deal about him, both as a historian and as a character!"

"Okay. I suggest, then, that we go over to his place. It's now, let's see, ten thirty. He assured me that we could drop by any time. There's no such thing as a short meeting with Monty, er ... Professor Montgomery, so I would count on a few hours, then we could take him out to lunch, and have you back here in time for you to be on your way by three o'clock this afternoon. Would that be suitable?"

"Yes. It sounds excellent! We can take my car."

"Good. Let's be off." We left the house, locked up and climbed into Stuart's car. Once in the car, I pulled out my cellphone, and soon I was speaking to Brierley. "Okay, constable. The clock is running."

I gave Stuart directions to Monty's place, and called Monty on the way there. He was waiting for us outside as Stuart drove his car onto the gravel area next to Monty's small Suzuki hatchback, I made quick introductions, Stuart handed Monty the keys to his car ("in case you need to move it"), and the three of us jumped into Monty's car. He drove us back to my place, let us out, waved farewell, and returned home. I got out three folding chairs, and was carrying them toward the huddle of shrubs to the left of the line of willows, when a police cruiser drove up, Brierley got out, and the cruiser went off again. We set up the folding chairs among the shrubs. It could end up being a long—and possibly fruitless—wait, but we considered it worth a shot.

After more than two hours had passed, my pessimism was growing. Maybe it was all just a fantasy. Maybe we were the dupes, sitting around waiting for something that just wasn't going to happen. Well, it would give Brierley a good story to tell. Just then, Stuart elbowed me gently.

"See that car there? It's the Ford Focus. That's the second time it has cruised past. Let's get ready."

On the next pass, the car drove silently into my place and parked where it was all but invisible from the highway, near the carport, and facing the street. By this time, I had my camcorder running. The driver emerged from the car and spent about fifteen seconds standing still, just looking around. He was about forty-five, balding, about five feet eight inches tall, wore jeans and a faded grey windbreaker, and looked athletic. He was also wearing what looked like driving gloves.

From the back of his car, he removed a black sports bag, and walked up to the house. He went straight to the bug on the window, removed it, and put it in his jacket pocket. After looking around, he walked down to the willow tree where the transmitter had been placed, took a garden trowel out of his sports bag, and began to dig it up. He lifted the transmitter out of the hole, removed one glove, appeared to switch the transmitter off, and then pulled the duct tape from the tree. He then placed the transmitter and the trowel back in his bag and zipped it closed. He emerged from the canopy of the willow tree, looked around again carefully, then went back to the house.

He set his bag down on the grass next to the step, tried the door handle, then withdrew a tool from his pocket. He had just begun picking the door lock when Brierley said in a loud, deep voice "Police! Stay where you are! Hands on your head!"

The man slowly raised his hands to above his head. Brierley moved up the path, approaching him from behind, but then things became confused. I heard Stuart murmur "No!" and saw him start moving quickly across the driveway. Just at that point, the man turned and moved with great speed. Almost in passing, and without breaking stride, he delivered a vicious chop to Brierley on the point of his shoulder. Brierley cried out and went down like a sack of sugar. The man ran across the front patio, heading for his car, and at that point he was on a collision course with Stuart. I'm not sure what Stuart had in mind but at just the wrong moment he temporarily lost his footing in the gravel. That was enough. The would-be burglar bodychecked Stuart heavily just as he was regaining his balance, and Stuart too went down as though he had been poleaxed. The car engine roared to life, gravel spewed from the back wheels, and Stuart scrambled out of its path just in time.

I'm no good in street fights, but by this time I was at the edge of the driveway and was carrying a fist-sized rock. I threw the rock, it struck the front window of the car causing a bloom of craze marks just to the right of the driver's view, but the car continued down the driveway, gravel still fountaining from the rear wheels. There was a loud clunk and scrape as the car lurched over the shallow curb, and then the tires shrieked as they bit into the hot asphalt surface, the car swung north, fishtailed once madly, then raced out of the village. The whole episode, from Brierley's challenge to the car disappearing up the highway, lasted less than twenty seconds.

Stuart had pulled himself to his feet and was cursing vigorously. We both went over to see about Brierley, who was still rolling on the grass in agony. We helped him to a sitting position, his face contorted in pain, but he nodded his head in response to our query on whether he was okay.

All I could think of saying to break my silence was, "The bastard got away!"

Stuart nodded but flashed a nasty grin. "Yes", he said to me quietly, so that only I would hear, "the bastard got away, but you have it all on video, his car has been badly marked, and we have that." Stuart pointed toward the sports bag still sitting on the grass where the burglar had dropped it.

"What?" I asked. "The bug and transmitter?"

"No", Stuart replied, still speaking quietly. "He put the bug in his jacket pocket. We do have the transmitter, you're right, but did you see what he did down there under the tree?"

I shook my head dumbly.

"You saw him take off his right glove and he pulled the duct tape from the tree trunk. And right after that, he absent-mindedly placed the trowel in the bag. We can probably get his prints off both the trowel and the duct tape."

At that point Brierley staggered up to us rubbing an evidently very sore shoulder. "I'm sorry", he said, through a mixture of pain, anger, and frustration. "This won't go well at all with Raymond." And he immediately set about calling in the incident.

Stuart shook his head, dismissing Brierley's apology. "That guy was strong", he said, "and he knew how to handle himself. It's my fault that he got away. If I hadn't lost my footing there, the bastard would still be out cold on the ground."

Brierley had moved off down the driveway and away from us while he made his report of failure. I looked at Stuart. "We know something else now, as well", I said. Stuart gave me a puzzled look and then his face cleared.

"Yes!" he said. "The second bug. He didn't take it, because he didn't know it was there, and he didn't know it was there because it wasn't his."

"Whoever placed it there", I said, "will find out about this little episode."

"Not all of it though, if Raymond keeps the information on that bug", and he pointed to the front window, "under wraps."

"Will he do that, do you think?" I asked.

"He might if we suggest it to him."

"I doubt that he'll be in the best humour", I observed wryly, "after having a nominally simple operation bungled royally, and in public."

"Yeah", Stuart agreed, "he'll be in a black mood, and he'll definitely want to grill us."

"Surely there's little we can tell him that Brierley won't already have spilled."

"Probably not", Stuart sighed, "but he'll likely consider it good for his soul just to put us, and especially me, through the wringer. But we can use his goodwill." Seeing my blank expression, Stuart continued. "To give us access to the fingerprints he lifts from the trowel." Here there was a pause. "I can't do anything officially, but I make it a habit of doing a lot of people a lot of favours. I can ask around about the 'man in the video' and we might get lucky just on that basis, but if we get those prints, I can call in a few favours and try to get some hard info on who that joker was, and maybe who he was acting for."

"I guess that will mean continuing to co-operate with Raymond", I said.

"To a point. But I plan to make it clear to him, using the little diplomacy I have, that this was his operation, not ours. We're not going to wear any shit that falls out because of this fiasco. And I think that we would be in a very different position right now if Raymond had agreed to my original suggestion: if the guy was going to break in, let him get inside, and have a constable in there already. Having people inside, and people outside, the chances of his slipping away would have been much less. But Raymond insisted on doing it his way. And I'm pretty sure he'll make it crystal clear that our involvement in any further investigation is now over. Period. But we, you and I, need a plan on what to do next."

It was my turn to look puzzled.

"You said it yourself, Richard," Stuart began, "that whoever planted the second bug will hear about this incident. What's he going to think? That just by sheer coincidence there was an attempt by someone else to break into your house? Remember that each of the people who had bugs planted had no reason to suspect that there would be a second bug."

"So why", I asked, "didn't the owner of the second bug also respond to our sting conversation? They would have heard it as well."

"I don't know."

Just then a police cruiser turned into my driveway. Brierley came up to us to take his leave. "I have to go and face the music now", he said glumly, and he walked toward the cruiser. As the police car drove off, I said, "I need a drink." I unlocked the house, and as we made to go in, Stuart took a handkerchief from his pocket and used it to pick up the black sports bag, which he then deposited behind the front door as we entered. Stuart also made a shush sign to me and I nodded. I went straight to one of my favourite wall cabinets, pulled out a bottle of VSOP and two glasses, and we headed for the back door.

When we were seated at the picnic table on the back patio and had taken a welcome first sip of our liquid platinum, I raised with Stuart something I had been mulling over since the previous evening.

"You're spending quite a bit of time here on my behalf, Stuart. I hope you're planning to let me know how much I can pay you."

Stuart waved off the matter. "No, seriously", I continued. "Nobody works for nothing, and one of the biggest mistakes of all is taking advantage, inadvertently or otherwise, of a friend's goodwill. So, please. Let me know what I can pay you."

Stuart eyed me strangely for a moment. "Okay", he said, putting down his glass decisively. "When this is over, I'll tell you what I would have charged a regular client, I'll discount that a bit, and then you can let me know how much of a stake that would represent in your mill."

I was dumbstruck. "Are you serious?"

"Absolutely", he said. "And now let's not talk about it anymore."

Just then, Stuart's cellphone rang.

"McLachlan", he said. "Hello Inspector Raymond", Stuart said neutrally, while giving me a meaningful look. "Just a moment please." Holding the phone down, Stuart said quietly to me, "He wants us both to come in right away. Sounds like he's in a poor mood."

I beckoned Stuart to pass me his phone. "Hello Inspector Raymond, this is Richard. I would like for us to come in one at a time. I really would prefer to have somebody at my house as much of the time as possible."

Raymond replied almost before I had finished. "No dice", he said coldly. "You will both come in and you will come in now."

"Inspector", I began. "Somebody just demonstrated every intention of breaking into my house, and being violent in the—"

"I'm not going to argue with you any longer, Mr. Gould. You will come in here now!" His voice had risen to just below a shout.

"Very well", I said. "But could you please send a constable out to watch my house while—"

"No, Mr. Gould! And I do mean now!"

The events of the day had been stressful and worrying, the events of the past week had bothered me deeply, Buck's death had kindled in me an intense anger, and now Raymond was really beginning to piss me off. But my years of working with sometimes awkward clients clicked in at the right moment.

"Inspector Raymond", I said slowly and evenly. "If you interrupt me once more, I will hang up on you. I will co-operate with you all you want, but I am *not* leaving my house unguarded. You don't know what that man we intercepted here was looking for, or whether he was working alone. You don't know what damage might be done to my house and its contents if they decided to return, break in, and look for whatever it is they want. You don't know that my house isn't being watched right now. Mr. McLachlan said he will come in right away, but if you want me to come in with him, then either you will have to send a constable to watch over my house or you will have to come and arrest me."

There was a long pause. "Very well, Mr. Gould. I will send a cruiser, leave a constable at your place, and you can ride back in the cruiser." And he broke the connection.

I handed the phone back to Stuart. "What do you think?" I asked.

"I think that Raymond is way overworked. Apart from himself, he has almost zero investigative capability. It sounds as though he hasn't got all the details from Brierley yet. But your place is a crime scene, and they haven't done anything to secure it, including looking after the one piece of physical evidence we have, which is sitting now in your living room."

Sixteen

The police cruiser arrived about ten minutes after Raymond's phone call to Stuart, just before four o'clock. Stuart and I discussed how long we would be at the detachment office (not sure), what Raymond would ask us (probably questions inspired by whatever he got from Brierley), and what Stuart and I should do, independently of the police, over the next little while. We reached a few decisions, all of them conditional on which way Raymond would go.

Since it could be dusk before we returned, I had switched on most of the lights in the house, and put down some food for Max. I had copied the video I had made of the intruder's retrieval of the bug and attack on Brierley and Stuart. But before we came in from the back patio, we discussed what we should do about the second bug. I said I wanted it removed. Stuart agreed, saying he thought that the interpretation of those listening would probably be that the police had found it and removed it.

The constable who came to provide a police presence at my house was large, beefy, and pimply, and had the gangly youthful air of someone who hasn't really grown up · yet. He looked like he had come to us straight from the police academy. He introduced himself as Jim.

"What's this?" The question came from the older man who had driven the cruiser, and he was referring to the black sports bag Stuart was holding.

"Hello Constable Harrison", I said, pleasantly but without any real enthusiasm. "This is the bag that was left behind by the intruder."

Harrison unbuckled his seat belt and began rolling out of the cruiser. "Okay. Give it to me."

"No. It's evidence", Stuart said, backing away slightly. He raised the bag to show Harrison that he was wearing a latex glove. "The less we handle it the better. Inspector Raymond is going to go ballistic as it is when he finds that it's been moved before the scene could be properly examined. If you open the trunk, I'll put it in."

Knowing that Raymond would be questioning us, being aware of the mood he was in already, and not wanting to have more Raymond ire directed at him, Harrison popped the trunk without objections, and Stuart placed the bag in it. The trip to the detachment was a silent one, apart from a somewhat pompous message sent by Harrison saying that he had secured the two "subjects" and was returning to base.

When we arrived at the detachment, Harrison took us straight through to Raymond's office. Raymond looked as though he had had better days. As Harrison slid quietly from the room, Stuart lifted the bag, placed it on the table, and snapped off the latex glove.

Raymond looked at the bag. "What's this?" he asked. I wondered briefly if we were hearing some sort of detachment refrain, good for all occasions. It took Stuart only a second to take in the implications of the question, and he then explained briefly. Raymond rolled his eyes, sending off waves of frustration, and murmured, "Oh, Jesus! No!" Evidently, Brierley had been so shaken up he had forgotten all about the bag.

Raymond sat down heavily, ran a hand through his hair, and rubbed his face vigorously. "Okay," he said in a pleasant conversational tone, "first of all, thank you both for coming in." We murmured our not-at-alls. "I see no point in interviewing you separately since you've already had quite a bit of time together, but what I want to do is get answers from you one at a time, so while I ask one of you questions, I would be grateful if the other said nothing at all." We both nodded.

Raymond's questions were in time sequence, and it was clear that he was following a chronology he had put together from his debriefing of Brierley, a debriefing that was undoubtedly somewhat spirited. He asked about timings, requesting that we be as specific as possible. He asked for details about the video I had taken. After noting that the video was less than five minutes long in total, including quite a few frames giving good head and shoulders images of the intruder, and included the attack on Brierley, the bodycheck on Stuart, and the car racing down the driveway and out onto the highway, I placed the copy I had made on Raymond's desk. I warned Raymond that there would be an unsteady section a few seconds long where I was throwing the rock I had picked up, and trying to operate the video camera at the same time. "Thank you", he said, looking up briefly from his notes.

He spent a lot of time on the details of the black sports bag, where it was when, who moved it from where to where, exactly how many people handled it, whether anyone handled it using bare hands. With regard to the bag, and where it was, Stuart filled in the time after the first cruiser had arrived to return Brierley to the detachment, until the second cruiser arrived to take us to the detachment, noting that we had moved the bag inside the house during that period. I also noted for Raymond that there was clear footage on the video showing the intruder putting the bag down, and confirming that it had not been moved after that until Stuart picked it up and placed it inside the house.

Raymond spent quite a few minutes making notes. He looked back through the seven or eight pages and then asked a batch of further questions.

"Okay, Mr. McLachlan, do you recall anything distinctive about the man's clothing?"

Even I could see that this was a test question, since everything was on the video. "No", Stuart replied. "He was wearing good-quality Adidas sneakers, white socks, faded jeans that looked like they might have been a designer brand, and a grey windbreaker, no logo that I could see, over a pale blue shirt. I believe that the shirt was short-sleeved, because I saw no cuff when he reached up to remove the bug from the window, and the jacket sleeve rode down at least to mid-forearm when he did that."

Raymond made notes, then looked up and nodded, as one professional to another.

"Did you see any distinguishing marks on the man?"

"No, but you can confirm that from the video."

"Did you check the contents of the bag?"

"No. I don't know what's in it, apart from the trowel and the bug transmitter. We saw him put them both in the bag."

"You did get quite close to him at one point. Do you recall anything at all from that?"

"Yes. He's a smoker, he has washed-out blue eyes, and he was probably, at one time, a dirty hockey player."

Raymond looked up from his notes, somewhat surprised.

"Okay", Stuart sighed. "Scratch the hockey comment. I'm still smarting from that bodycheck. I should have had the guy."

Raymond gave a faint smirk, but said nothing. "And when he drove away, where were you?"

"I was scrambling to get out of the way of his car."

"Do you think he deliberately tried to run you over?"

"No. He just made no effort to avoid me."

"Okay. Thank you", Raymond said to Stuart, then turned to look directly at me. "Now, why? Do you have any idea what he was after?"

Stuart and I had discussed this at some length earlier, and had come to a few conclusions, and my statement to Raymond drew on that discussion. "A week ago last Friday, I discovered a box, hidden in the wall of the mill, containing two rare books. Monty and I had given these books a cursory look that evening, but I placed them in a safety deposit box at the bank the following Monday. They are probably worth in the tens of thousands of dollars to a collector. I don't know whether the people who planted these bugs were after those books or not. If they were, I have no idea how they came to know about them, because until just now, only three people knew that they exist: me, Monty, and Stuart. Now you know as well."

"I'm a bit surprised that you are telling me this only now. Why would whoever has been listening not just have approached you and offered to buy the books, if that's what they were after? Why all the elaborate espionage?"

"I was hoping you would be able to tell me that, Inspector. I have no idea. But it does seem to me that the mere existence of the bugs points to someone having a greater need for information than for physical items. There's been ample opportunity, unfortunately, for someone to break into my house and search it, but that hasn't happened."

"Do you have an alarm system at your house?"

"Yes, but you know as well as I that all but the most expensive and sophisticated alarms can be disabled if someone really wants to do that."

"Do you keep money or valuables in your house?"

"No. I have some items that belonged to my wife, but they're in a separate safety deposit box in Toronto, along with insurance papers, will, deeds, and so on."

"Do you have any enemies?"

"There are people I don't like, and most likely there are people who don't like me, but I know of no situation that would induce anybody I have known or come across to go to these lengths."

Raymond questioned me for another fifteen minutes, tying up increasingly obscure and, I thought, increasingly less relevant points. He then thanked us for our time, said that there might be some follow-up questions, and called through to Harrison to take us back to my place and pick up the pimply constable.

As we stood next to the highway at the end of my driveway and watched the police cruiser drive off, I said to Stuart, "Raymond's investigation is going nowhere, but I'm not prepared just to sit on my hands while he stumbles around like a fly in a bottle."

"What do you want to do?" Stuart asked.

"What I should have done some time ago. Use my damn head. Apply my ability to analyse and solve problems. I need to put together a complete timeline of everything that's happened, all the detail I'm aware of, write down all the possible reasons I can think of for why certain central events happened and work out the implications for each of those reasons, try to see where there might be connections, try to see what information I need and how I could go about getting it."

"Okay", Stuart said. "Let's get started."

"I can't ask you to get into this, Stuart."

"Richard. Some bastard almost ran me over today. I'm invested in this up to my neck. So let's not waste time talking any more about it."

I nodded. "Thanks Stuart", I said and we began walking up the driveway to my house. The first thing we noticed was Stuart's car. A note on the windshield said *Thought you might need this. Clavis → Domus. Monty.*

"Crafty old bugger", I muttered, and then, "he's saying the keys are in the house", noticing Stuart's puzzled expression.

Still standing by Stuart's car, I said, "Let's figure out the best way of dealing with the second bug."

"Yes", Stuart agreed. "That means drafting your plan first. When we go in, we pick up some paper and pencils and go out to the back patio. We can draft a plan there out of reach of the bug. Let's see what we come up with, then we can work out the best way of removing the bug."

I unlocked the door, and noticed almost immediately on entering that Stuart's car keys were sitting on the floor below the louvred window that had been left open a crack. Within a few minutes, we were sitting at the patio table and had begun to jot down items.

It took three rounds of making and consolidating notes, but in a bit less than an hour we had a timeline of events, including information flows to and from these events, which of the events were planned (such as the planting of the bugs), and which might have been unplanned (such as Buck's death), and possible uses for the outflowing information. We had also produced a list, the elements in the list linked to one or more of the events, indicating who probably knew what at which points. This included uncertainties: there were things the listeners knew that probably we didn't know, but also things we knew that probably the listeners didn't, and we had to consider that the situation could be changing continuously.

"This is good", Stuart said. "It helps a lot. Excuse me for a second. I have to make some business calls." And he walked to the other end of the patio.

When Stuart had finished and rejoined me, I said, "I have some software for recording and displaying logic diagrams based on information of the sort we've just generated, and tonight I'll enter into it what we've got here. It'll make updating a lot simpler. But it's now seven thirty, and if I don't get some food into me soon, I'll pass out."

Stuart agreed that he realized suddenly how hungry he was as well.

"Fish done in tarragon and butter, with Florentine rice and fresh garden greens?"

"You smooth-talking bastard."

"You can be pyromaniac and cellar master again, and I'll play chef."

We had dinner delivered to the table as the sun set, and ate watching the zodiacal glow emerge subtly in the west, thanks to a moonless night and being far from light pollution sources. Despite the ongoing irritation of being spied upon, I enjoyed another kind of glow brought on by my share of a couple of bottles of nice Aligoté. Dessert was a snifter each of brandy.

It was one of those made-to-order late summer evenings. The crickets were going wild. There was not a puff of breeze, but the air was cool and humid and gentle as butterfly wings. We gazed out through the limpid sky and across the disk of our galaxy, still full of secrets. In the distance, one could hear the river whispering its own secrets in riddles as it slid over the dam. All around Greenvale, the glacial formations that defined the very shape of the village sat as dark but reassuring presences. The hill behind my house was curled up like some large benevolent beast, the inland equivalent of Puff the Magic Dragon.

"Tomorrow, I need to go back to Toronto, Richard. There are things I can't put off any longer. But I have to say that it would be nice to extend this moment indefinitely."

"That's fine, Stuart. You've already done far more than I could have hoped for or expected. I do want to remove that second bug, though, but apart from that I think I can take things from here."

Stuart sat up in his chair, and slowly put down his brandy. "Let's be clear about this, Richard. I'm going to see this situation through to its end. Although I'm going back into the city, there are a few things I'll do while I'm there, and I expect to be back here again for a few more days, very soon. As I said, when someone tries to run me over, I look forward to the opportunity to slam the bugger against a brick wall and ask him what the hell he's playing at. So, one of the things I will do in town is have a copy of that joker's photo, at best resolution, printed off from your video, and find out who he is. He's almost certainly got a sheet, so it shouldn't be difficult to assign a name to him and get a handle on his recent exploits."

"Well, thanks again Stuart, but remember that this is all going to be invoiced. What I want to do here is get things back to something close to normal, where I don't have to worry about bugs, imminent break-ins, and God knows what else. There's a huge amount I need to do at the mill over the next week or so, and it will need almost all my attention. So, I really do want to shut down that bug tonight."

"Yes", Stuart agreed, "I think we can do that. That work we did, at your suggestion, on analysing the information we have so far, is worth its weight in gold. It helps to bring us even with the opposition."

Stuart handed me a card. "This guy will visit you tomorrow. I've told him to call you on your cellphone before he turns up. He'll install a high-end surveillance system in and around your house." Stuart saw my impending objection and held up his hand. "Don't argue about it, Richard. We'll sort it all out later."

I nodded reluctantly.

Stuart then continued. "We might be able to assume, at least for a short while, that whoever is listening at the other end will recognize your voice but not necessarily mine, although if they're well connected, and they're watching us, they could soon identify me from my car plate. We can also assume, I think, that they'll get a handle on the capabilities of the local boys in blue, if they haven't already done that." Stuart paused in thought. "Everyone will know by now that this caper involves a murder. So, if they persist, we can be pretty sure that there's more involved than just an opportunistic attempt to grab a couple of books. When they realize, later tonight, that their bug has been neutralized, will they just pack up and forget about it? I doubt it, and I think it would not be safe to assume that they'd do that. Here's what I propose we do about the bug: We go into your kitchen and talk in general terms about 'it,' but make no direct reference to a bug. We mention Inspector Raymond in passing. Then we'll remove the bug. You then drive down to the detachment on some bogus errand, for example saying that you have some suppliers to visit over the next few days and might be out of the village intermittently, in case Raymond decides he wants to ask follow-up questions. To anyone listening and watching this house, they'll know that the bug has gone silent, and might be tempted to connect your visit to a delivery of the bug to the police. But instead of giving the bug to Raymond immediately, I'll take it with me to Toronto. There are people there I can consult who will be able to tell us very soon whether there's any information we can glean that would indicate who is listening. Do you agree with all that?"

"Yes, I do."

"Okay. Today is Wednesday. I have to spend two days away, but I'll be back on Friday." Stuart then handed me a small gizmo to detect bugs, and gave me a primer on how to use it. "I would use it every time you return to the house after you've been away for any length of time. If you find a bug, take a few photos of it and send them to me."

I nodded.

"Okay", Stuart said with decision. "Let's put our plan into action."

Seventeen

Thursday morning arrived bright and cheerful, just the opposite of how I felt. It was the day of Buck's funeral.

Although I wasn't looking forward to going, I wanted to attend. I knew I had to be able to draw a line beneath my short acquaintanceship with Buck, determine what lasting meaning it had for me, and just figure out how to let go. The simple fact was that, against all my initial expectations, I had grown fond of Buck. I could see that a longer term business link between us would have been possible, I was sure that we would have become good and comfortable friends, and I felt some considerable responsibility for his death. If I had been there that night, maybe I could have done something, maybe things would have turned out otherwise, less lethal, maybe, maybe.... Buck's parents would be at the funeral, and I knew that I would need to, and indeed wanted to, meet them and spend some time with them.

Despite the fact that I resisted doing so, I went to the mill early, and when my labourers arrived I outlined for them what I wanted them to do, and said I would be back late in the afternoon. The rest of the morning I pretended to do paperwork, but it was mostly a sham and just something to distract me.

It had been the police who had informed Buck's parents of his death, and I had to keep reminding myself that we were all dealing with the aftermath of not just a death, but a murder. Greg told me that Buck had a brother, Ivan, and gave me contact information. I had called Ivan, we had one of those twilight-zone conversations where everything seems a bit unreal, I asked whether Buck's parents needed any help getting to and from the funeral, and generally tried to be supportive and available. I managed to say to Ivan how much Buck had come to mean to me as a person, and he surprised me a bit by saying that Buck seemed to have that effect on people generally. I then felt somewhat guilty and angry with myself for being surprised in this way. Why wouldn't Buck have that effect? His natural quietness and shy reserve were very appealing. He had been one of the more open, genuine, and fundamentally kindly people I had ever met.

The funeral service was held in the local church in Greenvale, although the interment would be at the cemetery in Belleville where Buck's younger sister, victim of a car accident, had been buried some eight years earlier. When the time came, I dressed and drove to the church. Even though I was early, the church was already more than half full, and people were arriving steadily.

The service was short, simple, and fitting, but even then it was all something of a blur. I was lost in my own world of recollections, and regrets over all the might-have-beens. Then we were out in the bright sunlight. Jill and Greg were there, and Jill said to me that Buck's parents would like me to join a small gathering at their place in Belleville after the interment. About a quarter of the people at the service were, in fact, from Belleville, the remainder from Greenvale. A few of them were Buck's neighbours in the village, but most, I found out later, were people Buck had done work for. It seemed that he had had a hand in renovating just about every dwelling in the village. In due course, I joined a procession of about fifteen cars that set off down the highway toward Belleville, after getting directions for the cemetery and then for the Filmores' home. I drove on my own, despite many requests by people to join them in their cars and quite a few offers to join me in mine. It was a time for private reflection, and the thought of having to make conversation was just too much.

The interment was also short, simple, and dignified, and before I knew it I was standing in the Filmores' living room, sipping a soft drink, and, like everyone else, trying to find the right things to say. Several people guessed who I was and introduced themselves. And then I was face to face with Ivan.

Where Buck had been six feet two inches, Ivan was five feet eight. Where Buck's hair was blond, Ivan's was sandy. Where Buck had had brilliant blue eyes, Ivan's were grey-green. Where Buck was a rough-handed son of toil, Ivan was evidently someone who worked mostly using his head. Where Buck had been friendly and immediately lovable, the salt of the earth, Ivan was friendly but in a more remote and cerebral way.

"Buck had a lot of good things to say about you, Dr. Gould."

"Richard, please. I have a great many good things to say about Buck as well. I think he enjoyed working in the mill, and I had a sense that he could have become a right-hand man for me."

"Well, he didn't just enjoy working in the mill, Richard. He absolutely loved it. He always was good with his hands, and he had the ability to see what something would look like when it was finished long before it was anywhere near finished. He said more than once that he thought the mill would become the pride of Greenvale."

"Do you know why he chose to live in Greenvale? I never did ask him."

"He said it was the hills."

"The hills?"

"He said they inspired him, gave him ideas. I was never sure exactly what he meant by that. He had a powerful, even visceral, sense of the good and the beautiful. It gave him great joy to create pleasing and useful things with his hands. He didn't envy me for my academic accomplishments, but I sure did envy him for his ability to create."

"Well, I don't know what he saw in me, Ivan."

Ivan looked at me strangely. "No? Really? Well, I know exactly what it was. He didn't understand how you thought. He said to me that your notes and drawings were just about meaningless to him. But when he and you went out into the mill and you explained, showed him what was going to be done, he could see it right away. He said quite a few times that it was magic, and that you were a magician. I'm all but certain he felt that the two of you grazed the same pasture, but on opposite sides of a fence that you could cross but he couldn't."

Mentally I was kicking myself. It all seemed so clear now. *Why hadn't I seen that? Why hadn't I asked?* When it was so obvious after the fact that Buck was making such huge efforts to reach out, despite his reluctance and probably a feeling that he was on a different plane, why the hell hadn't I tried harder?

Ivan seemed to read my thoughts. "You shouldn't feel badly about any of this. Buck had absolutely no wish to become a Dr. Filmore, and he was always remarkably free of envy. I think he savoured every moment he spent at the mill. I'm just sad that he had way too few of those moments. I don't think I can recall Buck ever being so pleased, so delighted, in working at something as when he was at the mill."

"What's your background, Ivan?" I asked, perhaps too abruptly, but wanting to change topics.

"I studied physics at Queen's, took a master's at Toronto, worked a range of jobs for five or six years, but then I hit my stride where I am now."

"Where's that?"

"It's a little place called Quinte Fabricators. We have a total of about fifteen people. Do mostly metal fabrication for small industries. The guy who started it has a nose for anything that isn't quite right, and a knack for selling ideas. In the time I've worked there, I don't think I've ever done two jobs the same."

"Quinte Fabricators. I'm surprised I haven't heard of it", I said.

"I'm not. We do almost no advertising. Everything is by word of mouth, and by the boss's ability, essentially, to butt into someone else's business without offending."

We sipped our soft drinks, and let a comfortable silence prevail for a few moments.

Ivan took a different tack by saying in a refreshingly open way, "At some point, I would very much like to have a tour of your mill."

"By all means", I said. "I'm always interested in contacts with possible suppliers."

"Oh, no", Ivan said hastily. "I didn't mean that, and I'm sorry if I gave that impression. I really want to see what it is that Buck was so enthused about. But I also want to satisfy my own curiosity about a few things."

Given my recent obtuseness, I didn't trust myself to respond right away to his last somewhat vague conversational assay. I responded instead by saying, "It's still a construction site, but I gather that you might be used to that, so, by all means, you can come around any time."

"Excellent!" Ivan said. "I'll contact you soon about that." He sipped his drink, looked at his watch, then said, "Let me introduce you to my parents."

We approached a couple who were clearly the Filmores. They were both tall, slender, and erect. And although their faces were clouded by grief, they looked up expectantly as we walked toward them.

"Mom, Dad, this is Richard Gould. My mother, Andrea, and my father, Peter."

I had decided to steer clear of the standard formalisms for these occasions. Too often they sound hollowed out by use. But then I just stood there like an idiot for slightly too long.

"Thank you for coming, Mr. Gould", Peter Filmore said. "I know it's hard to find the right things to say."

"It's not that, Mr. Filmore. In the case of someone like Buck, it's not knowing what to say, it's finding where to start." Despite my best efforts, my voice became increasingly husky and unsteady, and I had to stop a bit abruptly. Mrs. Filmore teared up right away, but dried her eyes with determination and without affectation. I took an iron grip and continued. "Buck was one of the most natural people I've ever met, and it would be hard for anyone not to like him. We worked incredibly well together, and I'm ashamed to say it's only in hindsight that I realize I learned quite a bit from him."

Peter Filmore had not yet released his handshake, and his grip tightened here. "Thank you, Mr. Gould", he said in a strong, steady voice. "Buck talked to us regularly about working with you, and working at the mill, and I can't recall a time when he was more pleased with a job. He had a high regard for you, but I think it was also the mill itself. He couldn't seem to stop talking about it. I asked him a couple of times how long the job would go on, but he was always vague. Just last week, I asked him again, and he smiled and said that we'll see, that it could go on for quite a long time. I'm not sure what he meant."

There was pretty clearly a question in the air. "He and I didn't have a chance to talk about it, but I would have liked him eventually to be my miller."

Andrea Filmore had to staunch more tears at that point. Peter Filmore's grip tightened still more. "I'm sure that Buck would have leapt at that chance", he said. "As it was, Buck got a great deal of pleasure from working at the mill in the short time he had there, and I really want to thank you for that."

I, in turn, tightened my grip on Peter's hand, and when we disengaged, I turned to Andrea, enveloped her in a gentle embrace, and let her body pulsate against mine, as her grief found another path for release.

Ivan retrieved the situation. "Mom", he said gently, "Mrs. Andrews is here and wants to see you. And I think Richard needs to refill his glass." The Filmores and I exchanged weak smiles. Andrea's hand slid down my arm, and stopped for one last grip of my fingers before she moved away.

"Thanks, Richard. My parents both were not too sure what to expect. Buck's discussions with them, I think, left something that they weren't sure could ever really be closed off. At some point, would you like to come back here to Belleville and join us for dinner somewhere?"

"With pleasure, Ivan. I would love that. But I have a counter-offer. The mill will have a restaurant, and I'd be pleased if you could all join me there for a meal. I could give you a tour, show you everything that Buck and I worked on."

Ivan's expression cleared at that. "Ahh! Now! That is something I will accept immediately on their behalf. I think it should wait a few weeks, though."

"That's fine, Ivan. It'll be at least a few weeks before the restaurant is even close to opening. How about I keep you up to date?"

I stayed another half-hour. Jill caught my eye, and indicated that they were leaving. Ten minutes later, Ivan passed me a slip of paper torn from a small notebook, on which he had written his email address, and I said I would contact him as soon as I arrived home. He then led me over to his parents.

Peter and I exchanged the same firm handshake, but his smile this time was more relaxed, less laden by grief. Andrea gave me a warm hug, and softly said "thank you" into my ear.

At the end of the drive home, I realized that a rite of passage had occurred, that at one level, at least, I had said "adieu" to Buck. I let myself into the house, changed from suit to work clothes, and went straight to the mill.

Eighteen

During the following week, I spent about fourteen hours at the mill most days. The two labourers, plus an additional one to replace Buck, did most of the work that needed to be done to clear the way for the various other crews that came and went, while I seemed to spend all my time sorting out little problems. It took two days for the roofing to be completed, and Greg had his videographer, Jeremy, on the scene for several hours each day. At the end of that time, the mill wore a fresher smile, accentuated by the steel roof panels of dark cherry lipstick, chosen to mimic the colour, and as closely as possible the design, of the original roof. While the roofing was being done, that part of the electrical cabling and HVAC ducting not dependent on the floors being in place was installed along the walls. Practically before the roofing crew left the site, workers began tearing down the internal scaffolding, and they were finished just in time for us to do a cleanup before the concrete pour for the basement floor began. As the basement floor was being poured and was setting, scaffolding was erected outside around the two stone supports for the water wheel, and my three workers and I transported the components for the wheel from my house to the mill in a total of eight pickup-truck loads.

By this time, the activity at the mill had begun to generate a good deal of local interest, and twenty to thirty people stopped by every day to rubberneck. Greg had anticipated this, and we agreed that since almost the last of the heavy vehicles had come and gone from the site, we should start making the public face of the mill more attractive. An asphalt surface was laid for the parking area, a low stone wall was built around it using stone that matched the mill, tubs of flowers were set onto the wall, and a flagstone pathway was laid leading to the main entrance to the mill. Because it was an active construction site, the mill itself remained off limits to the general public, but that didn't mean that we couldn't tease them and whet their curiosity. We had an information board set up at the edge of the parking area, indicating what we were doing, what the end result would be, and when the whole thing was expected to be complete and the mill open for business. I noted with satisfaction that quite a few people spent time in front of this board, and more than a few took pictures of it as well as of the mill.

In the midst of all this, my application for a heritage property designation was approved, and the brass heritage plaque arrived. The following day, the sign that Greg and I had spent hours designing and arguing about also arrived. It was a large, solid, rectangular placard weighing several hundred kilos, red background the same colour as the roof, grey and red edging, and had the name "GREENVALE MILL" in gold capital letters sixty centimetres high, in a typeface similar to **ENGRAVERS**, set in the middle of the red background. When it was mounted on the side of the mill facing the highway, it was perfect, and I admit to an inward smile; increasingly, the mill looked like someone getting dressed for a big party.

Over a period of weeks, Greg had been busy with his high-end camera equipment. When he showed me some of the stills he had shot, they took my breath away. The photos were stunning. There were three-quarter shots of the mill showing great sweeps of cirrus cloud in an otherwise brilliant blue sky. There were detailed shots of parts of the stone wall around the parking area, and I could see that they were the forebears of similar shots that would include rogue dandelions, bunches of tall Johnsongrass, wild chicory, delightfully diminutive and demure wild barley, and anything else that would suggest the intimate thoughts, resting dormant for so long, of a hundred-and-fifty-year-old structure. There were shots in early dawn light, and shots at various times in sunset. There were dramatic shots, taken from the lagoon, showing the mill looming against the sky almost as a medieval structure. And there was a brilliant series of time-exposure shots that caught the mill resting in selenic languor beneath a huge harvest moon.

"Greg, these are fantastic", I said as we reviewed them one evening at his place. "We'll need to have a picture gallery in the mill."

"That too", Greg said, obviously pleased at his work. "Some of them are going here on my walls, and I expect you might want a few as well." As I nodded agreement, Greg continued, "But a lot of this is in aid of the publicity programme I have in mind." Greg hardly needed to elaborate, since I knew his instinct, and his acute eye, for publicity. It was my own responses to these pictures that surprised me. As much as I tried to keep a neutral and businesslike focus on the project, the mill as a multisided, almost living entity, kept asserting itself, but at another level, there was a feeling of deep satisfaction at having pulled back a coating of historical amnesia and peered in at the blurry glow emanating from the remnants of a past reality. Snatches of my former enthusiastic, almost manic interest in history lunged into the present, and I was suddenly there again with those great people I had idolized in my teen years: Heinrich Schliemann (warts and all), Leonard Woolley, V. Gordon Childe, Edward Carr, Geoffrey Elton, Robin Collingwood. Almost as an accusation, the question rose before me: *Where did all that go?* The feeling swept over me so suddenly and in such force, that it was clear immediately I needed to spend some effort thinking it through, and a chat with Monty would probably be in order.

That evening, Stuart called. "I'll be in Greenvale tomorrow mid-morning, if that's okay with you Richard. I have some news. I would also like to set up a satellite office at your place, but we can talk about that later", and we left it at that.

Just after my discussion with Stuart, my phone rang again. It was Monty. Despite the latish hour and the fact that I was tired, I agreed readily to have him come over. What to do about the cast iron frame for the water wheel at the bottom of the lagoon was becoming more urgent, and I was interested to know if he had had any further thoughts.

Monty skipped through the front door, carrying a stack of books and file folders, and clearly full to the brim in further thoughts.

"Richard!" he began, in more staccato urgency than usual. "I have a lot to tell you, so let me just run through it all first, then we can discuss points of detail." And when he said he had a lot to tell me, that was no understatement.

I have no idea how many showers must have been needed for Monty to rid himself of archival dust, but he had evidently spent many hours poring over venerable records. First, he had dug up an old account of the mill's water wheel, giving details of its design and casting. The account was by a local historian, of whom even Monty had been unaware, and was based on records that had since vanished, but it was as close to a pedigree as we could get, and much closer than I had ever hoped. It also turned out that the mill's water wheel was the only example the Polson Foundry had ever produced, and this had caught the attention of a number of historians and industrial archaeologists. Monty said that when he dropped the bomb that we had found the wheel and it appeared to be intact, several of these worthies had almost shat themselves. Just the act of recounting it again had Monty falling about in great titters of delight.

Monty then shoved all that to one side and pulled out a six-page, single-spaced typescript of the history of the mill as he had put it together. He had managed to research and compile an almost complete account of the construction, ownership, and operation of the mill, right down to its final and bleak closure after the fire. My question on where he had found all this stuff was waved aside, and his account thundered on. He gave me a copy, saying to read it later, that he had more to tell and couldn't stop now. There was another anxious flutter of manila folders, and the lights dancing in Monty's eyes signalled that he had reached the pièce de résistance for the evening.

"And now", Monty pronounced, in the sweeping flourish of an academic about to overwhelm his doubters and bury his critics, "I am delighted to tell you that we have full funding to raise and recover the water wheel! The only string attached is that we'll have to do a bit of public ass-kissing to help make a few politicians and bureaucrats look good, but some decent toothpaste, mouthwash, and lip ointment should ease that burden." He handed me an official looking document, requiring a signature and the submission of some estimates and promising funding, pending authentication, authorizations, blah, blah, blah, up to a quite generous limit.

I hugged him. What else could I do? "Monty, you are a marvel! Thank you and congratulations!"

When I loosed my grip on him, he did a little pirouette next to the desk. "I also went by the mill today, Richard, for the first time in a few days. It's…" and here, to his alarm, his eyes began to fill. Shaking his head in annoyance, he managed to get out, "It's beautiful, Richard. It isn't often that one can be present when history is resurrected like this. But there's still so much to do!"

"I know exactly what you mean, Monty, and I've had my own little tryst with History in the past day or so, and I needed to talk to you about it."

"With pleasure, Richard, but there are also those papers we must write."

We talked a little about that, Monty indicating that he had done a tad more thinking, me gently indicating that I would be under the gun for the rest of the week getting the next few major pieces of work done in the mill.

My tiredness must have been evident, because Monty wrapped the evening up quickly, and said goodnight, but not before we had made an arrangement to have dinner, and talk over a few things at more leisure.

I don't even remember walking up to the bedroom.

Next morning, Wednesday, I was out of the house by five forty-five. My labourers arrived ahead of the requested seven o'clock start time, I briefed them on the excavation for the lower patio, and work began in earnest. Within an hour I was pleased to see it proceeding at a cracking pace, accompanied by that colourful banter indicating workers who enjoy their work and who work well together. A whirlwind of tasks came and went, and at mid-morning I took a short break to call Stuart. He had arrived, was setting up his local office, had plenty to do, and would see me when I got home, whenever that might be. Just after lunch, the electrical installers arrived, and by the end of the afternoon, all the heavy electrical work had been completed, the equipment set up, connected, and tested. At seven o'clock, I declared it a day. The labourers left, delivering volleys of smiles, waves and insults, and drove off, each in his requisite pickup. As I was leaving the mill, before I switched off the lights, set the intruder alarm, and locked up, I gazed up and around the inside of the mill. It sent me a firm androgynous message, blending the soft, aromatic, exotic scents of fresh wood, and the hard, confident, metallic effusion from new electrical equipment, ready to kick some serious ass.

I arrived home just before seven thirty. Stuart was hunkered down at my desk, working. I ditched my safety boots by the door, and said, "I'm off to the shower. I smell like a bull elk three weeks late for rutting season." Ten minutes later, I re-emerged, abluted, clothed, and combed like a six-year-old in short pants ready for Sunday School.

"Okay", I said, "let me see if I can rustle up some grub."

"All looked after", Stuart said, dropping his pencil and rising from his chair. "I stopped at a place near Cobourg and picked up a nice game pie, some pickled onions, and a nice looking carrot salad. I'd love to say I made it all myself, but..."

This was like a gong to one of Pavlov's dogs, and I had two bottles of wine and two glasses in my fist before Stuart had even made it to the fridge. Within three minutes we were established at the picnic table on the back patio. The wine pumped new life into tired limbs, and kick-started work-addled brains. But it was the game pie that caused two palates to sputter to life. The meat was chunky, rich, and abundant, and had been complemented by generous hints of mango chutney, port, and an amount of thyme that clearly had been added by a sure gastronomic hand. The pastry was light but firm. After a hard day, it all tasted like ambrosia. When we had finished, I peered hopefully into my wine glass, but finding there only the bacchanalian wisdom of frozen sunshine, I directed my gaze at Stuart.

"So, what did you find out, Stuart?"

Stuart swirled his wine glass, and started looking fairly pleased with himself. "First, I know who our intruder is, and I know where he lives. Second, I know that he's been in regular contact with somebody local, that there has also been contact with somebody in the US, that that somebody probably lives in Pennsylvania, and the last contact our intruder had with whoever his controller was occurred the day we caught him removing the bug. Third, I'm fairly sure now that the two bugs were placed independently, likely by two different individuals."

This really had my attention. "Wow!" I whispered. "Details?"

"I'm going to ask you not to ask me how I know any of this. I can say that our guy seems to have gone to ground. He hasn't been back to where he lives for four days. I have someone now working contacts to see whether we can find out more."

We talked a bit more about it. Recalling the notes and logic tree we had constructed earlier, and the large number of question marks in those notes, I found that Stuart's new information didn't really change much, and provided no basis for ruling out any of the logic branches.

The next day produced yet another gyration, the nature of which became evident only slowly.

Nineteen

Stuart and I mapped out what each of us planned to do for the next two days, but while relaxing over digestifs we found that we were nodding off, so we cleaned away the dinner things and crashed. The next day, Stuart was going to continue working his contacts to see what more could be determined about the bugs and the buggers, while I would spend another day at the mill.

Morning broke to reveal a mild but mostly cloudy day; Monty telephoned just as I was about to leave for the mill. He asked about having dinner that evening, and said his overwhelming curiosity required that he try to bring himself up to date. After consulting Stuart, who declined to join us, I agreed and we fixed a time of seven at The Fox.

The day brought a succession of tasks, almost faster, it seemed, than we could complete them, and the mill was the scene of brute muscular effort, sweat, and the unfocused cursing that is generally believed to make work easier. Equipment deliveries continued, and a couple of outside work crews came and went.

At six o'clock, exhausted and our muscles telling us we had got a lot done, we packed it in for the day. When everyone else had left, I walked around the mill, visiting all floors via the utility ladders we still had in place, updating my sense of how things were coming along, and frankly just to have some private time with the old girl. I then went off to get ready for my dinner meeting with Monty.

Stuart had stuck a note on the fridge saying he had left the house at four thirty and would be back late that evening.

I met Monty at The Fox just before seven. He was his usual pink, scrubbed, elfin self, full of nervous energy. It had settled into a clear, mild, and windless evening, so we decided to sit out on the patio. The air had the golden glow of autumn, and the green valley that rolled out to the south below us had begun taking on its first tints of yellow and orange. In his trademark manner, Monty jumped right in, pretty much dispensing with any small talk.

"Richard! You're looking well. Must be all that hard work. So tell me about the mill first, and then about your 'tryst with history,' as you called it." He sat back waiting for my account.

I brought him up to date on the flooring, the equipment installations, the deliveries soon to arrive, and where I thought we were compared to where the plan predicted we would be.

"Well ahead of schedule!" he repeated excitedly. "When will I be able to have a tour?"

Shaking my head, I said, "It's still a construction site, Monty. I can't let you in just yet." But I walked him through the latest photos. Then, in an abrupt switch, typical of Monty, he said "Okay, tell me about you and Clio."

I told Monty about how I was spending increasing amounts of time lately thinking about my boyhood enthusiasm for history, how in the early years of high school I had all but decided that I would study history at university, but how my interests moved strongly toward chemistry and mathematics and so I ended up in engineering. "Don't get me wrong, Monty. I have no regrets about my career. It was successful and fully satisfying, as far as I'm concerned, but the time I've spent in and around the mill over the past weeks has made me feel, well, a bit like an archaeologist, and the enthusiasm I had when I was fourteen and fifteen has returned. This wasn't something I expected, but it's not unwelcome either. In fact, in my small amount of spare time, I've been doing a fair bit of reading. On what was happening around here at about the time the mill was built. On local industrial archaeology. It's mostly social history, because the country was so new then. We were all far from the action taking place in Europe. The US had almost a two-hundred-year lead on us and they were still struggling through their civil war about the time Adams got his mill going. So by comparison, things were deadly quiet here. But the mill, as a physical embodiment of history that stretches across a couple of centuries, is something that always seems to be before me."

"Interesting that you should make these comments, Richard. Especially just now." In response to my tell-me-more look, Monty leaned forward and began to expound. "Over the weekend", Monty began, "I was doing some work for several local museums. There are standards they have to meet, and I work for a number of museums periodically to help them prepare a statement of compliance. This time, I was looking at compliance to the conservation standard. It says that their collections have to be maintained adequately and not allowed to degrade. There's also a documentation standard, and I was looking at that in parallel, as a check that my statement on conservation compliance covered their collection. Well, I noticed something this time. This particular museum has an interesting but very spotty collection of personal letters going back about two hundred years. Many of these letters are of local interest only, historically speaking, and have no significance in a wider context, because they're incoming correspondence from people in Europe, and they mostly relate family matters and so on. This time, though, my eye was caught by a particular letter, written by one Carl Mason, and addressed to one Robert Bine. I decided to look at it only because it's the oldest letter in their collection. I copied the letter out completely once I had read it. It's a statement willing Mason's personal effects to his church, and it's dated October 14, 1796. The items in it that caught my eye were his reference to "our long trip from the south many years ago", and "my life here as written in my notes that I ask you to look after.""

Monty stopped to take a sip of his drink, and the look on my face must have conveyed my thoughts: *Where is all this going?*

"Bear with me Richard. I'm abbreviating all this as much as I can. So, I went looking at some old records. I found that there was indeed a Mennonite minister by the name of Robert Bine. He died in 1831 in Belleville. I also found that a Carl Mason died in Kingston on November 17, 1796, so about a month after the date of the letter. I then spent a frustrating day locating a church in Kingston that had received all the documents from Mason's local Mennonite congregation, when that congregation was amalgamated administratively with several others late in the nineteenth century. But the minister of the church in Kingston was quite nice. I told him about my conservation audit, showed him the request from the museum for me to do the audit just to confirm my bona fides, and indicated that I was following up on a few items. When I related the relevant bits of the letter to him, he said he had no detailed knowledge of these things, that it was all well before his time. He did say that there had been several large trunks that had been in a storage room in the manse when he took over, and that after a quick look to determine whether they contained things that could be important for the church he had sent them to the local museum, but that was years ago. It had started looking like the trail was just going to die out, but I asked him anyway who I could contact at the museum. He gave me a name, but then said that the museum was closed that day and the next, but that he had a key and volunteered at the museum regularly."

Another sip.

"So, he took me to the little museum, we looked around a bit, and then he located the trunks. We opened one, and found a mishmash of all sorts of stuff, but beneath an unpleasant looking set of old veterinary equipment there was a wad of notes neatly pressed between two wood covers, and held together by a length of ancient hide. We lifted it out carefully onto a desk, I looked at it from all angles for a few minutes, and then I asked if I could open it. He hesitated just for a second, then said okay. Despite using my gentlest touch, the hide crumbled almost immediately, but seeing just the first page was enough. It wasn't a diary, but it was an account written well after the events it related, and it was written by a Carl Mason. It was clearly an old document, but without knowing anything about Carl Mason, and without assuming that the two Carl Masons were the same person, one would have no reason to doubt that these notes might be more than two hundred years old."

I waited while Monty paused for another sip.

Monty resumed. "I said to the minister that this could have important links to my conservation audit, and that I would like to get a copy of the entire document. Before he could express concern, I said that it was far too old to place on a modern copy machine, and that I wanted to copy it by photographing it digitally a page at a time, but that that would mean taking it away. He eventually agreed to let me do this after I insisted he telephone Greg Blackett and confirm my identity. He did, Greg did, and so now", and here he reached into his documents case, "I have this copy! I haven't gone through it in any detail, in fact I haven't even read it all. The English is pretty shaky in spots, but I now know that Carl Mason arrived in Philadelphia from Rotterdam in September of 1727, that he made a difficult land journey from his homestead near Germantown to Kingston in

1781, and that he was accompanied on this trip by a man called Boersma. If there is really a link between the letter in the museum and the notes in the trunk…I know", Monty said, holding up his hand in mock surrender, "it's all tenuous and held together by a number of unproven assumptions, and it might be just one of those personal byways that the past hasn't swallowed without trace, but…"

Monty's face clouded, and he looked into his glass in apparent annoyance, as though discovering suddenly that somebody has been quaffing his drink without his knowledge or permission.

"So, as you can see", Monty continued, "I too have had a little dance with Clio. But she's stingy with her favours. This account, if it's true, is an interesting look, and a pretty rare look, into the late eighteenth century in these parts, and because the population was so small then there's always the hope that one will find some direct or indirect connection closer to home, to Greenvale or one of the other villages nearby. But, I am beginning to fear that we—"

At that point, Monty stopped and looked at me because I had just set my glass down rather heavily.

"Richard?" he said, noting my odd expression.

"It might be nothing, Monty, but Boersma is an anagram of Ambrose."

Twenty

Monty and I sat looking at each other for a few seconds, and then began saying, simultaneously, "but let's not jump to conclusions."

"What are the chances that this has anything to do with the mill?" I asked at length.

"Just on the basis of probabilities, I would say almost none, unfortunately", Monty replied. "I'm going to pursue it, though, not because of that small chance, but because it's a genuine bit of history and I want to see where it leads. But, let's just say there is a link. What would need to be true for that to be the case?"

After just a couple of minutes further consideration, I could see some fairly serious obstacles already, making it unlikely that there might be a straightforward "true" story here. I ticked them off on my fingers. "First, these two Masons have to be the same person. Second, if there are two families, one called Boersma and the other called Ambrose, there has to be some quite significant connection between them, but at the moment I can't see what that might be unless we start proposing other coincidences. Third, Ambrose isn't a particularly common name, but any Ambrose, to be of interest, would need to be very local to Greenvale, and over quite a long period of time. Fourth, there's a lot of time between a date of about 1795, when Mason and, one supposes, Boersma snuffed it, and 1930 when we knew there was an Ambrose around, or even between 1795 and about 1860 when Adams was setting up his mill. And I'm aware that the mill might or might not be the main connection of interest here. Fifth, if the names Boersma and Ambrose are linked only anagrammatically, then there's another level of splainin' to be done. Surely nobody in those days, and in this area, would have any interest or any need to dream up riddles to tease an unknown future. No, Monty, I think it's a mirage."

"You make a strong case against, Richard."

"Hang on, Monty. Do you *want* there to be a connection?"

Monty jumped as though a vindictive wasp had just located his privates. "No! Of course not!" he said with some heat. "And I will be led by the *facts!*" Here he paused and then continued more levelly, "But sometimes, where you go can depend entirely on how imaginative your hypotheses are, and how exhaustively you pursue them."

At this I smiled sheepishly and nodded to Monty. "Touché, Monty. I was always fond of saying to our junior engineers that when we assess a design or check the safety of something, we're looking for things that aren't obvious. So we need to peer into a design or a problem using considerable intuition, and when we ask questions, we're up against an ingenious old dog called Mother Nature. She always answers our questions, but she'll give us only one of three possible answers. Two of those answers, 'Yes' and 'No,' are acceptable. The third one isn't."

"What's the third one?" Monty asked.

"Maybe."

At that point, the server came to hover near us for the third time, and I grabbed the menu and said to Monty that I was suddenly hungry. We ordered, and our food arrived quickly enough to make me wonder, until I realized that we were two of only five people remaining in the place.

The gleeful and overeager critic in me having been subdued by a carbohydrate hit, I said to Monty, "Okay. Let's assume that Boersma and Ambrose are closely connected somehow. What would that imply?"

Monty hesitated, seeming unsure.

"Okay", I said, "let me try. I'm thinking partly on the fly here Monty, so bear with me.

"The first thing to do, always, is to be as certain as possible of the situation we're trying to assess. As I see it, our situation has three main elements: the books I discovered in the mill, the events at my house that led to Buck's death, and the documents that you found describing people and books. These three elements can be connected or kept separate by assuming some things. In particular, we could assume, as we're doing for the purposes of this discussion, that the people called Boersma and Ambrose are linked somehow. At one extreme, these three elements are three independent and unrelated problems. At the other extreme, they're all bound up somehow in a complex situation. Do you agree so far?"

"Yes, but obviously you've spent more time than me thinking about this."

"Probably true, Monty, but taking your previous injunction on hypotheses at face value, here are some hypotheses, preceded by some major assumptions. First major assumption: Mason's 'books' are the books from the mill. Second major assumption: Ambrose, the historical mill owner, is linked somehow to Boersma, but not necessarily by blood.

"Now, the hypotheses." And I rhymed them off. "There might be more, but that's what I can come up with at the moment."

Monty was nodding in approval. "You really should have become a historian Richard."

"No," I replied, as phlegmatically and deadpan as I could, "I was an engineer, something a lot more accomplished."

Monty giggled at this unexpected rib, and then made good-natured fuck-off faces and hand signals at me.

"But it does sound as though your earlier pessimism has dissipated."

"Not at all, Monty. I'm still sceptical, but there are things to be explained and we can't just set them aside in the name of scepticism. I guess the question I have for you is 'what do you think we should do next?' "

"I'm not certain", Monty replied. "What do *you* think we should do?"

"Well, there are a few things we *can* do that might give us more information. For example, I presume there are records on who actually did emigrate from Rotterdam to the US. Confirming that Mason was one of those people would solidify at least one piece of information, and it shouldn't be that difficult to do, if the date of September 1727 in his notes is correct. I suspect that a lot of that information will be available online now, and that really is an advantage of the Internet."

"Tell me about it!" Monty snorted. "In the 'good old days', any kind of field research like this meant travel costs, hotel bills, greasy diners, and having to smooth talk cranky librarians into allowing one to read dusty documents in poor light from a seat that would give anyone piles after just ten minutes." Monty popped a stray chip into his mouth and chewed it vigorously, exacting some imaginary revenge. "But I've vented enough spleen for now", he concluded. "What I plan to do is go over those notes closely, to see whether they suggest any other lines of inquiry."

We sat there, looking at the last forlorn dregs in our glasses. Monty ran a wiry hand through thin hair in apparent frustration. I swallowed my remaining wine and set the glass down decisively. Monty looked up, suspecting from my action that some new fact was in the air, and wanting to catch it before it flew past. "What?" he asked.

"Nothing", I said. "Except that I'm going home to look over again what we know, but this time to see what it is that we might not have and that would make all the difference if we did know it. Would you mind stopping at my place on your way home, so that I can make a copy of Mason's notes?" Monty nodded. We paid, left, and drove in tandem to my place. I went through the somewhat elaborate process of deactivating the alarm, I made a copy of Mason's notes, then Monty and I made a short checklist of the things each of us was going to do in the coming days.

Monty and I then spent about fifteen minutes discussing the water wheel at the bottom of the lagoon. I showed him the notes and drawing I had made on how I thought we could raise it at minimum risk of damage.

"So", he said, pointing at my hand drawing, "you have these twelve inflatable bags—what are they?"

"They're just that—specially made inflatable bags intended to lift heavy objects. They're designed to lift things from below, but we'll use them for lifting things from above using flotation. They come in different sizes, and I know where I can get used ones fairly cheaply."

"Are you sure it will work?"

"Can't see any reason why not, but that's why I'm going to test them twice, once in my shop here in the house, and once in the lagoon itself where I'll use one of them to try to lift a weight that's a twelfth of the total weight of the wheel from the bottom of the lagoon."

"How do you know what the wheel weighs?"

"I've made some estimates of dimensions, and I intend to check those by measuring parts of the wheel itself. Given the dimensions, I can estimate the volume of cast iron in the wheel, and since there are good estimates of the density of cast iron, I can get an estimate for the total weight. If my estimates are all on the conservative side, I will have more than enough lifting capacity."

"Good grief! Did you work this out by yourself?"

"No, Monty. I'm not that bright. I called on some real professional help."

Monty cocked his head at me questioningly, and then made some convulsive facial expressions and jerky arm movements, typically Monty, when I said, "Archimedes."

Monty is inexhaustibly curious, and he wanted to know more details, so I explained my idea of inflating the twelve bags separately and incrementally, so that we could ensure a slow and even levitation of the wheel from the bottom at minimum risk of stressing one part of it more than another, in case it was cracked somewhere. In answer to his question about air supply, I said simply, "a scuba tank". He then objected that this could only lift the wheel a foot or so off the bottom, since the lagoon is less than four feet deep, and I told him that that was the idea. "All we need is enough space to get a pallet under the wheel and then lift it out of the water using an industrial crane on the shore." Monty did a little dance of delight, and assured me that he wanted to be involved in every aspect of this operation. I could see talks to historical societies already taking shape inside his head. His curiosity thus mildly slaked but his interest massively primed, he looked reluctantly at his watch.

I bid Monty good night, and then returned to our earlier topic, opening the tablet entry I had begun on the Boersma-Ambrose business. Already, I had filled twenty or so pages in notes, but they were a mass of mostly unstructured jottings to get down ideas or observations as they came to me. Reading through them, I decided that some consolidation was needed, so I turned a page and rewrote them but under a set of headings that imposed some order. For some reason, I had a feeling that reading Mason's notes would help. I started into them, but realized quickly that the English, which was in a two-hundred-year-old style, would need more active brain cells than I could call on at the moment. So, I jotted down ideas for a few Internet searches that had come to me in an inspiration while talking to Monty over dinner. I also wanted to go back and look at the poem that was included with the two books; they seemed to be strange company, and although nothing registered at the time I first saw them, the more I thought about it the more puzzling it became.

Outside, I could hear a loon somewhere on the river, its long, mournful, evocative cry rising above the crickets' continuous orchestral tuning. I knew that if I went outside I would hear other night noises: the occasional but faint squidgy noise of earthworms, the rustling of small night animals in the grass, possibly a whippoorwill or a bobwhite, the distant cough of a deer high up on the hills, and, best of all, the distinctive call of the nighthawk. It would be easy enough to shed forty-five years, and imagine a ten-year-old boy hearing the same sounds, but in a different place and at a different time. Another chapter of *Foucault's Pendulum* seemed about the right challenge just then, and I had poured myself a cup of coffee and barely settled into a reading chair when Stuart returned. "Coffee? Brandy?" I asked, although my bet was on the second.

"Both, please", he said, but he immediately did a bug sweep that took about ten minutes. I passed him the coffee and one of the two brandies I had poured, he placed them on a small side table, then fell heavily into an armchair. Without much preamble, I gave him a short account of dinner with Monty. "Anything new at your end?" I asked almost mechanically.

"Yes, they found our burglar."

"Ah! Good! What's his name?"

"Jimmy Kralik."

"He can probably clear up a few things for us then."

"I doubt that", Stuart said, taking a gulp of coffee.

"Why not?"

"Because he's dead."

Twenty-one

My initial shock and surprise faded as Stuart jumped right in to relate, unasked, what had happened.

"The body was apparently placed in multiple layers of heavy plastic garbage bag, weighted at each end, and dropped in Lake Ontario. But whoever did the disposal didn't consider the volume increase as the body began to decay and bloat, and didn't use enough weight. The plastic bags didn't let anything escape. The bagged body floated to the surface. It was struck by a pleasure boat, and the propeller tore open the bags. The boat was just cruising slowly. A nasty shock to the woman driving it when she saw blood in the water and a chest slashed open."

"How did they identify it as our burglar?"

"Well, strictly speaking", Stuart said, "the local police who were called in after the body was found didn't know it was 'our burglar'. They just determined that it had been the guy who was the driver of a Ford Focus with a badly damaged windshield that was found abandoned about ten kilometres away."

"Hmm. I wonder whether Raymond will want to talk to us again."

"I doubt it", Stuart said. "My source said that Raymond had been informed once the local police caught up with the paperwork and realized that Raymond was working on a case that involved the same Ford Focus. So, as a test, I called Raymond, and asked if he had any further information he could pass on to us, just out of interest. He said 'no', and ended the conversation as soon as he could."

"This is becoming dangerous, Stuart."

He gave me a level stare for a few seconds. "It's always been dangerous, Richard. When somebody goes to the extent of bugging you, it's not safe to assume that they're just playing some prank."

"How did he die?"

"I don't know the details. But, obviously, it wasn't suicide, natural causes, or an accident, and that doesn't leave many options."

"So there must be a good reason for someone to want to kill him. Might it be because he had become a loose end?"

"That would be my guess."

"You mentioned that it looked like he had been in contact with someone in eastern Pennsylvania. Is there anything further on that?"

"No", Stuart said, "no further direct data. If we assume that all this activity was the result of some collector trying to get their hands on rare books, then we can look for well-known collectors. They would need to be serious and have some significant money behind them to consider getting into the game to this level. And if our burglar's death is evidence of a collector making sure his tracks are covered after a botched eavesdropping lark, then that collector is also determined and ruthless. I have someone making some initial inquiries along those lines."

"What about the second bug?" I asked.

"That one is odd. It's not a common device, and it's fairly high-end. We might be able to get more information, but…."

I ran a hand through my hair. "I don't know what I should be doing. Just hanging around makes me feel like a sitting duck. But I can't let myself get to the point where I'm afraid of my own shadow. I'm making sure that nobody talks about the safety deposit box. I'm not discussing any of this in emails. Beyond that, I'm just not sure."

"There really isn't much to do beyond that. I've done my poking around on the bugs in such a way that whoever is responsible now knows that we know they've been trying to snoop. I think the best you can do, Richard, is just carry on with your work at the mill. If anyone is paying attention to what you're doing, seeing that sort of activity will send a message that you aren't worried."

"It's all a bit of a cat-and-mouse game", I mused.

"That's exactly what it is. But there's a risk here for the party that starts off being the cat. They might find suddenly that they've become the mouse."

We discussed some of the details of my meeting with Monty, and although he smiled at my description of Monty's enthusiasm, it soon became clear that Stuart was running on fumes. I told him to go to bed, and he agreed without demur, saying he had another long day the next day and that he needed to get an early start.

"I have two short business meetings", he said in response to my query about what he had planned, "but then I want to push a little harder on follow-up activities about the bugs, and check in with the guy I have looking at collectors." He finished his coffee and brandy in two glugs, waved goodnight, and went off to bed.

Not for the first time, I gazed into my brandy glass, not really expecting to find inspiration, but this time I was surprised because after only two sips and some modest focus on the amber liquid, my fog of mild despair began dispersing, and a plan started forming in my mind.

Stuart was right. Focus on the mill. That was the tangible world right in front of me, and it was also a real project, involving real and substantial investment dollars, and there was a requirement for real returns to be forthcoming. So, the work had to go ahead. The assembly of the water wheel was a task that was coming up soon, and would be an impressive milestone event. Work on the water-level patio also had to be finished, since that levelled surface would be where the water wheel from the lagoon would be laid once it was craned up from the bottom, and where Monty would carry out his close examination of the wheel. All the construction work in and around the mill had to be completed, so that we could begin the first public tours, conducted for locals, who would be given preferential treatment, since these were the merchants and customers I hoped would buy the flour we were going to produce. This was Plan 1A.

Then there was the other problem, the problem of history and of *dramatis personae*. Apart from the effort that Monty would put into it, I also had to tackle the question of the books, come to an understanding of just who were these people Mason, Boersma, and Ambrose, and start getting my mind around the relevant history that had brought them together, here and now. It all came back to history. There was, of course, always the historical element in the sense of musty, ossified local history as it is usually understood, associated with the mill itself, the mill being the central tangible artifact that had ridden its own vector onto today's stage through more than 150 years of time. The artifact itself, considered only as a piece of current reality, laid out like a butterfly on a lepidopterist's table, with little or no meaning in isolation. For people in Greenvale, the mill carried some kind of significance, even if only as an object that had always been there, and everyone knew that it had a "history", although for most people that would probably translate to not much more than a vague feeling. *Is this all that history is?* I had gone back and begun to reread two of those books I had admired so much as an adolescent, the books by Carr and Elton, and in the process had come across a newer one by Gaddis. What did the history of the mill mean for me? Maybe it was time to find out.

But were I able somehow to go back and ride that vector, the mill's historical vector, through those 150 years, I would be able to see and know things that are hidden from anyone standing and looking at the physical mill today. There would be real live individuals, where now I had only names on a page, and most probably only a few of the names. Over time there would be background changes, imperceptible at any point called "now", yet large and intrusive against a broader temporal context, just as the building of mountains would not be a young boy's dream of a sudden buckling and heaving of the earth, and the excitement of unbelievable noise, but instead just an inaudible whisper spread across ages, and a topology that would be wildly varying and dramatic seen in geologic time, but which would always be, at any instant, just the same mundane and unchanging reality as was known the previous Wednesday, or the previous month, or the previous year. It would be like one of Einstein's *gedanken* experiments, a young patent office clerk riding a light beam. What could I see if I rode that vector, what could I know, what could I understand, how would my view change? And how was it all related to the shadow world of bugs and listeners that suddenly had snuck up on us?

Peering into my brandy glass again, this time in some dismay, I wondered almost aloud from where all that introspection had come (surely not the brandy glass?), and if I rubbed the snifter would I call forth some sort of historical genie, maybe even Clio herself?

Shaking off this Walter Mitty world, it was clear nonetheless that coming to terms with the historical aspect was essential, and that was Plan 1B.

Too tired to make any inroads at that moment, I locked up and went to bed, but the next day's main task was clear: collect a copy of the poem from the safety deposit box during lunchtime and begin a close study of Mason's notes that Monty had obtained.

The next morning, over a cup of strong coffee and some French stick with butter and apricot jam, I decided to spend fifteen minutes or so getting a feel for Carl Mason's narrative. It was about a hundred and forty pages of reasonably elegant handwriting, and in a quite small hand so that there were between thirty and forty lines on each page.

But then I thought, *This is foolish. It would take me an hour to read even a quarter of this. Better to leave it for when I have a bigger block of time*, although I had no real idea when that would be. So, I scribbled a quick note for Stuart, grabbed my project notebook and the drawings I would need, and left for the mill.

It was going to be a clear day, and there were signs that it would remain pleasantly cool. Just the day for manual excavation. When my three labourers arrived, I outlined what needed to be done and how to do it, and almost immediately they were hard at it. I had planned to spend the rest of the day working on the stairway connecting all the floors, and I was preparing to make a start when my cellphone buzzed.

"Richard, I was hoping I could catch you. Are you at home now?" It was Greg.

"No, I'm at the mill, Greg. What's up?"

What was up was that Greg's day had collapsed in chaos. Two meetings had been postponed at short notice, and he had the choice now of slogging away at paperwork or seeing whether there was anything he could help me with at the mill. It was the equivalent of a choice between cod liver oil and ice cream.

"Ah! Interesting, Greg. Do you have the full day free?"

"Yes."

"Well, I was about to start work on the stairway, but we could begin assembling the water wheel instead. It's a job for at least two people."

He jumped at the chance. "What do I need?"

"Jeans, some work gloves, safety boots, a hard hat, and also bring some sandals that won't mind getting wet and a bathing suit or pair of shorts."

"I'll be there in five minutes."

Going back to the table where I laid out my drawings and notes, I stowed the drawings for the stairway, and pulled out those for the water wheel. Outside, I heard Greg's car arrive with a flourish; evidently he was eager for a change of pace.

He strode in wearing safety boots and a hard hat, then stopped and looked around. "Look what you've done here! This is fantastic!" I realized it had been some time since he had seen the mill. The background smells of new wood, electrical equipment only a few weeks from the factory, concrete poured relatively recently, and the general scents of an active construction site probably had a greater background effect than he realized.

We went out onto the scaffolding that surrounded the two stone wheel supports, and I explained the job. He asked a few perceptive questions, I explained, he nodded, asked if we could complete the assembly today, and I told him that if we couldn't I'd have to fire him. This prompted a round of insults that collapsed in a spell of laughing.

Greg is a delight to work with. He always has energy, and I'm sure his positive outlook has got him through many boring village council meetings without shooting anyone.

My planning and my mock-up assembly wheel meant that there was no time wasted wondering how to do this or that. We got the first four spokes in place and bolted down in about forty minutes. The second set took ten minutes less, and after that we were doing a set every twenty-five minutes. When we had half the spokes for the wheel in place, we took a break. I went to check on the labourers, and they were heaving soil around to the tune of their usual banter. No problems there. I returned to where Greg was sitting and said I was making a quick trip to the bank. He nodded with his back to the mill wall and eyes closed while draining the last gulps from his bottle of water.

The trip to the bank took less than ten minutes, and on my return Greg was where I had left him. I sat down to join him.

"How are you doing compared to the schedule?" he asked, and I indicated that we were considerably ahead of where I thought we would be by this time.

"I guess that's your slave-driver mentality", he said, and I responded by flashing a one-finger salute.

"It's starting to look really good, Richard. From anywhere on the river now, it looks like an active building rather than a ruin." As he spoke, a boat approached on the lagoon. It was Jeremy, camera at his shoulder.

"I'm starting to hear some very nice comments on what's being done here", Greg continued. "There seems to be a feeling of civic pride that hasn't been around for a while. It was the red roof that did it, I think. Makes a dramatic statement that the place is functioning and cared for."

"I hope you pass back my regards when you hear things like that." There was a short silence as we aimed our faces, eyes closed, at the diffuse sunlight filtering through high cloud. "I'm hoping", I added, "to have some tours for the locals once the risks of construction are past, so that they can poke around in places that won't be accessible once we start operating. I want to try to get people onside, to feel that they have some kind of a village stake in the whole affair."

"I'm sure you'll have a good many takers. It'll be a very nice local gesture, Richard. And it looks to me like you're making all the right moves with the locals. Do you have any better idea of how flour sales might go?"

"More people are baking today than ten years ago. The local bakeries are all interested. On the face of it, it appears that I should be able to sell at least as much flour as I can reasonably produce, but in the end it can be hard to say for sure. It's a bit like polls before elections. But if you and I don't get back at it now, none of this will happen."

The wheel took shape during the day. Jeremy got footage from many different locations on the water. The afternoon flew past, but rather than being increasingly tired, as I expected I might be, my exhilaration surged at seeing an original water wheel—of my own design!—take shape against the side of the mill. Greg and I continued to talk and banter, although this fell off somewhat as the day advanced, since there was increasing focus on having all pieces of the wheel skeleton in place before we packed it in. As a marathoner gets a lift and taps into reserves when he first spots the finish line, the realization that we had just three more spars to install made the work seem lighter. When the final bolt was tightened, I walked back to the end of the scaffolding to see the entire wheel. It was magnificent. I walked around to where Greg was standing on the scaffolding and gave him a huge bear hug.

"We did it, you old bastard. Thanks. Just look at it!" And it looked entirely in proportion. The bottom of the wheel cleared the water by a little less than a foot, and against the rough expanse of the mill's wall, it looked made to order.

"No, thank *you*, Richard. It's been a long time since I've spent a day that gave me such a tangible reward at the end of it all. There really is nothing like creating something with your hands, at least every once in a while. But now, you're coming home with me for drinks and dinner."

"Hey, come on man, it's me who owes you. I couldn't—"

"Richard. Do I have to beat you into submission, or are you going to come quietly?"

I sniffed an underarm. "I'm scarcely fit to be stabled, let alone join polite company."

"Well, then," Greg said, "we stop by your place, you grab a change of clothes, shower at my place, then we all relax. Jill loves having you as company. I'll just give her a call to see whether we need to pick up anything on the way over."

My remaining resistance crumbled as Greg retrieved his stored home number and dialled. I could hear Jill's excited chirp from where I stood. I began collecting tools, and I made sure the brake on the wheel was well applied. We locked up the mill, stopped at my place, I ditched the hard hat and safety boots, turned on some lights, left a note for Stuart, put on some loafers, set down a plate of food for Max, and stuffed a change of clothes and my toiletry kit into a sports bag.

In five minutes we were at Greg's place. Greg and I clumped in through the front door, and were met by Jill in her swim suit. "I thought we might spend twenty minutes or so in the hot tub. It's heating now. That is, after you two have showered so that we don't all end up wallowing in testosterone soup."

Jill looks after herself, and evidently I had exceeded some time limit. Her expression suddenly became serious and she said "Oh! Should I take this off", glancing down at her swim suit, "or can I rely on you to do that?"

Greg emitted a huge guffaw and went off to look after wine, I blushed and went into a vocabulary stumble. Jill's laughter tinkled down the hallway, and she gave me a gentle shove saying, "Get into the shower! Guests first! Here", and she handed me a pair of men's swim trunks. "Come straight out to the hot tub when you're clean."

Ten minutes later, I joined Jill in the hot tub while Greg showered. Greg had built their hot tub into an extension of the deck that was cupped by a fold in the hill behind their house. From the tub, one could look south past the top of the house. The evening had turned fine. The high cloud was gone, the sky was unbroken blue, and we were headed for a cool, windless, late summer evening.

Jill was languid, lying with her head on a foam support, eyes closed. I took up a position directly opposite her. Without opening her eyes, she said, "I'm glad you were able to come over."

"It's always a pleasure, Jill. You're both so good to me."

She opened her eyes and looked at me for what seemed a long moment. "When Greg phoned you, and you said to come over to the mill, he was a kid who'd been invited out for a day at the beach. I don't know if you're aware, Richard, but you mean a lot to Greg. There's nobody else in the village he can interact with the way he does with you."

There was no time for a reply, because just then Greg came bounding down the deck, as though he was planning a dramatic entry into the tub, and Jill shrieked, half laughing, "Don't you dare!" After a few minutes, Greg and I settled down to a silent, eyes-closed soak, just the thing needed to avoid having stiff muscles the next day. We had worked hard, and I could feel the lactic acid stress dissipating even as we flopped there. The brightest stars had winked on just as we were thinking about leaving the tub. Jill looked up at them.

"I should really get to know the names of these stars. I was raised in Toronto, and it was rare that you could see anything in the night sky except airplanes. But here in Greenvale…" and she lapsed into silence as she looked across the sky. Turning to look at me, Jill asked, more as an idle conversational gambit rather than a serious question, "Do you know about stars, Richard? What are we looking at?"

"The knowledge of a rank amateur at best", I said. "But let's see. You can find Polaris, can't you? Okay, locate the Big Dipper, and find the two stars that form the side of the cup away from the handle. Now imagine a line going through those two stars and up into the sky. That line almost intersects a fairly bright star that has a piece of sky almost to itself. Find it?" A nod. "Okay, that's the pole star, Polaris."

"Shouldn't it be right overhead?"

"Only if we were at the North Pole."

After a moment, I continued. "Okay. Now look directly west. There's a bright star there, just above the hills. That's Altair. It'll set behind the hills in about half an hour. Now, if you follow along the hilltops toward the south, you come to another bright star, and it's also just above the hills. That's Vega. They're both easy to see but would be brighter if it weren't for the zodiacal glow, and if they were any dimmer we would likely have trouble picking them out at all. Now, if you cross the sky following a line that results in you looking almost directly east, you'll see two bright stars not too far from one another, almost on a north-south line. The one to the north is Aldebaran, and the one to the south is Capella. If we were to lie here for another couple of hours, four more bright stars would rise in the east: Procyon, Pollux, Betelgeuse, and Rigel. And with that you've just about exhausted my astronomical knowledge."

Jill and Greg both looked at me in some surprise. "Where did you learn all this?" Jill finally asked.

"At university, we had some optional undergrad courses. One of them was astronomy, and most of the lectures were given in the planetarium. I always had an interest in astronomy, probably partly because as a kid I was painfully shy, and the night sky asked no questions and passed no judgments. One of my uncles noticed me sketching star positions one night, and gave me a set of sky charts for my twelfth birthday. At one time, I could identify twenty or thirty stars easily, no matter what time of night or what season. It helped being raised in the country. No smog. No light pollution."

We fell silent, watching more and more stars switch on. The hot tub, the night, and the sky enclosed us as friends. The silence was long and companionable, accompanied by the crickets and the occasional water murmur as one of us shifted position in the tub.

Greg rose from the tub. "I'm getting hungry. I'll go and get the wine ready", and he stepped away, towelling himself as he headed for the house. I helped Jill out of the tub, went to change, and by the time I had returned to the dining room, Greg had the wine opened and poured. Jill had prepared lasagna and salad, probably enough lasagna for the two of them to have leftovers, but as it turned out just the right amount for a meal for three.

As it always does with them, my evening flew by. There was conversation ranging far and wide, much laughter, a few jokes that were slightly risqué, a bit of village and county politics, and of course questions about the mill.

Greg and I started fading at about the same time, and I began to make going-home noises. There was the usual post-dinner milling, I thanked Jill for the meal, and they both gave me good-friend hugs at the door.

I arrived back home just before eleven o'clock. Stuart was still not there; maybe he had decided to stay in town. No messages on my cellphone. I had rallied a bit in the night air, and decided that I would allow some of the wine to dissipate before going to bed.

After printing a copy from the photo of the poem I had made at the bank using my cellphone, I carried it to my favourite leather armchair. Max was on the back of the sofa, and he sneered at my pretension to tackle German poetry.

I looked over the eight stanzas, then began following through line byline. The German words all began coming back to me in a rush. A few others, archaic or more obscure, hovered just out of reach in some pseudo-Alzheimeric fog. I read the full poem through twice, and then a third time, speaking the words aloud. The familiar cadence of the language rose before me, and I slid further down into the chair, working through a rough translation of the first stanza.

> *Long have I loved Thee already, would wish to call thee Mother, recite to Thee as a gift an artless love song, Thou, the most beautiful city of all I have seen in the Fatherland.*

Rough and clunky compared to the elegant original, although it caught the essential meaning. But then…mentally, a furrowed brow. My translation was not quite right. I tried again. Still didn't fit. Something was wrong. I puzzled over it for another few minutes. It was a hand-copied poem. Maybe the transcriber had left something out, got something wrong. Two minutes searching and I came up with my volume of Hölderlin's poems, a gift from Werner all those years ago.

Leafing through the book, I soon found it. It was indeed Hölderlin's poem to Heidelberg, but then I quickly noticed that two words in the first stanza of the handwritten version were wrong. Checking through the rest of the poem, I found a total of fourteen words that were either different from the original or were added in the copy. Too many changes to be just accidental. I wrote out the thirteen words in the original that had been changed: *so, sich, tönt, auf, fort, wie, zu, in, die, schwer, die, umher, freundliche*. No matter in what order I arranged these words, and I tried for about ten minutes, they meant nothing, individually or collectively. I wrote out the words in the hand-copied poem that were different from the original, fourteen altogether, so one new word added: *aber, und, tief, laut, innen, doch, gut, bald, neugeborene, recht, ertönt, eine, nach, seine*. The same with these words. Similarly, no matter how I arranged them, no meaning jumped out, or even suggested itself, however faintly.

I struggled on for a few minutes, but fatigue was dragging me down, and I soon called it quits. It was eleven thirty. I locked the door, set the alarm, and then sent a text message to Stuart saying that I had done those two things. The hot tub had served its purpose; no stiff muscles, just a generalized pleasant lassitude. I crashed into bed, and the few drops of Lethean water that the spirits of the night splashed onto my lips had left the intervening six and a quarter hours as a complete blank when I emerged refreshed next morning at quarter to six.

Twenty-two

There must have been a fairly heavy rainstorm during the night; when I looked out the window at six o'clock there were leaves everywhere and the puffs of air skipping through the slit opening carried a delightful scrubbed and perfumed scent. The morning was roaring to life, the eastern sky was aswirl in the promise of a brilliant day, and my inward and outward smiles were irrepressible. After a wash and a quick shave, I fed Max and had breakfast on the back patio. The two sparrows that joined me, at the other end of the table, seemed to agree that it was a good day to be alive.

Stuart had not returned, and there was no message from him, but he always had been a cat that walked by himself. The to-do list for the day was just as long as ever, but for some reason that didn't bother me in the least, and I put it down to my sense that on the mill refurbishment track, we were now in the home stretch. I cleared away and washed up my few breakfast dishes, checked email, and then set off for the mill.

I decided that since I was quite early, at least an hour ahead of when my labourers would arrive, I would do a detailed tour of inspection, including making notes.

First stop was the river-level patio. All the soil removal was complete, and the stonework crew had built half the wall against the crescent-shaped cutting into the hill, mainly as a means of stabilizing the hillside against slips, but also for atmosphere. The river-level patio would be a fairly private place, not visible from the road, only partly visible from the river, and having an architect's thirty-degree view of the water wheel. The stonework was good. The stones' complete resistance to my pushing and pulling on them indicated that the wall had indeed the solidity of an arch that I had hoped for. It looked as though there might be another half day's work left to complete the wall, then about another half day to lay the rustically rough flagstones for the floor.

Next stop was the water wheel. It was in the state Greg and I had left it, and all the wood had become thoroughly wetted by the night's rain. A close look indicated that the treated wood had not minded the rain at all, and I found that it was easy to turn the wheel manually, indicating reasonable balance already, and few if any sources of friction. On this job, we were definitely in the home stretch.

The third stop was the aqueduct-like channel that would carry water to the top of the wheel. A local machine shop had built a piping arrangement, to my design, that would lead water from the sluice out to the top of the wheel, where the water would be distributed among a number of smaller pipes extending in parallel across a horizontal distance of half a metre, and these would supply water to the top of the wheel at a fixed rate and velocity. That had now been installed.

The fourth stop was the grain milling area inside the building. It would have been nice to use wooden power train components, and wooden gears, as had been the case in the original mill, but this was just not practical. The stone grinding wheels would be operational, and they really would produce a limited amount of stone-ground flour.

The final stop was not really a stop. The water wheel was set a bit more than halfway back along the mill from its downstream, or south-facing wall. This meant that the shaft from the wheel, the generator, the stone grinding wheels, and other equipment would be located in the upstream half of the mill. I ticked off in my mind all the features that were taking shape: the coffee bar and restaurant, the outside deck and awning, the internal window offering a view of the stone grinding wheels and other milling operations.

As I stood in the mill, the sounds around me were those of something that had awakened after a long sleep. The sun heating the roof panels and causing them to expand created a series of coughs, whispers, and muffled exclamations. Friendly lapping sounds from the river—the river water gently haranguing the dam on its way past—entered the mill and bounced around as a continuous private discussion. Birds were no longer free to swoop into the mill through an open roof, but they were happy to find perches, and I could hear sparrows, pigeons, swallows, swifts, and the occasional gull.

My tour of inspection complete, I finished the notes, just as my labourers arrived in a cloud of banter, followed closely by the stonework crew, and the day was a whirl of activity after that. At about eleven o'clock, Greg phoned saying that his afternoon was suddenly free, and that if I wanted to continue working on the water wheel, he could come right over. Of course, I jumped at the chance, not caring whether Greg's statement was strictly true, or whether he had just shunted aside a number of bullshit meetings. Greg turned up within minutes, full of enthusiasm, and we set to work right away, our efforts interrupted briefly about once an hour when I went off to check on the labourers and answer any questions they had about what to do next. At about one o'clock that afternoon, Stuart called saying he was on his way back to Greenvale, that he had found something significant, and that we needed to talk as soon as possible after he arrived. Just after three o'clock, Monty called saying he had uncovered an interesting document, and that I needed to look at it, sooner rather than later. Throughout the afternoon, people from the village dropped by the mill, peering over the fence, and asking me questions whenever I was outside and within earshot. Mostly, they wanted to know when they could take a look. I told them "very soon". Three canoes carrying local rubbernecks drifted into the lagoon in mid-afternoon, attracted by the stonework activity for the water-level patio, and by the sudden appearance, over the past couple of days, of the water wheel structure. I talked to them for as long as I could.

During the afternoon, Greg and I managed to fit about a third of the buckets to the wheel. It went like clockwork, and I could see that Greg was getting increasingly impatient, but out of excitement rather than frustration, to see the assembly work finished and to get the wheel operating. Jeremy came by during the afternoon and recorded the attachment of two buckets for his video record. Just before three thirty, Stuart called saying he was at my place, and I arranged to have our meeting at six. He said he had a pile of business calls to make and he wanted to start those before seven. So I called Monty asking if we could meet at The Fox at seven, he agreed but said, somewhat mysteriously, that we would need to find a secluded table. I agreed with aroused interest, since Monty is hardly a cloak-and-dagger type. That afternoon, my labourers finished the internal stairway, the last of the flooring, and began putting up drywall in what would be eventually the coffee shop/restaurant area and the offices. Late in the afternoon, the stonework crew announced that they were finished, and that they would have a crane and operator on site the next day to work on the stone wall that would enclose the lagoon. The same crane would also put in place, on the bottom of the lagoon, the footings for the underwater lights that would illuminate the side of the mill and the water wheel at night. It was also during the afternoon that those lights and the cabling for them arrived.

And then it was after five. The stonework crew had already departed, my labourers were just leaving, each proclaiming the others' incompetence and questionable parentage, but they all exchanged high-fives, hopped into their pickups, and drove off. Greg and I walked the new stairway, which was solid and had exactly the right proportions for the spaces it left and entered. We looked through the beginnings of the drywall work, and both of us could visualize a room full of tables and coffee drinkers. Outside, we walked down the steps to the riverside patio. Greg stopped in his tracks, looked around at the gentle arch of stonework leaning authoritatively into the hill, and complete with a half-dozen alcoves for mood wall lighting. He gazed at the rustic slabs that formed the patio surface, and then, as was the intent of the riverside patio, his regard was drawn over the lagoon, to the water wheel set against the commanding side of the mill, and then across the river and to the range of guardian hills in the east.

"Richard, this is fantastic! Not in my wildest dreams would I have imagined that this sad old ruin could be turned into something so dramatic and elegant! We're going to make a fortune from this place!"

Greg was overcome and in silence again, as his gaze traced out the same path once more. "I can work here all day tomorrow, if that fits your schedule", he said suddenly, and with a determination that struck me as comical.

"That would be excellent, Greg. We could finish the wheel. Are you sure you can manage it?"

He waved his hand dismissively. "I'll be here at eight."

"Great!" I said, "but I'll need to split my time between the water wheel and the lagoon. Tomorrow we raise the cast iron wheel from the bottom of the lagoon, and then the crane will install the flagstones for the underwater lights, and the wall for the lagoon."

I locked the security entrance to the mill then, Greg gave me a firm handshake that turned into a bear hug, and we went our separate ways.

Back at my place, I parked next to Stuart's car and clumped into the house. Stuart was working at the desk, his back to me, and he responded by a wave of the arm without turning around when I announced I would be back in ten minutes after a shower. On re-entering the living room, I found Stuart stretched out in an armchair, sipping a glass of whiskey. His appearance alarmed me. He was unshaven. His eyes were bloodshot. His face bore the signs of all-nighter weariness. But all this contrasted to his huge self-satisfied grin.

"Looks like you've been burning both ends of the candle, and then some", I said, not trying to hide my concern.

"I don't know how many ends this candle has, but you're right, I've been burning them all. It was worth it."

I gave Stuart a questioning look, without saying anything, and he continued. "I'm now fairly sure who was responsible for planting the second bug, but it cost my guy in Pennsylvania a fortune in whiskey. We're looking at a collector of rare manuscripts, as I expected. There's no proof, because he covered his tracks well, but like a lot of alpha types, he can't resist an opportunity to brag. My guy spent some time sussing out the whole scene down there, became reasonably knowledgeable about the rare biblical book business, and then started approaching people using vague statements on a few specific topics as bait. Most of the marks showed guarded interest or no real interest at all, except for this one guy who reacted like a hungry pike. Of course, there was the usual minuet when he feigned no interest at all and kept implying that he was going to walk away, but his eagerness to preen let my guy extract enough information to make a reasonable guess at the overall picture. So, our mark knows about 'somebody off in the sticks' who has a document the mark would like to acquire, but there's a complicating factor."

"Oh? What's that?" I asked.

"He already has a copy."

"But it's not unknown for a collector to have more than one copy of a rare book or document."

"No, but in this case, my man down there said he has an odd feeling about the whole business. So, for example, his interest, presumably in your document, is too intense, according to my man. There's something else going on."

"Do we know whether he knows that the document is here?"

"Depends on what you mean by 'here.' The fact that he planted the bug is a good sign that he knows something fairly specific, but I have no real idea what. He obviously believes it's located somewhere in Ontario. My guy is still working to find out how he knows that, since there are only four people here who are even aware that it exists."

"Well, so we thought", I said, "but evidently there's a fifth somewhere."

We both kicked that one around for a few minutes, but it was clear that no blinding insights were going to break forth suddenly. We then talked about where to go from here, and discussed several options. I said that I needed to update the information table Stuart and I had generated a week ago, and Stuart agreed, since we seemed to be moving into another level of complication.

"What is your guy doing down there now?" I asked.

"He's poking around using his cover."

"Which is?"

"Acting as an agent for a rare book dealer in Toronto."

"Won't the mark check on that?"

"It would be suspicious if he didn't, but don't worry. The dealer in question is a friend, and I've cleared this with him. If any calls come in, he'll field them for us."

"So, the mark must be playing his cards close", I said. "He seems to want to let on that his information is quite vague, and yet he knew exactly where to plant the bug."

Stuart nodded. "We can be sure that he knows the bug has failed or been located and removed. But he doesn't necessarily know that we know anything about the book he's interested in. He might be thinking that Fate has smiled upon him to send a rare book agent across his path from just the area he's snooping in. I expect he's also trying to figure out how to take advantage of this, and at the same time checking that he's not being played. If anything, he's likely concerned that another collector is trying to glean information on what our mark is up to. It's possible that another American collector would hire a rare book dealer in Toronto to poke around about a valuable item, but it's unlikely that that poking would extend as far as contacting the competing collector directly."

"So", I mused, "he planted a bug to get some sort of information. Maybe he hopes that I've come across something and don't know its value, and that he'll be able to lift it for a song. Or maybe he just wants to try to pilfer it and whisk it across the border."

"Those are both possibilities", Stuart said. "But, as I said, by now he knows that either the bug has been found and removed, or that it has just failed. Either way, we have to assume that he has, or will have, a watcher on the job. But I think we can also assume that, even if our mark knows that it is indeed you who has the book, our mark doesn't know its exact physical location. If there is a watcher, that watcher will know now that we have serious security in place, and that planting another bug will be tricky. He probably also knows that trying to break in would not be wise, first because of the security, and second because he has no hard evidence that the book is here in the house."

"So he's not likely suddenly to lose interest in your guy, since that might be now the only link he has to the book."

"That's the logic", Stuart said. "But it's a complicated game. Nobody is sure how many players there are, and nobody but us is sure which ones are cats and which ones are mice."

I had to smile despite myself. "You're enjoying this, aren't you?"

"Wouldn't miss it for the world."

I left Stuart to his business calls and went off to meet Monty at The Fox. He was already there when I arrived, and he had dragged two tables together on the patio and spread out various papers on them, weighted down by bricks against the light breeze. The sun was reaching low in the sky, approaching the western hills, and a pale amber light flooded everything, giving it a different substance and reality, that glorious and slightly nostalgic end-of-season valediction. It was a mild day, cool enough for long sleeves but not requiring more. We ordered something to drink and cast an eye over the menu before Monty dived straight into the paper.

"Okay, Richard", he said in an almost conspiratorial way, "I've found something important."

Twenty-three

It was Thursday. Stuart's business calls of the previous evening indicated that he needed to be back in town for the day, and he had left by the time I surfaced. A note scrawled hastily and placed next to the kettle said that he would be back ASAP, probably fairly late that night.

There was a huge schedule of work to be completed during the day, and I was becoming increasingly worried that I had tried to cram in too much. The mill was bathed in gorgeous pink morning light when I arrived, as if trying to assure me, 'Don't worry laddie; it's in the bag.'

While the operator was setting up his big crane, I carried the inflatable lifting bags and the modified scuba tank down to the riverside patio. In just a few minutes, I was in the water and fastening the lifting bags to the cast iron wheel. Within a half-hour, I had them all attached and had begun to inflate them. Soon they had expanded to the point that they blocked all direct view of the wheel from above, and I had to go completely underwater to check on things. Inflating the bags was easy enough, but making sure they were inflated uniformly was rather tedious. Just when I began to become a bit concerned, the tops of the bags suddenly broke the surface of the water. Sure enough, when I ducked down, I could see that the cast iron wheel had lifted completely free from the bottom of the lagoon.

It now took only about ten minutes for the crane to raise, swing, and lower the heavy pallet to a spot just to one side of the wheel. The pallet was lowered into the lagoon, with effort I moved the floating assembly of lifting bags and wheel over top of the pallet, deflated the bags, and the wheel settled gently onto the pallet. Throughout all this, Jeremy had been working like a madman, taking footage from all angles, as well as having a camera fixed on the general location of the wheel in the lagoon, and running the whole time the retrieval operation was in progress. I removed the bags, and the crane operator lifted the load about three feet above the surface of the water, and slowly swung it over to the riverside patio, where he set it down delicately. I unhooked the lifting cables. The first job was finished.

By this time, my labourers had arrived, and they gave a round of applause, cheering and whistling in their usual carefree adolescent fashion, as the pallet was gently set down onto the patio. By comparison, placing the flagstones for the underwater lights was simplicity itself. We placed the first flagstone. I timed it at 15 minutes, and it went off without a hitch. There were twelve flagstones, so I guessed that lodging the remaining eleven should take a bit less than three hours.

Monty and Greg arrived and went directly to look at the cast iron wheel. Monty tried unsuccessfully to restrain his St. Vitus dance of excitement, and within seconds he was on his knees and had pulled an assortment of small tools out of the bag he had brought along.

"Good God!" Greg said in astonishment. "It's a huge mother, isn't it!" It covered all the central section of the patio. We asked Monty if he needed anything else, or any help, but he had already passed through the portal into the land of forensic history, and was beyond reach.

Greg and I set to work assembling the remaining bits of the wooden water wheel, and the work went quickly. By ten thirty, we had all but two of the buckets attached. At that point, I was called away to get the next craning job started, since the flagstones for the lighting had all been placed.

There were sixteen sections of lagoon wall structure to be placed, and we could probably do them all in one session, but the work would most likely stretch out to six o'clock or a bit later. So it was important to get started right away.

My contractor had devised a good scheme for the lagoon wall, had cast and finished all the custom wall sections, and they had been delivered the previous afternoon. The crane lifted and placed the first section. Twenty minutes. So the whole job would take a good six hours.

Back at the water wheel, Greg and I finished bolting in place the final two buckets, and sat back to look at our handiwork. Greg bore that puffed up laughing and crying look of a new father.

"What now?" he asked.

"Now, we start balancing the wheel", and I explained how we would do that.

Within about an hour, we had the wheel balanced, so that when it was placed arbitrarily at any rotational position, it would stay there and not tend to turn one way or the other.

"So, is that it?" Greg asked.

"Is that what?"

"Are we finished?"

"Let's put it this way: It's not the end and not even the beginning of the end."

"Okay Winston, what's left to do?"

"Well", I replied, not trying too hard to conceal a smirk, "we have six commissioning tests to do before the wheel can go into operation", and I rhymed them off. "We won't do them in just that order, and we have something else to do first."

"What's that?"

"We'll set the wheel turning at low water flow and eyeball it for anything that seems amiss."

"Can we do that today?"

"How about right now? Better get Jeremy over here."

If Greg's earlier expression had been "new dad glow", he now radiated an aura of first eye contact and recognition.

We went to collect Monty, since he couldn't be left out of an event of this significance, stopping on the way over only to watch the swing of the crane as it moved another wall segment well clear of the patio and out over the lagoon. Monty met us when we were partway to the riverside patio, at the corner of the mill. His smile was so broad it looked painful, and he danced about like a hitherto unknown mathematician who had just proved the Riemann hypothesis.

"Richard! Richard!" he began excitedly, evidently trying to express a half-dozen complex thoughts all at once. "It, it, it's okay! It looks fine! I can't find any cracks! Holy shit, Richard!"

Greg and I exchanged glances, each of us concerned that any more excitement might carry Monty into complete nervous overload. I explained to Monty what we were about to do. He looked anxiously back and forth between the cast iron wheel and the wooden wheel, the perfect picture of a two-handed academic, conflicted over equally exciting, but mutually exclusive options.

Suddenly he overcame his stasis. "Okay!" he pronounced decisively. "I can't miss this! But, but, Richard! Holy shit!" and the St. Vitus bug had him again in its grip.

Jeremy had filmed the placement of three sections of the lagoon wall, and was now setting up three microphones: one right next to the wheel, one near the corner of the mill at the point where he had set one of his cameras, and one inside the mill itself. Jeremy had also placed a second camera right next to the wheel, and looking up at an angle past the buckets, through the spokes, and to the water flow coming in from the sluice.

The water flow would ultimately be regulated from the control panel inside the mill, but on this occasion I would open the flow manually since the scaffolding extended far enough back to the sluice to be able to do this. The others were assembled on the mid-level of the scaffolding. The wheel contained, by my estimate, about 2400 kilos of wood, and the whole thing would weigh about a hundred kilos more when completely wet but without water in any of the buckets. So, my calculations indicated that when I opened the valve, the wheel would slowly begin to turn, even though there would be no power delivered to the generator, and that the whole thing would be gripping and dramatic. After checking that Jeremy was ready, I gave him a signal to start his cameras and opened the valve to allow about 10% of full optimal flow.

Immediately, water began splashing into, and then out of the bucket directly facing the flow nozzles. I had imagined this moment so many times, and had done so many calculations for it, that nothing came as a surprise to me. The others, however, were transfixed. Slowly, the wheel began to turn. The sound being made initially by the water changed as the first bucket passed out of range of the flow, and water began filling the next bucket. The wheel slowly picked up speed. Now the third, and about ten seconds later, the fourth bucket began to fill. I glanced over at Greg, Monty, and Jeremy on the scaffolding. That great tutelary spirit of technology, the one that stirs the loins of everyone nearby when some first like this occurs, the one that has the power to raise goosebumps the size of Ping-Pong balls, now was doing all that but also was painting a communal smile on every one of the upturned faces. The wheel speed continued to increase. The regular chug-chug as water flowed into consecutive buckets was moving up the frequency register. Then, suddenly, there was the accompanying splash-splash, as the wheel moved to the point where water from the buckets was being emptied into the lagoon. The noise level increased. Greg gave me a high-octane thumbs up. Monty went into a closed loop holy-shit chant.

When the wheel reached what looked like a steady rotation, I climbed down onto the same level of scaffolding as the others, and peered closely at the wheel. The buckets swung past the scaffold framework in Swiss-watch precision, and I could see no variation as they did so, indicating that they were all aligned and properly fitted on the wheel. As the buckets moved past, it also appeared that they were filled to about the same extent. There was no wobble that I could see anywhere. There was no squeaking or groaning. None of the spokes was deflecting, bending, or twisting as far as I could tell. The axle was rock-steady. The spokes swung past in both metronomic and geometric regularity. I looked at Monty and Greg. Monty was mesmerized. Greg's gaze was flowing across all parts of the wheel, taking in a scene that was completely outside his experience. Our eyes met and I gave him a huge smile. His return smile was at least as broad. We both knew we had brought something to life, had resurrected a river dweller gone quiet for a hundred years. And it was a hell of a good feeling, throat lump and all.

I let the wheel turn for about ten minutes, then shut off the water. The wheel began to slow, and I timed the period from the moment I shut off the water to the instant the wheel was still: a minute and forty seconds. That piece of information, and the video record of the wheel's deceleration, would provide the basis for a rough estimate of the friction and other losses the wheel was seeing. We stood there for a moment, listening to water drip off the wheel.

Monty came over to me. "Richard...I...I...I don't know what to say. I'm ashamed that I feel like a kid with a new toy."

"You shouldn't be the least bit ashamed, Monty. Just enjoy the feeling. When you build something and it works, that's exactly how you should feel."

"But I didn't build anything, I didn't do anything."

"Monty. We're all in this project together. You provide moral support, and moral support from someone like you is worth at least two more pair of labourers' hands."

He went all gooey, so I rescued him by suggesting that maybe he should get back to the other wheel. As though he had suddenly come out of a trance, or some distant Merlin had lifted an evil spell, he blinked a couple of times, looked sharply toward the patio, muttered something like, "you're right, what the hell am I doing?" and skipped off down the scaffolding.

The placing of the lagoon wall was more than half done, and it looked as though they would be finished by six o'clock. I indicated to Greg that we should go take a look, and he followed me down the scaffolding steps, but looked back at the wheel three or four times, the image of the great thing in such stately and dramatic action still clearly burning brightly in his mind. We walked back to the corner of the mill, and watched the crane swing another section across the lagoon and slowly lower it into place. It looked as though adjacent ends of the sections in the water were sitting virtually in contact with each other, and the tops of the sections were at almost the exact same horizontal level. The line of the wall swung out from a point just upstream of the shoreward stone support for the sluice, and swept past the mill in a long graceful elliptic section.

"Looks like it's coming along well", I said.

Greg just looked along the line of the wall without saying anything. Eventually he murmured, "What a day!"

"What do you mean 'What a day?' " I said in remonstrance. "The day is scarcely half over. There remains work to be done, my man." And so we went back to the wheel and did two of the commissioning tests: the calibration of flow through the piping and header from the sluice, and a bearing check. By the time that was complete, it was pushing four thirty.

"What now?" Greg asked.

"Now, I think we go in and check on the drywalling." When we got inside, we found that most of the heavy work on the drywalling had been completed. Only taping, plastering, and sanding remained. Expanses of drywall on three sides of the room were broken by rough hewn but finished heavy wooden beams, and offset by expanses of ancient brick. Three long, equally rough hewn beams stretched the length of the ceiling. All the wiring and piping had been done already, we were now in a space that was recognizably commercial, and Greg's entrepreneurial buttons lit up. By the way he looked around, squinting slightly, I could tell he was visualizing the finished restaurant and coffee bar space. Ceiling and sconce lights would go in next, then flooring, then large items of kitchen equipment, then the painters would do their work. After that, tables and chairs, cutlery, china and porcelain, and the larger kitchen utensils would be delivered. The anticipation was palpable.

Greg was taking all this in basically at a glance. "Richard, we should be able to start at least the coffee-shop service here in about a week."

"And that's exactly what's on the schedule. Tomorrow, my labourers will be building the outdoor coffee shop deck and putting up the awning. There will be events of real interest happening at this mill pretty much every day for the next week, and I hope we can have paying customers coming to have a gander at every one of those events. Remember the outline plan we had for this stage of the work, for getting people involved? We really should update that and do some more detailed planning.

125

We're probably behind on some of the things we should be doing. Would you have time this evening to get together to do that?"

"Absolutely", Greg said with emphasis. "Come up to our place when we're done here. Jill is off to her book club tonight. She'll be sorry to have missed you."

"Well, if she's not too late I can hang around for coffee and a schnapps when she gets home."

The engine note of the crane changed suddenly, interrupting our discussion. I looked at my watch. Five forty-five. We had spent far more time here in the mill than I expected. Stepping outside, I could see the crane operator emerging from his cab, and my one labourer climbing out of the lagoon and onto the riverside patio. The lagoon wall now cut a long elegant arc across the water, leaving only a short two-foot gap near the river bank at the downstream end for outflow. The third, and biggest, job for the day was now done. At about the same time, Monty came up to us, his countenance wreathed in intellectual victory, and said he was leaving for the day, that he had taken almost two hundred detailed photos that he wanted to examine at home, that he would be back first thing in the morning, and that, if possible, he would like another two days to complete his examination of the wheel.

By quarter to seven, the crane operator was ready to depart, my labourers had all roared off in a cloud of friendly invective, Greg had driven away to get pizza for us for later, and I had locked up the mill. The rest of the evening flew by in something of a haze. Back at home, there was a message from Stuart saying he would be in Greenvale again by mid-morning the following day. There was a backlog of emails from all sorts of people looking for an update on progress at the mill. And there was Max waiting for his dinner.

I hadn't collected my mail that day, but possibly I could do that on the way home from Greg's place.

I arrived at Greg's just after eight o'clock. As usual, his home was an oasis. Piano music, I think by Clayderman, filled the rooms at just the right volume from his superb sound system. There was wine opened, mixed olives for nibbles, and the pizzas were just coming out of the oven. On the table, I noticed the detailed chart of events at the mill, and preparations for them, that we had constructed, incorporating Greg's care and his eye for detail, and on which he had already made quite a few annotations. Greg emerged from the kitchen, swept up a couple of wine glasses in one hand from the sideboard *en passant*, and motioned me to a seat within reach of wine bottle, olives, and chart. He was evidently a bit tired, but still pumped up, and there was a strong residual glow in his eyes from the events of the day. We worked, drank, ate, talked, and in about an hour we had reviewed all the events in the chart. The entries were now covered in red ink, and Greg said he would make the changes on the computer file and run off a couple of clean copies. Greg then made the case that, apart from consultation, he should be left to take care of all the commercial and publicity arrangements related to the mill. I agreed without argument.

We discussed some specifics as we finished the pizza. Jill returned just after nine, and Greg found the energy to lay out for her, in detail, the day's events, his hands sculpting the air as he spoke. As he paused to take a sip of wine, Jill winked at me, obviously delighted to see Greg so charged.

On the way home, I stopped at the post office. There was no mail of interest. As I pulled into my driveway, the car lights swung across the front patio, and patches of weeds danced in the beams with impunity. I had a pang of guilt at not having spent enough time on this patio, enough time weeding the stonework, enough time tending the garden that had kept me supplied in such an abundance of luscious vegetables over the entire summer. "Later", I muttered, then ducked ignominiously into the house, disabled the alarm, locked the door, dropped the mail on the table, was already shedding clothes as I entered the bedroom, slid gratefully into bed, and was out like a light.

I awoke suddenly—instantly wide awake. It was just after three thirty. A ridiculous but unshakeable sense of victory filled my consciousness. After a few minutes, I turned on my dim bedside reading light and thought about things. My euphoric sense surely couldn't have been caused just by the events of the day, although they really were signal and satisfying. The reactions of Greg and Monty, and the expressions on their faces were by themselves worth the day's effort, but that wasn't the explanation either. Switching off the night light, I waited for the remaining fatigue from the day to pull me under again.

I didn't need to wait long.

Twenty-four

There were eight days to the event on Greg's list identified as "Mill Sound and Light." We had talked about this one enough, the organizational items needed for the event were now in place, and the roles that Greg and I were to play would be simply enjoyable and not need a lot of preparation. It was getting the mill itself ready for the big event that preoccupied me.

The drywalling and painting of the restaurant space was now complete, and we had the doors and windows of the place open fourteen hours a day to get rid of the fresh paint odour. The flooring was in. The stoves, ovens, large fridges, working surfaces and the pots, pans, skillets, ladles, tongs, and other kitchen utensils had been delivered and were being put in place. I had worked summers in restaurant kitchens while at university and am a reasonable cook myself, Greg had acquired some experience from the Pavilion in putting together a kitchen, but we agreed that we would not just try to wing it. We hired a consultant, who worked with us for a month and would stay on for a month after opening. Our consultant, Ms. Ferris, was in her mid-forties, businesslike to the point of being abrupt, but her eyes missed nothing, and it was clear from her expression when she looked around the mill that her passions were food, service, and motivated staff. She insisted on a full tour, in terms that hinted at someone being holed below the water line in the event of refusal, and her eyes lit up as we walked past the milling machines, just newly installed. We entered the kitchen, she stopped, scanned the room with a laser glare, and I felt my sphincter-control effort climb dangerously.

"Who designed this kitchen?" she demanded.

My heart sank.

"This is first rate! We'll have this written up for the trade press!"

She moved around the kitchen, commenting *sotto voce* and nodding her head periodically, and I could see her visualizing the ergonomics of food preparation.

To assist us in finding a restaurant manager, Mrs. Williamson suggested to us the name of a young woman, and we could be certain that she would have an IQ in the top five percentile as well as nerves of steel to merit that recommendation. After a half-hour interview, Ms. Ferris said she was good, so we took her on. She would also run the coffee shop. Jill's young brother, Michael, was an aspirant chef, full of piss and vinegar and having good qualifications but little real experience. Ms. Ferris checked him out as well, and Michael told Jill later that if his exams at cooking school had been as difficult as that interview, he would now be driving a truck. Ms. Ferris gave him a hesitant pass, saying that he had a good attitude, a good feel for *la cucina*, what he lacked in experience was balanced by his enthusiasm, but that there would be risks and a lot of work and guidance needed if he were taken on.

Greg voted not to hire him, fearing the problems that can come with relatives and perceived nepotism. I was in favour of taking him on, and we met partway by asking Ms. Ferris to draw up a training and evaluation schedule for a six-month probation period. Michael was ecstatic and not the least bit upset about a probationary position. So now we had a chef. Greg was still concerned and wanted to know what my role would be. He felt that I might consider my vision for myself to have been somehow usurped. In fact, I was most interested in being the majority owner of a successful venture, and it was the vision for this venture that concerned me most.

Throughout this period, I had struggled against cold feet: after all, it was a long way from my original idea of just a flour mill, to what was threatening to be an industrial empire and one-size-fits-all social venue, but Ms. Ferris waved this off, tut-tutting at my faintness of heart, and said that we were on a good track. It's true that this change in scope was planned and controlled and not the result of insidious creep. It's also true that costs were trending down the middle of my range of predictions, and we were ahead of schedule, and anyhow it was way too late to have second thoughts now. I do confess, however, to following a somewhat euphoric-panic sine curve for a few weeks.

There were a thousand small things to do. Ms. Ferris was at the centre of the action, juggling multiple tasks with the ease of a Leonard Bernstein conducting a school choir. Curtains had to be put up. Linen had been acquired and had to be subject to a storage and inspection routine. We had to finalize laundry arrangements. The last details of waste disposal had to be organized. Our consultant had planned a menu strategy to test our front-end assumptions about clientele, and to aim for a point not too high but not too low, while leaving greatest room to adjust. We had three trial restaurant sittings, the purpose of these trials being to gauge the reactions of the diners, but also to test and optimize the flow of food from freezers and fridges, through the kitchen, to the tables, and then the removal of plates, glasses, cutlery from the tables, so that the whole thing looked smooth and effortless, and neither too fast nor too tardy. We checked indicators of customer satisfaction. We checked noise levels. We checked for odours. We checked our arrangements to be able to provide guaranteed vegetarian and vegan meals. We checked endlessly, it seemed, for tripping and slipping hazards. We checked procedures for maintaining the restrooms. We tested the coat-check operation. We checked the dumb waiter delivery to and from the lower patio. Just about the time we were feeling checked and mated, Ms. Ferris smiled and was happy, so we followed her lead.

The days flitted past, far too quickly, it seemed. Then, when there were just two days to Mill Sound and Light, Ms. Ferris told us to piss off.

"Go home", she said. "Rest, read, play field hockey, do some gardening, watch birds, anything but worry or think about the restaurant. You've done all that you can do. The next time you come back, you need to be relaxed and confident." It was good advice.

I found myself, unaccountably and unusually, at home in the middle of the afternoon. Max was unimpressed at this abrupt and barbaric change in the order of things.

Stuart returned that afternoon from one of his longish stays in Toronto. His business came in batches, and he had just finished a particularly tightly bunched batch of jobs. I knew he worked mostly on his own, farming work out to a small band of trusted operatives when necessary. I also knew that his jobs were greatly varied, but I didn't ask for details, and he didn't offer any. This time, although he was obviously tired, his mood was upbeat, and he filled me in on what he had been doing for us over the past few days. There was quite a bit to relate.

He had traced Ambrose. Gerard Mark Ambrose had died penniless in a hospice in Barrie in 1974. Stuart had found sufficient records to be sure that this was the Ambrose associated with the Greenvale mill. There was a son, Ian Ambrose, and Stuart was still trying to track him down. Our burglar, Jimmy Kralik, had been a small-time villain who had popped up regularly at various places and in shady contexts across southern Ontario. He had been shot once in the head. It was considered to be an execution, but the police had followed a short investigation trail to a dead end. I filled Stuart in on what we had been doing, but it became evident that he had a mound of other work to do, so I left him to it.

Having all this time on my hands, I found myself casting about somewhat, not sure what to do. But then I decided that this was the ideal slack time to take a look at the document Monty had unearthed. Retrieving it from my desk, I sat down to read.

Carl Mason had produced his diary, or life story, in sections, which were headed *My Origins*, *My Youth*, *Land and Sea Voyage*, *My Life in Philadelphia*, *Journey to British North America*, *Life in Upper Canada*, and *Late Days*. I opened to the first section and read.

> *I know not, with any certainty of recollection or through documents, the year of my birth. But I divine it to be the Year of Our Lord 1709, since I believe I was of age eighteen, nine years after the death of my mother, when I disembarked from the* James Goodwill *in 1727. I believe this date to be true, but have no means of confirming it with certainty due to circumstances that overcame me, as I will tell.*
>
> *My family werked a small holding of land in the countryside, and we were able to remain together, werking this land, only through great travail and in the face of recurring misfortunes. Our nearby village was said to be small and poor, but I travelled to it just once and thus have no firm recollection, even as to its name. From the village, our modest house was a small distance removed, the equal of about a hundred and fifty chains, in measure I learned at Philadelphia, or about two miles, in measure of today. Our life was difficult, and we knew hardship in many forms. As my father related, two of my four brothers died 'ere they reached the age of four. One of my two sisters died as an infant. My mother, a humble, caring, God-fearing but delicate being, succumbed to neumonia after an injury while I was in what I judge to be my ninth year.*
>
> *My father and his brother strove to sustain us. When I attained the age of sixteen, or seven years after my mother's death, the differences in outlook between my father and his brother, which*

grew over the years, became a gulf that none could reconcile. My father's brother departed. There remained then my father, me, and a sullen brother of the name Peter. Short weeks after the departure of my uncle, we knew that my brother had also left his family home. What became of any of my two other siblings I do not know.

My father was a stern man, who would now be called a Pietist, competent at husbandry, but often sullen, taciturn, one who imposed his own harsh rules, and was without the leaven of any humor. How he did it I know not, but he had placed in store some small resource, and he told me one day to pack my few things for we were embarking on a great journey to a new life. Where that was, and the path which led us to it, I will relate presently.

To that point, the life I had known was one of husbandry. By day, we labored from first light to twi light, and our reward was then a simple meal taken around one candle. My father could not read. He attended church meetings but rarely, and learned many biblical passages which he was fond of reciting to himself. He instructed me as best he could in religious matters, but he was mostly solitary and a man of few words, and my burden of labor was too heavy to commit time to religious contemplation. As a youth I was unschooled and could neither read nor write.

There was another page or so of similar details, but I left them for the moment to do a quick computer search, and was delighted to find that records of immigrant arrivals in eighteenth-century Philadelphia had been digitized and were available online. It took me very little time to confirm that a ship called the *James Goodwill* had docked in Philadelphia on September 27, 1727, having sailed from Rotterdam, stopping in England at Plymouth, and my interest quickened considerably. A bit more searching gave me the list of passengers who disembarked from the *James Goodwill*, and I downloaded it. There was no Carl Mason among the names. After some further digging, I found a number of academic papers on immigration to Penn's Woods. They filled in quite a bit of material, describing the horrific conditions some of the passengers had to endure while crossing the Atlantic, the quite large losses of passengers due to illness during the voyages, and a caution that the records from that period varied considerably in quality, that none should be taken at face value if they were to be applied to an important end use, and that independent confirmation of information on dates, etc. was the best and most prudent course, although that was often impossible. So, Carl Mason might have been on that particular ship, but the records didn't show it, or he might have been on a different ship arriving on a different day or even in a different year.

Turning back to the diary, I skipped to the section *Land and Sea Voyage*, and read on.

I never was to learn what my father did with our home. We left one morning and walked away. We were many days on foot, and we passed through towns and cities, and through some attractive countryside. We walked without speaking. My father knew only the destination, but we followed the large river after we reached Mannheim and still he asked the way many times. We had to turn back a few times since we went astray more than once. We slept in fields or in barns. We ate what we could and when we could. Some days, we traded a day's werk for food. We both became gaunt. My foot wear fell to pieces.

Twice we were threatened by highwaymen, but my father was quick to anger and he put his large walking staff to good use. In sum, our journey was many weeks. The large cities were strange and noisy to me, and I found them unpleasant. But we also passed through a long, steep-sided valley, and the aspects it presented I recall as being most pleasant. At length, we arrived in Rotterdam, and there was much discussion, bargaining, and some shouting before we found places on a ship. My father immediately disliked the captain of that ship, and refused to agree on paying passage, so we began again looking for another ship. It was chilly and damp in Rotterdam, the nights were cold, and many days passed before my father agreed to passage on the James Goodwill. *I recall being greatly confused at the time, wondering why we were enduring this hardship, and doubting my father's faith that we were headed for a better life.*

Finally we sailed. Within a short time, what turned out to be a waking nightmare had begun, and seasickness plagued many. Conditions in the sleeping areas were beyond description. The sounds of mass retching made sleep difficult, but the vile and acrid air and the disgorged food which soon caked everything was scarcely barable compared to the sweet air and the water for bathing that we had found along the great river.

We had two days respite in Plymouth, and some attempt was made there to clean the ship, but when we sailed again, this time carrying even more souls, the nightmare resumed. About a week after we had left Plymouth, the first death occurred. The first of two great storms fell upon us, and the fearfull noise of crashing water mingled with anguished wails begging the Almighty for deliverance filled the bowels of the ship. More people died the following week. A few weeks later, a lassitude overtook my father. Four days later, he also died. The morning of his death, he carefully passed me the few gold coins that remained to us, and said that his end was near. I objected, wishing that he was wrong, but he rallied with that stern mien I knew and said in a firm voice, that probably cost him his remaining strength, that it was His Will, that I must accept it, that I must carry on, that I must take his clothes and foot wear after he had been received by the Lord, that I must safe guard the trunck that had been entrusted to us in such anxiety by its owner, and he gave me his final blessing as a good and faithfull son. He drifted in and out of a most troubled sleep for a number of hours, and finally departed me late that afternoon. Within an hour, his remains had been dropped over the side of the ship, and as I recited the sole fragment of a prayer that I knew I bade him adieu. I was now alone, and I wept silently, not knowing whether for myself or for my father.

It was an odd document, but one that could not help but be touching. I simply could not imagine walking a total of five hundred kilometres, without wayside indications, without any understanding of geography, without even knowing the names of successive towns, and having to ask constantly where I was. It was impossible to imagine then embarking on a sea voyage that seems to have lasted many weeks, perhaps months.

This was a different time, in that a sea voyage, or even the sea itself, would be a great unknown, beyond comprehension, for someone who had lived their life in valleys, hills, plains. In a time when most people had no coherent view of the world that anyone today would recognize, apart from that offered by religious faith, changes of this sort would be a trip into the irrational, and deeply fearsome for most. It was a different time, and the people were made of different stuff. It was also clear that this man and his father had walked through part of what is now Germany, so his original name could not have been Mason. This whole business was beginning to look more complex. I skipped to the section *My Life in Philadelphia* and read some more.

My first sight of Philadelphia was a most welcome one. After we sighted land, to our great joy, and with much giving of thanks, our ship followed the shore for two days. We sailed up a long and wide passage, and in the end the city rose before us on high land in the distance. Being now without my father, and laden by a trunck I had given my solemn word to take with me and keep safe, I was mindfull of the need to find a means to support myself. Husbandry was all that I knew, and I resolved to make use of that. My father had entrusted to me the small sum of gold coins that remained to him when it was clear that he would not live to complete the sea voyage. Almost everything we possessed was paid to the captain of the ship for our passage and food, if such that we ate could be said to be food, and I was confused and distressed as I watched my father's body being dropped over the side of the ship. My father left this world some three days after the captain declared that we had already sailed more than half our full distance, so there was no refund or recompense to me. It took me some time to understand this, since I knew no English then, and there were few people on the ship who understood both English and German. Without my father to provide the support I was acustomed to, I felt alone in the world, being far from people I understood, and not yet knowing that I had the support of Our Good Lord, a blessing that came to me later in my life.

It had been but three days prior to my father's death when our recent friend, a man from Rotterdam I believe, had also been taken to the bosom of Our Lord after an unpleasant illness, and he had pleaded that my father should swear to take care of this trunck and its contents. My father had done so, since there was no other civil path to tread, and he caused me to swear the same oath when he was near his own end. I honored that oath and have retained and safe guarded the trunck faithfully throughout my life.

When we were ashore in Philadelphia, I was asked to make a mark on paper to state that I had arrived, and that I would be a citizen of Penn's Colony and given land to werk. The land given to me was near Germantown, and my belief was sorely strained by surprise to see how much land would be mine. It was very fine land as well, covered with large trees that had to be removed before I would be able to grow crops. I remember werking hard in the season remaining that year, but soon had to shelter during the winter in the home of another who had arrived some time before. We had the same language and so were able to converse, he provided me food and adequate shelter in return for werk, and although he was not a pleasant man, I survived my first winter and returned to clearing my own land when the weather changed.

In but a few months, I had learned ennuf English to trade and make my own way. It was several years before I learned to read and write, but I strove to acheave this when I observed the fate of those who did not aquire those skills. It was four or five years before my standing in our community was recognised. By then I had built a small home, had cleared more than sufficient land to provide for a family, had purchased an old horse that would serve, and was able to prove the worth of my husbandry skills. I had been in Penn's Colony seven years when I took a wife, although I was regarded as too old and there was much gossip. It was only two years later when my beloved Christina was taken from me during the birth of our son Rolf. I remember it as a dark time, and it was to become darker still, since Rolf proved himself to be idle and worthless. When Rolf reached fifteen years, by my estimate, there was a violent argument, and to my shame I beat the boy without mercy when I learned of his plan to spirit the trunck to Philadelphia and sell it. He left me shortly thereafter, and I never cast eyes upon him again. May the Lord forgive me this heavy sin, which I continue to regrett every day.

Compared to the life I remember in my former land when our family was one, my years in Penn's Colony were easier. There was much hard labor, and there were lean years, but I was never under threat of being forced from my land and I was not under threat of war or general disruption. In my spiritual weakness, which is the lot of imperfect man, I wished betimes that Our Good Lord might have chosen to spare my beloved Christina, but then I would forthwith chasten myself saying that His Will was thus and I must be content to obey.

During the years that Providence chose to allot to me in Philadelphia, I maintained the trunck, the care of which I was charged with on the James Goodwill. *Since I had sworn to my father, as he lay dying, a solemn oath to do that, it was for me the natural thing and the only right thing to do and required small effort. Since I did not change lodging after I had built my dwelling, keeping the trunck was no burden. My understanding was given strength, and a small measure of Divine favor was revealed to me, when I first looked into the book which the trunck contained. I discovered that it was a miracullous text, most beautifull to behold, and although I could not read it, since I was able to read only English, I had seen German text in the possession of other residents near Germantown, and I came to know that the trunck contained a Holy Werk, and that the task of keeping this Werk safe and intact had been assigned to me. From then onwards, I felt myself graced that such a privilege had been laid before me by our Blessed Good Lord.*

In Philadelphia, I had indeed much to be thankfull for, and my faith in Our Lord and His Divine Purpose grew. It was during this time that several kindly citizens of the colony, who had also come to this new land from Rotterdam, befriended me, and it was from them that I gained an ability to read German. I came to regard this also as part of Our Lord's Great Plan, and I was humbled, for this led me to obtain one of the greatest possessions a believer may aquire: a copy of the Holy Scripture. It was from Christoph Sauer, a man of worth and estimation, and someone with whom I had a small old country connection, that I purchased my Holy Bible. It was printed in Philadelphia and in German, of which my understanding was still halt, but my copy was handed to me by Christoph Sauer himself close to Christmas in the Year of Our Lord 1743, and I was obliged to force upon him the sum I had set aside over long periods before I could feel I had the right to possess such a treasure. I trembled in gratitude, and in the fire of my ardent belief, when I first opened my copy of the Blessed Scripture and was able to read

Am Anfang schuf Gott Himmel und Erde. Und die Erde war wüst und leer, und es war finster auf der Tiefe; und der Geist Gottes schwebte auf dem Wasser.

I tremble still when I recall that day, and such is my thankfullness, such is the beauty of the Scripture of which I am the humble and gratefull steward, that I look into it but rarely, one time each year, and that only with the most strenuous care, and have committed many passages to memory, always desiring and hoping that my copy of the Holy Scripture might remain ever pristine and unsullied by the defilement of human touch. These two books, that assigned to my care on the ship and my own Holy Scripture, I continue to maintain with all the care and diligence and reverence in my power, since I regard the custody of these volumes as a duty willingly borne but also as a privilege bestowed upon me.

This section of his memoir went on to describe at greater length other aspects of Mason's life in Philadelphia, and I skimmed over it quickly. He spent several pages describing his good fortune at having such rich land and the skills to work it. He wrote about the carpentry competence he acquired in building his own house and furniture, and how he was able eventually to trade on that competence by making items of furniture of increasing elegance and quality during the winter months, for those who were all thumbs. I skimmed through a good many parts of his memoir, knowing that I would read every word in due course, but was struck more than anything by the spirit of the age that came through in the words.

He wrote many pages on the ferment that was growing in Philadelphia, making observations that would surely be gold dust to historians of the time just before and just after the Revolution. But he also recorded his own misgivings once the Revolution had begun, fears that the new republic would not last and that retribution would be severe, fears that order would not be maintained and that things would descend into the sort of chaos that he recalled so vividly from the Palatinate and how he had hated and feared that tumult. He expressed fears that the dream which had become true for him in Germantown would unravel, that his life of working his land and living in peace and free from interference or disruption would not endure. He recorded his first thoughts about a trek to British North America, and how a few others had begun thinking along these lines.

I was keeping an open mind on the question of whether this document was authentic. I thought that it might be difficult to prove that it was. But if it was not authentic it might be fairly easy to prove that it was not. Something I wanted to discuss with Monty was the task of identifying the information needed to establish its actual origin. But assuming for the moment that it was authentic, what I was reading was reflections on a way of life that had passed out of existence more than 200 years ago. Like the mill, this text was a concrete artifact, existing in the present, but deriving from an actual past, where it had also existed as the same object but in a different present. Neither of these artifacts, not the mill and not this old text, could be understood, really understood, without having some sense of the spirit of the time. To characterize my grasp of this spirit in terms of a clothing metaphor, I was as a new-born babe, without clothes and without real understanding. Once again, I could sense that V. Gordon Childe, Geoffrey Elton, Edward Carr, and Robin Collingwood were with me now, encouraging me on.

Twenty-five

The big day—Mill Sound and Light—was bearing down on us.

We had tested everything. It all worked. It all did what it was supposed to do. And on a brilliant, sunny Monday, the first Monday in October, we produced our first commercial flour. Through sweat, hard work, and some luck in avoiding the pessimistic eventualities I had accommodated in the planning, we were about four weeks ahead of our worst estimate schedule, and a little more than two weeks ahead of the best estimate date.

We had used Marquis, an almost heritage wheat grain, since quite a bit of it was grown in the region, and more than a dozen local individuals and bakers had said that they would like to see Marquis flour, and, more importantly, that they would buy it.

I had examined our first flour product closely, and we had two experts pass judgment on it. "A little finer than necessary", they said, "but excellent." But the proof of flour is in the bread. So I made about twenty kinds of bread. There were loaves of different sizes and moisture contents. There was French-style bread, Kaiser rolls, baps, sourdough, herb breads, onion bread, Greek olive boule, ciabatta, focaccia, and pizza base. It all had a slightly branny quality, as expected, but the crust and the crumb looked good, and, according to my tasters, the taste was perfect in every case.

That test completed, we then ground five hundred kilos of flour for samples, and gave them away to prospective customers. The rest of the arrangements for getting the mill well known in Greenvale and nearby villages had taken four days, and Greg and I planned them down to the last tiny detail. Greg spent many hours putting together the audio tracks for Mill Sound and Light using his sound system. I spent one sixteen-hour day in my kitchen.

At three days to go, the new oak door to the main entrance was hung, and it had the same impact as Cindy Crawford's beauty mark. Literally everybody who entered the mill hesitated to admire the door. Two days prior to the big day itself, we had the last of the craning work done. Bundles of scrap wood that had formed the pallets for all the items of equipment, and which had been stored temporarily in an area to the north of the shipping door, were craned onto a truck to be taken to The Fox, where Jasper would cut them into firewood. The cast iron wheel was lifted from the riverside patio and placed in the area vacated by the pallet wood. Finally, a single large crate of tables and chairs was lifted from its delivery truck and lowered onto the riverside patio, where I uncrated and placed them during spare hours. In the fading light of that long day, I finished the wooden enclosure that served as a blind to close off the cast iron wheel from view, checked all wooden handrails for splinter hazards, gave the several dozen flower boxes a good soaking, swept the visitor parking area and the lower patio, checked all the land-based lighting once again, and loaded soft drinks into the fridges.

On the morning of the big day, Greg and I were both at the mill at six o'clock. The restaurant space was now populated by solid, attractive, pioneer-design tables and very comfortable chairs. The kitchens, a small short-order galley arrangement associated with the coffee bar, and a larger closed-off space to serve the restaurant and which included a walk-in cooler, were now fully equipped. Greg and I tied up a large banner along the back wall of the dining area in the mill's hallmark shades of grey and red, on which "Welcome to Greenvale Mill" would greet anyone who entered the room. There were strings of small decorative lights mounted in random bunches on the walls and on some of the tables. Signs on the walls and doors invited and led people on self-guided tours of the kitchens and food-preparation areas. Access to the rest of the mill would be closed for the evening of the big day, but in the days to come we would be having controlled and guided tours throughout the mill. We installed and tested speakers for the sound system on the outer mill wall at the second-storey level, and on the upper deck and lower patio. We had eighteen speakers, to produce a wall of sound but avoid the unpleasantness of two deafening point sources. Greg and I did a test of these speakers and a final test of the underwater lights, the mood lighting in the alcoves at the riverside patio, and the foot-level lighting to illuminate the steps between the upper deck and the lower patio.

At about eleven o'clock, Jill and I arranged the armsful of flowers she had brought. At twelve thirty, I went home for a short rest and to change.

Jeremy caught on video virtually every aspect of these preparations.

Greg and I both led the tour that started at four o'clock. We were distinctively attired. I wore highly polished black shoes, a matte grey suit, a plain white shirt, and a tie in the mill's signature shade of cherry red. Greg wore oxblood loafers, tan trousers, a cream shirt, a jacket the colour of golden ripe wheat, and an outsized paisley bowtie in primary colours. We must have looked like an odd pair. Our tour group included business people, municipal politicians, several bakers from surrounding local towns and villages, my three guardian spirits (Mrs. Williamson, Jasper, and Lonny), Monty, and the local school principal, and they all entered freely into our caution-to-the-winds approach to the evening. We walked them around the outside areas, then led a detailed tour that followed the path into, through, and out of the mill, that would be taken by grain as it was converted to flour. At the end of the tour, each of them received a token one kilo cloth bag of flour, the bags all carrying the name "Greenvale Mill Flour" in the lettering and colours that the commercial product bags would bear. There was a good forty-five minutes of detailed and intelligent questions about many aspects of the mill itself and about the flour-making operation. And I noticed with satisfaction that the eyes of many of the tour guests roamed the physical structures inside the mill, and many were drawn to tactile encounters with the stonework and the exposed beams. The old girl had huge drawing power for everyone. Toward the end of the tour, Mrs. Williamson caught my eye, and gave me a warm smile and a nod of congratulation that said, in every way except the literally spoken words, "Well done, Dr. Gould!" At the end of the tour, Lonny sidled up to me and whispered, "Fecking brilliant!" Jasper spent a long time giving the dining area and kitchen spaces a critical professional examination. He was the last of the group to move outside for the light snack we had arranged just for this group. He approached me, and my hand disappeared into his huge outstretched meaty paw which then closed as though powered by the hydraulic system of a large Caterpillar, and he gave one authoritative shake while staring directly into my eyes. I briefly wondered what to say should he offer to wash my feet.

It was mid-October, and dusk arrived quite early. Jeremy had set up cameras at five locations, and they ran all evening. At six thirty, the mill was thrown open to everyone in the village, and Greg had made sure that the event had been preceded by saturation multimedia advertising. About a hundred and twenty people turned up. The visitor car park was full. There was every attire from jeans and lumberjack shirts to dress jackets and long evening gowns. Each person entering was handed a single sheet saying what would happen when, and inviting them, for the initial half-hour, to wander about, look at everything that was open, and saying that both Greg and I would be available to talk about whatever anyone wanted to discuss. We mingled as best we could, but I felt as though lost in a school of krill. We had set all the lighting to mood level. The upper deck and the lower patio were magnets for people to collect and chat, and although it was an unseasonably warm evening, it was too late in the year for us to be bothered by mosquitoes or bugs. The sides of the mill were bathed in soft cream light. The water wheel was almost in obscurity, but was lit just sufficiently so that people could make out its shape. I was swamped by questions, comments, and congratulations.

At about seven o'clock, Greg started the audio, which consisted of a collage of easy listening tracks he had selected, and was played at a volume loud enough to be recognizable and enjoyable but too faint to make conversation any strain. At seven thirty, Greg took over as MC, and within a minute had the entire assembly in the palm of his hand. He introduced Monty, who gave a short but impassioned and animated exhortation on the importance of local history, but almost lost it when he turned to indicate the mill as the embodiment of his main point. He recovered nicely behind a nervous laugh, and somehow managed to suppress any holy-shit reflex. Greg introduced a representative of the heritage organization that had provided funding for the refurbishment, and she gave a pretty short speech that thanked me, the investors, the village council, and all the residents of Greenvale for such a "gorgeous and satisfying project". The next up was the village clerk, an imposing man who projected a commanding *basso profundo*, was head of the local Toastmasters, who spoke for barely two minutes, but left few dry eyes by the time he finished. Greg then introduced me. I spoke of the past six years, mentioned many people by name, described the mill as the project of a lifetime, and ended by saying that

I hoped to see many of them over the coming months in "our mill". I was overcome by the response, and as I moved back from the illuminated speaking area, Jasper in acknowledgement dropped a huge hand, indistinguishable from a five-ton weight, onto my shoulder.

Greg was being the impresario, his arms pumping the air, bounding about in enthusiasm, flashing a fifty-megawatt smile, and enjoying the evening immensely, even more so as it was obvious that everyone else was as well.

"And now", he said, all the introductory fluff being out of the way. Long pause here. "The star of the show!" He turned to pass a theatrical sweep of the arm over the mill behind him, then he turned back to the audience and slowly moved his gaze across the crowd, playing them all shamelessly.

A loud drum roll fell as a torrent from the speakers and gradually faded over a space of about ten seconds. At the same time, all the mood lighting slowly dimmed in tandem with the drums. Everything became still, dark, and quiet. For five seconds there was all but total silence. The river murmured to the dam upstream. A dog barked somewhere in the distance. Someone almost suppressed a cough. The night sky, full of stars, looked on peacefully.

Suddenly, a blast of light bathed every feature of the mill, pouring from the floods on land, and erupting upward in a great surge from the underwater pots in the lagoon. Simultaneous with this burst of light, the initial majestic bars of trumpets from "The Great Gate of Kiev" filled the night. There were *ooohs* and *ahhhs*. People looked about and exclaimed. There was pointing and gesticulating. A few people just responded, eyes closed, to the music. At about thirty seconds from the end of the piece, Greg gave out a loud whistle and began applauding, and everyone joined in. There was hand clapping, cheering, whistling, laughing, and some damp eyes, and this carried on through the music, the applause coming to a crescendo with the final great finish of trumpets, drums, and gongs. Despite Greg's editing to cut the playing time from just under six minutes to just over three (editing that would be undetectable to all but those who knew the piece reasonably well) Mussorgsky and Ravel had done us proud. The applause continued, but then began to fade as the lighting on the mill façade waned.

The light dimmed increasingly, until it was almost at its earlier intensity. Just then, someone shouted excitedly, "Look! The wheel!"

Everyone on the lower patio turned to look at the water wheel. Anyone else who could do so hurried down to the waterside. Those who couldn't rushed to the south end of the car park from where the wheel was visible. The lighting on the mill walls had returned to subdued mood levels, but, in dramatic contrast, brilliant light streamed upward from selected pots in the lagoon and flooded the wheel. There was the sound of splashing water, and the wheel slowly began to turn.

More music now was flowing from the sound system, and after only a few bars, an uncharacteristic but delighted cry rose from Mrs. Williamson.

"Oh how lovely! It's the *Water Music!*"

Excited chatter broke out, as people continued to look at the wheel which was picking up speed. Soon the wheel was turning at a constant rate. The *Water Music* faded, and Greg said into the portable microphone, "There are soft drinks and nibbles inside the restaurant and at the upper deck. There's more than enough for everyone. Richard, Monty, and I will be available for anyone who wants to talk to us. Thank you all so much for coming. Please feel free to stay, mingle, look around, and enjoy the evening. We won't have an occasion like this again for quite some time."

The music now went to the playlist Greg had prepared, and it covered many styles and centuries. Michael Praetorius rubbed shoulders with Luciano Pavarotti and Peter Dawson. There were dozens of cameo appearances. Eugène Gigout's organ music flowed richly from the speakers, and Jeremiah Clarke's trumpet voluntary soared into the night. Queen rocked everybody from shoe soles to hair follicles, and Charles-Marie Widor's toccata awakened in the crowd at least a half-dozen closet conductors. I looked around at the company. Some jabbered happily, and would have done so had there been no music at all. Some stood in groups of twos and threes, half listening, and half talking. A small number of people took up solitary positions, most of them having eyes fixed on the water wheel, and smiles passed repeatedly over their faces as the music leapt a couple of centuries, or a couple of decades, or revealed another old friend. It would have been a pleasure to devote some time just to people-watching, but I didn't have that luxury, since it seemed that individuals were lined up most of the evening to speak to me, and that was just as good.

About twenty percent of the people in attendance drifted away early, as is usually the case for any gathering. Another seventy percent had drifted off by ten o'clock. Of the dozen or so people remaining, most continued to chatter animatedly, giving every appearance of settling in for the night, reluctant to let go of the moment. Greg and I moved among them, both of us just as unwilling to relinquish such a beautiful evening. All these people had become my friends. Jasper was the first of that group to leave, and as he shook my hand yet again, he said quietly, "Dinner on me. Any time." Lonny hugged both me and Greg unashamedly, and said, "Bloody marvellous. The next time I redecorate the store, I'm going to hire you two for the reopening." Across the room, Mrs. Williamson was saying her farewells to Greg, and they shook hands for a long time during the leave-taking, talking while they exchanged warm, polite smiles. She then crossed the room directly to me, and put her hands on my shoulders.

"I'm very rarely at a loss for words, Richard, but I really don't know what to say." She looked at me, smiling, for a long moment, her eyes liquid from the pleasure of the evening. "Thank you, thank you. I haven't enjoyed an event this much in years." I was then pulled into a strong embrace. She disengaged, took my right hand in both of hers, and said, "See you in the library", while the smile from a stimulating four hours still played around her lips.

And then by eleven o'clock, it was over. Jeremy had packed up all his gear and left. Just five of us remained: Monty and his wife, Greg, Jill, and me. Monty and Mrs. Monty, historical soulmates, were doing a close examination of an exposed oak beam. Greg and I looked at each other, ready to assess the evening.

"So, that went all right, I think", Greg said.

"If you like that sort of thing."

"Oh? What would you have changed then?"

"Well, the music was a tad *ordinary*. And I definitely would have rethought the choice of MC."

"How about the location?"

"Not sure. A bit dated, wouldn't you say? Old school? Pompous?"

"You might be right, but it did bring out the lookers."

Jill looked from Greg to me and back. "Knock it off, you two. Just because you've both picked up clear invitations to park your shoes under a number of local beds", she said smiling.

Greg and I, both still riding the high, didn't hold back the smartass responses. "Dirty job, but someone has to do it." "The very stuff of 'The Miller's Tale'." And this carried on until we both collapsed into schoolboy laughter. Jill just shook her head in indulgent mock disgust. Greg turned an ear to the speakers, then stepped over to the amplifier, turned up the volume for *The Blue Danube* waltz which his playlist had just reached, scooped Jill up, and swept her around the room in some flamboyant ballroom steps, fragments of her laughter trailing behind. Monty's wife broke into applause and glanced over at Monty, who had put on a don't-look-at-me face.

All attention refocused suddenly at the sound of the champagne bottle I had just opened. Five glasses were soon filled, I pulled a plate of pâté from the fridge, and a couple of sticks of French bread that I had placed in the cupboard earlier.

"We've had an interesting diversion here tonight", I said, "even though the work starts again tomorrow. But tonight is still tonight, so let's all toast the future."

We clinked glasses energetically, intoning, "To the future", each took a large chug, and then we did some serious work on the bread and pâté.

Mr. and Mrs. Monty drifted off to look at yet another beam. Jill was standing between Greg and me. "The work begins tomorrow? So what's next?" she asked.

"What's next", I said, "is that we get this place producing income. We start milling grain in earnest. Next week is practically solid tours for customers. We have three interviews with journalists lined up. One of those is a television journalist and involves two politicians. There's already commercial activity on the website, and I need to respond to all that. We have joint advertising to set up with at least five bakeries. We'll be visiting a half-dozen small local shops and supermarkets over the next three weeks to finalize supply arrangements with them, and that'll be followed up by in-store promotions for the spots that have agreed to stock our flour. Tomorrow, this coffee shop will open for trade for the first time, and about thirty people have agreed to come in during the day to help make the place look busy. I have six speaking engagements lined up for business groups around the area over the next month. On Wednesday, I'll be in Prince Edward County to organize joint bread and cheese, and bread and wine evenings, both here at the mill and at the cheese and winemakers. And we have orders now for flour that we need to start delivering tomorrow."

"Wow! Sounds like you have it well in hand!"

"Actually, Jill, I'm taking nothing at all for granted until we have firm orders for at least our present flour-producing capacity, since that'll be our only source of income over the winter, and winter is almost upon us. Oh, and I nearly forgot, Greg and I have some house calls to make next week."

There was a two-second pause while Jill, puzzled, looked from Greg to me and back as we sipped our champagne in unison and in deadpan seriousness.

"Well!" Greg said. "All those lonely women!"

Champagne spilled generously, as Greg and I fell about laughing, Jill's look of overstrained indulgence being just too much.

Twenty-six

Saturday was brutal, since I got less than four hours sleep the night before. After arriving home just shy of midnight on Friday, I was back in the mill kitchen at four the next morning, making bread for the Coffee Shop Opening Day. Didn't *have* to do it. The part of me still clinging mentally to pillows and sheets didn't *want* to do it. Did it anyway. Glad I did. But I had the feeling that it really was tempting fate, making so many different kinds of bread in the new ovens. They had been run for a while at temperature, and trial batches of bread had been done, but this was a much larger scale and there was always a chance that some of the bread would be a flop.

As it happened, the gods and goddesses of breadmaking were with me. By seven thirty, when Karen, our restaurant manager and coffee shop organizer, arrived, I had easy background music playing, and the entire space was filled by the heady aroma of fresh bread.

"Wow!" she exclaimed, stopping just inside the door and sniffing eagerly. "What have you made? It smells *gorgeous*!"

"Hi Karen. Well, we have ciabatta, focaccia, *pâte à choux*, and milk scones, and the baguettes will be ready any minute. No time to make muffins, I'm afraid."

"Oh God, don't worry about that! Anyone smelling this won't want to be within half a mile of a muffin!"

Karen busied herself right away with rustic coffee shop table settings, and put on three large pots of coffee. But not before stealing an end of *pâte à choux*.

I had thought that the morning traffic through the coffee shop would be sluggish, but after the previous evening it seemed that many people were fired up to come by for an initial kick at the gastronomical tires, and for a bit of hot stove league discussion of the night before. Saturday was always a busy day for Mrs. Williamson, but despite that she rolled in half an hour before the library opened, and sampled bread with her morning coffee. By nine o'clock, the place was almost two-thirds full, and there was a steady in and out flow. Karen moved into a brisk and very competent routine of making coffee, serving, and collecting cups and plates. By ten thirty, the bread was more than half gone, and I went home to crash.

At two thirty, I broke the surface of a huge lake of molasses and grappled with the usual jumble of *Where am I? What day is it? What's happening?* and so on. A quick shower and hot, black coffee swept aside most of the confusion, and the piece of focaccia I had spirited home, dipped in oil and balsamic, tasted good and would see me through nicely to dinner. I recalled the long list of things to do I had rhymed off to Jill the night before, and went to my desk to check the printed list. We were in good shape. Very little preparation remained to be done for any of these tasks. Greg and I really had done our homework well. So, I turned back to The Great Puzzle. I already had a file on this, and every time I turned to it, I needed a notepad at my elbow. The list of open questions was depressingly static, and I looked through them hoping that more or better questions would be in place. Nothing jumped out.

Against all these questions, what did I have that was solid?

The short answer to this was "pretty much the same as last time I looked: Nada". I needed more basic information, but the only path forward at the moment seemed to be to dig further into Mason's life story. I took it out of my desk and began reading part of the section entitled *Late Days*.

> *If I was born in the Year of Our Lord 1709, as I believe to be the case, I am 85 years of age as I write this. I ceased doing the heavy werk of farming ten years ago, as it became much too onerous for me. My land is good, has been husbanded well over the years, continues to yield bountifull crops, and is werked for rent by a young neighbor who lives slightly closer to Meyer's Creek than I do. With some help from that young neighbor, my husbandry skills are now applied indoors, and I produce a cheese that is in demand in our region. I thank the Good Lord that my health and physical condition remain sturdy, and that due to this I am able to continue carpentry, which I enjoy greatly, and the result of which must be reasonably good given the amount of werk I must sometimes turn away. For these manifold gifts, I give thanks anew every day, while still feeling a keen pain and regrett over my shamefull treatment of my son Rolf. I continue to entreat Our Lord to watch over my Rolf, and to forgive me my mistreatment of him, my only child, and now lost to me.*
>
> *In this world, this vale of tears, corruption is everywhere about us. We ourselves must struggle against The Evil One continuously, but those things that give beauty around us also need our considerable skill and effort in order to prevent, or at least to restrain the decay that affects all flesh and all material things. My efforts over many years to preserve the two books entrusted to my care have been a task that I shouldered willingly and even with increasing devotion and eagerness over the years. How they can be safe guarded when I am no longer here is something I have given long thought to. My links to our church, the solid stone building which I helped erect and to which I have freely given much labor, provide a way, and will involve a true labor of love. I have begun that werk now, and I can see and dearly wish that when it has been completed my blessed books may see a safe and undamaged passage through many more years.*

I had already turned the page to continue, when a vague question mark drifted before me. In the eighteenth century, how would one preserve something as susceptible as books when one was no longer around to provide active care? What was he going to do? Monty and I had already seen that, without any ill intention, the trunks we found in the local museum had essentially zero care devoted to them, and the condition of their contents was almost entirely in the hands of chance. And this was within an institution devoted to preservation!

I pondered the text before me for a few more minutes, then I read through the last paragraph of it slowly and carefully. Nothing leapt out at me, but I did decide that I would see whether I could identify the church that Mason wrote of, and whether it was still standing. There was little chance I would turn up anything useful. Initially, I thought of trying to do it all online, and began an Internet search, trying to look up all the churches in the region, to see which ones were old enough to have been contemporary with Mason. There were four: two in Belleville, one near Thurlow, and one near the tiny hamlet of Corbyville. It was approaching three o'clock, the day was cool but fine, so I decided to do it the old-fashioned way: actually get out there and look. It was less than a half-hour drive to Belleville, so I would check Corbyville, which was on the way, then check Belleville, and finally look at Thurlow.

The church in Corbyville was in the process of being converted to a house, after what appeared to have been a small fire, so I was down to three. The large church in Belleville had evidently been remodelled many times, and was no longer in essence an old church. That left two and a maybe. I was on the Thurlow side of Belleville now, and in ten minutes I was down to one and two maybes because the Thurlow church was boarded up. The small old church in Belleville was indeed a stone church, a fieldstone church, and it was clearly old. A blue heritage plaque stood in front of it on a steel pole to the right of the central entrance.

I expected the church to be locked, but it was open, and I went in. Inside, the church was melancholy, the well-known story of a building once greatly loved and a strong community focal point, but now an almost forgotten house of assembly because the old community was no more, existing now instead as atomized individuals each sitting in front of a television, each completely focused on a smartphone, or each in a separate vehicle getting drive-through coffee. Churches always seem relaxing to me, and this one was no exception, despite its melancholy air. The lancet windows were small, had a pioneer elegance and were fitted in mock–stained glass. The floor consisted of planks in sizes that have been unavailable for many decades, at least twelve inches wide and probably two inches thick. The pews were solid, functional, and darkened by age. The stone in the walls was visible in the upper sections between the windows, but covered in panelling elsewhere. The ceiling was an open beam construction, and a sprinkler system had been fitted to the beams, reasonably unobtrusively. A small oil stove sat in one corner near the entrance, but was apparently no longer used judging by the well-camouflaged electric heaters placed strategically along the walls. The space to the other side of the entrance housed a coat rack.

My slow progress down the aisle had taken me about halfway to the front of the church, and I jumped as my reverie was shattered.

"Can I help you?"

Since I was the only person in the church, I imagined it must have been the voice of….But when I turned I could see a spare man carrying a napkin and wiping crumbs from his shirt.

"I'm sorry to disturb you", I began.

"Not at all", he said, moving toward me. "I happened to notice you entering the church and wanted to see if there was anything I could do."

"Probably not", I said, already starting to make my way back to the door. "I was trying to see whether there are any traces of a local resident from very long ago, but I suspect that I've deluded myself more than anything."

"Well, I'm Reverend Carswell. I've been associated with this church a very long time."

"Actually Reverend, when I say 'a long time ago', I mean more than two hundred years ago."

Carswell was unfazed. "Do you have a name?" he asked.

Deciding to play along, even though I now had the sense that this really was a dead end, I said "Yes. The man was Carl Mason."

Carswell nodded once, and began walking to the front of the church. "Come with me", he said, and I followed him up the aisle, and up the single step to the space behind the pulpit. There was an old piano to the far right, and a large solid altar in the centre of the church draped in a heavy white cloth.

Carswell lifted the cloth from the altar, and began to fold it with exaggerated care, but I wasn't watching him. I was looking at the altar itself. It was solid and completely authoritative, massive, but at the same time elegant, built with exquisite care, and unaccountably appealing. It took me only a few seconds to realize that its dimensions were golden ratios. The altar was in oak but the wood colour had darkened considerably. Brushing my hand along the top of it, I could tell right away that a great deal of talent and care had gone into its construction.

"This might be what you're looking for", Carswell said, pointing to a spot a few inches below the overhanging top and to the far right. Looking down, I could see a small brass plate, on which was engraved

Built and Donated by
Carl Mason
His Treasure to the
House of the Lord
A.D. 1796

I'm sure I didn't breathe for at least a minute.

"Are there any more details about this altar, or the particulars of how Mason donated it?" I asked expectantly.

Carswell shook his head sadly. "There are probably more than enough fingers on one hand to count all the people around here who have ever even heard of Carl Mason. I myself have no information except the most trivial snippets. I'm intrigued to find someone like you, who I don't know and have never seen in this church or in the community, expressing interest in Carl Mason. It's me who ought to be asking you for details."

As he made this short speech, Carswell was looking at the altar, not at me, as though lost in thought.

"Are there any records at all about this altar? I believe that Mason died in 1796. Do you know if he built it here in place, or if he built it somewhere else and then had it brought here?"

"I have only a dedication statement made by a friend of Mason's in 1797, apparently a few months after Mason died."

"Would that friend have been someone called Robert Bine?"

At this, Carswell looked up sharply. He studied me for a long moment, then said, "Do you have some time free just now, Mr., uh…"

"Richard Gould. I live in Greenvale. And yes, I do have time. But first, would you mind if I took some pictures of this?"

Carswell waved me forward in invitation, and using my cellphone I took about fifteen pictures of the altar, from various angles, including three shots of the small brass plaque.

I nodded my thanks to Carswell, who then led me out of the church and to his residence next door. He introduced me to his wife, a short, sprightly lady, who had a bright twinkle, a ready smile, and a cheerful little cackle that I couldn't help but respond to.

"Please come through, Mr. Gould", he said, leading me to his small study, which had floor-to-ceiling shelves on every inch of wall not occupied by window or door, all of which were crammed full of books, files, and reports. When he had cleared a chair for me, he reached for a filing box on a shelf behind his desk, pulled out a manila file, and extracted from it a copy of a sheet of elegant penmanship writing. "The original is in our museum, locked away, along with everything else from the eighteenth century." Carswell handed me the sheet. I read.

> Carl Mason was an estimable man, a humble servant of Our Lord, a devout believer, and a friend. He did not task me, request me, or propose that I stand here before you and speak these words. He was much too modest to conceive of such. I say what I say because he was a dear friend.
>
> I knew Carl for the twenty years he lived here in Upper Canada. He spoke not at all of the past, saying that it was indeed past. I do know that his past was varied and difficult, but that he considered it a time he had lived through for Christ as best he knew how. He lived in the present and for the future, and he lived for his fellow beings. This church, which contains Carl's love and sweat in its fabric, was a centre for his life. Many of the beams above you were hewn and finished by Carl. The pews were of his design. Many of the stones in the walls about us were laid by Carl.

And today, I honour my friend by dedicating this altar. It was the last piece of wood working that Carl completed. He devoted six months to it. The cares that he shouldered willingly or out of duty, and that concerned him of late, were his silent wishes for his son Rolf, his need to assure himself that the land he had worked so well and loved so dearly would be passed on to a worthy husbandsman, and especially his concern over his few effects which were modest but cherished. During his final months he at last found release from these worldly cares.

The dedication of this altar is in words of Carl's choosing. I give thanks to Our Lord for the time granted me to spend with Carl, and I give thanks that this gift from him will now remain among us.

It was signed by Robert Bine and dated February 18, 1797. I passed the sheet back to Carswell without comment, but reminded myself to request a copy of it before I left. Recalling the details of the altar, I said to Carswell, "It seems to me that the altar would have been far too heavy to handle as a completed object. It looks as though it might easily weigh three or four hundred pounds, perhaps more. I'm assuming that Mason completed the altar in sections elsewhere, then transported them here and assembled it in the church."

"That I don't know", Carswell said, shaking his head.

"It looks remarkably fine, for something more than 210 years old. Do you know if it was ever damaged and repaired? Knocked about perhaps during a church renovation, damaged by water leaks or by fire?"

Carswell smiled briefly. "Any renovations to this church have had to be done by members of our congregation themselves. We have no money for such things. To my knowledge, there has never been a fire in the church. Nor, to my knowledge, have we ever suffered water leaks or damage. I confess that I'm not sure why you might be asking all these questions."

"I'm sorry", I said quickly. "I didn't mean to be nosy. History has been a long-time interest for me, and I've come across several references to Carl Mason in the past little while. My curiosity is something I've never learned to rein in."

"I see", said Carswell, smiling politely, but not really seeing at all.

"I've taken up too much of your time, Reverend, but I'm grateful to you. At some point, I would very much like to have a copy of that dedication address."

"That's not a problem", Carswell said, appearing suddenly to leave a world of reverie and taking on a brisker manner. "I can copy it for you right now."

Carswell handed me the copy and we shook hands. He led me back through his home, past his delightful wife who cackled for reasons that I failed to grasp, and he accompanied me to my car. I thanked him again, and as I opened the door, and he began to make his way back home, he stopped, and turned wearing a somewhat speculative expression.

"There was a small repair done to the altar about three years ago. The top surface seemed to be degrading, and had taken on a rough feel. One of our young parishioners did the work of sanding and then treating the wood to bring it to the same aged colour as the rest of the altar. He took almost three weeks to do it, but did an excellent job. Ames, I think his name was. Yes. Robert Ames."

"Does Mr. Ames still live in this area?" I asked, as neutrally as I could.

"I don't believe so. He seemed to appear out of nowhere, took a fairly active part in the community for six or eight months, and then disappeared just as abruptly."

Seeing my expression, Carswell added, "but that's not uncommon for this area, in my experience."

I thanked Carswell again and drove back to Greenvale, thinking over what I had learned. Much of that evening I spent at the mill restaurant, where the mood was upbeat. I had a quick word with Karen, who was clearly delighted at the custom we were seeing, and who warned me that the wine cellar would be drained in less than two weeks at the rate it was being poured. She gave me a listing of what had been consumed and what remained, and I promised to top it up in a day or two. I also spoke to our chef, Michael, who had taken to his role as a fish to water. Asking him obliquely about his probationary status, I soon got an enthusiastic response, that close observation and guidance was exactly what he wanted. At about eleven thirty, I returned home, worked for an hour on the mill's business plan, and then turned in.

The surge of awareness hit me in the middle of the night, like an electric shock.

Twenty-seven

It was quarter past three, and I was standing in my bedroom next to the bed, fully awake, not entirely sure how I had risen so quickly, but definitely feeling like a man on a mission, someone to whom all was about to be revealed.

Through the doorway, I could see that the door to the guest bedroom was closed, inviting the assumption that Stuart had returned, something confirmed later when I found his note next to the sink: *1:45. See you at breakfast. S.* Pulling on jeans and a golf shirt, I went downstairs. The top of my large desk held neat piles of drawings and project notes, and a file containing the business plan for the mill. Placing all these on the floor, I lifted out from various drawers the Hölderlin poem and my sheets of doodles for it, Mason's life story and the few notes I had made on it, and a fresh pad of squared paper and turned on my laptop.

The Hölderlin poem was most interesting to me, because it was the most obscure and the most intriguing. My notes on the poem were a bit chaotic, perhaps not surprising since they had been made quite late after a generous dose of some of Greg's excellent wine. Starting over, I lined up the words in two columns, the one on the left being the words in the original poem that were not in the copy, and the column on the right being the words in the copy that were not in the original. I worked on the arrangements of the words in the left-hand column for about twenty minutes, and concluded, as I had previously, that there was nothing there. Then I turned to those in the right-hand column; same result after another twenty minutes. Then I combined the words from both columns. Nothing.

Next, I tried arrangements of the first letters from the words in the left-hand column, first looking for combinations that meant something in English, then in German. Two vowels and eleven consonants didn't look promising, and after fifteen minutes I gave that up. Then I tried the same for the words in the right-hand column. Here there were five vowels and nine consonants, and a few possible words began appearing almost immediately. The English words *regular, blind, grail, legend, genius*, and a few others popped out right away, but in each case what was left behind was rather a jumble of letters that couldn't be arranged into any supplementary words that made any sense. Working further, I came up with a total of about twenty-five words, but no revealed wisdom.

I tried the harder task of constructing German words. After a bit of effort, I had formed twelve words: *teilen, Grund, leugnen, Beleid, braun, Graben, treiben, Berlin, glauben, leer, Gebruder,* and *entlang.* But in each case, the letters remaining were just a jumble. Hardly surprising, I suppose, since there was nothing logical or systematic about how I had identified these words. I decided to try to find another few words, this time focusing on nouns, and kept shifting the letters around. While doing this, I had to resist the strong sense that this was all stupid, that I was grasping at whatever straw the wind happened to blow past. Sometimes, one just has to suck it and see.

Gesund popped out, not really a noun.... *Natur* popped out. *Leine* popped out. And then *Stein*. This rang a bell. I checked the letters remaining after s-t-e-i-n had been removed: b, l, n, e, r, a, g, d, u. From these remaining letters, the word *berg* suggested itself, and since this is a common word component in German, I decided to separate it out and see what was left: l, n, a, d, u. The name of a town or location, perhaps? I reached for the atlas. Landuberg? Ludanberg? Couldn't find either of those anywhere in Germany. Not much hope here.

Then I separated out b-u-r-g. The letters remaining: l, n, e, a, d. *Eldanburg? Elandburg? Aldenburg? Ladenburg?* No Elandburg or Eldanburg, but not surprising since they both sounded odd. No Aldenburg, which *was* surprising. But there was a Ladenburg. Looking it up in the atlas; my heart stopped. It was only about ten kilometres from Heidelberg.

I sat back in the chair with a sense of exquisite frustration. There must be something here, but I couldn't see it yet. *Why Ladenburg? What was there that might be significant?* I was about to start a more detailed search on Ladenburg, when I jumped as the possible link between Mason and Stein struck me. *Is it possible that at one time Carl Mason could have been a rough English equivalent of a German name—Karl Steinhauer? Karl Steinmetz? Or how about just Karl Stein?* Turning to my computer, I pulled up the passenger list for the *James Goodwill* and scrolled down through it. There he was: Karl Stein. "Holy shit", I murmured, realizing that this Montyism might have something behind it.

So, what was going on here?

The first possibility, and one to be kept firmly in mind, was that this was all a chimera, that I had constructed a fantasy, something that had no real world meaning whatever. *Okay. Park that in full view for now. What might support another interpretation?*

There was Mason's statement that he and his father followed the great river after they passed through Mannheim. He was likely referring to the Rhine, since the Rhine passes through Mannheim, and my atlas indicated that Mannheim is only about ten kilometres or so from Ladenburg. *What else had Mason written?*

Looking back through his life story, a number of the pages of which I had marked by sticky notes, I found it: Mason's description of Christoph Sauer as "someone with whom I had a small old country connection." Opening another computer file, in which I had copied information about Sauer, I looked through it impatiently. Sauer's dates were 1695 to 1758, so he was fourteen years older than Mason. And Sauer was born in—*Holy Shit!—Ladenburg!*

And what was it that caused me to spring out of bed as though stung by the intellectual equivalent of a scorpion? *Something from yesterday? Yes, a name. Robert Ames. Why? Who was Robert Ames? What might the name* Robert Ames *mean, refer to, imply? It seemed to have no linkage to—*

And then I froze anew. *Rob Ames* was an anagram of *Boersma* and of *Ambrose*.

Okay. Let's try to make sure we really are not going in circles here, not deluding ourselves about turning straw into gold thread, or creating silk purses from porcine body parts. Back to the parked item, and let's step through this systematically. Start first with the apparent links to Ladenburg. Could all these links be simply spurious, just nonsense? It was starting to seem unlikely, since there were now enough connections that an explanation based just on chance was under serious strain. *All right. If it isn't nonsense, what does it mean? Supposing that the person who made these changes to the poem really was coding a message?*

Well, surely our messenger wasn't just pointing out that these two men, Sauer and Mason, originated in the same local area, or that the man who printed one of the two books I had discovered was born just ten kilometres from where the other book was printed. At some period sufficiently far in the future, today for instance, anyone could easily check on where Sauer was born because Sauer is a historical figure, but how could one know or even care about Mason? If our code writer really was just highlighting such an obscure coincidence, then this was all the product of a fevered mind, done for no obvious reason. No, there must be something else. But what? Was there something of interest somewhere in Ladenburg, and if so, what?

Back up. The doctored poem couldn't possibly have been placed with the book by Mason, since he was dead before the poem was even written. So, if the altar had been chosen by Mason as a safe place for his books, any assumption that the association between the books and the poem involved Mason posed a problem. If Mason was attempting to consign the books to some higher care, and keep them away from the ravages of the elements and people, he would have kept the fact of them being placed in the altar a secret. Nobody else would have known about them, except the individual who added the doctored poem. This must have been done sometime in the first few decades of the nineteenth century, at the earliest. There was one candidate for this: Mason's good friend Robert Bine. But it was far from clear why he would do this, why he would go to all the trouble of adding an elaborate coded message to something that was meant to remain concealed until the time was right for it to reappear. I needed to look more closely into whatever details of Robert Bine might exist. Then it occurred to me that Bine was an unusual surname, but that Bein was not unknown and that *Bein* also forged another German connection!

But wait, if Bine, or Bein, knew about Mason's books in the altar, maybe he knew about something more as well. Perhaps Mason's purpose was to preserve not just his own two books. Perhaps he felt some responsibility for that "something more". Could it be that late in Mason's life he passed on to Bine the responsibility for not only the two books but also his suspicions that there was more? More what? And why was Ladenburg involved?

No. Stop! This is all just the most tenuous supposition. There might be something to it, but better not to warp out too far into outer space!

In the light of what had happened the day before, it then occurred to me that the whole Ambrose-Boersma nexus was taking on a new urgency. *Could it be just coincidence that the man who called himself Ames appeared out of nowhere, worked for a while on Mason's legacy object, and then vanished again just as quickly?* Of course it was possible. In fact, for isolated events, chance or coincidence was sometimes the best and simplest explanation.

Or maybe not. Here, I struggled with a thought that felt as though it wanted to remain unformed. It seemed as though Mason directed his last energy toward completing the altar in the little church. Perhaps the repair work was just what it seemed, and Ames came, refinished the altar, and left. But Carswell had said that the little congregation was impecunious, and most work and repairs had to be done using contributed labour and materials. As an erstwhile unknown, and having apparently no connections to nor investment in the community, Ames would hardly have stepped up and done the work for nothing. So?

So, he got paid some other way. He couldn't have nicked valuables from the church, because that would have been discovered. At that point, I hit something of a dead end, so I went back to the question of what the code writer might have been doing.

If there was indeed a code writer, he was trying to keep something from being lost. *Was he leaving a trail that would lead someone bright enough to the right spot, or was he leaving a warning about something?*

Suppose it was the first of these. What information was he coding? Nothing obvious came back. Something to do with Ladenburg, but beyond that...?

Suppose it was the second. Suppose he was warning against somebody or something.

Blank.

Time check. It was five fifteen. I'd been at it for two hours.

I struggled with all this for another half-hour, then concluded that I was searching for something that wasn't there. Our messenger wasn't trying to warn someone in the future about something. But the idea of being aware that at some time in the future there might be someone to worry about made a sort of retrospective sense. If these books were being sought by whoever was doing the bugging, then one might be able to work backwards from a list of likely collectors. It was a long shot.

Another twenty minutes of computer searching had turned up some odds and ends, but it was guaranteed that these results were neither complete nor definitive.

Top of the list was something known as The Green Collection, but it was pretty easy to rule that out. These were serious above-board collectors of biblical documents, and were very obviously not in the least fly-by-night or doubtful. There was also quite a bit of publicly available information about them and their collection.

Then we came to the others. They were really just names seen through a mist. Ardrey. Barton. Steyr. Billinton. Charlton. Burns. Everett. Torrey. I scrolled quickly through the bits of information on each of them. Slim pickings indeed. I was about to give up on the whole thing when I noticed something about Burns. He lived in Philadelphia. Interesting, but not proof of anything.

I opened a Word file, copied the information from all eight of these names into it, and saved the file.

I heard a toilet flush. Checked my watch. Six forty.

"Richard. You're up early." Then, glancing at the paper storm as he came down the stairs, Stuart said, "Looks like you've been up for a while. What's wrong?" This last question asked in some concern.

"Good morning Stuart. You're up early too given that you weren't in bed much before two."

Rising from my chair, I went straight to the kitchen. "Coffee?" Without awaiting an answer, I filled the maker, added coffee, and hit the big red button.

"So", I said. "While we wait for the elixir of life, tell me a bit about Pennsylvania and the arsehole we've been filling with alcohol down there."

"Richard. What's going on?"

"Well. We've been, or at least you've been, casing a guy down there. Who is he?"

"Yeah. Yes, we have been watching a guy pretty closely, but—"

"His name wouldn't be Burns, would it?"

We stood there, looking at each other as though we were both strangers, and it was a weird and unpleasant feeling.

I raised both hands in surrender. "Okay. Look. Stuart, let's start over. I think this thing is getting to me. I've had a bizarre night. I think I've found something, but I can't be sure. I want it all to be over, and I've had a feeling for the past week that I really would enjoy beating the living shit out of somebody, smashing his face to an unrecognizable pulp."

After about a fifteen-second delay, I walked over to Stuart.

"Stuart, for my own mental health, I need to find a way through this. Come and talk to me."

So, in response to his questions, I laid it all out for Stuart: the doctored poem, suspecting a code, looking for patterns, finding a clue that appeared to have led me to the real and original identity of Carl Mason, the logic behind looking for a second message, but behind it all the worry that this was just bullshit, that I had manufactured something out of thin air.

"I don't think it's bullshit, Richard. The name of the guy in Pennsylvania is indeed Burns. He's slippery and apparently dangerous, but then we suspected that already. We have a lot of suspicions, but no hard facts."

Here, there was a short silence before Stuart continued. "If you were able to find out that Burns is the guy in Pennsylvania, when I had deliberately kept his name from you until we had something firm, that changes quite a few things. You realize that, don't you Richard?"

"Yes, I do."

Stuart rose, grabbed a mug, filled it, came back to the table, and stood beside me for a moment. "Before we get into any of that, though, I need you to show me more about what you've done here. I just had one of my feelings, and I never ignore them. Maybe we can dig up some hard facts after all."

Starting from the top, I walked through everything I could think of that was relevant, and went over the events of the past twenty-four hours in detail. I told him everything I could remember about finding the church in Belleville, about my discussion with Carswell, about the altar as I saw it. I showed him the pictures of the altar I had taken using my cellphone. And I told him about my strange and sudden wakefulness a few hours ago.

"Why did he build an altar?" Stuart asked. "Wasn't there one there already?"

Of course, this was a question I ought to have asked Carswell. "I don't know."

"Do you know exactly when this chap Ames did the work at the church?"

"No", I said. "According to Carswell, it was about three years ago. Why?"

"Because, even though I'm getting the feeling that somebody knows a great deal about all this, there appear to be things that don't fit, or pieces that are missing. You had an intimation about this some time ago, and I ignored it. Well, time to fix that. Here's what I want to do."

Stuart then told me about a guy he sometimes uses on jobs. He is mostly a polymath recluse, but is also a genius at doing electronic searches for almost anything. "I want to give him a job looking for anything related to any of the problems, situations, people, names, and so on that we've come across in all this. He's been able to find things about other people, even things buried in those people's own files, when those people themselves had given up the situation as hopeless. In particular, I want him to look for any records—letters, newspaper clippings, changes in title deeds, particular chatter among the collectors of biblical arcana, auction records, acquisitions by local museums—anything that would define more clearly what we know compared to what others appear to know."

"Is what he does all legal?" I asked.

"Next question?"

"Okay, I agree, let's put this chap of yours to work." We then spent about half an hour generating a list of search terms that Stuart's guy could use to get started.

"How long would it take him to do his searching?"

"He's a demon for work. Once he gets his teeth into something, he often works day and night until he finds the results he needs. It's too early to call him just now", Stuart said, sliding the folded sheet of search terms into his shirt pocket, "but in a couple of hours I'll call him and set him to work. If he hasn't too much else going, he can probably have this job done in two days."

"You're obviously thinking of some particular situation that a search might throw some more light on", I said, presenting it as an oblique question.

Stuart nodded. "Yes. Let's suppose, just as a trial, that the people we're thinking of, whoever they might be, are also looking for something."

"Like what?"

"Well, like the books themselves."

"But somebody hid those books in the mill. They should know exactly where to go looking for them."

"No, whoever hid the books knows where he hid them. But who are the *they* we keep referring to? What if the person, or the people, who hid the books, has gone missing, is incapacitated, is now dead? Or has gone deep into hiding? In any of those cases, whatever is known by the people who hid the books would be out of circulation, inaccessible to anyone else, anyone else who might want to know what is known by whoever hid the books. It's the possibility that the people now listening and looking might be 'other people,' is what I want to explore."

"This is all just theorizing, right?" I prompted.

"Yes. But let's see if it leads anywhere."

"Where might it lead?" I asked.

"Well, if there's some connection between all this and the mill, someone wanting to play information catch-up might want to eavesdrop on the people who have some intimate connection to the mill."

"People like me", I said. "This is a possible link to the first bug."

"Yes. That has always bothered me. We can be pretty sure that Burns is behind the second bug, although proving it is another matter, but the first bug is still something of a mystery. But it might be not just you who would be affected."

Here, I didn't try to hide my confusion. "Who else?"

"What about Monty?"

"Oh shit! Surely I haven't dropped Monty into this by association?"

"I know that that's a larger concern, Richard, but it's the immediate implication of all this that interests me, and what it might tell us."

"And that is?"

"Well, to find out we go and check whether Monty's place has been bugged."

Twenty-eight

Since it was still not even seven o'clock, and too early to call Monty, Stuart and I decided to have breakfast, outside again. The air was now quite cool, but after the addition of socks, shoes, and sweaters, we were the equal of any October morning. The summer birds had fled, and the first of the winter birds were flitting about and loudly voicing their territorial and generally feisty challenges. The hills were a riot of colour: flame red sumacs, rusty brown ferns, feverish yellow poplars and birches, ash in muted shades, delicate tan in the black locust fronds, vines climbing fences like brush fires, and maples capturing every region of the spectrum apart from blue-violet. I knew that out there, somewhere, there were likely dozens of puffballs to be discovered, that the first clumps of Michaelmas daisies would be appearing, that milkweed plants would be slumping in despondency now that the monarchs had departed, and that Moloch squads of devil's paintbrush would be strutting their tarty but appealing stuff.

Because we had time, I went for broke. French toast, but with one hell of a twist: finely chopped and caramelized Vidalia onions, an impossible looking amount of chives, a large handful of chopped bacon, a generous portion of freshly ground pepper, and a hint of fresh rosemary.

I was in my element. The morning's mind-bending technicolour presence, the simple but profound tactile and olfactory pleasures of food preparation as the first step on the ascending scale to cooking and eating, were like an approach to the pleasure dome in Xanadu. The finely diced onion hissed excitedly as I dropped it into the large skillet on the barbecue. In a second pan, the chopped bacon sputtered and snapped, slowly releasing the fat that would be used to cook the combined egg mixture. The aroma rising from the chives was subtle and refined compared to that of its kick-ass cousins, garlic and onion. I couldn't resist running my fingers over the rosemary and then sniffing the heady aromatic whisper it left on my skin. I put Stuart in charge of converting to toast, over the hot lava rocks, the thick-cut, unbleached white bread made from the mill's own Marquis flour. I whisked together the eggs and other ingredients, poured the mixture into two hot skillets on top of the toast, and in five minutes we had breakfast steaming on our plates.

Once Stuart tucked into this feast, it looked as though he was never going to stop.

During a gastronomic lull, when Stuart's mouth was sufficiently clear both to come up for air and to speak, he managed to articulate, around the remains of the previous bit of toast, "Good God, Richard! This really is excellent! How do you come up with these combinations?"

"Not difficult, and this really isn't such a radical combination. I just throw together things that seem to have a good chance of getting along, and then adjust. But, for me, the key is not to be afraid to load up the herbs."

"Well, I suspect there's more to it than that. I wish I could lash up stuff like this."

"There's no reason why you can't, Stuart. It's really just a question of confidence."

"But don't you have the occasional failure?"

"Sure. Sometimes what comes out smells or tastes anywhere between iffy and disgusting, and it has to go into the compost. But that doesn't happen too often, and you get better at figuring out what just won't work after some practice."

We finished, even if somewhat reluctantly on Stuart's part, cleared things away, and then settled down to a spell of planning. This took much longer than I anticipated, because a considerable number of possibilities emerged once we started thinking through the whole thing systematically, and some of them were unexpected. This was an exercise both Stuart and I were familiar with, Stuart from the preparations he had to do prior to taking some action on something that could affect his clients, and me from the planning and projections that I always had to do on technical projects. The way these approaches complemented one another was something of a surprise to both of us.

The immediate points we worked our way through and around was the potential reaction Monty could have to a suggestion that he might have been bugged, whether and how we might inform the police, and how our own thinking and actions might be constrained by the implications of such a discovery. My feelings on this were not comfortable, since I had the sense that we were sliding slowly but more deeply into a dangerous swamp. But, at the same time, we agreed it was highly unlikely that the problem would just go away if we ignored it.

A few minutes after nine o'clock, I emailed Monty, saying that I was doing some long-range planning for installing the cast iron wheel at some point in the future, and there were a few things I wanted to check with him. I said I would be having some lunch at The Fox at about twelve thirty, and asked if he could join me. I then went back to fleshing out some of the notes Stuart and I had made after breakfast. Five minutes later, a ping announced the arrival of an email message. It was Monty.

"I'll be there", he wrote.

If Monty was surprised to see Stuart with me at The Fox, he didn't let on. After he had settled himself, complete with the obligatory bulging file folder, I came straight to the point.

"I'm ashamed to say that I wasn't honest with you, Monty. I couldn't find another way of having this discussion on neutral ground." At this, Monty's expression clouded over, he looked uncertainly from me to Stuart and back, but waited for me to carry on.

"I've found something that changes the way we view the whole business of those books and the mill, but first, I need to tell you that my house was bugged. Listening devices", I added, in response to Monty's puzzled look. "We can go through the details later, but the important point right now is that the new information I have opens the possibility that your house might have been bugged as well. This is very disturbing for me, as I'm sure it is for you, and it's something that I never expected and certainly didn't intend."

There was an extended silence here, while Monty gazed into the distance, thinking furiously, his expression hardening in response.

"What are you really saying, Richard?" Monty asked. "Are you trying to figure out whether I might resent it all, or that I might be fearful, or become angry? Because I'm feeling all those things now, but not against you. If my house has been bugged, do you know who the bastard is who would have done it?"

"Before we try to logic our way forward, Monty, what we really need to do is determine whether in fact your house has been bugged. But the choice here is yours and my own discomfort doesn't matter. You might not want to know. You might just want out of the whole mess, and I wouldn't blame you a bit for feeling that way. But—"

"Richard", Monty interrupted. "Why would I not want to know? I do feel in a fog, I admit, because this is something new to me, and I expect it will be a bit like being burgled—the strong feeling of violation comes a little later. But if somebody is snooping into my life, you can be damn sure that I want to know the details. So, what are you proposing?"

"We're suggesting that I scan your house for bugs", Stuart said in a mild tone. "If there is a bug, then that will confirm a number of things. If there's no bug, it won't necessarily negate anything, but neither will it mean that we can all sigh and relax."

"How long would it take to scan for bugs?" Monty asked.

"About ten minutes", Stuart responded.

"Okay. Let's do it right now. Marjorie is out with her autumn leaves walking group this morning. But can you fill me in on what led you to this outlook?"

I took about fifteen minutes and walked through the whole thing for Monty as succinctly as I could. He asked a few questions, Stuart and I gave him the best short answers we could, and then he nodded and said, "Let's go."

Stuart outlined how he thought we should go about it.

"From now on, we take nothing for granted. So, I think you should leave here first, Monty, go into the village and visit the post office, or buy some sausages, or something. Take about ten minutes. Then go to Richard's place, knock on the door, then leave in a few minutes when nobody answers, and go to your place. I want to watch and see whether anyone has followed you here or follows you away. When you get to your place, just wait for us. Richard and I will arrive separately, Richard first. I want to check your place from a distance before you arrive to see whether we have any watchers, and I want to make sure that there are no tails on either of you. So I won't appear to arrive at your place until sometime after you are both there. When you both arrive and go inside, just talk about something unimportant and not having anything at all to do with what we've discussed. By the time I knock at your door, I will already have done a sweep outside. If I tell you that I have something in the car that you might be interested in, that means I've found something, and you both should come outside. But if I don't turn up at all after Richard has been there twenty minutes, that means that there's something else involved, and you should both come straight back here. Okay?"

"Got it", Monty said, the hint of a conspiratorial smile tugging at the corners of his mouth, despite the fact that he must have been experiencing some considerable turmoil.

Monty left, and Stuart went outside, stood by the door of The Fox, and appeared to be making a call on his cellphone. I left, went to the mill which was closed apart from the coffee shop because it was Sunday, pretended to check the security system, and walked around the outside of the building. When I arrived at Monty's place, Monty's car was there, and he let me in when I rang the bell. About fifteen minutes later, Stuart rang the doorbell, and when Monty opened the door Stuart said through a bright smile that there was something quite interesting he really wanted to show Monty in his car. We began to walk through the door, but Stuart held up his cellphone and jabbed his index finger at both of us. After a short spot of incomprehension, I pulled out my cell and Stuart pointed to the sill of the window right next to the door. I laid my phone there, and then Monty did the same.

Then we both walked out to Stuart's car and climbed in.

"I'm sorry to say, Monty, that there is a small listening device just above your living room window. And that business with the cellphones is indeed a paranoid precaution, but justified all the same."

We looked at each other in some renewed trepidation, despite the fact that we knew in advance of this possibility. Monty pursed his lips and muttered, "Son of a bitch!" Then he looked at Stuart and asked, "What next?"

"Next, I want to sweep your car and the inside of your house."

At this, Monty's expression reflected true personal offence and violation. "Really? Isn't that taking paranoia too far?"

"There are two people dead. One of them was likely an unintended result, but the other was an execution. We have to assume that there's someone out there who is completely serious and ruthless. So it's better to be super cautious than to walk into something unpleasant just because we happened to have our eyes shut."

"What about my car?" I asked.

"I've already checked your car."

"Okay. Let's do it", Monty said with sudden resolve.

Stuart spent half an hour doing an exhaustive check all through Monty's house, and then sweeping his car. At the end of it, Stuart pulled out his notebook, turned to a blank page, and scribbled *Back to The Fox*. So, after Monty and I retrieved our phones, we all climbed into our cars and headed to the pub.

Back at The Fox, where trade was now picking up, we sat and looked at each other in silence for a few minutes.

"I must apologize Monty", Stuart said. "I should have thought ahead to this and forestalled this intrusion into your life. I'm sorry."

Monty waved this away. "After Buck's death, we all knew that we were in the midst of something sinister. It's my fault as much as anybody's that this situation has crept up on me. But instead of focusing on blame, can you make a guess at how long I've been bugged?"

"I can't be sure", Stuart said, "but likely it goes back to the time when the bug was planted at Richard's place, or sometime later, perhaps when we rumbled the bastard who came to retrieve it. I would say not longer. The trouble is, we don't know how long the bug at Richard's place was active."

There was another longish and fairly uncomfortable silence. "So what do we do?" Monty asked.

For the first time I could remember, Stuart was hesitant. "I have to admit", he began, "that at this point I'm really not sure. Would it be too much to ask that you give me a day to work through all this?"

Monty nodded, without enthusiasm. We ordered three mugs of beer in the hope that that would inject some cheer into the situation. It didn't.

After agreeing to meet at The Fox again at noon the next day, we finished our beer and sloped off.

Back at my place, Stuart said he had some calls to make and wanted three hours to himself, so he went off to his room. I tried reading, but couldn't focus. So I went out for a walk, leaving a note for Stuart, intending to visit the coffee shop and have a word with Karen. When I got there, the coffee shop was heaving in customers, and I was pretty much forced to make the rounds of all the tables to have open-ended chats with the people seated there.

Karen was busy bustling to and fro, and I extricated myself from the crowd to have a word with her.

"Things going okay, Karen?"

"Couldn't be better", she smiled, glowing from the exertion of steady work. "This place seems to have the ability to put people in a good mood."

"Well, that might just be novelty value. We'll see what happens in a few weeks."

"I wouldn't be so quick to make that judgment", she said. "It's the space itself, I think. It has a very different feel to it."

We talked a bit more, and it was clear she was in her element, something that reassured me. Looking at my watch, I was surprised to see that it was already five thirty, and checking outside, I could see that the day had faded. Making my excuses, I left.

Having set out to take a walk, and having got only as far as the mill, I decided to follow a more extensive route through Greenvale. Although Greenvale is not Königsberg, it does have quite a few bridges, and it is possible to walk a surprising number of different routes. The houses in Greenvale are set at locations dictated by the varied terrain. Some of the routes among these houses are close to the river, while others provide more commanding views at various distances up the sides of the hills. There is no common alignment of houses because of the complex curvature of the folding and undulating hills, so the houses have the appearance of sitting where they were dropped. At dusk, which we were fast approaching, as lights in the houses came on, the effect was that of ornamental lights strung whimsically along the hillside, set almost at random, like seeds cast the old-fashioned way. It made the village immensely attractive, at least to me, and during my walk I stopped often and spent a lot of the time looking up, down, and across the valley.

At length, it was just about time to return home before it became completely dark, and I crossed the most southerly bridge in the village and started back toward my place. To my right, partway up the hill, was Greg's lovely house sitting largely on its own, well spaced from neighbouring houses, and showing only outside lights since Greg and Jill were spending a few days in Montreal.

I felt, more than saw it, and immediately sensed that something was not right. It was just the hint of a shadow. I fell back behind a large lilac bush and called Stuart.

"I'm just down the street from Greg's house, Stuart, and I think somebody is moving around outside it."

"Where are you in relation to the house?"

"About a hundred feet to the east, just up from the river, and a bit south of the house."

"Stay hidden. Don't do anything. I'll be there in less than five minutes." The connection was broken immediately.

I focused on the house as closely as I could, but in the gloom it was hard to make out anything. The movement was really only a hint of a shadow, and whoever it was they must have been dressed entirely in black.

The sound of a car approaching slowly reached me before I could see anything, and then I realized that the car was coasting, engine and lights off. It was less than a minute before Stuart materialized right beside me. I hadn't seen or detected him coming at all.

"What's that?" I asked.

"Infrared camera." And he immediately aimed it toward the house. He operated the camera for at least a couple of minutes until I could bear it no longer and whispered "What are we going to do?"

"Nothing", he said without looking at me. Then after a few seconds, "I want to make sure I get as much footage of this charlie as I can. After that, we wait to see where he goes, and we follow him."

The figure moved around the outside of the house for a few minutes more, then disappeared behind the north side. A few moments later, the figure emerged at the corner of the house, appeared to look both ways along the lane that passed in front of the house, then slid back into the darkness.

"Well, well", Stuart said, still looking through the eyepiece and filming. "I recognize that guy, and you'll never guess who it is."

I looked sharply toward Stuart.

"It's Constable Harrison", he said.

There wasn't time to respond, because just then a car slid soundlessly into view, descended the driveway, and moved off down a shallow gradient to the south without lights. "Prius", Stuart whispered. Then he handed me his keys. "Let's go back to my car, quickly. You drive. We're following him."

We let the Prius move about a hundred feet away, before I put Stuart's car into neutral, and we began coasting down the lane after it, lights off. The Prius headed toward the main road, its headlights were switched on, and it turned south. We waited until the car vanished around a corner, then I started the engine, switched on our headlights, and followed. The Prius drove about a kilometre, then turned off onto a side road to the right.

"Where does this road lead?" Stuart asked.

"It crosses two concession lines, then stops in a T-junction at the third."

"Do you know anyone who lives down here?"

"Yes. Constable Harrison."

Twenty-nine

Inspector Raymond lived in a nicely kept bungalow halfway up one of the promontory hills to the south and east of Greenvale. The graceful sweep of flower bed at the front of the house, illuminated by the outdoor lights but now settled down for the winter, spoke of a serious gardening hobby. Raymond was neither pleased nor displeased to see us, and he had agreed, although reluctantly, to our visit when I had phoned him ten minutes earlier. He had asked what we wanted to talk about, but I had said it was important and not something I felt comfortable relating over the telephone.

On the way over to his place, we discussed our approach.

"Helpful and deferential, right down the middle", Stuart had said. "What we have to say is probably the last thing Raymond wants to hear, so there mustn't be any hint of 'I told you so' or any suggestion of incompetence. I doubt he will accept any offer of help from me, but I intend to make the offer anyhow."

Off duty, Raymond looked relaxed in jeans and what was evidently a favourite old sweater. He invited us in, asked us to find seats in his surprisingly large sitting room, and then went off into the kitchen saying over his shoulder that he was getting coffee and asked if we would care for some. We both declined. On the mantel, there were pictures of two boys, presumably sons grown up and moved away. I was drawn immediately to the wall covered in bookshelves, and was looking down the rows when Raymond returned.

"Very nice collection", I said.

"Too bad I have so little time to read them. What can I do for you?"

I indicated to Stuart that he should take the lead.

"We have learned two things today that I'm sure shouldn't wait until tomorrow, so we've come to brief you this evening, and I'm sorry for this disturbance."

Raymond nodded a neutral acknowledgement.

"I will say in advance", Stuart continued, "that neither of the two pieces of information we have is good. I'll give you all the background, but first I want to tell you just what we've come across. This afternoon, we discovered that Monty's house has been bugged, for how long I don't know. And about twenty minutes ago, in the course of an evening walk through the village, Richard noticed somebody prowling around Greg Blackett's house. He called me, I joined him, and I have footage of the prowler here in infrared image. The prowler was Constable Harrison", and as he said this, Stuart held up his infrared camera.

Raymond almost spilled his coffee, and his face hardened in anger, against whom I couldn't tell.

"Show me", he said sharply.

Stuart played the recording twice for Raymond, who viewed it poker-faced. He took one last mouthful of coffee, set the cup down carefully, said "Fuck!" almost under his breath, rose, and retrieved a notebook from his desk in the corner of the room, and, once he was seated again said, "From the top. Everything."

It took a little less than an hour to relate all the background to the two events and to answer Raymond's questions. Raymond filled many pages in notes, and when he had looked through his scribbles and found no more questions, he picked up a cellphone that was lying on the coffee table. We could guess what the other half of the conversation was.

"Brierley? It's Raymond. Things are quiet I assume? No, no. I want you to come here, to my house. Yes, immediately. We have something to do. That can wait. Just come here right away." He ended the call and placed the phone back on the coffee table.

"If there's anything I can do", Stuart said in a low-key voice, "please just ask."

Raymond sighed, as though weighed down by all the cares of the world. "No. I think it best if you both just stay out of the way. But, thank you for bringing this business to my attention so quickly." He appeared to hesitate here, then continued. "On second thought, there is something, but I must ask you to do it exactly as I say." And then Raymond asked Stuart to check for bugs at Greg's house. His instructions were to touch nothing, not to remove any bug that he might find, and to text him a one word message when we had finished: "Yes" if we found something, "No" if we found nothing. "And please don't make any assumptions", he warned.

We both left right away, in order to be gone when Brierley arrived.

Stuart drove us straight back to Greg's place and did a thorough check. He then sent a text message to Raymond. "Yes." We drove back immediately to my place.

It was just after nine o'clock when we arrived, and Stuart said he wanted to make a few more calls while the hour was half sensible. I wanted to go over our timeline of events, which now, after several more revisions, had been expanded to include a projection of possible future events, their causes, and their implications. It was mostly guesswork, but we had tried to make it out-of-the-box thinking, and we were more interested in any suggestions and implications that might emerge from our postulates. We had no hopes that some single cosmic revelation would rise up from them.

I spent about half an hour going over the sheets, making notes where it seemed that something was incomplete, was now less relevant, or seemed to be just wrong. On a clean sheet, I began doodling. At first, they were just, well, doodles. But after ten minutes, and a couple more sheets of paper, some sort of shape appeared. The events we had observed were effects, and might not have been the only effects. The effects were Buck's death, Kralik's abortive attempt to retrieve a bug from my place, Kralik's death, the placement of two bugs at my place, the placement of a bug at each of Monty and Greg's places, and Harrison's involvement as a prowler.

No meaning rose out of the doodles, and I asked myself just what I had found. Nothing.

I dropped my pencil in frustration, and sat there going over the few notes I had made in the past thirty minutes. *You're trying to do too much reasoning based on too few facts*, I said to myself, and taking a hard look at that sentiment, it was difficult to disagree. The only source of original hard information I had was the life story by Mason, so I had to go back to that, even though I was not hopeful of finding anything further.

Lifting Mason's document and my increasingly thick file on it from a desk drawer, I began skimming through the life story from the beginning, looking for any hint of text that might help me. After forty minutes, I had advanced to the section *My Life in Philadelphia*, and although I recognized some of the passages easily, having now read portions of the text three or four times, I went through them again anyway. There were discussions of neighbours, of local politics, of Ben Franklin's ill-fated *Die Philadelphische Zeitung*, and how Mason and his German-speaking acquaintances were disappointed when it folded after less than a year's publication. He spoke of the occasional shortages of goods that were experienced. He wrote about the local mores, and how he thought that manners were decaying as the population rose quickly. He wrote at some length, and in approval, of the energy and the business enterprise that was evident everywhere in Philadelphia. Near the end of this section of the story, and when I was about to move on to the next major segment of the narrative, a fragment of a paragraph caught my eye:

> *and though I have no good record of the passage of time on the* James Goodwill, *time which delivered to me such discomfort and anguish, nor am I able to set in good time order the many events I can recall, when I compare those fearsome weeks at sea to my life now, greatly more comfortable and offering hope, I do wonder at how things might have been for the original owner of the book, had he lasted the journey. There was only his brief note, which I was unable to read then, and am still unable now.*

My tiredness evaporated instantly. *Note? What note? And does "am still unable now" mean that he had the note, whatever it was, that he had retained it while he was in Philadelphia?* Thinking back, I could recall clearly the evening Monty and I checked the contents of the box I had found in the mill wall. Apart from the two books and the sheet of paper bearing the doctored poem, there was nothing else in the box. The second implication was perhaps even more profound. "His brief note" implied that the original owner of the book was able to write, and so able to read as well. The ability to read and write was not common at all in the eighteenth century in Europe.

The phrase "which I was unable to read then, and am still unable now" implied (perhaps?) that Mason had seen this note either while he was still on board the *James Goodwill* or sometime after he disembarked. Probably the latter. So, where was the letter now? Was it now lost? Had it been left behind in Philadelphia? Is this one of the sources that our eavesdroppers had found?

Just as I was trying to take this in, another implication lit up. What did he mean "am still unable now"? By his own testament, Mason was not able to read until some time after he had settled in Philadelphia. So this statement about the note was probably a quite late one, penned at the time he was writing his life story, likely as a fairly old man. But he could read German as well as English, as was proved by his description of the faith and awe he experienced at reading, in German, the first words of Genesis. So why could he not read the brief note?

I filed away that little puzzle in order to concentrate on the first item on tomorrow's to-do list: go to the safety deposit box and look through the book for any brief note that might be slid between its pages. Without having any idea what was in the note, there was no way of telling whether it would lead forward or just provide a side comment. The second item on the list could be dealt with right away. Jill and Greg were due back the next evening. I sent a text message to Raymond: "I'm assuming you will inform Greg Blackett about the bug on his house. Please tell me when you plan to do this because I would like to be there." Greg would find out that, under Raymond's orders, Stuart and I had found the bug at his house. He might infer from my absence or silence that I thought the fact of his house being bugged was unimportant, and I definitely didn't want that.

It was now past eleven thirty, and time to call it a day. I packed away Mason's story and my file, straightened up the remaining files and papers on my desk, and was about to turn in when Stuart burst from his room and called out: "Richard! There's news from my hacker!"

Thirty

Monday morning I was at the bank in time to be first in when it opened. On the way, I reflected on what the hacker had sent us the previous evening and the follow-up discussion Stuart and I had over breakfast. Stuart's man, his hacker, had come through in spades, having identified a couple of dozen documents and fragments of documents, in four languages, that could be relevant. Stuart was going to spend part of the day printing copies and following up on a few suggestions made by the hacker. I didn't ask where the information had come from or just how the hacker had retrieved it, but put my faith in a comment the hacker had made to Stuart: "people have an irresistible urge to post stuff on the Internet or to boast about having it, no matter how trivial, how ridiculous, how libellous, how erroneous, or how inflammatory the material might be. Many claim to be amazed at this, saying that nobody could be that stupid inherently. But it's all part of the Internet personality, which is so contagious one can catch it from the ether. There's no cure, and lawsuits and imprisonment are a partial treatment at best." I suspected, however, that the hacker's success also had something to do with the fact that people do not lock things away in hardened steel vaults having walls a foot thick and no electronic pathway in.

A pleasant bank employee led me into the safety deposit box area, brought me my box, and said I would have privacy for as long as I wished. I opened the box, saw that everything was as I had left it, except that the books seemed to have taken on an increased mystique. Wedging the Catechism between my briefcase and the Sauer bible to avoid it being damaged in any way by falling open too far, and pulling on soft cotton gloves, I began leafing carefully through the book. It didn't take long. About a third of the way through the document, there it was. A single sheet of ancient and now rather fragile paper filled on one side by handwriting.

Not wanting to miss anything, I used my cellphone to photograph the two pages that enclosed the letter and the letter itself. Having done that, I looked more closely at the letter. I expected the writing to be in German, for some reason, but realized quickly it wasn't German. It was Dutch. *So that was why Mason couldn't read the note.* I could guess at the meanings of some of the words because of the cognate links between German and Dutch, but not nearly enough to read the flow of meaning reliably. After checking that the image of the letter I had captured using my cellphone was good enough to produce a legible paper copy, I closed the book, replaced everything in the safety deposit box, locked it, and then called for the bank employee.

Outside the bank I checked my watch. I had to spend a couple of hours at the mill, but there was just time to do one more thing first. I called Monty and asked if he had a moment. I received the familiar enthusiastic "yes", and fifteen minutes later I was at his place, where he met me at my car in his usual state of apparent purposeful agitation.

"Simple question, Monty. Do you read Dutch?"

"No."

"Okay. Do you know anybody who can read Dutch?"

"Yes", Monty said brightly and without hesitation. "One of my old academic collaborators, Henry Newhouse."

"Doesn't sound Dutch."

"No. But his real name does. Hendrik Nieuwenhuizen. He's emeritus from Queen's, lives in Belleville, sails on Lake Ontario from last ice to first ice, and spends a lot of time on his *Meisterwerk*, documenting the War of the Spanish Succession."

"Surely that one's been done to death?"

"Not as far as Henry's concerned. The work of fourth-rate hacks thus far, is his judgment. Aims to set it all right. Scales will fall from eyes, and so forth."

Monty began dancing about when the conversational lull extended to three seconds. "Why do you need somebody who reads Dutch?"

I explained my discovery to Monty and how I had come across it, and he gestured impatiently for me to come inside and discuss it at length. I just pointed to his window, and he gnashed teeth in frustration. "Your place?" he suggested.

"Yes, okay, but I can't spare a lot of time. I'm needed at the mill in less than half an hour." Monty's expression indicated that half an hour was more than enough time, and it was just a question of talking a bit faster. But then I had a second thought.

"Do you think it would be possible to see Henry later today? I ask because instead of going to my place now when we don't really have enough time, we could both go to Belleville this afternoon, assuming that both you and Henry are available. We could talk on the way."

Monty was already jabbing at his cellphone. "Henry. It's Monty. Likewise to you, you old bastard. Well, thank you, and a pox on your house as well. No, I don't care what kind of pox—small, medium, or large—just so long as it's unpleasant. Yes. A question. Would you have some time free this afternoon? Probably about an hour. Three o'clock should be fine. See you then, at your place. Yes." Monty ended the call.

"Excellent, Monty. Thanks. If you come to my place at about two fifteen, we can go in my car."

Monty chuckled in delight at the prospect of fitting one more thing into a day that was probably already bulging at the seams. We agreed to postpone the lunch at The Fox we had arranged the day before, and I texted Stuart to let him know.

Back at the mill, I checked in at the coffee shop, which was still half full of people who all seemed to have ordered bacon sandwiches. Could be something in the water, I supposed. After saying hello to a dozen or so people and asking after various friends and family, I went into the mill itself. The sound of machinery working was like the voice of an old friend.

I was supervising the milling process because I was the only one who had any kind of training in what's involved in grain milling. It wasn't a lot—four weeks in total, gained through close observation of three millers who had together close to a century of experience. Thankfully, the batches of flour I produced with the help of a local young lad all passed muster every time I had them checked. Eventually I developed a feel for the process and started testing the flour regularly in the best way possible: by using it to bake bread. And, with fifteen years of serious amateur breadmaking behind me, I did know what I was doing there.

The local lad—Graham (rather fitting, I thought, since his name also designates a kind of flour)—soaked up knowledge of the process, and I had to pull him back from his fixation on perfection. Together we developed a concise flour-milling formula exactly suited to our mill, along with a number of straightforward tests on samples taken at different points in the process. Getting the characteristics of these samples right gave us assurance that we had the overall process right. (A thankful nod here to Walter Shewhart and the basics of statistical process control.) Graham was almost ready to be left on his own to do large batches, but both he and I were seeking that sweet spot on the professional comfort scale, and sensing that it was within reach.

Going through a full assessment of the process—something we decided to do once a week for the time being—took the two of us a surprisingly long time, about an hour and a half, including time to document the assessment. But by the end of each such review there was absolutely no stone unturned, a metaphor that proved irresistible when it occurred to me. By the time I left the mill, just after noon, Graham and I had three days worth of milling planned and felt assured that it would come off hitch-free.

I drove home from the mill to get ready for my trip with Monty to Belleville. I made several prints of the letter that I had photographed and put them, along with several pages of my notes, into a small leather documents case. Then I went to see what Stuart was up to.

Stuart had printed out thirteen documents from the twenty-seven his source had flagged for us. Two were in German, three were in Dutch, and most of the rest were in English. There were two in Spanish that Stuart had yet to download. These documents varied from about half a page to twelve pages. They would need close study. Stuart and I discussed them briefly, but he said his German and Dutch were too poor to warrant spending a lot of time on them, and that he would defer to me. Besides, one of his other projects had begun to go sideways and he needed to spend a day getting it back on track. It seemed to me that things were beginning to move, and I sat down for half an hour to get my thoughts straight for the interview with Hendrik.

I had also asked Stuart whether he had heard from Raymond, but he just shook his head, "I'm not going to ride him. He's just been handed a huge steaming pile of shit, and he'll want to deal with it in his own way."

About twenty minutes before Monty arrived, a call came in on my cellphone from Raymond.

"Good afternoon, Inspector."

"Hello Mr. Gould. I just wanted to let you know that I will be meeting Mr. Blackett at his house tomorrow morning at ten. You're welcome to come along."

"Thanks, Inspector. I'll see you then."

The connection was broken without ceremony.

Monty arrived spot on time, as expected, I grabbed my documents case, and we set off for Belleville. Monty was his usual bubbling, cheerful self, and I got him onto the topic of interest easily enough.

"Tell me a bit about Hendrik, Monty."

"What do you want to know?"

"Just general stuff. What's he like? How did you get to know him? What are his areas of interest? Things like that."

"Well, he's a very generous man, both personally and academically. He lost his wife to Alzheimer's disease a little less than a year after he asked for emeritus status, and it took him a long time to get over it. For a while he thought of returning to Holland, but when he went back for an exploratory visit, he concluded quickly that he had changed too much. His areas of interest have always been thirteenth to early nineteenth century Dutch political and economic history, including special attention to Dutch colonial adventures. We got together initially because I went through a period when I was interested in developments in commercial and naval ship design and naval armaments in the seventeenth century. He's a pleasant person to know, and has a well-stocked mind, so I kept in touch."

"Does he still visit Holland?"

"At least once a year, to research his projects. And probably to visit family, but I'm not sure about that."

"Do you still collaborate with him on papers?"

"Not on serious academic papers, no. But we have written articles together for non-refereed journals. Mostly just for fun, but a few of them have uncovered stuff that was unexpected."

"Do you think he'll be interested in the things I want to discuss with him?"

"Hard to say. He has enthusiasms that are hard to predict. He's usually not big on religious history, but I've found that he knows more about the Dutch Reformed Church than some academics who specialize in the topic. I expect he'll be interested in the Dutch angle."

"What approach would you recommend?"

"It's best just to give him some quick background, then let him peruse the papers you've brought. He's not shy about asking questions. He says quite often that there are few stupid questions, and that the stupidity arises when people don't ask questions. Oh. And call him Henry, not Hendrik."

"All right. Got it. By the way, Monty, has Inspector Raymond got back to you on what he proposes to do about your bug?"

"Not yet. But he said he would speak to me tomorrow about that."

I thought I knew how that tied into recent events, but I didn't say anything to Monty.

Henry Newhouse lived in a largish bungalow at the eastern edge of Belleville, not far from Lake Ontario. The house and gardens were dripping in Dutch TLC. The flower beds that stood sentinel in front of the house looked as though their edges had been trimmed using a scalpel. An assortment of trees and shrubs, immaculately pruned, dotted the grounds as though they were bashful trainees in an arboretum. The house itself was spotless, painted white against Lincoln green trim, and as I found out somewhat later, the back garden was an absolute oasis, providing a sheltered outdoor work and study area, complete with a library trolley on which the books needed for the day could be rolled out from inside. This area for study, and obviously also for outside entertaining, was enclosed by a brick wall about four feet high, and this wall was sandwiched in turn between trelliswork and vines rising to eight feet on the outward-facing side, and by movable panels on the inward-facing side, spaced so that the brick was attractively visible between the panels, on which there were scenes reproduced from works by Anton Pieck.

When Newhouse answered the door, I was unprepared. He was a solidly built man, about six feet six inches, had brilliant blue eyes and faded blond hair that had once been straw gold. He had a deep voice inflected by a faint Dutch accent, a slow delivery, a deliberate manner, and a completely charming presence. Except for the charm, which can come in many forms, he looked and behaved as the antithesis of Monty. Monty made the introductions, and Newhouse invited us in.

His living room was decorated, but not overmuch, by some well-known paintings ("Reproductions. They're every bit as good as the originals which should be safe and cared for in a museum in any case"), tasteful bits of Delft china, and a floor-to-ceiling bookcase in which the books were arranged by size in a way that made the collection itself almost an artistic room decoration. A close look at the titles, however, revealed that these books were in no way some interior decorator's idea of bibliographic eye candy; they reflected a life filled systematically by informed and intelligent thinking, and had been assembled deliberately and to a plan.

"I suggest we sit outside in the back garden", Newhouse said, moving that way himself and not expecting objections or alternatives to be voiced. Although the day was on the cold side of cool, Newhouse's garden was well protected, and even the low October sun made it surprisingly and pleasantly warm.

"Can I get you anything?" Newhouse asked as we settled ourselves. "I have a good selection of cold beers, *oude* and *jonge genever*, white wine, or some lemonade that I just made." Monty and I both opted for the lemonade, and Newhouse went off to get it. His chairs and his patio arrangements were such that one could relax or work at equal ease. Looking up, one gazed into the branches of a large silver maple, now almost bare of leaves, but on the flagstones underfoot there was not a single fallen leaf, let alone gangs of them huddled fugitively in corners. Newhouse re-emerged carrying a tray, three glasses, and a large jug of lemonade. One taste of it convinced me right away that Henry Newhouse probably never did anything slapdash or in half measures.

"You like it?" he asked through an engaging smile.

"So much so", I replied, "that I would like to get the recipe from you."

He laughed in acknowledgement of the compliment, said, "but of course", and it was clear immediately to me that I wanted to get to know him better.

I rose carrying my tumbler of lemonade and walked around the patio. It was large, about ten metres square. The warm mixed browns of the bricks in the low wall, the tendrils of vines, now trimmed back but still bearing a sprinkling of fiery red leaves, the soft grey and rose limestone flags underfoot, the large dark terracotta planters scattered carefully at random, the solid cast iron table painted white and having just enough curlicues to avoid it being stilted or boring but not so many that it was fussy, the substantial wooden chairs and cushions on which were depicted scenes of windmills, canals, and poplars, these all defined a space that begged to be lived in.

"This is truly a wonderful outdoor space. It makes my patio look like sick kitsch." A quick glimpse over the wall and through the trelliswork revealed a large manicured vegetable garden, now tucked in for the winter.

"I doubt that your patio is either sick or kitsch, Dr. Gould."

"Ah! I see Monty has prepped you."

"Not at all. Monty never tells me anything that it might be useful for me to know. In fact, Monty does and doesn't do exactly the opposite of what he should and shouldn't."

Monty chirped to life here, cackling at the complimentary insult.

"No, I read the local papers, and the accounts of your mill, and a few years ago of your house, were quite impressive."

"Well, thank you, Dr. Newhouse."

Newhouse waved this off impatiently. "Henry, please. And I presume you prefer Richard."

"Yes. What I was going to say was that if you're interested, you're welcome to come to Greenvale anytime for a tour."

"I would like that very much. By the way, what kinds of grain do you mill?"

"At the moment, we're milling Marquis and Neepawa wheat, but we don't mix the flours. They're packaged separately. We'll see how this goes."

"And I assume that you try your own flour in different sorts of bread?"

"Yes. I'm kitchen testing it all the time."

"How many kinds of bread have you made?"

"About forty altogether." I hesitated slightly. "Do I detect a question here on whether I've made any Dutch breads?"

"Very perceptive, Richard. Yes, I would be interested."

"Well, it's not really bread, but the first thing I tasted, years ago, on my first day in Holland was *poffertjes*, and I make them fairly often."

"*Poffertjes?*" Newhouse eyed me in renewed scrutiny. "There are very few people here who have even heard of *poffertjes*, and you are the first non-Dutch person I know who says he can make them. Dare I hope that you also make Dutch apple bread?"

"Yes, I do. And *volkorenbrood*, and crunch bread, and *roggebrood*."

"My dear chap!" Newhouse boomed. "We have many things to discuss."

"How about we look at the document Richard brought, Henry?" Monty interjected in his typical nervous agitation. "Let's focus on that instead of this potterpees, or whatever the devil it is."

"*Poffertjes*, Monty. *Poffertjes*. It's a culinary delight, not some tinklepan you slide under your bed for nocturnal emergencies."

"I'm only saying, Henry—"

"Yes, I know what you're saying, you gustatorily challenged old carpetbagger."

Following Monty's suggestion, I gave Newhouse a two-minute backgrounder, then laid out on the table the single sheet of the letter and the notes I had brought. Newhouse looked through them all carefully, smiling when he reached the copy of the letter that had slept in the Catechism document probably for two hundred and eighty years.

"Hmmm. This Dutch is almost certainly from the eighteenth century, and written by someone who had more than a trivial education." Newhouse read on in silence for some time. "Interesting references."

After five minutes more, Newhouse laid the sheets in front of him and looked at me.

"I'm assuming, perhaps uncharitably, that you know little or no Dutch, Richard."

"It's safe to assume none."

"Okay. What I will do is give you an off-the-cuff translation right now, and then we can talk about it. But since this document isn't long, I will also prepare a more careful written translation and send it to you later today or this evening. Would that suit you?"

"That's far more than I expected. Thank you. Can I pay you for this?"

"A tour of your mill will be fine."

After a few minutes more, Newhouse cleared his throat and began to read a translation, halting every few words to find the right phrasing: "My dear father was so distressed that I failed to bring about his dream of having an educated and erudite son. The terms educated and erudite meant something to him within the confines of the established church. He revered our great Dutch predecessors Rodolphus and Erasmus, and like them he hoped for learning to be applied to wide and noble purposes while being guided by biblical ideas. And it was from Rodolphus that he took his adopted name, but in Dutch and not in Latin.

"Long have we known religious persecution, and to escape it, to worship as we must, we moved often. My father's interests took him to the Palatinate, where a great historical process was being pursued. The collection of documents he made was his own attempt to take part in this process, to study, and to record. In this he struggled. Whenever he read any well-argued text, he despaired at his inability to see, no matter how he tried, fine but significant distinctions of the sort Erasmus made apparently without effort. He urged me to know the items in the collection. As he grew older, his entreaties became more urgent. As he realized that his time on this earth was nearing its end, he implored and begged me to carry his work forward.

"Without connections to any established house or institution, he, and I in turn, have been able to sustain his collection, and it is truly admirable, only by the grace of Fate, which, at any time, could deliver it whole to various undeserving noble families, or indeed could see it all destroyed. Loving my father for the sincere, caring, and devoted man that he was, I have taken steps to protect the collection, while taking care directly of one very valuable item. By the Grace of God, my father's work, what he devoted his life to, will be safe where I have placed it, unlikely though the location might be, in the sacred bosom of this delightful and ancient town, so near to the academic city of my dreams.

"Should I pass from this world prematurely, I would beseech the good Lord to have this document received by hands that will carry our work forward."

We looked at each other in silence for some time.

"That's the best I'm able to do on an impromptu basis. The document has a good deal of inherent ambiguity, deliberately so I would say, but there are also several words that could have more than one interpretation, and I need to think about them for some time. But I'll send you a good translation later today."

"Thank you Henry. I need to think about all this. Could I ask you to keep the entire matter confidential for the time being?"

"Yes, of course. I assume that this is part of a work in progress to which others might like to lay some claim?"

"Something like that. I promise that I'll fill in the blanks as soon as I'm able."

"Good. In the meantime, I have something to chew on. I like a good mystery."

"A question of information, if I may?" Henry inclined his head toward me, inviting me to continue. "I am aware of Erasmus, but I know nothing about Rodolphus. Who was he?"

"Ah!" Henry beamed. "Rodolphus Agricola was a fifteenth-century scholar. Brilliant. Extremely learned. Preceded Erasmus."

"So when this man says his father adopted Rodolphus's name but his name in Dutch, that means…what?"

"Well," Henry began, "it sounds a bit anachronistic to me, but I'm assuming that it refers to the Agricola part, and my interpretation is that he adopted the name Boersma."

I pondered this quietly until Newhouse changed the subject, asked me about my background, and listened with interest as I related my educational and engineering career in less than five minutes. After minimal prompting, Newhouse went into a short discourse on his own work, becoming quite animated about the War of the Spanish Succession. "So much still to document. So many nonsensical misconceptions to debunk. So many little mysteries to try to unravel. That's the real stuff of history, Richard, not grubbing around in the kinds of decayed, treacherous, and rusted-out industrial footnotes that seem able to bring Monty here to the point of ejaculation."

Monty rose predictably to the bait, "If you got out more often into the open, where the real physical markers of history exist, instead of locking yourself away in airless vaults, you might possibly avoid your current guaranteed fate of becoming an irascible, emphysematous, old irrelevance."

This carried on for a few minutes, until the supply of hot verbal magma died down.

We talked a bit longer about Newhouse's academic career. He had had several sabbaticals in Holland, and he still owned a small flat in Utrecht, where he had been born. I asked him conversationally about aspects of Holland. He said that there were things he missed and things he didn't. "But the main things always to recognize are that one can never escape who one was, and one should never try to deny who one has become. I enjoy immensely having two home countries. I wouldn't think of giving up either."

Newhouse asked if we would like more lemonade, or a nibble, and I took this as a hook on which to start hanging our goodbyes. I thanked Newhouse for his trouble, as we exchanged a warm handshake, and told him that he was welcome at the Greenvale Mill any time. He assured me that he would take me up on the offer, and I sensed that it was a real promise, and not one of those nice departing commitments that are forgotten before the car has been started.

As we left Belleville and drove toward the glacial hills south of Greenvale, I said, "That was very illuminating, Monty. Thank you."

We talked a bit more about how and when his and Newhouse's academic paths had crossed, and Monty said without prompting that Newhouse had one of the best historical instincts of anyone he had ever met. "He disparages what I do on a kibitz basis, but because of his deep interest in Dutch economic history, there are few industrial historians who would come out best in a serious dispute with Newhouse."

We drove on in silence for a few minutes and as we approached a filling station I said to Monty, "I should have used Newhouse's facilities before we left. I'm going to pull in here." I stopped in front of the entrance and said, "Back in a minute."

Inside, I went to the toilet, locked myself in, and got out my cellphone.

"McLachlan."

"Stuart. It's me. I'm at the Shell station twelve kilometres south of Greenvale. A car followed me all the way down to Belleville, including a lot of side street turns almost until we arrived at Newhouse's place. There was another car parked half a block from Newhouse's home, and it's now following me back to Greenvale. What do you suggest?"

"Did you get both plate numbers?"

"Yes."

"Okay. Can you wait there for a few minutes until I come down?"

I agreed, we hung up, and I took my time emerging.

I beckoned Monty from the doorway to the sales area of the station, and he climbed out of the car and skipped over.

"Do you want anything?" I asked. "Drink? Chocolate bar?"

"No thanks", he said, somewhat puzzled. "Are you getting something?"

"Yes. I'm going to get a small bag of Smartfood", which I then did, fumbling incompetently and for a long time with my change at the cash. As I was opening the bag and looking around cluelessly, my shadow, who had parked to one side of the building, came in and went to the magazine rack. Less than two minutes later, Stuart stormed in through the door, raised an eyebrow at me, and I inclined my head toward Mr. Magazine Rack. Stuart put on a heavy scowl, stumped over toward the magazines, and bumped heavily into the shadow.

Before Magazine Rack could say anything, Stuart said roughly, "You need to watch where you're going, bub."

Magazine Rack looked sharply at Stuart and began to say, "It was you who—"

"Then I guess maybe you need your eyes tested", Stuart barked.

They glared at each other like rutting males, then Magazine Rack backed down and headed for the door. I walked over toward Stuart who whispered, "Straight back to Greenvale. I'll arrive about five minutes after you."

Although I knew something was going on, I had no real idea what. I winked at Monty, who was completely nonplussed, we went back to my car and drove the remaining few minutes to Greenvale in an uncomfortable silence. I delivered Monty home, then returned to my place. Stuart turned up ten minutes later.

"What was all that about?" I asked.

"This", Stuart said smiling while holding up a fairly bulky wallet. "I'm going to find out who this guy claims he is."

"Shit! Did you lift his wallet?"

"No. Of course not. We just found it in the street, and like good citizens, we'll put it in the mail addressed to the person on this driver's licence. Andrew Robic."

Stuart wiped down the wallet ("Just a precaution. It's almost impossible to get usable prints from leather"), put on latex gloves, then removed all the contents of the wallet and lined them up on the desk. Then he photographed them all using his cellphone.

"Should be interesting for him when he comes to pay his motel bill."

I had to chuckle at this. "Yeah. What's he going to say? 'I had it this morning. Must have lost it while I was tailing one of your village's citizens.' "

But the weak attempt at humour failed to lessen my deep, growing concern.

Stuart replaced everything in the wallet, I got a padded envelope from my desk, Stuart wrote in block capitals on a small piece of paper *FOUND IN THE STREET*, put both items in the envelope, sealed it, and addressed it using the information on the driver's licence, which he had also copied into his notebook, along with both licence plate numbers.

"I need a drink", I said, "and then we should get ourselves a nice dinner. I have everything we need here for spaghetti carbonara. Would that do you?"

"God, yes!" Stuart exclaimed with enthusiasm. "I haven't had that in ages."

We selected a Bardolino, and I put Stuart in charge of opening and pouring. The spaghetti took little time to prepare, and within twenty minutes we were tucked in and Stuart was obviously enjoying it all. When the plates were empty and removed to the kitchen, we shifted to the sofa and big armchair.

"That really was excellent, Richard. Thanks."

"You're welcome, Stuart."

There was a longish pause while we tried to make the two bottles of wine become three. It didn't work. Again.

Stuart looked at me levelly. "I would guess that in about ten minutes, if I don't say something first, you're going to tell me about your plan to get this albatross off your back."

Once again, Stuart had read my mind.

Thirty-one

Over the last of the wine, Stuart and I discussed my frustration at the entire situation: the buggings, the shadowing, the sinister awareness that the search by somebody for something would not end until they had found it, and behind it all the appalling, pointless, mechanical, and enraging fact of Buck's murder.

"I know how you feel", Stuart said. "I've had to live with this kind of situation several times, and I've seen clients struggle with it many times."

"I'm just tired of sitting around impotently, feeling like a target. I think it's time I took a more active role."

"What did you have in mind?" Stuart asked.

"Well, we could have someone beat the shit out of one or both of these shadows, try to get out of them what they're after and who they're working for, and at least send a message that we're finished being toyed with. If nothing else, it might get someone's attention, cause them to think twice. I, or someone, could go to Pennsylvania and confront this merchant who might be calling the shots, tell him that if he doesn't back off someone's going to get hurt, and that someone might be him. Or I could just try to lure someone out into the open."

Stuart pondered my suggestions for a good minute. "The first option works sometimes. But if they don't know anything, we would just be making matters worse, and it could also just turn into an open war. The second one is a naked threat, and to be effective, the person threatened has to believe that the threat is credible. The main problem here is that someone is devoting a hell of a lot of resources to obtaining something, and setting aside for the moment the possibility that the kingpin in all this is a wild narcissistic monomaniac, the something that's being pursued has to be worth a lot more than two moderately valuable rare books." There was a pause here, and seeing Stuart gaze into the distance and tap his thumbnail against his front teeth made me wait to see what else he might say.

"The possibility of luring them out into the open is interesting. What were you thinking of specifically?"

I took a moment. "I agree that something big is involved. Has to be. So we can regard the two books I found as being just an indicator of something larger, whether that something is real or imagined. What it might be, I really don't know. I'm presuming that what's going on is the following. There are two groups looking for something, probably the same thing. One is being driven by this guy Burns in Pennsylvania. Another is associated with the shady name of Ambrose. I suspect that these two groups are aware of each other, but that neither has a good idea what the other knows. Both are probably looking for that one piece or few pieces of information that will lead them to whatever the motherlode is. Both of them know about me, and they might suspect but don't necessarily know what I know. If one of these two groups became convinced that the other had come across the critical piece of information, and if that new knowledge led them to act in a specific way, then they would reveal themselves, and probably betray just what it is that they know or don't know."

Stuart had suddenly begun paying more attention. "Follow that thought further", he prodded.

"Okay. Let's look at the Sauer bible first. I can't see any connection to anything else important. It's a German bible. It was printed based on Luther's translation, and using typeface brought to the US from Germany. About a hundred and fifty of the original twelve hundred copies are known to exist. Quite a few of those are in institutions, so presumably are permanently out of circulation. But it's likely there are other copies floating around still, many of them possibly in poor shape, but available if one put enough money on the table. If there's any connection to anything larger, that connection almost certainly exists in Philadelphia, right in Burns's backyard. If all that's true, he wouldn't need to be rooting around up here. So, I think the Sauer bible is not the key. That leaves the Catechism. We can be pretty sure, I believe, that the man Mason had both these books in his possession for quite a long time. But at some point, they passed into someone else's hands. Our best guess for this is someone associated with the name Ambrose. We know that Old Man Ambrose is dead. We know—because you found the evidence—that he had a son Ian, but there seems to be no trace of him. I think that somebody else local is involved. I think also that that somebody and Burns's guy both came across the same or very similar information about the Catechism at about the same time. But for some reason, neither of these two knows where the book is."

I hesitated here for quite a long time. Stuart waited for me to continue.

"There's something here", I said, "that's of fundamental importance, and I'm not seeing it. But I know it's there. I've had this feeling many times in my engineering career, when some clever mathematical manipulation was needed, and when I finally found it, the problem I was worrying over simply fell apart."

Another pause.

"Newhouse's translation should be in my inbox by now. I want to go over it carefully and take a look at the documents you've been digging out and printing. And I want to look at all this against the list that we've been keeping of actual and possible events. Somewhere in all this…"

Pulling myself out of this incipient reverie, I rose and walked to the liquor cabinet. "I'm going to have a cognac and then go to bed. Tomorrow morning, I need to go to Greg's place to hear what Raymond has to say. Will you join me in a nightcap?"

Stuart didn't say anything right away. "Yes", he said finally but without enthusiasm. "Sorry. Yes. Definitely. I'm hesitating here because there's the possibility of a good plan in what you just said. But let's revisit the whole matter at breakfast."

We didn't have a nightcap. We had two. And I put on The Spencer Davis Group, and the evening came to a pleasant if indeterminate end.

Overnight there was apparently a dramatic development in one of the other projects Stuart had on the go. When I came down at six forty-five, Stuart was already up, had had coffee, and was in the middle of an intense telephone call.

"So, you agree?" he barked into the phone. "All right. That's what we'll do. Need anything more from me? Okay. Call me if there's any problem, and I do mean *any* problem."

"Trouble in paradise?"

"Really, you don't want to know", he replied.

"Have you eaten?"

"No. I've been on the horn here continuously for the past forty-five minutes."

"How about a western sandwich?" I asked tentatively.

Stuart brightened considerably at this. "I could do some serious damage to that."

I whipped up two massive western sandwiches, and we hunkered down over them.

"Mmmm. This is really good. Why did you waste all those years as a plumber when you could have been cooking?"

"Could have had something to do with avoiding fifteen-hour days, petulant staff, one a.m. quitting times every night, and maybe $25 000 a year, if you're lucky."

We finished the sandwiches, poured out more coffee, and by then each of us was evidently working through his day in his head.

"I won't be able to spend time this morning carrying on from our discussion last night", Stuart said apologetically. "I still have a pile of calls to make."

"Not a problem. I'll take a couple of hours to go through Newhouse's translation and your documents, and then I have to go over to Greg's place. We can catch up later."

Stuart nodded agreement and moved off to begin his calls.

Newhouse had sent his translation as an attachment at about ten o'clock the previous evening, along with a note in his email:

I enjoyed your visit yesterday very much. We must schedule a repeat soon. My translation is attached. The original Dutch appears to be a couple of hundred years old, so there are a few interpretation problems, but I believe I have captured everything important and that any distortions are minor.

Newhouse's revised text had only a few changes from his impromptu translation. I read it twice carefully, then filed it.

I lined up on my desk copies of the documents Stuart had printed. Most of them seemed not of great interest, although I would probably need to go through them all in detail at some point just to be sure. Two were commentaries on Question 80 in the Catechism. Two were in English and were commentaries on work by Menken, one was in German and recorded the loss, in a fire, of a copy of a Dutch translation, and one was in Dutch, and was an account of a discussion with Jacobus Isaac Doedes. Doedes had located in 1864 the sole copy known to remain of the 1563 first edition of the Catechism, a copy that is now in the rare books collection at Utrecht University. I had to rely, at least for now, on the Google translation of this Dutch document. The document itself must have dated originally from sometime before 1897, which is when Doedes died. This account, by an unknown author and which had been posted relatively recently online, noted the author's recollection of Doedes's statement that he had the sense much more material existed, but that he was unable to locate it.

It wasn't much to go on.

Time check. Eight thirty. I had about an hour and a quarter before I would have to pack it up and go to Greg's place.

A ping signalled the arrival of an email. Partly because I was floundering a bit, I broke off to check it. It was from Stuart. *Another message from my hacker. He's found three more items. Attached.*

Looking through the attachment, I found that one of the items was an unpublished research paper from Utrecht University that had recently been posted online. It was in English, and scrolling through it quickly indicated some interesting background. Something to be looked into later. The second was a note attributed to Isaac le Long, the first person who undertook a detailed study of the Catechism. It was in German and appeared to be discussing the distribution of first edition copies of the Catechism. Once again, something to be studied later. The third item was an Ontario death certificate for one Ian Ambrose. That one stopped me cold.

The registered date of death was given as the date the remains were found, although the medical examiner had said that actual death was likely several weeks earlier, but a reliable date could not be established. Looking down through the text, I found the assigned date of death: September 18, 2010. The body was identified from a wallet found with the remains.

Some careful thought and checking was needed here. The date was far earlier than any of the events that were of real interest to me. Possibly it was a different Ian Ambrose. I needed to check with Stuart. If we had birthdates or ages from more than one source and they agreed, then this most likely was the Ambrose of interest to us. Otherwise, did that mean that the Ambrose trail had gone cold? I turned to my listing of events and followed through. If we could not identify "our" Ambrose, then support for the idea of a second group of watchers became much thinner, a good explanation for one of my two bugs became problematic, and the link through Ambrose to the mill became murky.

It was nine fifty when Greg opened the door for me. It was clear he wasn't happy, but he greeted me as usual. I entered and nodded to Jill who returned a faint smile.

"How much has Raymond told you, Greg?"

"Virtually nothing. I know it seems to involve an attempted burglary—not the kind of thing one gabs about over the phone."

"I don't want to cause problems with Raymond, Greg, but I'll give you the thirty second account before he appears. On Saturday night, I was out for a walk. I saw somebody prowling around your house. I called Stuart, and he came over right away. We got footage of the guy on an infrared camera, and we followed him to his place when he left. We reported the whole thing to Raymond immediately, he agreed to allow Stuart to sweep your house, and we found that a listening device had been planted on one of your windows."

Anger was hardening Greg's face, but he remained outwardly calm.

"The unexpected news is that the prowler was Constable Harrison."

Greg's face twisted into a grimace, and he spat out, "Shit!"

"Here's what I suggest, Greg. This was probably at least as great a shock to Raymond as to us. Let him have his say, and treat him with kid gloves. We can ask about actions once he's said his bit."

Greg looked at Jill, who appeared stricken, and they both nodded.

Jill recovered her hostess role. "Would you like some coffee, Richard?"

"Could I have a soft drink instead? Whatever is handy." She looked at Greg who shook his head and she went off to get my drink.

Raymond arrived a few minutes after ten, there were pleasant greetings all round, and everyone settled in the living room. Raymond declined anything to drink.

"I won't beat around the bush, Mayor Blackett. Someone has installed a listening device at your home."

"Is it operating now?" Greg asked.

"As far as I know, yes. And I'm hoping that whoever might be listening is aware that we know about this little game. We can't be sure who installed the device, or exactly when." Seeing the confused look on Greg's face, Raymond glanced at me and said, "We are questioning someone now about trespassing. We have no proof that this trespasser also installed the bug, but regardless of that it's not going to go easy for him. What I propose to do is go and remove the bug now, and we can then continue our discussion in private."

Greg nodded his agreement, Raymond went outside, and through the window we saw him handing a small package to Constable Brierley who then carried it to the cruiser and drove away.

Seated in the living room again, Raymond continued. "I can't tell you how angry and frustrated I am that this has occurred. That one of our own people might be implicated makes it all ten times worse. Now, instead of me trying to second-guess what you might want to know, please ask me whatever questions you wish to and I will answer as best I can."

"Do you have any inkling as to who might be behind this?"

"None."

"Is there anything you can discover from the bug itself that would lead you to the people involved?"

"My technical people say it's unlikely, but they're going to examine it carefully anyway. Ludicrous as it might seem, anyone can buy one of these bugs off the shelf from a hundred different outlets."

"Is there a way to prevent someone from coming around and planting another bug?"

"Short of staying home and alert day and night, there's no guarantee. You can beef up your security system. And there are means available, and they're cheap and reliable, to check for bugs regularly."

"Do you have any idea what they might have been listening for?" This question was from Jill.

"No. None. It could be business or political espionage, as far-fetched as that seems. Or it could be something else." Here I had the feeling that Raymond was making a deliberate effort not to look over at me.

There were two questions on the what-happens-next theme, which Raymond partly answered by saying that he was continuing to investigate. Jill asked if he would keep them informed as much as possible on breaking news, and Raymond said, "yes, of course". Raymond looked from one to the other of them, as the silence lengthened.

"Unless you have other questions, I should be off."

"Thank you for coming around, Inspector, I appreciate your time."

I sat with them for a while after Raymond had left. That unclean feeling of personal violation filled the room, and I knew what they were going through. They knew that I knew as well, and this seemed to help them.

"How do you get past this?" Jill asked in a voice loaded in frustration and anger.

"You rely on your friends, Jill. I'll say straight up that if you're like me you'll go through a period of strong anger. That will pass, but it will take a few days. In the meantime, you and Greg might want to talk to the guy Stuart referred me to. He upgraded my security system, and that alone made a difference for me. I was doing something proactive rather than just sitting around seething."

Deliberately to change the subject, Greg asked how things were going at the mill. I expanded at some length, talking about the sustained volume of custom at the coffee shop, how Karen was ecstatic at the way things were moving ahead, how well Graham was coming along as our miller, how we had just filled our first commercial orders for flour, and that so far we had had almost a hundred people buy two-kilo bags of flour through the retail shop. I warmed even more to the subject when I related how we had begun supplying power to the local utility, and expected to receive the first of our monthly cheques in about three weeks.

After fifteen minutes of this, they both seemed to be in a more balanced frame of mind, so I began to make time-to-leave noises.

"Almost forgot", Jill said. "My book club is looking for a different location for our next meeting. I suggested holding it in the mill and they all went wild. The book we're reading isn't that good, in my opinion. It's about family intrigue and double-cross, and an atmospheric place like the mill would give us a fallback to salvage the evening in case everybody trashes the book itself. Could I arrange that with you?"

When five seconds passed, then ten, and I didn't answer, both Jill and Greg looked at me questioningly. I managed to say, "yes, we could arrange that. Just give me the date." But in my mind I was already back home. The equivalent of a mathematical manipulation had just lit up in my head. Maybe this books and bugging problem was about to crumble. But if my thought was as significant as it seemed to be, by this time next week I would be in Germany.

Thirty-two

By the time I arrived home, it was after eleven. At two that afternoon, I had a tour of the mill and an interview. At four thirty, a meeting was scheduled in Belleville to explore how links between the mill and four local bakeries could be forged to everyone's advantage. At seven o'clock, after their day had finished, I had arranged to meet a cheesemaker and two local winemakers in Picton to set up wine, cheese, and bread evenings at each of our various establishments.

Even though that didn't leave a lot of time to begin fleshing out the thought that had occurred to me at Greg's place, I began working on it with determination.

The information on the Ambrose body was sketchy, but included the statement that Ian Ambrose was reported to be fifty-five. That was consistent with independent information obtained earlier concerning the Ian Ambrose we believed to be associated with the mill, so they could be the same person. If Stuart could get access to the data from the wallet found with the body, that would likely nail things down one way or the other. So that item went on the to-do list.

Taking the information from the hacker's email at face value, if the individual died in 2010 at age 55, he would have been born in 1955. A check of births in Ontario yielded four possible Ian Ambroses who had been born that year. If there was a brother, he could have been younger or older. But given only a surname, there were too many possibilities, since the brother could have been older by some unknown amount, maybe ten years, or even more. He could also have been younger, but since Ambrose *père* had died in 1974, very much younger started to seem unlikely.

A different approach was needed. Just as I began trying to identify different ways of tackling all this, a thought occurred. It didn't need to be a brother. It could have been a son.

Starting at the age range 25 to 35, and therefore the years 1980 to 1990, when Ian Ambrose might have become a father, I began looking again at births. During that period, a total of twenty-nine children had been born to fathers named Ian Ambrose. Fourteen of these children were sons. Limiting the birth locations of these fourteen to southern Ontario reduced the total to ten. Two of these births had been in Kingston and one in Belleville. Taking a chance on Belleville, I came up with the name Joris Ambrose, and thought immediately of a poem by Robert Browning. Galloped indeed. The name Joris rang a bell, but it was all becoming a tenuous chain of let's-suppose-for-the-sake-of-argument assumptions.

I leaned back in my chair, searching for other possible links. Something was tickling a reluctant synapse somewhere, but I couldn't pull it out. It would have to wait for now, because I needed to be at the mill in twenty minutes. I jotted down some notes, closed the whole Ambrose file, and placed it back in the desk drawer, hoping that it would ruminate like a good file should while I was away. Then I collected my documents case and headed off to the mill.

It was a superb autumn day. The sky was brilliant blue and a sparsely scattered litter of cumulus clouds stalked each other playfully across it. The trees were now bare, and the wind huffed capriciously in light gusts, giving the deep blue water surface on the river a knurled appearance, contrasting nicely to the calmer water inside the lagoon. The wind picked threads of water from the water wheel and drew them out into strings of small beads, some of which came as far as the lower patio where they would strike the face, refreshingly, of anyone standing watching.

The tour and interview wasn't expected to be contentious, and it was not. The mill itself is a happy face, a good news story, so nobody is tempted to dig deep to find the real dirt. There isn't any. I had read some of the writer's stuff, but in contrast to her pointed and concise writing style, her speech was surprisingly elaborate and adorned by curlicues. She was relaxed and easy to talk to. As was the case for every interviewer or reporter I have dealt with on the topic of the mill, the apparent mismatch between my engineering background and the mill restoration was of great interest to her, and I was asked to expand on it at length. This writer apparently had some knowledge of carpentry and stonework, and to complement the number of pictures taken by her photographer, she asked numerous questions on why or how I did this or that. I had the impression that she enjoyed the interview, but one never knows until the end product is printed. After an hour and a half, we shook hands, she and the photographer drove off, and I headed for my appointments with bakers, winemakers, and cheesemakers.

It was after nine o'clock and completely dark when I returned home, pretty much bagged. Stuart's car was in the driveway, and despite being tired, I wanted to go over a few things with him. I noticed that I had left the light on in the carport, but I could turn that off from inside. I locked the car, and started across the gravel driveway. A moan came from the carport. Then Stuart's voice. "Richard. I'm over here", also from the carport.

Blood had run down the left side of Stuart's head, and onto his neck and shirt collar. He had a nasty bruise on his left cheek, and he was standing over a prone figure on the carport floor. The figure moaned and moved.

"What's happening?" I asked, alarm evident even to me in my voice.

"The security system detected movement outside the house. I came out to have a look and caught this joker snooping. He came at me and I had to lay the bastard out."

"Who is he? Do you know?"

"No. Can you cut me two twelve-foot lengths of that polypropylene rope?" Stuart pointed to a coil of rope hanging on a peg on the carport wall.

We tied the guy up, hands and feet, and Stuart pulled viciously on the rope as he tightened the knots. "I need to sit down", Stuart said, as he stumbled and reached for the wall as support. I steadied Stuart so that he could lean against the wall, then got a chair from the front patio for him. He sat down heavily and said "thank you."

"I'll be back in a second", I said. Returning with a cold bottle of water, I handed it to Stuart.

"Thanks", he said, and drank half of it practically at a gulp.

"I'm calling Raymond and an ambulance. I've had it to the teeth with this fucking nonsense." Stuart could only nod. I started to make the 9-1-1 call, but Stuart raised his hand, shook his head, and said not just yet.

I hesitated. "Are you okay?" I asked.

"Yes. This prick hit me one hell of a crack."

At that point, the intruder rolled and said, "Untie me."

I walked over to him. "What did you say?"

"I said untie me."

I kicked him in the stomach. "If you want to say something, say who you are and what you were doing here."

Stuart had now regained some strength. "You won't get anything out of him easily", he said. I assumed this meant that Stuart had already made an initial attempt, and I was sure that he could be much more persuasive than me. Stuart drank most of the rest of the water in the bottle. He had just replaced the cap when his phone must have vibrated, since he drew it out of his pocket.

"Yes?" There was then a long pause, evidently as information came from the other end. "Okay. Thanks." Stuart ended the call, put the phone back in his pocket, and rose from the chair.

"On your feet", Stuart said to our trussed prowler, and he pulled him up violently and slammed him against the block wall of the carport. "Okay, Davie boy. I think you had better start talking." At the sound of "Davie", there was a slight flicker in the prowler's eyes. "Oh yes", Stuart said. "I know that you're Davie McCrae."

Turning to me, Stuart said, "Go into the house and get the longest-handled pair of pliers you've got, a crowbar, and some duct tape." In less than two minutes I was back. Stuart had placed the prowler between two vertical pieces of two-by-four fixed to the carport wall. A heavy crosspiece of wood was fastened to the two-by-fours about three and a half feet from the floor. Normally I used this device to store odd lengths of wood. Stuart was pushing the guy's bound hands down between the wall and the crosspiece.

"There. Wouldn't want him to fall down and hurt himself now, would we? I was saying to Davie here that we could do this the easy way or the hard way. Davie seems to want the hard way, which is fine by me. Rip off a piece of duct tape and cover his mouth." I did that. "Good. Now I'm going to be trying to convince him to have a friendly chat with us, but if he pulls anything stupid, just tap the crowbar right there", and Stuart indicated a point on the guy's shoulder. Then, with one swift and violent

189

movement, Stuart pulled down the prowler's pants and underwear. The defiant expression was replaced by one of apprehension.

"I want you to know right away, Davie, that I am entirely serious. If you want to answer my questions, just nod. Now, who are you working for?" Stuart said, as he closed the jaws of the pliers lightly on one of Davie's testicles. There was a sharp sucking in of breath, but no real sign of co-operation. Five seconds passed. Then there was a long suppressed roar dammed up behind the duct tape as the plier jaws tightened.

"Who are you working for?" Another delay followed by another suppressed roar, longer this time, as the jaws tightened and held. Davie was now breathing heavily, and sweat ran from his face. "You have two of these", Stuart said conversationally. "When the first has been squeezed to a pulp, we can start on the second. It could easily take an hour." A short delay while Stuart looked at him and waited. "No? All right. Have it your way", and the jaws once again slowly began to tighten.

This time, there was what sounded like "No! No!" from behind the duct tape, and Davie was nodding vigorously.

Stuart pulled the duct tape off roughly and said, "Start talking right now."

There was heavy breathing, and then Davie began in a quavery voice. Stuart released the testicle and drew the pliers away.

He talked volubly for about three minutes. It seemed then that the flow was about to dry up, but when the pliers moved back threateningly toward his groin area, that was enough to fan the dying embers of co-operation back to full flame.

Stuart questioned him for about fifteen minutes. At length, Stuart stepped back, reached into his pocket, pulled out what looked like a cellphone, and pressed a switch. "It's amazing what one can do these days. This little box can record up to two hours of almost anything, but in this case it's been conversation. Your conversation, Davie. Now, we're going to turn you over to the local police. We have images of you prowling, and the whole little minuet between you and me, including you striking me with the piece of pipe, is all on disc. You might be tempted to complain to the police inspector that you were tortured. I wouldn't do that, if I were you. If you do, I'll know because the police will ask me, 'Did you torture the suspect?' If I hear that, my answer will be 'No', of course, but then things will turn nasty for you. You saw how easy it was for me to identify you. I can operate that network the other way just as easily, and put out the word that you squealed like a little piglet, answered all my questions, told me all I need to know. That bit of news would make its way back among your crowd, including the people you were doing this job for. You know what would happen then, don't you Davie?"

Stuart looked at me, nodded, and I called 9-1-1. Stuart pulled up Davie's pants and laid him down again onto the floor in the middle of the carport, and beckoned me outside.

"It's best if you say that when you arrived home, chappie here was already tied up, and you called 9-1-1. No matter what they come back with, just stick to that story, that he was tied up when you arrived and you don't know anything about what might have happened before then." Stuart looked at his watch. "It's nine thirty-five now. Let's agree that you arrived home at about nine twenty-five, or nine thirty. I'm sorry that you became involved in this sordid shit Richard."

"How did you—" I began, but Stuart interrupted.

"I took a half-dozen pictures of him on my cellphone then sent them off to a guy I know."

While we were waiting for the police to appear, I told Stuart about my searching for the brother or son of Ian Ambrose, and gave him the details. Stuart perked up somewhat, although he still looked ghastly, half his face being covered in caked blood. He was on his cellphone right away sending a text message. When he had finished and switched off the phone, he told me what he had done. "If my contact finds anything about this Joris, he'll send the result to both you and me by email. So keep an eye out for incoming emails over the next little while. Raymond is going to question me at length, but I suspect that he'll let you go fairly soon when you tell him that you arrived after all the action had taken place." Stuart also handed me the little recording device and asked me to put it in a safe place. I picked up the pliers and duct tape, including the piece that had been over Davie's mouth, and carried them and the crowbar back inside, where I placed them in the utility room at the back, then I locked the recording device in my desk. A few minutes later, a police cruiser pulled into my driveway.

Brierley stepped out and exchanged a few pleasantries, then we went to look at our trussed turkey. Brierley applied handcuffs, then cut the wrist and ankle bonds, led Davie to the car, bundled him in, then came back to us.

"Tell Raymond that we will both be at the station in about ten minutes", I said, "right after these guys", and here I indicated the EMS vehicle that had just arrived, "clean up and check Stuart."

Brierley radioed in this news, and apparently got approval for our plan, then drove away. While the EMS guys were unloading their gear, I shot several pictures of Stuart's injuries using my cellphone. It took the EMS crew about fifteen minutes to clean up Stuart's face, apply some bandages, and check him for fractures. The attendant said that everything looked okay, but that Stuart really should be checked by a doctor, and then they left. Stuart and I climbed into my car and I drove to the police detachment.

Stuart's prediction was correct. Raymond, who seemed to be in an uncharacteristically upbeat mood, questioned me for about ten minutes, told me to stay clear of the areas where the struggle with the prowler had occurred at my place, told me not to touch the recording equipment on the security system, and then let me go. I arrived back at my place in a strange mood: tired but also belligerent. I needed to unwind and get some distance between myself and the recent violence, and a good double brandy seemed just the ticket.

After a first gulp of brandy, followed by two or three genteel sips, the world had begun to come back into focus. I cued up an assortment of gentle music on my sound system, starting at "Sheep May Safely Graze", then pulled out the notes I had been working on nine or ten hours earlier, and switched on my computer. I did a search on Google for Joris Ambrose and was not really surprised to find nothing of interest. I then did a bit of doodling. Two names were before us: Burns and Ambrose. Conceivably, just one of them could have been responsible for all the crap that had occurred, but that seemed unlikely. There were just too many instances where bugs and the like had been duplicated, and why would one person want to do that? Burns was a collector, apparently a very determined one. The Ambroses were a big question mark. It seemed unlikely that they were serious collectors. Maybe they were just treasure hunters? Maybe they were seeking what they were seeking on behalf of someone else?

A ping signalled the arrival of an email. It was from Stuart's contact: *Picture of Joris Ambrose attached. Shady but no record. More info to follow later.* I saved and printed the picture. Just then my stomach rumbled, and I realized that since breakfast I had consumed nothing apart from a small glass of wine, about two ounces of cheese, and the brandy. Telling my stomach to put a sock in it for a few more minutes, I returned to my musing. Time to formulate some theories that could actually be tested.

Mason had hidden his books somewhere, but not in the mill since he was long dead before it was built, so whatever hiding place Mason had chosen, somebody must have found it. Suppose it was the Ambroses who found the books. Suppose that they had worked as systematically as they could through all the places where Mason might have stashed the books. Suppose that one of those places was the church in Belleville. Suppose that Ambrose Junior wangled the job of refinishing the altar, and took the opportunity to search the entire church. Suppose that he found the books. *But then why would he be looking for them now, if indeed it was him doing that?*

This one stopped me. I walked around the problem for a few minutes, and was about to try another tack, when it occurred to me. Suppose Ambrose Senior hid the books somewhere, like in the mill, but didn't have time to tell Junior. As far as Ambrose Junior would be concerned, given that Ambrose Senior was now dead, the books would be lost again. There was a possible connection here, and now that I had a physical image of Ambrose Junior, I could test part of this suppositional chain. Tomorrow, I said to myself, I'm going back to see Reverend Carswell.

Almost immediately, another thought occurred. Suppose that Ambrose and Burns are both aware that someone else is looking for what each of them regards as his to take. They might both be trying to find out who the other is and how much he knows. If one of them had hired the guy who had killed Buck, that would have sent a clear message to the other that there was a competitor out there. Ditto for the death of Ambrose Senior. But one step at a time. Talk to Carswell again first.

It was now just after midnight, and as I was making some last notes Stuart was returned in a police cruiser. He looked as though he had just been bled by an over-enthusiastic barber.

"Stuart. Coffee? Brandy?"

Stuart flopped on the sofa in genuine exhaustion. "Brandy, please."

"I'm surprised Raymond kept you this late when it was obvious you'd been through a lot." I must have said it in an accusatory tone.

"It wasn't him. It was me. I insisted that he go through the whole thing tonight, get it all over with, except for the inevitable few follow-up questions. Glad I did. Glad to have it all behind me."

I handed Stuart a generous brandy. "I was just going to get myself something to eat. Nothing too heavy, given the time, but I haven't eaten for more than twelve hours. I was going to stick some fruit and vegetables into the juicer. Would you like some?"

Stuart just nodded, I dug out the necessary provisions from the fridge, and soon had two large glasses of vaguely rusty red liquid for us.

We drank the rest of our juice in silence, then settled back to the brandies. I explained my ruminations to Stuart and told him my plan to visit Carswell again in the morning and what I hoped to learn. Stuart nodded approvingly. "With any luck, we can start luring out these buggers, just as we discussed a few days ago. Can we revisit this plan over breakfast? I'd like to make sure we have the full picture in mind and that we don't miss anything before we start putting a show on the road."

"Suits me. Shall we say huevos rancheros with some spicy strips of steak on the side for breakfast?"

It was two exhausted but smiling faces that saw the remainder of the brandy go to a good home.

Thirty-three

Despite the late hour the previous night, I awoke at seven thirty, fully refreshed, after a deep, dreamless sleep. Stuart was still out cold, so I walked to the mill to have coffee, say hello to the early clientele, and check with both Karen and Graham. Even at that hour, surprisingly to me, there were about a dozen people having coffee. More were expected later. Karen was her usual self. She repeated to me once again, not even trying to hide her delight and pride, that the stretches of downtime sitting alone in an empty restaurant, that she had expected to see in a new operation, just hadn't materialized here. A full schedule was evidently lifeblood to her. Similarly, Graham was all smiles. I had heard independently that our initial flour customers were pleased with both the product and the service. Graham and I talked about the possibility of a customer appreciation day once we had been operating some milestone span of time, such as six months. Michael had put out the word that the mill restaurant was having an impromptu French bread celebration day, and fresh baguette, butter, and apricot jam would be ready at nine, pain au lait at noon. Michael hoped it would lead to a small blip in the morning's trade. Karen expected the place to be swamped.

I finished my coffee, said hello to a few people, then took the opportunity to check all the readings we were logging to monitor the operation of the water wheel, the milling equipment, the power delivery to the grid, and internal power use. To my delight, they were all right down the middle.

Back home, I set about preparing the ingredients for breakfast (cooked the tortillas, chopped the onions and chillies, and prepared the tomato sauce), then put on some coffee hoping that the scents wafting through the house would penetrate as far as the Land of Nod.

They did.

Stuart came into the kitchen, washed, shaved, and looking a thousand percent better than the night before, providing one discounted the angry purple smudge on his left cheek. "I'm starving", he said. "What can I do?"

"Just set the table, pour us each a large glass of juice, and get ready to butter some toast when it's done, but otherwise relax. We'll eat in about five minutes."

The eggs and spicy steak strips were cooked in parallel. In no time we were each seated in front of a blowout three-egg plate of huevos. We were obviously ready for it. Not a word was spoken for almost ten minutes.

"Shit, Richard! You've now spoiled me rotten. When this caper is over, either my culinary life will be free fall back to Dullsville, or my restaurant bill will take me into the financial red zone. This is fantastic. I've never had huevos like this."

"Well, it's easy enough to do. You can do it too. You just need to stop being an idle bastard and take the time to practise." This occasioned a general exchange of insults and some vigorous maligning of parentage.

"I'll clean up the pans", Stuart said, "while you get out your notes and then we can do some planning."

The various sheets were spread out over the table, and we both took time to bring ourselves up to date. "Here's the theory that has been suggesting itself to me", I began. "Mason wanted someplace safe where he could consign his precious books. He chose to build the altar in the little church in Belleville as his legacy to that congregation and he put the books inside the altar. The altar itself is of brick-shithouse construction: the top alone is too heavy for even one very strong man to lift on his own. I know that because I've done some calculations based on these photos I took of the altar and on the density of oak. I'm not sure who Mason thought would retrieve the books or when, but in the spirit of his time he likely just consigned them to God's care, and had faith that they would see the light of day again when the time was right. I speculate that a young man, who went by the name Robert Ames, ingratiated himself with Reverend Carswell so that he could undertake the refinishing of the altar top. While he was alone in the church doing that job, he probably searched the place top to bottom, and in the process found the books that Mason had placed in the altar. He then spirited them off."

"How does this man Ames fit in?" Stuart asked, openly puzzled.

"I think Ames's real name is Ambrose. He found out, somehow, that Mason had built the altar, and he also knew, somehow, that Mason had something valuable in his possession. I've tried to track everything physical associated with Mason. The house he lived in, just outside what was then Meyer's Creek and is now Belleville, burned down early in the twentieth century. But what Mason had was something that he personally cherished greatly, so he would be unlikely to leave it in a place that could be reduced to ashes, or would become the property of someone who was completely unknown to him. So, the conclusion is that he must have lodged it somewhere else. The church would be a leading contender."

"We've covered this ground before. If Ames retrieved the books, surely he wouldn't be looking for them now."

"You're right, if it is him looking for them, and if he still has them. Here's what I think. Robert Ames is really Joris Ambrose. He's the son of Ian Ambrose. I suspect that Burns was also hot on the trail of these books, or at least of something associated with them, and being hot on the trail of the books, his trail and Joris Ambrose's trail were bound to cross. Joris probably suspected that he was more visible than his old man, so he gave the books to Ian, who hid them somewhere but didn't tell Joris where, before they both went underground to stay clear of Burns. Burns went after them, and located Ian, but Ian died of a heart attack, probably triggered by Burns's interrogation, and obviously before Burns could find out where the books were. Now Joris doesn't know where the books are either, so he's bugging all the places that he thinks might give him a clue, while at the same time trying to stay low and off Burns's radar. But both Burns and Joris know that the other is around, because of all the events that have led to police activity." I paused here to see whether Stuart had anything to add.

"Okay, this is a nice variation on our previous thinking", Stuart said slowly. "As a theory it's plausible, and I can't find any holes in it."

"I think the first thing to do", I said, "is to determine whether Robert Ames is actually Joris Ambrose. Reverend Carswell should be able to do that for us. If Carswell can't do that, or if Ames is not Ambrose, then we're back at square one. But if Ames is Ambrose, then we're closer to knowing just what's going on."

"But how does all this link up to the books? Where's the connection between Mason and Ambrose?"

I paused here for a moment. "I've spent a lot of time thinking about this. There are four possibilities I can see, but I won't go through all the tedious details. I think the most likely one is a family linkage from Ambrose back to someone who trekked with Mason from Pennsylvania."

We both sat and pondered this for a while.

"Okay", Stuart began. "I agree that the first step is to determine whether Ames and Ambrose are the same. If they are the same, then we try to locate Ames. If we find him, we have three courses of action. We can tell him that you have the books but that he won't be getting them, they'll be going to an institution." I was about to object, but Stuart held up his hand. "Or, we can sweat him, saying that we know he's responsible for Buck's death and is behind some of the other problems that have arisen, try to get out of him just what he's been doing, and what it is that's been so important for him to spend so much time and effort on all this. One potential advantage of this is that it might lead us to be able to determine which actions can be traced back to him and which to Burns. Or, we can just say that we're turning everything we have over to the police. I'm just thinking out loud here, so please jump in."

I nodded and summarized what I thought at some length.

Stuart was nodding slowly; it was obvious he was going over the thinking carefully. "If we're planning to locate Ambrose and grill him, we need to keep in mind that if, as seems likely, he's tied to Buck's death, then the stakes are high, he has little to lose, and we need to assume that he could be quite dangerous. Also, if we're going to grill him, we need to make sure we have all our facts straight, and we need a strategy that includes anticipating his answers and always being ready with another question no matter what he comes out with."

"Yes", I agreed. "That means that I need to go over all the material carefully."

"Both of us need to go over it. I have to say that I think it should be me doing the interrogating. I've done a lot more of it than I expect you have. It also means", Stuart added, "that we have to be as certain as we can that he doesn't see us going to visit Carswell, and we have to hope he didn't see you visiting Carswell the first time."

"What about Burns?" I asked.

"What about him?"

"We can't assume that he's just sitting idly by. He, or at least his goons, are out there somewhere. He's probably also watching Ambrose, who, in turn, is probably doing the best he can to watch Burns. But Burns likely has the upper hand because I expect he has more resources behind him. So Burns is probably the cat. But neither of them can be entirely sure what the other knows, so they're both likely watching to see whether the other inadvertently tips his hand on something. Sooner or later, it will turn deadly. When one of them gets what he wants, or at least gets access to it, then the other will suddenly be somebody who is no longer useful but knows too much. That might apply to me as well. So, my thinking is that I need to find some dirt that really will stick to either of them, but especially to Burns, so that I can insert the police between me and them. At the moment, I've got nothing."

Stuart suddenly had gone very quiet.

"What?" I asked.

"Something you just said", Stuart replied.

I waited, then he continued. "You said you think Burns has more resources behind him. You're right. But, in fact, the apparent mismatch between Burns and the Ambroses is so great that it's not credible."

"And?" I prompted.

"And so, it seems unlikely that the Ambroses are acting on their own behalf."

"Maybe they're agents for another collector?"

"Something like that, yes."

"I did wonder about that", I said, "but I'm not sure what supports that thesis."

"Nothing specific that I'm aware of, but then absence of evidence is not evidence of absence."

In a less charged discussion, I would have stuffed this commonplace profundity up Stuart's nose, but we were actually trying to cross something of a mental minefield in the dark. And I took the flicker of humour, especially in this absurd and dangerous area, to be a good sign.

"What this means is that there could be multiple watchers on us", Stuart said. "So, here's what I think we should do in preparing to visit Reverend Carswell."

We discussed a plan, made some changes, and then jotted down a few items. I called Carswell and arranged a meeting the next afternoon at about two. Stuart booked a rental car at a location on the outskirts of Belleville for first thing the next morning, then went off to look after a couple of his other projects. Max, who was sitting on the back of the sofa, and had been watching us all this time, evidently concluded that what we were planning wouldn't work, yawned, climbed down onto a cushion, and went to sleep.

It was now just past noon. As I had promised Michael and Graham, I went back to the mill, and we went through a mini-review of the past few days and the next few days. As I had promised Jill, I went to her place and made arrangements for her book club meeting in the mill. As I had promised Monty, I met him at The Fox and we sketched out two of the papers he was itching to draft. The mill was now beginning to receive substantial amounts of mail. A lot of it was junk, some was just business related and fairly routine, but some was material that deserved attention. I spent an hour going through all that, another hour clearing things off the mill website, and a further hour collecting autumn bounty from the garden and putting parts of the garden to bed for the winter. There were several excellent squashes ready to be picked, cabbages and onions to be brought in, a surprising number of stubborn tomatoes still defying the cool nights, chives that were tougher than their tender spring forebears but still useful for a lot of things, and quite a bit of straggly basil that would make good pesto. All this came to two large bushel baskets of produce that I set by the sink and began cleaning.

At six thirty, Stuart emerged. "How be I treat you to dinner tonight at The Fox?" he asked.

"How be I make a nice butternut squash and shredded chicken risotto and we call on a good sweetish wine to help wash it down?"

The Fox took a rain check.

Thirty-four

Thursday dawned in that steely brightness of an autumn day on the long and languid slide to winter. We had had a frost overnight, not a lethal one for most vegetables, but enough to paint delicate white beards on the ends of the long grasses. My harvesting the day before of chives and basil had happened none too soon.

Breakfast was a late and pedestrian affair: bacon, toasted walnut bread, and jam, since one can't live by huevos alone. Brilliant autumnal light chugged in from the east, transforming the ground floor space into a gold-suffused apiary whose walls and woodwork were kissed by solar honey. It was midway between two of those seasonal farewells that occur through the year, a silent and seamless flow of events giving rise to that bittersweet feeling, a feeling captured best, I think, by the German word *Sehnsucht*. "Longing" doesn't reflect the depth of the feeling. "Nostalgia" isn't right, and "yearning" and "wistfulness" both miss the mark. There's a special mood associated with changes of seasons, and the mood for each of the changes is different. Although each season has its enchantments, not many people release winter unwillingly. Spring unfolds the miracles of animal birth and plant renewal, and although the transition from spring to summer can bring a sense of the loss of freshness and innocence, at the same time it involves a tingling expectancy of the power of new life to deliver on great promise. The real undercurrents of *Sehnsucht* appear as summer transitions to autumn, and autumn to winter. The tug of the former change comes to me most strongly in my garden, when I have soil under my fingernails, baskets full of vegetables, a compost pile stacked deep in withered leaves and roots, the reluctant ebb of a butterscotch sunlight tide, a frosting of cirrus clouds in a high blue sky, and the world whispering to me through my circumscribed little patch of stardust, "I've done what I said I would do, now I'm tired, and soon I will sleep." But the change from autumn to winter is more wrenching. Demeter's grief is at hand, the Great World, having spun, is now receding and it peers back at me through a deepening cosmic mist, taking its leave. "I have enjoyed our trip around the Sun, but now my time is through. Take care, little brother. I pass you to the arms of a new year. Goodbye."

"Are you okay?" Stuart asked. "You look like you just lost your entire family in a flood."

"I'm fine. It's just the closing grip of senility and the quicksand of retirement."

"Hey?"

"More toast? It's good with a thick smear of *Sehnsucht*."

"Richard! What the…?"

"It's almost ten o'clock. Your car rental place opens in half an hour. I'll give you about an hour and twenty minutes lead time, then I'll set out." I had already decided that I would spend that time communing a bit more with my garden. "You have the list of places I'll be stopping at?"

"Right here", Stuart replied tapping his shirt pocket, but evidently still struggling to make sense of our recent exchange. "First stop is the garden centre. You should see me parked at the filling station just this side of it, but I'll call you when I've picked up the rental to let you know what make, model, and colour to look for."

"Good. I'll spend about fifteen minutes in the garden centre. Then I'll carry on through the rest of my five planned stops and not pay any attention to where you might be."

"Got it", Stuart said. "I'll be in regular touch, and we can call or text each other at any time if something occurs that might upset the plan", and he got up, picked up his windbreaker, and headed for the door but then stopped and looked back. "You sure you're all right?"

"Yes. Nothing that some soil under my fingernails won't cure. Go. See you back here sometime this afternoon."

Another hour left the vegetable garden almost completely harvested, neatly edged, and resting. Another fifteen minutes saw the large basket of mixed produce washed, trimmed, and draining in the mud room at the back of the house, a space that has separate temperature control, where I keep boots, a large chest freezer, and a utility sink where I regularly wash tools and vegetables.

Twenty minutes later, the garden centre came into sight as I crested the low hill marking the beginning of the long descent into a wide shallow valley. At the southern edge of the forecourt to the Shell station, which sits almost in the middle of this valley and not quite a kilometre to the north of the garden centre, was an olive green Altima, just as I expected. The view from within the Altima, up and down the highway, was unobstructed. I pulled into the garden centre, and spent ten minutes poking around the place and talking to the owner, then bought a bag of mulch, which I actually did need. The large outside display area was well stocked in planters of all types, but walking past the rows of trellis material, I could look out through the latticework at the parking area in front of the garden centre without being seen. At this time of year, and mid-week, custom was not brisk, and there were only eight cars parked there. One of them was the Altima, but I couldn't see Stuart. I looked at trowels and stakes, frowned in concentration, and tried to appear as though I was struggling over deciding whether I needed them. Five minutes later, I carried my bag of mulch to the car, and prepared to resume my route toward Belleville. Looking around as I got ready to turn back onto the highway, I noticed that the Altima was no longer there.

My second stop was in the nasty bit of strip mall just within the outskirts of Belleville, where I went into an auto parts shop and bought an oil filter for which I had absolutely no need. My third stop involved doubling back to the edge of town, where I pulled in to a tourist information kiosk. It was closed for the season—I had known this—but nevertheless I peered in the windows, tried the door, and scowled. Back in my car, I headed for my fourth stop, a delightful clothing store in the middle of Belleville, Harry's Emporium, where everything is always an unholy jumble. Harry is an exceptional septuagenarian who seems always to know exactly how many items of which kinds of clothing he has, and can find them unerringly in the well-mixed non-descript piles. I spent about five minutes in Harry's, then came out, and almost immediately received a call from Stuart saying that we were on track. I got into my car, and moved on toward my fifth stop. Driving slowly down a main street in Belleville, I pretended to be searching for an address, ignoring the impatient horns from cars behind me. Several cars from further back in the queue pulled out and passed me. At the last minute, I accelerated and went through a set of lights just before they turned red. There was an angry blare of horns behind me, but I paid it no attention, took a sharp right turn, sped down the street, did several more turns, drew up behind Belleville City Hall, and parked in a multi-storey car park next door, where I sat in the car and waited.

My cellphone rang.

"Hi Stuart. Everything okay?"

"Yes. Come out of the car park now and take side streets to your meeting with Carswell, but park at least two blocks from his house. And let me know when you're about to leave Carswell's place." Within ten minutes, Carswell opened his door to me. It was one fifty.

"Sorry I'm a bit early, Reverend."

"Not at all, not at all. Come in, come in, Mr. Gould. Nice to see you again." A familiar cackle tumbled through from somewhere in the house. We settled in Carswell's study. "What can I do for you?" he asked.

From the envelope I was carrying, I pulled out a photo and handed it to Carswell. "I would like to know if you recognize this man as Robert Ames."

Carswell needed no time to respond. "Yes, yes. That's him." He handed the picture back to me. "Why do you want to know, if I might ask?"

"Yes, by all means, Reverend. I believe that he's related to a former owner of the Greenvale mill, and since I'm trying to put together as complete a historical picture of the mill as possible, I want to try to contact him. Putting a face to a name is one step in that."

Carswell nodded without saying anything, but I was pretty sure he wanted to know, to satisfy his own curiosity, how I had got a picture of a man whose address I had admitted during my previous visit I didn't have. "I'm trying to trace Ames through his past connections, and I'm afraid to say that he hasn't always been completely on the sunny side of the law. That's how I got this picture, in a roundabout way." Sliding the picture back into the envelope, I asked, "Would you happen to know anyone Ames might have worked for while he was in this area, or where he lived?"

"I don't know where he lived. Apart from the days he spent working on the altar, and even then he kept very much to himself, I probably saw him only six or seven times in total. But I believe he did some occasional work for Charles Brossard's landscaping company. Beyond that, no I really don't have any information."

I would now need to contact Brossard, but I could do that by telephone. Carswell and I made some small talk. He asked me how things were going at the mill. I thanked him for his interest, and spent a few minutes giving him a short summary. "I don't know if you or your wife do any baking, but you've been generous with your time and I'd like to leave you a small something." I pulled a two-kilo bag of "Greenvale Mill" flour out of the cloth bag I had carried in and offered it to Carswell.

"That's very kind of you Mr. Gould. Thank you."

"I don't want to keep you Reverend, so I'll be off."

Carswell accompanied me to the door, we shook hands again, and I left. Walking back to my car, I called Stuart. "I've just left Carswell, and I'm walking back to my car."

"Good", Stuart said. "The coast is clear, but to be on the safe side, can you leave Belleville to the east, find a route that circles around, and then come into Greenvale from the north? Call me every fifteen minutes or so to let me know where you are. I'll see you back at your place in about two hours."

It was about twenty past two when I left Carswell, and I converted the need for a long trip home into an excuse for a nice potter through the countryside. Shortly after four o'clock, I parked in the carport. Stuart was not back yet. It had been twenty minutes since our previous telephone discussion, so I called him again. "Stuart. I'm back home."

"Good. I'll see you shortly. We have a few things to talk about."

The sun was hovering just above the western hills, and we were heading for quite a cold night, so I spent the time pulling the last of the carrots and parsnips, cut the remaining three cabbages, and dug the last few hills of potatoes, before pulling roots, turning soil, digging in black earth from last year's compost, and putting the rest of the garden into hibernation until April. I had just finished washing the vegetables when Stuart returned. As a complement to all this late harvest, it seemed fitting to drain the last of the wine from a few barrels, at least symbolically. Stuart and I settled down to a glass each of meaty red.

"What did we net?" I asked.

"By the look of it, a couple of flounders trying to masquerade as barracudas. I have a lot of pictures to print, just as soon as I finish this excellent red."

I asked Stuart what happened in Belleville.

"Quite a bit, but I'm guessing you're referring to the little exercise at the intersection. When you ran that red light, my guy was waiting in the cross street and shot into the intersection pretty smartly. Must have missed your rear bumper by not more than a few inches. The guy tailing you couldn't get past, and just managed to stop without hitting my guy's car. They had a car horn pissing match that you probably heard. My guy jumped out of the car and started waving, pointing, shouting at the merchant tailing you, the other guy got pissed pretty quickly, jumped out of his car, and in the excitement my guy planted a bug and homing device in the tail's car. Well, it almost came to blows, but then the local fuzz turned up, my guy complained to them, 'Can't even come out to the country for a nice drive to buy some apples without coming across assholes like this', and his story was good. He had a basket of apples on the back seat, along with a receipt for them from that morning, he was driving his own car, he had a local tourist map and had visited a trout farm about ten kilometres away where he made enough impression to be remembered. Your tail had a rented car and had nothing to back up his explanation ('a drive in the country') for what he was doing there."

"Where were you?" I asked.

"Just down the street. I shot an insane number of pictures of streetscapes, old buildings, and whatnot, to cover the three dozen close-ups of your followers, and the pictures of their cars at various places in Belleville."

"Followers?"

"Yes, there were two of them. As far as I could see, they made no signals to each other, their actions were not co-ordinated, and each of them seemed to be unaware that the other was there. I think they were working independently and had no connection to each other."

"What did we learn then?"

"Okay. The second follower stayed clear of the fuss in the intersection. He sat back and observed, but another of my guys was observing him."

"Another of your guys? Christ Stuart, who's paying for this army of agents you're fielding?"

"Richard, I said before, don't worry about the cost. We'll sort it out later. If we begin worrying about it now, we'll start cutting corners, and miss out on information. You're just going to have to trust me."

I stared at him unhappily for a moment before finally agreeing.

"All right", Stuart resumed, "my second guy then followed the other tail around Belleville. My guess is that the guy was attempting to pick up your scent again. After fifteen minutes, he gave up, parked, and made a call on his cellphone. It looked like quite an animated discussion. Then he drove to a tiny coffee shop in the east end of Belleville, and he met a guy there. My man was able to photograph them, and he sent it on to me", and Stuart showed me the picture on his cellphone.

"Shit! That's Ames!"

"Yes. I didn't know it then because I hadn't received the picture yet, but I made a guess and instructed my man to ditch the follower and find out where his coffee shop contact went. He traced him to a small run-down farmhouse way off any main road outside Picton."

"So now we know where Ames lives", I said brightly.

"Not necessarily. Now we know where Ames went this afternoon. He might or might not live there, but your guess is probably correct." Seeing my expression, Stuart added "We don't want to get down the road and find that an unwarranted assumption has led us off into the weeds."

Evidently, rigour in Stuart's line of work didn't extend to avoiding dreadful mixed metaphors.

"That seems to indicate that the other follower, the one who was outfoxed at the intersection, was working for Burns."

Stuart nodded. "Yes, but probably at some remove. Burns might well be using one or two intermediates."

"What's next?"

Stuart drained the last of his wine and gazed at the empty glass in a mixture of appreciation and disappointment. "Right now, I'm going to download my pictures and send the best ones of our two followers off to see whether they can be identified. Then I want to find out whether the bug in the other guy's car has yielded anything. Then, I want to plan for an unannounced early morning visit to Mr. Ames."

"What can we get from Ames at this point?"

"I hope we can rattle him badly, and get an idea of just what's so important, what has made him go to the extremes he has. But we can talk about this later. I want to deal with these pictures." And Stuart headed off to his lair.

For a few minutes, I sat there in something of a fog. Having decided that cogitating or ruminating would turn up nothing new, I went to finish cleaning the vegetables I had pulled, then set about preparing a huge pot of minestrone. It would have to sit for a day or two, but within half an hour the aroma filling the room was one of the many standard varieties of "essence of Italian kitchen." Without consulting Stuart, I then began preparing a beef vindaloo, and pulled some naan from the freezer to thaw.

I had guessed at half an hour, but after twenty minutes Stuart glided downstairs on the upward flowing curry waft, his feet barely touching the floor. "Please tell me it's a vindaloo."

The nutty aroma of the basmati was overlaying the heavier, richer, more complex earthy scent of vindaloo, already promising more than a hint of subcontinent fire. A ping warned of hot naan in readiness.

"Grab four cans of lager from the cooler, Stuart. By the time you have two poured, we can serve."

The fate of the first half-glass of lager would have made many a magician envious. Soon, lips and tongues were anaesthetized, and the unique glow of Indian curry reminded two abdomens that while chargrilled pepper steak has its place, it doesn't lay sole claim to the centre of the culinary universe. I had prepared enough for two smallish helpings each, together the equivalent of one good-sized helping each, but taking it in two parts avoids eating too much too quickly and makes the meal much more satisfying. The end result was pans and plates wiped almost to clean room standard and two happily sated fifty-somethings. Stuart raised his glass, saying "First rate!"

We finished the lager at a snail's pace, but finally Stuart said, "Much as I would prefer to do something else, let's prepare for tomorrow. You still have my recording of our encounter with Davie McCrae?"

"Better than that", I said. "I made a transcript."

Stuart sorted out the pictures he had placed on my desk before dinner, while I ran off two copies of Davie's transcript. There were several photos of the follower who had led Stuart's guy to Ames at the coffee shop, that follower now having been identified by Stuart's connections as Dean Stephenson. But apart from leading us to Ambrose, the name Dean Stephenson meant nothing and generated no further useful information. The farmhouse was pretty much out in the open, but there appeared to be enough cover for it to be approached unseen, with some luck, from the south. Stuart said that would mean an early start so that we could find a not-too-obvious place to leave the car, and time to approach the farmhouse and watch for signs that Ambrose was at home, and up and about.

We agreed that each of us would set about reviewing the transcript, making notes on things each thought could be significant, and each compile a list of questions. All that took about forty-five minutes, then we compared what we had done, sat together at the computer, and came up with one list of questions and one set of supporting material. By ten thirty, we had finished, and we each had a copy of the two items to review. I agreed that Stuart would take the lead the next day, and that if he wanted me to intervene he would provide a clear opening.

"Are you ready for this, Richard? I don't foresee any genital work, but if you prefer, I can do it alone."

"No. I'm coming."

That decision turned out to be a good one.

Thirty-five

We found the right place after only about ten minutes of looking, an old brick barn. Long abandoned, possibly for seventy years or more, it was covered in brambles and vines. Part of one wall had collapsed. The roof was gone. But still it soldiered on, wouldn't give up. It was a testament to the past, and to past practices of solidity and durability which had now all but vanished, but it could be seen also as a critique of today's rushed and just-good-enough practices, and to the myopia that failed to see what power a combination of these approaches might have. I couldn't help thinking of the mill, how it had gone from being a ruin, an eyesore, a forlorn and discarded and unconsidered relic, and had been returned to a central part of Greenvale's village life in less than a year. *What was the difference, then? Could some structures be revived, put to use again, but others not?* My own vision for the mill, which was and is complex and has changed over time, was something I'd have to examine seriously and honestly at some point. The mill had always had for me, as its central element, a not-well-defined but tremendous pride. But beyond that, the mill's significance was complex yet nebulous, and this made me view the present lamentable state of this barn as a proxy for something that was vaguely greater.

We had driven the car off the rough back road and into the property occupied by this old barn. The ground was solid and dry, and we were able to park the car between the barn and a large clump of cedars where it was all but invisible. It was just seven in the morning, we were booted, jacketed, hatted, gloved, and thermosed, ready for the approach to Ambrose's farmhouse, several hundred metres away, and ready also for as long a wait as necessary until we knew he was at home, and were reasonably certain where he was in the house.

The day was ideal for what we had in mind. The sky was heavily overcast and only a thin grey light seeped through. Heavy mist hugged the ground, murmuring its early winter lullaby, and limiting visibility to not more than a quarter mile. There was no wind. The temperature was a few degrees above freezing. All this only mirrored my apprehension on what we were undertaking, but I had resolved to shove my concern as far out of consciousness as possible.

Stuart carried a backpack that contained a selection of his toys. "We don't know anything about Ambrose, not really", he said. "Maybe he feels entirely secure here and has nothing to check whether his perimeter is being penetrated. Or, maybe he's a complete paranoid and the place is bristling in sensors. Rather than guess, we'll check." Which we did, and found nothing.

We had moved up to a pair of fir trees, about a hundred metres from the house. I scanned the house using Stuart's binoculars. From this distance, everything was visible, although still a bit hazy, partly shrouded in mist. "One car. No lights in the house that I can see. No outside propane tank that I can see. Possibly he uses wood for heat." The house was a practical but unimaginative structure, a squat, two-storey affair, wood frame, at one time painted white but now showing large, grey, patches of overseasoned wood where the paint had peeled, blistered, or just conceded its battle against the elements. On the ground floor, we could see two windows, draped in the sad modesty of grey lace curtains, old and dusty and carelessly drawn, on each of the two sides of the house that were facing us. At the west side of the house, there were two wooden recliner chairs placed on a sort of veranda that seemed to be a concrete or stone pad, cracked and uneven, protected by a sloping roof supported at its outward end on four fieldstone pillars. The house sat on what looked to be about four acres separated from the surrounding land on three sides by a wire fence and facing a gravel road on the fourth. On the southern approach to the house, there was a large knot of hawthorn bushes on our side of the fence, and about eighty metres from the house. We decided to move to that spot and wait. On the other side of the fence, between the hawthorn clump and the house, four large old lilac bushes sat stripped for the winter, testimony to a long gone yearning on someone's part for a little beauty and delicacy. These bushes formed a line, the bush nearest the house being about ten metres from it. If we moved up to the lilac shrub closest to us, then angled our way carefully to the left, we would be facing the southwest corner of the house and, because of the narrow angle, have the least exposure to a sightline through any of the windows. We completed the riskiest part of our advance, crossing the fence, and settled prone behind the lilac bush furthest from the house.

Just in time, too, because almost immediately someone appeared from the rear of the house and made his way to a small outbuilding. "Ambrose", I whispered, my eyes fixed to the binoculars. He reappeared from the outbuilding a few seconds later. "He's carrying an armful of wood."

Ambrose went back into the house. About thirty seconds later, wisps of smoke began to rise from the chimney. Evidently he was setting a fire in a stove or fireplace, probably a stove. Stuart and I both guessed that the stove would be in the kitchen, and that this was probably at the rear of the house, close to what we now saw must be the woodshed. If this were the case, as long as Ambrose was busy in the kitchen, likely he would have no view through the two windows closest to the corner of the house we were facing.

There were clumps of tall grass close to our chosen corner of the house. Stuart slipped off the backpack, and I placed the binoculars in it. We made our move, and we flattened ourselves behind the grass clumps. From that location, we could just see the entrance to the woodshed, and a few minutes later Ambrose made another trip there. Once he had disappeared into the woodshed, we sprinted the last few metres to the house and stood at either side of the front door, where we were not visible at all from inside the house. We were now close enough to hear telltale sounds. We heard Ambrose re-enter the house, and heard the back door close, not too loudly, but probably on a spring. We heard the clatter of wood being dropped. We heard clanking sounds, stovetop lids being removed and replaced as Ambrose fed the fire inside. We heard water splashing, possibly Ambrose doing primitive ablutions in a small sink or basin. There was a sneeze. Then, nothing for a while. Stuart and I looked at each other intently. Had he gone back out the back door, for some reason? Did he have any reason to come around to this side of the house from the outside, and if so, from which direction? His car sat just to my right at the end of a weed-infested gravelled lane, of sorts, leading from the road. Looking at the ground nearby, it was evident that somebody, at some time, had entered the house through the door we now flanked, but it was impossible to conclude that this was the preferred, or even the most likely way.

Then there was a sound of a plate or bowl being removed, probably from a pile of other plates or bowls. We heard a spoon clinking in a mug. Coffee or tea being stirred? Breakfast being made? There was a soft clunk. Stuart and I looked at each other. It occurred to me unexpectedly, and I mouthed to Stuart, "toaster." There were sounds of cutlery being used. There was a belch. Then nothing for a few more minutes until we heard rather heavy steps becoming louder. A lock was turned, and the door between us swung open.

At a speed I didn't expect, Stuart grabbed Ambrose by the front of his shirt, slammed him against a veranda post, then swung him around hard against the wall of the house. Ambrose struggled and attempted to break free, but a quick blow to the solar plexus put an end to that. I held the door, Stuart frog-marched a gasping, unco-ordinated Ambrose back inside, and into a sturdy Mennonite kitchen chair, against the wall, wrists being bound to the chair arms using lengths of rope that dangled from loops on the outside of Stuart's backpack. All this took less than ten seconds.

Ambrose was clearly still in pain. He looked at us venomously. Stuart did a quick search and pulled a cellphone and a set of keys from Ambrose's pockets.

"Who the fuck are you? What are you doing in my house?"

"You're saying you don't know who this is?" Stuart asked casually, inclining his head toward me, and removing his gloves.

"No. Why should I?" Ambrose barked defiantly.

"Liar!" Stuart said softly, and delivered a hard, open-handed slap across Ambrose's face. Ambrose uttered something between a roar and a groan.

"You know very well who this is", Stuart shouted. "You've been spying on him for weeks."

Ambrose worked his mouth experimentally. A trickle of blood appeared at one corner of it. He looked back and forth between us.

"You guys are in deep shit. You can't just break into my house and assault me."

"No? Well, you can't go around bugging people. You can't murder young men. So I guess we're just evening up the score a little."

"I never—"

"Spare me the bullshit!" Stuart roared. "I'm about an inch from proving that you were behind the murder of Buck Filmore. I know your connections to Jimmy Kralik and Davie McCrae. Your link to Constable, or rather ex-Constable Harrison. When I turn all this over to the police, you, my arrogant friend, will be done like fucking dinner."

As the names were rhymed off, a faint hint of fear shimmered across Ambrose's face.

"But that's a matter between you and the police. We're here about something else today. You're going to tell us what you've been looking for."

"I don't know what you're talking about", Ambrose said, perhaps a little less confidently. He had barely finished this statement before two more hard slaps across the face were delivered. His head lolled a bit, and he had trouble focusing for a few seconds.

"I predict, Mr. Joris Ambrose, that your face and teeth will give out before my hand does. But that's up to you. Now, I'll ask again. What have you been looking for?"

"I'm looking for what's mine."

"Okay. That's a start. And what is this thing that you claim is yours?"

"I don't need to explain myself to you."

Another vicious slap across the face.

"You didn't think", Stuart began, "that you were just going to be able to continue snooping and spying and attempting break-ins, and nobody would react, did you? Surely you're not *that* stupid."

Ambrose worked his mouth a bit more.

"Let me tell *you* a few things then. I know that your grandfather owned the mill in Greenvale at one time, but abandoned it. I know that your father died of a heart attack under circumstances that were pretty odd. I know that you lived in the Belleville area for a few months under the name of Robert Ames, and that you did a peculiar bit of work for Reverend Carswell. I know that you hired Davie McCrae because he told me so himself. And I'm pretty sure that whatever you're after is more significant than Auntie Vera's antique china soup tureen. So, tell me what you're looking for. If we have it, then we can come to some arrangement. If we don't, then you can go and look elsewhere and leave us in peace."

"Why should I tell you anything? You might just—"

"Just what, Ambrose? Might find it and sell it to someone else? If we had it, how do you know we haven't already sold it to somebody else? And to answer your question about why you should tell me anything, well, just look around. You're not in a good spot right now, and you're facing two guys who are completely fed up with your poor man's James Bond act. I'd say it was in your every interest to tell me what I want to know. You can refuse and get the shit kicked out of you a bit more. But an easier way for me to put a stop to all this is just to call the police and tell them where to come and get you, while I send in everything I have on your antics in an unmarked manila envelope."

"Go ahead. I'll tell them it was you who did this to me."

"Ah! I see. But you do realize, I hope, that the tip to the police won't come from me. It will come from a public telephone somewhere in Ontario. So nobody will be able to verify your absurd little accusation. And you think that because we've been the victims of your nonsense, that the police will automatically believe you? Think again, my friend. Nobody will find any evidence of us here. And you'll discover that we both have solid alibis for the time in question."

"We'll see ab—"

"What's that!" Stuart roared, and raised a hand again.

"Wait!" Ambrose said quickly.

After a short delay, Stuart said to me, "What do you think?"

"There's a much easier way", I replied, in a weary voice indicating that this was all a waste of time and I was tired of it. "It won't get us what we want, but at least it will get this prick permanently out of our hair."

"Oh? What?" Stuart asked conversationally.

"Well, accidents happen. Man falls asleep, wood stove or stovepipes overheat, man is overcome by smoke, house burns down, very sad but quite common when wood is used as fuel."

"You wouldn't", Ambrose said, but no longer so cocky.

I leaned over and glared at Ambrose. "All I have to do is remember Buck Filmore's face, and there's not much I wouldn't do to a piece of dog shit like you."

Stuart put on a nasty smile and began to nod. "Very neat. I like it. Gets rid of our problem. Saves police time. No loose ends. Very neat, indeed."

There was a hint of panic in Ambrose's face now. "Not as neat as you think. It wouldn't get rid of the other—" Then he stopped abruptly.

"Wouldn't get rid of the other what? What other? The other guy?"

Even though all his defiance was now gone, Ambrose sat there silently.

"What other?" Stuart repeated.

Silence.

Two more violent slaps across the face.

Head lolling, eyes half closed, Ambrose mumbled, "Burns."

"Burns? Particularly appropriate name under the circumstances, don't you think? Burns who? Tell me about Burns."

Ambrose began recovering from the last two blows. He looked from one to the other of us, worked his mouth, swallowed.

"You wouldn't get away with this", Ambrose said, in a voice that was not at all convincing or convinced. "They would find evidence of me being bound."

210

"Oh, no. Because we'll cut the bonds and remove the rope. And then you'd have your chance to escape. Right? Wrong. Because before I cut the bonds, and after we're sure we have a good fire roaring, I'll put a sleeper hold on you to guarantee that you'll be out for at least fifteen minutes, even though it's more humane than you deserve. So you'll be done even more like dinner."

Stuart paused, evidently pleased by his own extended metaphorical performance, but appearing to think the thing through. "Okay", he said to me, "go get a couple of large armsful of wood."

I started resolutely toward the kitchen door.

"No, wait", Ambrose said in alarm. There was a long pause then. "I'll tell you."

And he did. It took almost fifty minutes, and a bit more coaxing, but he confirmed that events were close to what we had surmised. He confirmed that there were two books at the centre of it all. He confirmed, in response to vague questioning, that notes prepared by Robert Bine had started his grandfather on the search decades ago. He confirmed that he, Joris, had finally found the books in Carswell's church, that his father subsequently had hidden them somewhere when Burns was breathing down their necks, but that then the old man died. He was afraid that Burns had got the hiding place out of Ambrose Senior, but when nothing changed he concluded that this didn't happen. He confirmed that he and his father had been working on behalf of someone else, but apparently he thought he could stiff this someone else and skip out with the loot at the last minute.

Finally, although there were plenty of questions, there were only a few loose ends that Ambrose was likely to be able to tie off.

"Tell me about Jimmy Kralik. Why did you kill him?"

Surprise in Ambrose's face. "I didn't kill him!"

"Was it Burns?"

"Must have been."

"Had you told Kralik the details of what he was trying to lift from this man's house?" Stuart asked, indicating me.

"Yes. A mistake. Burns probably pumped Jimmy dry, then finished him off."

"Okay. What are the details of these notes of Bine's that your grandfather found?"

"Grandad was something of an amateur historian. Spent a lot of time rooting around in local museums. I think that's how he came across it. I don't have any document, and I've never seen one."

"But there must be more to all this than just the two books", I said. "What else is involved?"

"I don't know. But Grandad referred to 'the big prize.' I don't know what he meant by that."

"Who is the guy you're working for?" Stuart asked.

"I know nothing about him. He uses the name 'Smith'. I don't ask because he pays."

"And what does he want you to do?"

"Deliver the books."

"That's it?"

"Yes. That's it."

"But you thought you might keep them for yourself."

"What would I want with some old books? No. I thought I could find someone else who would take them for a better price, or maybe Smith would pay me off."

"Dangerous game."

"Yes, but once you've gone beyond a certain point…"

"Where does Smith live?"

"In Europe."

"Big place. Where exactly?"

"In the Netherlands, I think."

"You think?"

"He gets in touch with me only by email. The messages come from Internet cafes, or something similar, and the country designation is usually NL. I've tried to track him down, but his messages always come from different places."

"So you have no idea at all?"

"No. I did have one telephone discussion, right at the beginning of all this. Might have been Smith. The voice was disguised. He talked about deadlines. He kept referring to speed and secrecy."

"How did he locate you?"

"He contacted my father originally, said we were distant relatives. As far as I'm concerned, it was just bullshit."

"But he was willing to pay."

"Yes. He paid."

Stuart looked at me. "Anything else?"

"No", I said. "I think that's it."

"Good", Stuart said, pulled the recording device out of his pocket, and switched it off.

"What's that?" Ambrose asked.

"I find that as I get older, my memory has become less reliable, so it's always good to have a verbatim recording." Stuart looked over at me. "Okay, get the wood."

"Hey, just a minute!" Ambrose said in alarm. "I told you what you wanted to know. I kept my side of the bargain."

Stuart looked at Ambrose, at me, and then at Ambrose again. "You've told us something, but for all I know it's just bullshit. Everything you've said has to be checked, before I believe a word of it. And as for a bargain." There was a short silence here. "Bargain?" Stuart said to me. "Do you recall anyone agreeing to a bargain?"

I shook my head and started for the kitchen door.

"Wait a minute! What do you want?"

I stopped. Stuart looked at Ambrose. "I can't think of anything you have that I want. Your problem is that you don't know enough to be useful, but you know too much to be harmless. You're a headache, a loose end, a liability. It's nothing personal. No. Wait. It's very personal. But either way, it doesn't really matter." Then to me, "Get the wood. No. On second thought, go check upstairs." In a few minutes, I was back. "He has a computer", I said, "and quite a few files in boxes, arranged so they can be packed and moved within a few minutes."

"All right", Stuart said. "Collect them all and take them out front. I'll call Bill once we're finished here and tell him to come and pick us up."

In less than five minutes, I had everything placed outside the front door.

"Okay", Stuart said. "*Now* go and get the wood."

As I approached the back door, Ambrose had begun to shout "No!" and to thrash about in the chair, trying futilely to loosen his bonds. Stuart approached him, dragged the chair away from the wall, and placed hands and arms carefully about Ambrose's face and neck.

I waited outside for thirty seconds, then came back in. Ambrose was unconscious.

"You go and get the car", Stuart said, handing me his keys. "If chummy here resurfaces, I'll put him under again. Once we're gone, it will probably take Ambrose only about fifteen or twenty minutes to free himself. But I have his cellphone, and in a minute he'll have no land line. I also have his car keys, but we'll disable his car just in case he knows how to hot-wire it."

I started back across the fields to get Stuart's car, while Stuart unlocked Ambrose's car, released the hood, and went to work using a knife he had taken from his backpack. I had Stuart's car in front of Ambrose's house in about five minutes. We loaded the computer and papers, and drove off. A cold rain had begun to fall.

"Do you believe him?" I asked Stuart.

"Yes. Most of it. But something's not right."

"What?" I asked.

"Considering what's happened, he's not enough of a hard-ass to be up to the violence. He tries to put on the right act, but I'm not convinced."

"So, what's going on?"

A delay here. "I'm not sure", Stuart responded. "I need to look at the details of his answers, but I have a suspicion that he's being played."

"Burns?"

"Could be", Stuart replied.

We rode in silence for another ten minutes.

"All this really makes me nervous", I said, looking straight ahead.

"It makes me more than nervous", Stuart said. "It's all very distasteful. It makes me no better than the scum I have to deal with. But, sometimes there's no other way. Soon, though, I think we'll be able to neutralize Ambrose." Seeing my sharp look at him, Stuart elaborated, "I mean we'll be able to take him out of the game permanently without touching him."

"How?"

"We get at him through Smith, and with a bit of luck we can neutralize Smith as well."

We rode in silence for quite a long time. As we approached Greenvale, I asked, "Who's Bill?"

"Bill is a wild goose."

Thirty-six

In our so-called modern world, magic doesn't get a fair deal. It's all around us, but far too few people see it. We become so used to dressing everything up in explanations, invoking physical rationales and mechanisms for why a thing is what it is or does what it does, that we no longer realize what we're actually doing. In the process, we lose sight of the fact that the explanations themselves, in their turn, can just paper over, provide an artificial coating to, or even misrepresent or mask completely, the underlying numinous reality, something we can be pretty sure is there, but cannot ever really know despite what we think our explanations tell us. We live within a fabulous kaleidoscopic world that we understand in a way that's stunningly metaphorical, yet too many people think of metaphor, if they give it any consideration at all, as just a quaint literary device, irrelevant to the real modern-day job of working, taking holidays, and discussing weather and sports. If I bump something and it falls to the floor, that happens because of gravity, of course. But then the explanatory responsibility is just shifted one step forward to the something we call "gravity." There is no question that when we postulate things like "gravity" and the postulates turn out to have some quantitative substance, we do make intellectual headway, but often we are simply shifting to a more refined metaphor, and not, as we might think, coming up with anything final or absolute. Then there is time, the "familiar stranger" as Fraser has characterized it, and its role in ordering the events of our lives. We look back at a time series of past events, and we find it easy to construct a conveniently unique rationale for why that particular path was followed, without recognizing the narrative fallacy we have thereby fallen into, and how that fallacy impoverishes our view of the immense number of possibilities inherent in the world.

Those engaged in blinkered activity, or as Russell saw it, focused on the job of rearranging matter at or near the earth's surface, might not see it this way. But anyone interested in something more fundamental will embrace willingly the breathtaking scientific advances we have made, while at the same time remembering to engage in the serious business of wondering. That person, the wonderer, is quickly led back on a parallel path through a long chain of thinkers all the way to Plato, Aristotle, Parmenides, Anaximander, Thales, Pythagoras, and Zeno. At least some of the confusion those venerable gentlemen wrestled with becomes understandable, at least some of their insight and foresight becomes admirable in its audacity, at least some of their wonder becomes something to share. Learning to live in some comfort with the uncertainty and confusion all of us always face, whether we want to acknowledge that condition or not, is a humble strength to be acquired.

An Uncompromising Place

An airplane leaves the ground, in Toronto in my case, familiar objects fade to a blur as we climb away, then are obscured completely by clouds, those meteorological, metaphorical, and mythical entities. In this instance, as the clouds part eight hours later, we are circling Frankfurt—magically—and I can imagine, and soon am able to see, half-timbered houses, fields and villages that have their own stories to tell, and in general speak of a distinct and present destiny that emerged, following a unique path, along a historical course very different from the one I just left. I discuss this with few people because the resulting blank looks are too often as hard and accusatory as stone walls. There is puzzlement, dumbfoundedness, incomprehension, because to many people there's no difficulty, it's all just geodesy and aeronautics and history, so what's to explain? And they look at me as though I have just grown a second head, or suddenly had the contents of the first one drained. Probably by an alien.

These thoughts reminded me where a larger part of my interests really lay, that I should not allow the world of waterwheels, flour, and the intrigues they had invited, to claim too large a piece of my mental universe.

We land, park at the gate, and soon (this is Frankfurt, after all) I'm at the baggage carousel waiting for my luggage. My few hours of savouring metaphysical disconnection are over.

After Stuart and I left Ambrose, Stuart dropped me at my place, I transcribed the sections of the recording that were of use, and then wiped the memory completely and permanently clean following Stuart's instructions. I then had a much-needed shower, more to remove psychological contagion than physical grime, went pretty much straight to the mill, and did a complete and thorough rundown on every part of the grain milling operation. It was with a good deal of pleasure that I found equipment operating exactly as intended, production on schedule, customers talking and gesticulating in the coffee shop, and, most of all, animated and enthusiastic staff. After all that, and since I was feeling in the mood, I announced to the coffee shop crowd that I was about to make some bread, and would consider any requests. A cacophonic response ensued, through which requests for pretty much every type of bread on my repertoire were shouted out. I opted for cheese bread and Greek boule with red onion and olives. After the sordidness of the morning, to do something as civilized as make bread in my own kitchen was like deliverance from a nightmare. The feel of the extra old cheese as it was being grated, the texture of the dough as I mixed it—getting the water content just right—and then kneaded it (having passed on the big mixer and dough hook), the heavy, rich fragrance emerging from the cheese bread dough as it was rising, the captured sunshine odour of the olives as they were pitted and chopped, the staccato crunch of the onion being sliced and then the roller coaster olfactory ride as it passed all the stations along the route to caramelization, the delicate grassy tang of chopped parsley, the satisfying sight of fully risen loaves sitting in a row, the increasingly strong waft of dough becoming bread, and then the triumphant moment when fully tanned loaves of bread emerged from the ovens, responding in just the correct tympanic note when their bottoms were tapped. Karen carried the first of the loaves into the coffee shop almost before they had cooled enough to be cut, and a cheer went up, the kind of cheer one feels might precede a riot. I joined them all for a slice of each, and watched as several people avidly set the stage for what was sure to be later indigestion.

Stuart had headed straight to Toronto where he handed off the computer for one of his geeks to gut, and spent some time going through the files, all of which he scanned and most of which he then shredded and burned. Two days later, he was back in Greenvale. A check with Raymond on whether there was any progress he could report brought back a curt "No", but no questions on our whereabouts or activities arose, and there were no suspicious looks. Stuart didn't tell me one way or the other, but I would bet that he had one of his guys watch Ambrose practically from the time we left him. We concluded that Ambrose was rattled enough not to try anything stupid.

This flow of thoughts—pleasant, not so pleasant, and indeterminate—was pinched off as I noticed my navy blue bag, hugged by its rainbow strap, slide down onto the luggage carousel. Grabbing the bag, and reflexively feeling the stubble on my chin, I headed through the green Nothing to Declare gate and into the airport concourse.

A hand gripped me strongly just above the elbow of the arm not dragging the case. "*Kommen Sie mit uns bitte, mein Herr. Keine Unruhe.*" And then in heavily, comically accented English. "Come with us, Sir. Please don't make any troubles."

"Since when did they start letting second-rate hack scientists into the *polizei?*" I asked, without breaking stride and continuing to look straight ahead.

When I finally did turn to examine him, I saw, as expected, that the man beside me wore no uniform, and the blond hair streaked in white, high forehead, angular cheekbones, strong nose, and bright blue eyes were unmistakeable.

"*Werner, Du blödes Arschloch!*" I boomed in a North American cellphone voice. "*Wie lang bist Du aus dem Gefängnis?*"

This brought a number of disapproving looks, whether because of the unpleasant swear word, the unsocial volume, or the alarm at being so close to a recently released felon, I wasn't sure.

We faced each other and exchanged a rough hug. "*Herzlich wilkommen in Deutschland!* Come. This way", Werner said. "I have my car."

Werner and I chatted amiably as we walked toward the parking area, Werner popped a couple of coins into the *Automat*, and we were soon in his BMW. In ten minutes we were clear of the airport area, and heading off toward Königstein. It was a clear cool late autumn morning. The air was full of the smells of fields, forests, and orchards settling down for the winter.

"Good flight?"

"Uneventful, as it should be, but packed."

"You have to tell me all about your retirement adventures. The pictures you sent look, well, unlike you. I can't imagine you owning a working mill."

"Lots of time for that", I said, "but I also have something important to do here in Germany."

"Well!" Werner said with enthusiasm. "How about some breakfast? I know how much you dislike airline meals. You probably haven't eaten since yesterday afternoon."

"As long as it's not pancakes and maple syrup."

"*Ach Nein! Du Trottel! Ein schönes deutsche Frühstuck! Was sonst?*"

"*Mit Bier und Wurst und Speck und Spiegeleier und Bratkartoffeln?*" I suggested.

"Yes, with beer and sausage and bacon and fried eggs and pan fried potatoes."

"Doesn't sound half as good in English."

A natural pause occurred while I watched the heavily wooded hills roll past.

"How's work you old *Gauner*?" I asked.

"*Gauner? Was soll das heissen?* You cut me to the fast, Richard!"

"Quick", I corrected.

"Quick what?"

"It should be 'you cut me to the quick'."

"*Scheisse!*"

"Don't worry", I said in bright encouragement. "Even though you're not an Otto Jespersen just yet, you're coming along nicely. How's work?"

"I'm where you were two years ago, Richard. But next year, in fifteen months to be exact, I will be in pension, er, in retirement."

"Why not now?"

"A number of reasons…"

"Of course. There always are. But why not now?"

After a pause, Werner continued. "In fifteen months, Gudrun will retire. She wants to sculpt full time. Can't wait."

"How is Gudrun?" I asked quickly, looking forward to seeing her again.

"Fine, but she's hiking in the Alps with two friends, back in two weeks. Came up at the last minute. She hesitated, wanted to see you, but I told her to go. We'll talk to her on Skype tonight."

"And what will *you* do when you retire?" I asked.

"Sketch", Werner said, but oddly without much enthusiasm.

And I remembered his work. "Sketch" came nowhere close to describing it. Almost all pencil or charcoal. There were winter scenes, leafless trees, stark and still against steel-grey skies, having just the right hint of that compulsive urge to insanity that can come over one at midnight on the Baltic. Or forests and meadows, portrayed in greys, but still bursting in implied colour. Or birds, rendered in fantastic detail, down almost to individual feathers. Or still life, fruit having indeterminate outlines, huddled together in vague delight and shimmering in a flood of sunlight. Or surrealist views of water: stagnant ponds, flowing streams, puddles, small waterfalls, reflecting water's myriad moods. Or drawings of old industrial sites, like the *Völklinger Hütte*, full of power, focus, and purpose, even though frozen in death.

"Do you have a project?" I inquired.

"Two, in fact. One, to draw whatever strikes my interest. Two, to draw faces of old people. I want to be like Monet and his water garden."

"Well, if you wait twenty years, you can sketch me."

"No, you're ready now", Werner said in perfect deadpan. "Might even be a bit late."

I smiled an inward touché. "How's work?"

"Good", Werner said, somewhat ambiguously. "I enjoy working, always have, a bit like you. But too often I'm doing again the same thing I did last year or five years ago. I've started letting go already. And you know what happens when you get into that, that, *wie heisst es, Verfassung?*"

"Frame of mind."

"Yes! *Scheisse!*"

"Yes, I know what happens. You can't let go fast enough."

I had been to Werner's place several times before, mostly straight there from the airport, but this time we had taken a route that I didn't recognize. Impossibly lovely villages flitted past every few kilometres. The smell of wood smoke was noticeable every now and then. The steep roofs, the solid house structures, the Fraktur script on the buildings, triggered fond memories and made me smile.

Werner made a sharp turn to the left, we descended a hill along a narrow lane, the landscape opened onto the plain of a river which I assumed was the Main, and about half a kilometre along we pulled into the parking area of a *gasthaus*. The name *Gegen Alles* was emblazoned across the front in gold lettering.

"Interesting", I said, unbuckling my seat belt. "I haven't been here before."

"No. It opened only a year and a half ago. It's owned by a chap who used to pilot barges up and down the Main, got tired of that, had some cash, and decided to open a *gasthaus*. Although it's actually a *wirtshaus*. He couldn't give up the barges entirely, so he picked a place on the river where he can at least watch them. Good beer garden at the back overlooking the river, the food is *gut hessische Küche*, the wine's exceptional, and I've been here often enough that Gerhard now knows me pretty well."

"Well, why are we wasting time sitting here gabbing?"

Inside, the place had high ceilings, light tan walls wedged in place by dark muscular oak beams, a dark tile floor, and fresh corn dollies (or *Strohengeln*, as they call them in Germany) fixed to the walls in splayed fan patterns. A large *Kachelofen* squatted in one corner, like an ogre minus the attitude, ready to pump out sufficient heat to blast everyone from the place when it was fired up. Pictures of river scenes were hung on all the walls. Over the doorways, quotes from Goethe encouraged drinking and carousing. The wall and ceiling beams were decorated at their points of intersection by wood carvings of small game, and one almost expected Peter to enter any second followed by the hunters carrying the Wolf. The tables were massively constructed in heavy, age-darkened walnut, as were the chairs, everything looking a couple of hundred years old, or at least timeless. But the strongest impression, the one I probably relished most each time I came to Germany and on entering the first pub or restaurant, was that sharp, rich, aromatic, scent, elusive to definition, of German cooking in the air. It was neither bold nor refined, in the various ambiguous impressions, complimentary and insulting, that those terms could invite, and in fact the usual olfactory adjectives always failed miserably for me.

"*Herr Wirt!*" Werner shouted. "*Bist Du offen, oder ist heute Ruhetag nochmals!*"

"*Komme gleich! Reg Dich nicht so auf! Um Gottes Willen!*" And saying that, the owner made his placid way toward us.

"*So eine lange Warte!*" Werner complained. "*Es ist ganz möglich hier vor Durst zu sterben!* Gerhard, I would like to introduce a colleague from Canada, Richard Gould."

Gerhard's face cleared. "*Ah! Aus Kanada.* Then welcome to Germany. But I'm afraid my English is not good."

"*Danke!*" I began. "*Ich bin immer froh wieder in Deutschland zu sein, und ich glaube wir können uns sowieso ziemlich gut verstehen.*"

"*Um Gottes Willen!*" Gerhard exclaimed through a delighted smile, and asked how long I had lived in Germany. We eventually got everything straight, and Gerhard was happy and relieved not to have to abandon German. He asked me where I had learned German, and I explained the piecemeal way I had come to it, and apologized in advance for being rusty.

"*Aus der Übung? Um Gottes Willen! Du sprichst Deutsch viel besser als dieser Sau Preuss!*" waving a dismissive hand at Werner. The effect on Werner of being called a Prussian pig was predictable, and quickly brought on another exchange of guttural shots across the bows, until Gerhard turned to me suddenly and asked, "*Was möchtest Du essen Richard?*"

I ordered the works and a litre of Bitburger. Gerhard nodded approvingly, then turned to Werner wearing a barely tolerant scowl, saying that he supposed Werner would go for his usual cheapass two slices of day-old rye bread and a glass of warm tap water.

The mugs of beer arrived immediately, and the server said the food would be there "*gleich*".

"*So Herr Pensionär! Zum Wohl!*" Werner said, raising his glass. I nodded in acknowledgement and then dispatched a third of the beer. As good as her word, the server returned with our heaped plates of food.

Not a lot was said for the next few minutes. The owner came by asking if everything was in order, and our full mouths and hand signals indicated definitely yes.

I brought Werner up to date on my last year of work, the projects I undertook, the whole business of winding up a thirty-year career, and how I felt about it all now. He ran through some of the work he was busy on, and I had to say to myself that it all sounded rather flat and uninteresting.

"What's the other business you need to do while you're here?" Werner asked.

"I'm following leads from the sixteenth century", I said enigmatically. "I'll tell you all about it when we're at your place."

We finished breakfast, making it all but certain that the next meal would be at least seven or eight hours in the future, and then, somewhat unconventionally, I ordered a glass of local wine, which Werner countermanded immediately by an order for half a litre and two glasses. While we waited for the wine, we both stepped out into the garden. Tables and chairs were stacked at one side and covered by a tarpaulin. The vines that in summer would have enclosed the area from the sides and from above, and made it a private and verdant space, were now pruned back. Underfoot there were large rough terracotta tiles, and a brick wall about a metre high defined the sides of the terrace and its long dimension that faced the river. Rising above that wall along the sides were strong metal supports for the vines, and training wires extended across the top at a height of about two and a half metres. The river did its best to sparkle in the wan sunshine, and the engines of a receding barge thudded powerfully as it moved slowly upstream. The previous night's crop of fallen leaves murmured anxiously in one corner, as though to shelter each other from the inevitable broom and pan. Not for the first time, I was envious of the centuries of lived-in landscape, cultural accretion, and physical imprint that make Europe distinctively what it is.

During the rest of the way to Werner's place, I glided across that mental map where the unaccustomed regains its familiarity, where the response to a mass of digesting carbohydrate translates to a soft glow, and where a confused and frustrated circadian rhythm tries to impose a reality that is now over six thousand kilometres and six time zones distant. Werner's home sits on what used to be the edge of Königstein, on a largish plot of land that slopes downward toward the street. Two large beech trees stand in front of his house, and a giant sour cherry broods in one corner at the back. The house itself looks older than it is, and came into Werner's possession as the result of the previous owner's broken marriage. He has had quite a bit done to it to tone down the modern aspects and make it look a bit more like a traditional German country home. The pièce de résistance is the patio at the back: large, private, green, allowing shade at the height of summer and sun at other times. It is basically where Gudrun and Werner live for as much of the year as possible. After putting my things in "my" room, changing out of travel clothes, and having a quick wash, I went onto the patio to refresh my memory of it. It was still the oasis I remembered. Gudrun's multi-level herb garden had grown even larger, and although it was in end-of-season state, it was still prolific. The sounds of a civilized community going about its quiet life enclosed this space and filled the air around it.

"If you have things to do, Werner, I'm more than happy to be left here just to doze in the sun. A couple of hours napping now is the best way for me to get past jet lag. So, please, don't feel you need to entertain."

Werner put up token resistance but then said that, yes, there were a few things he should do, and he would be back by four o'clock. "We'll have sauerbraten tonight, so you can have as little or as much as you wish. Unless you'd prefer something else."

I signalled complete agreement to sauerbraten, and noticed that despite my still full stomach, my mouth watered all the same in anticipation.

Werner fussed a while, asking if I had everything I needed, if I knew where to find things, to feel free to help myself, and would have carried on if I hadn't ordered him to "*verschwind*".

After Werner had left, I took my computer out of my luggage, logged into his wireless connection, and sent an email to Stuart, saying that I had arrived safely, and that I would be in touch regularly.

Thirty-seven

That evening, we had our sauerbraten, homemade *käsespätzle*, a delicious mixed salad, and an excellent Riesling from Volkach. I couldn't resist sniffing repeatedly the sharp, but rich and complex essence rising from the thick cuts of sauerbraten. I didn't eat the *käsespätzle* so much as let my taste buds luxuriate in the surprisingly sophisticated taste and texture—a combination of simple noodle mix, paper-thin onion slices browned in a hint of oil, then the two mixed together and tossed in a hot pan, heated through and seared slightly, and finally strewn with grated Gruyère. All that plus the mountain-spring freshness of the eight-component salad, and the intense floral nose and perfect acid-ester-sugar balance of the Riesling had me wondering, yet again, at the unpopularity of German cuisine outside the Germanic countries. The meal ended—all too soon for me. We then settled into a long Skype conversation with Gudrun. We spoke of many things, but spent what I thought was a surprisingly short time on the topic of their son, Klaus. When I asked after him, Werner said "Klaus is Klaus", an ambiguous pronouncement that brought no rebuttal from Gudrun. "He's in Thailand now. Not sure just what he's doing. He finished university, but then was very restless. Worked for six months, but was unhappy and unsettled. Decided to do some travelling." There seemed to be a vague air of censure about what was seen to be his meandering life path.

"He's young", I said. "He has to make his way in a world that's very different from the one we faced when we were his age", but I stopped there, not wanting to be seen as offering gratuitous advice. We talked about that, and the discussion recovered its sunny aspect when we all relived our twenties. After more than an hour, Gudrun signed off reluctantly, but not before extracting a promise from me to visit again soon. Werner and I plunged into an even longer session going over pictures of the mill and the whole history behind how I became involved in it. This included a long grilling by Werner on how I approached and handled the retirement thing, something he was evidently in the process of getting his head around. Werner was fascinated by the photos showing the mill moving from a ruin to a working operation, and questioned me, one engineer to another, for almost half an hour on the design and construction of the water wheel. There were some brilliant stills from the big opening night, pictures of Karen, Michael, and Graham at work, smiles splitting their faces, shots of the kitchen and of fresh loaves just out of the oven, and a series of photos that made a virtual tour through the mill from receiving the grain to bagging the finished flour. Werner paused over the twenty or so photos of the various pieces of equipment in the mill, and I could see that he was deriving almost as much vicarious, and I thought envious, pleasure out of the mill as a design and construction project as I had done hands-on. Werner asked for high-resolution files for a number of Greg's stunning exterior shots so that he could produce and frame large prints.

"Something like this would be impossible here in Germany", Werner said, and there was more than a tinge of something in his voice that was not easy to define. "In the first place, there are few, if any, ruined mills to recover, and in the second place, one would never get permission to do this." I thought this was a bit overplayed, but said nothing. "Gudrun will strangle me when she realizes what she has missed."

"Not at all", I said. "We can easily arrange an online walk-through of all this when she's back here and I'm back in Canada." Werner hesitated a long time over several of Greg's stills. "Look", I said. "I can transfer electronic copies of these to you right now and you can have a few of them printed tomorrow. If you think that you still need high-resolution files to work from, we can do that later."

Werner then somehow contrived to embark on a long discussion of his work and his life, and I recognized the signs of someone trying to come to terms with a big change and at the same time get a lot of unruly ducks lined up. He had shown me Gudrun's workshop in a room generously supplied in windows at one end of their house, and it seemed clear that she was well ahead of him in the psychological business of changing boats. Her working space had that controlled confusion that speaks of intellectual ferment, energy, focus, and creativity. Stifling a yawn, I looked at my watch and could hardly believe that it was almost one thirty in the morning. We both headed off to bed.

Werner had booked some time off work, and the next two days flew past, despite my efforts to grab them en passant and slow them down a bit. Königstein is in prime walking country, and each day we did a walk of more than ten kilometres. It was easy to see why Werner looks so fit. Although it seemed like we were keeping up a good pace, we were continually passed on uphill stretches by hikers, men and women, who were a good fifteen years older than either of us, and who offered a pleasant, "*Morgen*", while showing no signs of either laboured breathing or a glistening brow. On both these days, lunch was soup and bread in a forest *Hütte* that would not have looked out of place in the seventeenth century. During my last full day with Werner, he baited his angling hook using a number of veiled questions about breadmaking, so we dug into Gudrun's recipes. I found a good-looking one for *Haselnussbrot* (hazelnut bread), we checked that Gudrun had all the other ingredients, bought some hazelnuts, and that evening I taught Werner how to make bread. Cut in thick slices, toasted under the grill, and coated generously in honey, I thought it was not bad, but Werner was bursting from proprietorial pride. During a lull in his bread panegyric, I asked if I could borrow his camera to go out first thing in the morning and get some pictures of his house, the neighbourhood, and views over Königstein.

The next morning was clear and still. I went out onto Werner's fantastic patio and took a dozen or so shots. I then moved around the corner of the house, zoomed in on the car parked out front using Werner's top-end telephoto lens, and took another dozen pictures of the car and its driver. A gateway at the rear of Werner's property led onto a path that rose to the crest of the hill behind his street, and from there I was able to take some very nice pictures looking over the central part of Königstein. Back in the house, I downloaded the pictures, deleted them from the memory card in Werner's camera, and emailed six pictures of the car and its driver to Stuart.

I think Werner was secretly grateful that I successfully argued against his driving me the following morning to the main railway station in Frankfurt. He took me instead to the local station where a good connection to Frankfurt was available. In the ticket hall, I purchased a single fare to Frankfurt. Rejoining Werner, I agreed to his suggestion to have a cup of coffee. There was a nice breakfast place that had some outdoor tables, and we took our coffee out there, making us the only ones braving the chill.

"Thank you so much for taking the trouble to visit, Richard. The next time you come, you must accompany Gudrun and me on a walk, perhaps through the Black Forest. And I look forward to seeing more pictures of your mill."

"I've enjoyed this visit very much, Werner. Not many of us manage to keep in touch for as long as you and I have. And if you come to or near Toronto at any time, let me know. I can meet you and whisk you both off for a visit in Greenvale."

Werner nodded and smiled, a bit sadly, I thought. Gudrun not being here, me leaving, his working life inexorably coming to an end, his effort to think his way into retirement not proceeding in the expected Teutonic synchrony, they all seemed to be weighing on him a little. We talked in a desultory way about our immediate plans. And then it was time. We returned our cups, and walked into the small station concourse. A firm handshake held longer than normal. Another strong hug to match the one on my arrival. Wishes to be well. Then Werner turned and walked decisively out the door toward his car. There was the usual letdown on parting from a good friend, but I realized that it was more that just that. I felt uncomfortable, ill at ease, apprehensive, and was unable to shake a sense of foreboding. This was so at odds with my usual feelings of elation at being able to sink once again into German culture that it left me irritated and despondent. But being honest with myself, I knew the reason. To remove danger from my life and from the lives of my friends, I had taken on a powerful enemy. Sooner or later, I would need to outflank Burns, outsmart him, strip him of all advantage. There was the possibility of a direct confrontation. There was the possibility that the only solution would be to take him out.

Never in my life had I considered physical violence against anyone. The mere thought left me shaken.

At Frankfurt, I bought a ticket onward to Heidelberg, picked up a copy of *Die Zeit*, and walked to the platform. The train would leave in about half an hour. Enough time to read and watch.

Thirty-eight

My university studies did not include a stint at Heidelberg, alas. But then, neither was I a resident student at Bologna, Oxford, Valladolid, or Toulouse. I used to rage inwardly, and it still irks me, that there is so much that could be learned, seen, done, experienced, yet my powers are so puny, and there is so little time, that I could never realize anything more than the tiniest sliver of this panoramic and glorious potential.

The train journey from Frankfurt to Heidelberg, or more generally along the Main and Rhine Valleys, was one I had done quite a few times, but it has never stopped being fresh for me. Now, in the late autumn, the air was almost like a vessel, filled to brimming by liquid sunlight. Ploughed fields, bare trees, and regiments of naked vines sailed past the carriage windows. A few cyclists were out, there were dogs walking muffled owners along paths through the fields, and the last flocks of birds wheeled above the sleeping land in preparation for the big journey south.

At Mannheim, a cold damp wind gusted down the platform as I waited the twenty-five minutes for the connection to Heidelberg. Only a handful of people were pacing slowly, waiting for the same train, and trying to keep the cold from seeping into their bones. Fragments of mist swept threateningly past office buildings that huddled and shivered in the chilly air, and crows cawed somewhere in the middle distance. This only heightened the sense of impending winter.

Stuart had been adamantly opposed to my making this trip, although he agreed that we were coming close to the key elements of the puzzle, that we were probably well ahead of Burns, and that, if we made the right moves, we had a good chance of shutting the matter down permanently.

"The risks are too great, Richard. We're dealing with determined criminals. They wouldn't have the least compunction about wiping you out. You, in contrast, have no field training, and couldn't protect yourself in any serious close combat encounter. The logic is there, but given the practicalities, the act itself would be madness."

"So give me the tools", I replied.

"Give you years or decades of capability and experience in a few days? That's like me asking you to turn me into an international expert on dormant faults before the end of next week."

"What's the alternative, Stuart? Sit around like meek arseholes and wait for someone else to be injured or killed? You know damn well that that's the *only* alternative, and it's just not acceptable."

"It's not the only alternative. You and I have gone through a number of variants—"

"Yes", I interrupted, "and we haven't found any way of operationalizing any of them. So, let's not pretend that there's some kind of magic pathway here."

Stuart's eyes were blazing and we were both breathing heavily in incipient anger. This was not what should be happening.

After a few seconds of cool-down, I began again, in a more level voice, banishing as much of the heat as I could. "This is what they want, Stuart. They want us frozen in inactivity. I know that it's risky. I know that they're ruthless bastards. I know that I might be an easy target. But they won't be expecting me to turn up suddenly in Germany, and we can try to arrange things so that they don't know about what I'm doing until it's too late. A wonderful young man had his life cut short for no reason except the avarice of some egomaniacal prick. I can't just sit around and do nothing. Which one of my other friends might be next? I can't just wait for something like that to happen. So, I'm asking you, please, help me find ways to make the risks of this venture as low as possible."

Stuart looked at me hard for a long moment, then rubbed his head angrily in frustration. "Okay. Okay. Against all my better judgment, we'll try to work out something. But can we do that this afternoon? I need a couple of hours to think it all through."

A *Deutsche Bahn* ICE ripped through the station, and shattered my reverie. I looked up at the platform indicator. Five minutes more until my connection arrived.

Elements of Stuart's advice, which I had stored in my laptop and printed out, came back to me.

Stay alert! Be entirely, all the time, right in the moment.

Make mental notes of everything (people, cars, sounds, odours). Your brain should hurt from the effort. Recall regularly the mental lists you made a half-hour ago, that morning, the day before. Compare them to what is in front of you now.

Run through, at least once a day, the list of people's telltale actions that we developed, and look for them in those around you.

Be aware of options for action, yours and the other guy's. Don't forget that women are physical adversaries. Treat them as such.

Be on the lookout, everywhere, for things you could use (or that could be used on you) as a weapon: a chair, any tool or metal object, a part of any item of furniture or any loose piece of wood, a pen, a spray can, anything breakable, a wall plug, hot liquid (or irritating liquid, like vinegar), anything substantial (a brick, a stone, a glass jar), anything hard having sharp corners. Be especially aware of anything that might be a threat to your eyes, your ears, or your gonads.

Be aware of the space you're in. Make sure you know all the entrances and exits, be familiar with all areas within the space (including up and down), and never assume that there is nothing behind a door or around a corner. Determine how you (or someone else) could take control of the space. Be aware of any reflective surface. It can be an advantage or a risk.

Know your state of fear or anxiety. When you find real fear or anxiety in yourself, do exercises to logic over top of it.

Assess the psychology of any situation.

227

Relax and empty your mind whenever you have the opportunity, but only for a specific period of time and only whenever it is safe to do so (for example, when you are able to lock yourself in your hotel room).

I hadn't believed Stuart, not entirely, when he had said that the amount of effort needed to focus closely for long periods is hard to imagine. Well, now I knew. Standing here on this platform, adrift in thought like an idiot, I had been every bit the sitting duck that Stuart had feared. Looking again along the platform, I took note of the people. An elderly couple (late seventies, both stooped, white hair, the man having a tremor in his left hand, the woman carrying a cane) was consulting the carriage indicator. Two men in suits (one sandy hair, dark brown suit, grey coat, athletic, medium height, the other grey hair, tallish, overweight, charcoal suit, dark green coat) paced slowly. A woman and a young boy (she about forty, medium-length black hair, first streaks of white, square face, high cheekbones, he about five years old) sat eating sausage and bread rolls. A young man (about twenty-eight, cropped blond hair, jeans, blue sweatshirt), a backpack at his feet, was examining a copy of the *Frankfurter Allgemeine*. Thinking back to the station at Frankfurt, and further to the station near Königstein, I had noticed none of these people there. *How many carriages had there been on the ICE that had just roared through?* Didn't count. *Without looking, where is the train on the next platform coming from, going to, and when is it arriving?* Didn't know. *Come on Gould! Wake up!*

My mind went back (but this time under close supervision and without losing track of what was happening around me) to my discussions and sessions with Stuart. He walked through dozens of possible encounters and we made notes on them afterwards. We set up several scenarios on how things might go right, and then we produced perhaps forty variants on how they could go wrong, in some cases badly wrong. More notes. The sessions extended to cover days. Nerves became taut. I got things wrong. We went over it again. And again and again and again.

I complained.

Stuart dropped his pencil in frustration and concern. "Look, Richard. Your life could depend on this. Probably will, although I surely hope not. This stuff is hard, very hard, and getting it exactly right is much harder still, but hard as it is, it's even more important that you do get it right. We're not in some make-believe world here. It's not going to be a case of some"—and here he searched for an apt metaphor, eventually coming up with something silly—"some superhuman Henry Hudson who rows to the shore of his namesake bay, walks two thousand kilometres through bog and forest to a settlement, and eventually faces his mutineers back in London. Hudson died. That's what I don't want to happen to you. So please let's do this again."

My train was announced, and a few minutes later it entered the station. From the carriage indicator there would be six wagons plus the engine. As the carriages drifted past, I got an impression of how many people were on the train: first carriage, about twenty; second carriage, about ten; third carriage, about fifteen. The train stopped when the fourth carriage was in front of me, that being the carriage where my seat, number 68, was located. I glanced up and down the platform. Everybody waiting had moved up to the train. Nobody was looking at me.

The doors opened, I climbed aboard and found my seat, settled, and took out my copy of *Die Zeit*. Then I stopped and thought back. Had I missed something? "Think it through", I heard Stuart say inside my head. What young man, dressed as a student, reads the *Frankfurter Allgemeine*?

The train started off; it would be about fifteen minutes to Heidelberg. I was travelling fairly light, one smallish bag with wheels, but easy enough to carry if need be. Quite a bit of what I had brought with me was back at Werner's place.

I would be off the train first and move quickly to some area in the station concourse where I could watch who did what, who met whom. The ridiculous hat was rolled up and stuffed into my coat pocket. At this time of year, and this time of day, traffic in Heidelberg station would be just about as light as it ever would be; few if any tourists, well away from any rush hour, not a weekend, nothing special about the day. Still, there would be people. I thought through again the request I had made to Werner when we were setting all this up. The interview, the visits to two professors, the tour of the Max Planck Institute for Nuclear Physics, the historical walking tour of the older parts of Heidelberg. All window dressing, but having good cover stories and arranged seriously through one of Werner's contacts. The brakes of the train shrieked as we came to a stop in Heidelberg *Hauptbahnhof*. I stepped off the train and immediately ducked behind a pile of freight sitting on pallets on the platform. The change took about five seconds.

I limped but moved quickly to a small place just opposite the tourist information office that was serving bread, coffee, and cakes. Just at the point where the station concourse connects to the platform area. I picked up a sunflower roll and a large napkin, ordered a large cup of coffee, and found a spot at a small table against the wall. My coat, which had been grey on the train, was tan now that I had reversed it. The large ridiculous hat was pulled down over my head and almost covered the heavy glasses through which I appeared to be reading the paper. In fact, there was just enough space between glasses and hat brim for me to see who passed from the platforms into the station concourse while I appeared to be engrossed in yet another journalistic account of the goings-on in Brussels. I felt unbelievably idiotic, but played the part anyway. I saw three of the seven people who had boarded the train in Mannheim pass into the station concourse and out toward the city. Two more went past. Then the second of the two men in suits strode by and outside, waving for a taxi. I took an awkward sip of my coffee, as though engrossed in what I was reading. The young man wearing his backpack walked just into the station concourse, stopped, and looked around. He was approached by an older man, bald on top, black fringe, large bags under his eyes, heavy set, and wearing a stylish black leather coat. They smiled at each other, shook hands, and walked off to stand chatting near one of the exits from the station.

There were a number of items in the paper that I really would have liked to read, but instead, I timed myself. About six or seven minutes to a page. A sip of coffee. Check my watch. Be unconcerned.

The two by the exit continued to chat but I noticed that both of them were scanning the station.

This little game went on for another twenty minutes or so. The two both looked at their watches, and did a slow circuit of the concourse. They passed within about ten metres of me, eventually returning to their spot next to the exit. A few minutes longer, and they both left the station after one last look around the concourse.

I stayed where I was. Half an hour passed. Then an hour. It was an effort to stay focused, but the strong coffee helped. After an hour and a quarter, I pretended to drain the last of the coffee from my cup, folded my paper, picked up my bag, and walked to the book stall just opposite one of the exits from the station and appeared to be examining trashy novels. I could see neither of the two who had been standing next to the exit. Picking a time when nobody was waiting for a taxi but there were several empty taxis parked, I strode out of the station, waved at the knot of taxi drivers, and climbed into the first taxi in the queue.

The driver hopped in, closed his door, and looked at me in his mirror.

"*Zur Max Planck Institut, Saupfercheckweg*", I instructed. The driver nodded and we set off. After we had cleared the area in front of the station, I pulled out a small pocket mirror and began dabbing at one eye using the corner of my handkerchief.

"*Allergien?*" the driver asked, glancing in his mirror.

"*Nein*", I said, my voice dripping in irritation. "*Augenwimper*", letting him know that I was trying to fish out an eyelash. He smiled in sympathy, nodded, and went back to his driving, while I mumbled to myself in frustration at not being able to remove the offending lash. Judging from what I could see in the mirror, it looked like there was nothing following us. After turning several corners, we began climbing toward the Max Planck Institut. Nothing was following. I mumbled "*Gott sei Dank*", and put away the mirror and handkerchief.

The Max Planck Institute for Nuclear Physics in Heidelberg is a group of low unassuming buildings, and the taxi wheeled up next to the front door.

"*Könnten Sie ein Paar Minuten hier warten? Ich komme gleich zurück.*" The driver nodded, I said "*Danke*", and climbed out. At the desk inside, I identified myself and asked to confirm the time for my appointment the next day, although I knew exactly when it was. The young woman tapped a few computer keys, and said that yes, it was in order, that I was expected at two thirty, but could I arrive at two fifteen to allow time for the security measures?

Back in the taxi, I asked the driver to take me to the *Hotel am Rathaus* in a small street off the Market Square. At this time of year, the hotels were typically less than half full, and soon I was flopped on the bed in my locked room ready for a nap that would set me up for the afternoon and evening.

At about three o'clock, I was out again as a tourist. There was a cold wind blowing up the Neckar, a condition that amply justified my being well-muffled and walking with my head down. I spent twenty minutes listening to the organist practise in the *Heiliggeistkirche* in the *Marktplatz*, strolled along the *Hauptstrasse*, stopped to enjoy a glass of wine at the *Palmbräugasse*, then carried on to the *Universitätsplatz* where I spent forty minutes in Lehmanns. Werner had ribbed me about my reading, saying that nobody he knew except me tried to read Thomas Mann and Hölderlin for pleasure, and that maybe I should try what normal Germans read. To counter my somewhat pouty objections, he suggested the *Krimis*, or police novels, by Wolfgang Burger, or those by Ursula Meyer. Lehmanns had a good selection, so I picked up two by each author, hoping to find things in them that I could use as the basis for a good argument with Werner. From Lehmanns, I headed toward the river, crossed over *Hauptstrasse*, yielded shamefully to a common bias and scowled in cultural offence at the Starbucks Coffee shop as I passed it, then returned through the *Altstadt* along *Untere Strasse*. I stopped for another glass of wine at *Café Knösel*, where I looked through the books I had bought and had to give grudging acknowledgement to the value of Werner's suggestions. I read the first few pages of Burger's *Heidelberger Requiem*, and found myself engrossed.

A stomach rumble prompted a reflex glance at my watch, and I was surprised to see that it was almost six thirty. I had had nothing to eat since breakfast, and planned on a reasonably early dinner, since I wanted to go over quite a bit of material in my hotel room that evening. Consulting my map, I decided on *Zum Roten Ochsen*, which was close to my hotel, planning to do a circuit of the *Kornmarkt* and a walk past the old *Akademie der Wissenschaften* on the way there. There was a decent scattering of people out and I adopted their strolling speed.

Zum Roten Ochsen is a genuine old Heidelberg institution, and outside the tourist season it is claimed back by the locals. As I walked through the door, I entered a pleasantly noisy fug and was guided to a table out of the way in one corner. *Zum Roten Ochsen* is essentially just two rooms: a main room that one enters from the street, and a second room off to the right that one stumbles into by descending a half-flight of steps. This lower room appeared to be where the locals collect, drink, and sing. The walls were dark panelling, and held many closely hung pictures, signed and unsigned, of visitors and guests going back decades. I had asked the hostess who seated me initially whether there was a picture of Fermor here, since he remembered this particular inn as a highlight of his walking trip through Germany in 1933, but it was clear that she didn't really know what I was talking about.

"*Guten Abend. Zum Essen? Trinken?*" I looked up to see a classic German maid: blond hair pulled back, brilliant blue eyes in an open face, fair skin, and late adolescent breasts pumped up by her traditional gathered décolleté top to a vision of fecundity.

"*Beides*", I managed to say, and ordered a glass of dry Riesling while she placed a menu in front of me, smiling unaffectedly, and saying she would be back in a few minutes. At the table next to me, toasts and the clink of beer glasses punctuated the background hum, and a wave of inviting food aromas swept over me as plates of schnitzel, *steltze*, and *saumagen* were delivered.

And then I did one of the things I enjoy doing most: I sat there, sipped my wine, waited for my food, and just soaked up the surroundings and the sounds of people living. An image of the mill's coffee shop fluttered behind my eyes, but it was out of place in the current setting and I tucked it away. People came and went in a slow, steady stream. To my relief, I recognized nobody in the room. My meal of pork loin arrived, brilliant blue eyes asked if I wanted another glass of wine, I said not at the moment, and I settled in to a slow enjoyment of the food. An older lady stopped at my table ten minutes later, asked if everything "*schmeckt*", to which I replied by a full-mouthed nod. She asked if I was a student, to which I said simply "*zu alt*" (too old). She barked a dismissive laugh, and said that then I must be studying German. "Always, but that's not why I'm here", I replied enigmatically in the most colloquial German I could manage. She said, "Ah, I see", complimented me on my German, and moved off to check on another table.

At just before eight o'clock, I stepped outside. There were still quite a few people about, but I walked quickly back the couple of hundred metres to my hotel, stopping twice to look around, check on who was nearby, and what they were doing. Back in my hotel room, I retrieved the thick sheaf of notes from the inside pocket of my case, settled at the desk, and began to work.

It was only prudent to assume that the other side knew I was in Germany, and that they were out there somewhere. It looked as though I had given them the slip at the station, but that would be little more than a temporary thing. They would pick up my trail again. They would probably take considerable pains to stay in the background. If they didn't expect to find out something from my presence here, then they wouldn't be here in the first place. So, it was our working assumption that they felt I might know something they didn't, that possibly I knew the location of the "big prize", which Burns might know about and was itching to get his hands on, and that they had to give me enough room to lead them to it. But the more I behaved like a tourist, and the more I pursued the image of someone working on a technical or historical field project and doing research in support of it that was unrelated to any of Burns's interests, the more they were likely to begin having second thoughts. The only thing I was reasonably sure of, in an oddly vague way, was who "they" were. "They" almost certainly would be exclusively local talent. They would have pictures of me. But I didn't expect to see Burns here, at least not until he thought we were in the endgame. He would be somewhere close, but would stay well out of sight. Despite the fact that we were in Germany, Burns still had the advantage, because of the resources he had available. Stuart's reservations about all this came back to me. For months now, Burns had been an ominous presence in my life, but from the time I realized that there was enough information to link him to Buck's death, my active hatred of Burns had been kindled.

After working on my notes for almost three hours, I put them all back into the file, replaced the file in my case, and went to bed. Tomorrow would be a busy day.

Thirty-nine

Breakfast was a buffet, the usual small German hotel affair: excellent, relaxed, and as voluminous as one wanted it to be. Since there was a good chance I wouldn't get lunch, I chowed down on scrambled eggs, sausages, cheese, cold meat, yogourt, and a bread roll, enough to carry me through the rest of what was likely to be a long but interesting day.

The first item on the list was to arrange a meeting with Heinz. Werner had given me Heinz's name "in case I wanted to have a friendly drink", said that he was an independent software troubleshooter who had made a name for himself and now was based in his hometown of Heidelberg but worked for clients all across Germany. I contacted Heinz by email, he replied almost immediately with enthusiasm and a complimentary reference to Werner, and we arranged to meet at noon at the *Reichskrone*. In the three and a half hours before that meeting, I headed off with my camera, visited Robert Bunsen's statue in front of the old chemistry faculty on *Hauptstrasse*, then made the longish walk to the *Bergfriedhof* to locate the graves of Bunsen, Carl Bosch, and Leo Königsberger. Too bad that Kirchhoff was not buried there as well. It was a cool but fine day, and the cemetery was quiet and pleasant. I located the graves without rush or trouble, took my photos, and then just wandered around for a bit. In all this time, I kept an eye out for anyone tailing me, following Stuart's tips. Nothing.

At eleven o'clock, I headed back into town, and arrived at the *Reichskrone* about fifteen minutes before noon. It was no trouble at all locating Heinz. Werner had said, "look for a youthful middle-aged man bursting in vitality", and there he was, sitting in a quiet corner of the pub. I smiled and he waved me over as he stood, his hand stretched out. He was about ten years younger than me, slightly taller, had short wavy brown hair, and looked disgustingly fit. I took a seat having a view of the pub entrance and most of the interior. Nobody came in immediately after me. Nobody appeared to be paying any attention to us. Two youngish men came in about ten minutes after me, but left shortly after that. It looked as though I wasn't being tailed.

"You must be Richard", he said in fluent but distinctively accented English. "Welcome to Heidelberg."

"You must be Heinz. Sounds like Boston. MIT?"

"Wow! Nobody has found me out quite that fast. Yes. I spent three years at MIT. But more to the point, what's your poison, Richard?"

"Ha! I haven't heard it called that too many times in Germany. Dry Riesling."

Heinz's wave was a cross between an enthusiastic request to join the party and a centurion's command, and the waiter hurried over. Drinks were ordered, and the waiter responded predictably to Heinz's twinkle. Twenty seconds later, two glasses of wine appeared before us.

"*Zum Wohl!*" I offered.

"*Zum Wohl!*" Heinz replied, "*und herzlich wilkommen in Deutschland*", quick sip of wine, "although I understand from Werner that you're no stranger here", Heinz continued in German.

I gave him a quick summary of how my links to Germany developed, he nodded while giving me some friendly but undisguised scrutiny, and then complimented me on my German. Rather than make self-deprecating noises, I just said that I hoped soon to be able to fool at least some Germans into thinking that I actually was German.

"Instead of 'soon' and 'some,' I would say 'now' and 'many' ", Heinz said giving an impressed nod. "But Werner was very vague about what you're doing here."

"Yes", I agreed. "He was vague because I didn't tell him much", and then I gave Heinz a quick sketch on chasing down details of sixteenth-century religious documents.

"A bit outside a chemical engineer's expertise, isn't it?"

"Far outside, but it's a long story I was dragged into that began in Canada and has links to here and the US. I hope I can sort it all out in the next week or so."

"Sounds deliciously cloak-and-dagger. How come shit like this never happens to me?"

"Believe me, this is shit you really would not want." I guess my emphasis gave more than a hint of a dark side, and we both sipped our wine while the conversation quietly changed gears.

I was fairly sure that Werner had indicated what else I would be doing in Heidelberg, and Heinz nodded understanding as I outlined my meeting at the Max Planck Institute that afternoon, and the interviews with two professors the next day.

"And you will actually be writing up stories based on those interviews?"

"Yes", I nodded. "I've always enjoyed writing, there are small electronic publications that were quite interested in the material I suggested based on some digging online, and having that as a reason to do the interviews adds extra interest."

We talked about his work for a few minutes, I ordered two more glasses of wine for us, and then I took the leap.

"Would it be too much to ask a small favour of you, Heinz? I know it sounds odd when I've known you less than half an hour, and feel free to say no."

"That depends on the favour. Will I need a gun and a cyanide pill?"

I outlined what I wanted.

"Schwetzingen! No problem at all. Tomorrow?" I nodded. "Agreed!"

We sipped our wine.

"Tell me about your mill", Heinz said with enthusiasm, catching me off guard. Seeing my reaction, Heinz chuckled and added, "Werner is dead jealous of you. I could hear it in his voice over the phone."

The postcard version took ten minutes.

"Wow! How cool is that? Do you have any pictures?"

I pulled out my tablet and soon had several choice shots for him to look at.

"You lucky bastard!" he said at length. "That wouldn't be possible here."

I asked Heinz about Heidelberg, and he gave me a five-minute rundown of his experience as a native son. "When my father died two years ago", he said in conclusion, "the family home came to me. I thought of selling it, but then reconsidered. I have good memories here, Heidelberg is pretty central, Angela loves it, and, hey, we have to live somewhere."

Heinz glanced surreptitiously at his watch.

"I'm sorry", I said. "I'm keeping you from something."

"No", he protested. "I'm thinking more about your appointment in thirty-five minutes."

We drained our glasses, and I beckoned the waiter and paid. Heinz gave me his card and said to call him about the details for the next day. "I've enjoyed this", he said over a firm handshake. "We need to do it again, but next time at my place."

And then he was gone, striding off in single-minded Germanic purpose. From my tablet, I sent an email to Werner saying that I had just had an interesting meeting and a drink with Heinz, thanking him for the introduction, and asking him a few questions.

Putting away my tablet, I walked down to *Neckarstaden*, found a taxi, and headed off to the Max Planck Institute.

Dr. Gert Eisenegger was short, slim, had longish white hair, and spoke in a surprisingly deep and resonant voice. Of course, I had looked up his background before leaving Toronto, and it was impressive. I took to him immediately.

It was clear that he had no real idea why I was there or what I wanted, so I handed him a sheet on my background while explaining what I hoped we could discuss over the next half-hour. He relaxed when it became clear that my German was as good as his English. He relaxed further, and visibly, when he saw the items on nuclear physics in my background, and even more when I began the discussion by explaining my interest in one of their current projects, at the same time displaying a reasonably deep understanding of the project. From that point, he was unstoppable, and if his enthusiasm was as infectious among his staff as it was for me, I could see why he was a group leader.

He didn't so much talk as deliver a polished and exciting seminar, passing me charts, plots, and photos at just the right times, as though he were saying, "And you can see from this slide that...." I took copious notes, but at forty-five minutes when I began to make time-to-wrap-it-up noises, Eisenegger passed me a plastic-bound glossy package covering everything he had talked about.

I thanked him generously, promised him a copy of the end product I would be producing, and collected my things.

"Please come back any time, Dr. Gould." There was then a slight pause. "Perhaps we can keep in touch", and he handed me several of his cards.

The young woman at the reception desk called me a taxi. We made one stop on the way, I selected bottles to make up a case of mixed good-quality French red wines, paid, and copied from Heinz's card the address I wanted the clerk to send it to. At quarter to four I was back in my hotel room.

My case was where I had left it on the luggage trestle, way off and out of the way in the corner of the room, but looking down behind it I could see the small plastic bead sitting on the grey floor carpet, instead of being nestled into the leather seam on the left-hand top corner of my case where I had placed it. Possibly it was the maid's doing, but I thought not. Someone other than the maid had been in my room. They had opened my case. So that meant they had gone through all my notes.

I wondered what they had thought about the fifty pages of material on Robert Bunsen photocopied from various sources, another sixty pages on Gustav Kirchhoff, a twenty-two page appreciation of the life of Leo Königsberger, and not a hint of anything on sixteenth-century religious documents.

I smiled.

But I knew that all this was just putting a brave face on things. Behind everything, behind the violence and sleaze that had descended on Greenvale, most of all behind Buck's death, was that bastard Burns, and increasingly I found myself willing to embrace any means to get him permanently out of my life and eliminate him as a threat to the people I cared about. Along with this, however, a deep, bright, hot desire was burning in me for revenge.

Forty

Schwetzingen Day.

After a leisurely breakfast, I packed my rucksack, repacked my case, pulled on my jacket and gloves, and walked into town. At the railway station, I dropped off my suitcase in left luggage, then went into the men's room and shut myself in one of the stalls. There was an entrance directly from the railway station to the bicycle rental shop, and I went in and picked up the bike that I had booked and paid for over the phone the previous evening. After adjusting the seat, checking the tires, making sure that I had tools and a tire repair kit, I wheeled the bike outside.

It was a pleasant day, the light diffuse but bright through a hazy sky. The blue and silver Lycra cycling outfit, the red and black helmet, and the wraparound sunglasses were only a partial disguise, but they would cause at least a temporary break in identification. I pulled on my backpack, hopped on the bike, and rode off. Leaving the station forecourt, I found the street leading in the direction of Schwetzingen. Traffic going into Heidelberg was heavy, but in the direction I was headed it was light. After about half a kilometre, I checked in the handlebar rear-view mirror, something I had specified when I ordered the bike. Traffic came up behind me, followed for a few moments, then passed when the opportunity arose, but at the moment there was a taxi, a Peugeot delivery van, a grey BMW, and a blue and black Mini behind me. After another kilometre, I checked again. Grey Mercedes, black Passat, red Opel. Another half kilometre: late model Renault, motorcycle, but the red Opel was still there. Not far to go now. A kilometre further: still the red Opel, hanging quite far back, but nothing else.

The road swung gradually to the left and I was in Pfaffengrund. Residential streets drifted past on both sides. Soon, I passed under the E 35, and signs to Eppelheim appeared. *Eppelheimerstrasse* was just ahead, but there was now a separate bicycle path to the right of the roadway. The road once again swung gently to the left. The bicycle path branched here. One branch followed *Eppelheimerstrasse*. The other carried on straight through a set of steel posts about three feet from each other and forming a barrier across the path, and followed a course across open fields. I took the open fields branch. In my mirror, I could see the red Opel come to a stop, wait a few seconds, then screech off further along *Eppelheimerstrasse*. About three kilometres ahead, the bicycle path would enter a beech wood, and I would be lost from sight to whoever was in the red Opel.

Some of the haze lifted. The sun came out and shone in wan approval. I smiled and cycled on unconcerned. But I didn't rely on them losing me. All along the way to Schwetzingen, they could track me, provided they had a good set of binoculars, provided they had a good map, and provided they kept their cool. Maybe they wouldn't meet one or more of those provisos. Well, in that case, tough luck. They'd just have to go back and report failure.

At a steady leisurely pace, it took me a little less than an hour to reach Schwetzingen. Cycling through the town, I found the *Schlossplatz*, located a small restaurant off to one side, and continued cycling around the *platz*, looking. I soon found what I was looking for, and at the same time, saw a red Opel pull hurriedly into the parking area to one side of the *Schloss* entrance. I dismounted, pushed the bike to within about ten metres of the restaurant, locked it to a bike rack, and went into the restaurant. I checked the menu board on the wall, then went through to the toilets at the back.

I had been in the men's loo about a minute when he walked in.

"Heinz! Good to see you again. How are tricks?"

"Tricks are fine, especially after I saw that case of wine you sent me. I have to insist that you take it back. It's too much."

"Now Heinz. You've already forfeited a morning, and it will probably take you, being German and an accomplished cyclist, another, oh, fifteen minutes to cycle back to Heidelberg. If anything, I owe you another case."

This banter carried on for another half-minute. "I'm sorry that you have to climb into my clammy cycling gear. But let's make the change."

I hesitated for a moment, and Heinz raised an eyebrow. "I have to tell you, Heinz, that I believe I was followed here. It's the red Opel parked across the *platz*. I don't want you to become involved in this crap any more than you are already, so I hope that you will be able to lose them on the way back if they decide to try to follow you."

Heinz was nodding and smiling. "Some of my clients are the most anal, secretive, and paranoid people on the planet. This little scene here pales into insignificance compared to what I sometimes have to do in my work for them. Stop worrying. My route back to Heidelberg will be so far from any road, and so obscured that not even a helicopter would be able to follow me. I've cycled all around this area for years. I know it better than the back of my hand. I will email you when I've returned, to report on any activity."

I nodded and thanked him, but was still concerned. "You realize that if they lose you they might just go and wait at the bike rental location."

"The company you rented from has four locations in Heidelberg. I can return the bike to any one of them. Or, I can call them from my home saying that the bike isn't working properly, and they'll come and pick it up. They won't be watching my place because they don't know who I am. Stop worrying. I'm not uncomfortable with any of this."

Ten minutes later, wearing blue and silver cycling clothing, a red and black helmet, wraparound sunglasses, and having his street clothes in my now otherwise empty rucksack that he was carrying on his back, Heinz unlocked the bicycle, climbed on, and headed back to Heidelberg. As I watched carefully through a window in the restaurant, I saw the red Opel pull out of its parking spot and follow. I gave it fifteen minutes, then stepped out of the restaurant.

In the second rucksack, which I now swung onto my back, and which had been carefully folded within the one now returning to Heidelberg with Heinz, I had three changes of clothes, my tablet, toilet kit, and one of Wolfgang Burger's books. So I was all set. The trip by local bus from Schwetzingen to Ladenburg, without going through Heidelberg, was long and a bit tedious, but a pleasant ride. Following our route as best I could on the most detailed local map I had been able to find in Heidelberg, I could tell when we were coming close to Ladenburg. It took some coaxing for the driver to let me off the bus in what seemed to be the middle of nowhere, and it was a good thing that he was carrying on from Ladenburg because he definitely wouldn't forget me. I stepped down onto the side of the road, the bus set off again toward Ladenburg, and I began walking. The day had become increasingly overcast during the past couple of hours and within fifteen minutes it began to drizzle.

Even though I had done some Internet searching earlier, and had located three possible places, it still took quite a long time to narrow it down to just what I was looking for: a small, isolated inn, *Gasthaus im Wald*, off the road and not far from the tiny settlement of Rosenhof. By then, I had been out in the rain for some time and I almost certainly looked bedraggled, although my high-tech rain gear made sure that the wet was all external.

Perhaps there had been a forest when the *gasthaus* was first built, but now it sat among just a dozen or so large beech trees in otherwise open fields. It was inviting in a basic sort of way, and there was a single car parked to one side of it, probably belonging to the owner.

From the outside, and as I found out later from the inside as well, *Gasthaus im Wald* had that timeless look that one becomes used to in Germany. It might have been built anywhere between fifty and two hundred years ago. It was a three-storey affair, had a set of what would probably be, in season, attractive flower gardens in front, and a large vegetable garden at the back complete with what looked like gardening outbuildings. A decorative porcelain sign on the door said *Knock and Enter*. My hesitant knock brought a "*Herein!*" from within, and I opened the door and stepped in. Inside, the entrance floor was stone flags, the walls looked like walnut heavily darkened by age, and a small counter that appeared to double as a bar was staffed by a plumpish woman who was peering down, through long but now faded blond hair, at the papers she was working on.

"Oh, you poor dear!" she said as she looked up and saw me.

"But certainly!" she replied to my query on whether she had a room available. "Let me show it to you straightaway. You must get out of those wet things without delay." Rather than protest, I took off my rain hat and jacket and hung them up on pegs above a space that looked like it was for muddy boots, while she continued to fuss and cluck solicitously that I should follow her. The place seemed to have four large guest rooms, numbered 2 to 5 for some reason, on the first floor, which would be the second floor were I back in Canada. She fussed a bit more but I said it all looked excellent and just what I needed. She repeated with emphasis that I had to change into something dry, and that when I had done that I should come down and have a restorative schnapps, this kind of thing being essential in Germany where the evil elements engendering colds, sickness, and worse, lurk under practically every bush.

Although my shirt had remained dry under the rain jacket, I changed it anyway to avoid another round of tutting and clucking. Descending to the ground floor, I found that Frau Rohde, as she had introduced herself, was in the small adjoining room pouring out two measures of peach schnapps. She waved me in, herded me to a seat, picked up her glass and intoned loudly *"Zum Wohl"*, presumably to strike fear into the hearts of the evil elements that were doubtless gathering for the kill. The schnapps really was excellent, genuine essence of peach rising to entice my nose as I lifted my glass in turn.

Frau Rohde turned out to be an accomplished conversationalist, and had soon extracted from me my name (shamefully, to me, not my real name), where I had started out from that morning, and what my interest was in these parts. I went into a short exposition on the Roman history of Ladenburg, saying that I was particularly interested in Emperor Vespasian and his times, and wanted to get some first-hand knowledge of Ladenburg, or Lopodunum, at the time when he was emperor. I added, in what I hoped was a conspiratorial tone, that others shared my interests and that those others would be fired by alarm and jealousy if they knew I was here doing serious study. She nodded knowingly, saying that my confidences were safe with her. She went on to say, however, and with a note of sadness, that very little residue from those times remained, but expressed great pride in Ladenburg's long and distinguished history, a local view that I was to learn was held rather fiercely. The unspoken but invidious comparison to the upstart Heidelberg hovered in the air until I recognized and validated her statement by my own hint that the time between now and the fourteenth century, the beginnings of Heidelberg's pre-eminence today, was just a surface flush compared to Ladenburg's far more substantial historical roots.

She flashed an approving smile and refilled our glasses. *"Sie sprechen aber ausgezeichnet Deutsch. Für ein Engländer."* I thanked her for the compliment on my German, and didn't bother to correct her assumption of my nationality. We chatted for another twenty minutes or so, during which time I learned that she and her husband had both been born in Cologne, that they had moved to Ladenburg many years ago when he took on his dream job at the Benz Automuseum, and that they had run this *gasthaus* as an aside. He, alas, had died suddenly four years back, but had left her financially secure. The *gasthaus* was almost a hobby, but was fairly busy in season and allowed her to meet a wide assortment of people very different from her friends and acquaintances in Ladenburg. Our glasses having been drained, Frau Rohde glanced at the mantel clock and asked me if I had plans for dinner later that evening, and if not she would be pleased if I could join her for *hirschgulasch*. I accepted quickly, saying how much I enjoyed *hirsch*, to which she gave me a large dimply smile, said we would eat at six thirty, collected the glasses and schnapps bottle, and bustled off.

Back in my room, and having two hours until dinner, I took out my tablet, was pleased to find that the access claimed by Frau Rohde did indeed exist, and once I had logged on, I saw immediately an email from Heinz.

"Uneventful journey", he wrote. "Woodlands beautiful this time of year. No sign of poisonous red flowers. Package delivered unobserved and subject remains incognito. Managed to take several photos of unhappy driver. Attached. Let's get together again when you are available."

Once I had stopped chortling, I sent a long email message to Stuart, summarizing my activities of the past few days, telling him where I was now, that my case and most of the things I had brought from Königstein were in a left luggage locker at the Heidelberg railway station, that I planned to do background reconnaissance for two days, and then begin the next phase of what I had to do in Ladenburg.

On the tablet were all the notes I had made over the past few months, running to several hundred pages now, but organized so that important individual items were easy to locate. I also had a picture gallery that included all the individuals we had photographed, plus pictures of Burns and Ambrose, as obtained by Stuart through some means. I reviewed, first, all the material I had on Ladenburg, then went over once more all the documents that had come to me via Mason, and the results obtained from the searching done by Stuart's hacker. Having not looked at it at all for a few days, I was prepared for the possibility that something new would pop out, but that didn't happen. There was nothing here to change my view of things, even though the same uncertainties remained. Despite all my work, and even if my basic presumptions were correct, I could not avoid the real possibility that I would be unable to locate what I wanted, that it would be there somewhere but beyond reach. Even more negatively, I could be completely wrong, that the whole business was just a chimera, that the "big prize" didn't actually exist, in which case all this would have been a waste of time but would still carry all the potential personal danger. But there was no point whatever in continually revisiting that particular chipped tooth.

I looked over my plan of action, what I would do two days hence. It must have been the thirtieth time I had done so, and still I could find nothing to add or change. Just after six o'clock, my time, a reply arrived from Stuart:

Send me the plate number of the red Opel. I'm looking at detailed maps of the area around Ladenburg. Please tell me specifically where you are now in relation to the buildings in Rosenhof. Also, please email me just before you leave to go to Ladenburg, and give me an idea how long you expect it to take to get there from where you are now.

Remember that a plan is based on a set of assumptions. The set might be incomplete. One or more of the assumptions might be wrong. Don't become blinkered by an expectation that things will go as you foresee. Try to work out why and how they might turn out otherwise, and what you will do in the event of each of those variants.

Burns's location is not known. My man has not seen him for three days in Philadelphia. Please be very, very, careful Richard.

I acknowledged receipt, since Stuart was obviously concerned. But then it was time for dinner, and the rich sauce of a *hirschgulasch* was something to banish any concern.

At least for a while.

Forty-one

It was evident from the moment I left my room that Frau Rohde ran a competent kitchen. The aromas gracing the air that rose to meet me were good enough indication. The table was set for two, a bottle of local dry Riesling had been opened, and on the side two cheeses were warming on a cheeseboard that they shared with a generous heap of walnut halves.

"Good evening, Herr Rowntree", Frau Rohde said cheerfully as she emerged from her kitchen carrying a plate of pâté and coarse-grained dark bread. "Please take a seat and help yourself to wine and pâté. I have one more thing to attend to and then I will join you", and she vanished back into her kitchen.

I poured wine for both of us, perhaps a bit presumptuously, and then spent a moment moving around the dining room to look at the pictures on the walls. They were an eclectic assortment, including what seemed to be family photos from two generations or more, and quite a few paintings: one of the attractive brick building housing the Benz Automuseum, one of a luxuriantly flowering fruit tree next to what I assumed was the Neckar, a rendering of *Gasthaus im Wald* at the height of summer, resting in a jigsaw of sun and shadow beneath the beech trees, and a brilliant, almost impressionistic view of the Alte Brücke in Heidelberg at sunset.

"They're all by my husband. It was his hobby for more than forty years." I turned quickly, not having heard her enter.

"They are superb", I said. "Did he sell many?"

"No. He gave away a few, but he wouldn't sell them. I never really knew why. You seem to know something about painting."

"No, not really. I used to do a lot of sketching and watercolour work, but that fell away once I began my professional life. Are there others hung elsewhere in the house?"

"A few", she answered. "Most of what he did is stored in the attic."

"How many?" I asked out of idle curiosity.

"More than five hundred."

"Good heavens!" I exclaimed, almost involuntarily.

"Yes. I'm not sure at all what to do with them. But come. Let's eat. We can discuss this later."

This considerable cache of art was something that Werner might well be interested in knowing about.

Despite the fact that we were separated by a slight linguistic barrier, because of my less-than-perfect German, and by a cultural difference of uncertain magnitude, and that we were almost completely unknown quantities to each other, the evening was a delightful and effortless social occasion. Frau Rohde was able to steer the discussion with great skill, demonstrated a sophisticated sense of humour, was not alarmed by an occasional silence, and had a remarkable grasp of German literature. She probed my own knowledge of German literature, seeming to be pleased at what she found, and asked some perceptive questions about English literature. She also expressed regrets about not pursuing more education herself, but put that down to the realities of a past time, place, and circumstance that she appeared to be seeing somewhere in the distance.

My concern over a possible mismatch between pâté and *hirschgulasch* turned out to be groundless. The pâté was light and delicate, and in no way capable of stealing the considerable gustatory thunder of the *gulasch*. Together with homemade *spätzle*, red cabbage, and homemade red currant jelly, it formed a meal that I was sorry to see end. We lingered over cheese, coffee, and schnapps until it seemed the right time for me to suggest that I had some work to do and should excuse myself and get on with it. Frau Rohde asked me a few practical questions about my schedule and I told her that I expected to be needing the room for three nights, including that night. In response to her next question, I said that, yes, I would be delighted to have evening meals. She said that if I wanted to use a bicycle, there were two in the garden shed, the key for which was on a peg next to the front door. I thanked her but said that tomorrow I would be walking. When I added that I wouldn't need breakfast in the morning and expected to be leaving early, we had a short animated discussion, but in the end she relented. She refused my offer to help clear the table, so I thanked her for a superb meal and bid her goodnight.

It was my hope that the rain would continue into the following day, since that would allow me to bundle up in rain gear to the point where I would be unrecognizable. My plan for the next day was to explore the outlying parts of Ladenburg, familiarize myself with the layout of the town, and ask around about local walking routes. I would also be looking for the red Opel, not that I expected to see it, and would be checking closely for any of the people I had come across over the past week, such as the watcher near Werner's place, the sandy-haired youth from Mannheim station, and the driver in Heinz's photos.

I worked until half-past midnight, reviewing Mason's material yet again, my plan for the next three days, and the collection of photos on my tablet of everybody I wanted to avoid but might come across. When I did turn in, the combination of *hirsch*, wine, and schnapps dropped me immediately into a deep sleep from which I emerged refreshed just before six o'clock.

After a quick wash and shave, I crept downstairs at about six fifteen. On the table in the hallway sat a small bag labelled "Herr Rowntree", It contained a boiled egg, a bread roll generously stuffed with meat, and a lump of cheese. So she had prevailed after all.

As I had hoped, the sky was heavily overcast and there was a steady drizzle. The waterproof laminated local map was tucked in my pocket, but I knew it practically by heart. From *Gasthaus im Wald*, I made my way along several hedgerows, across two fields along farm tracks, and joined the footpath beside a stream called the Kandelbach.

As I expected, there was nobody out in weather like this, which was why I was astonished when, fifteen minutes later, two cyclists whipped past me. It wasn't so much that they were cyclists, but that they were singing. And, finally, it was *what* they were singing: "Take Me Home, Country Roads". It occurred to me that John Denver and Gene Kelly made an odd pair. Overcoming this unexpected musical interruption, I continued following the Kandelbach footpath, and eventually walked along the streets once I entered Ladenburg. I soon reached the Neckar where the Kandelbach empties into it and then continued walking along its bank. There were few people out, due to the continuing drizzle. The postman was making his rounds, two workers were digging a hole in a nearby street, and a young man passed me walking a dog. I had stopped to look across the Neckar, and my gaze followed the boy and dog almost automatically. The boy was clearly not happy at being out in the rain. The dog, on the other hand, was enjoying the outing greatly, possibly just from the knowledge that the longer they stayed out, the less happy the boy would become. This odd notion of canine anthropomorphic sadism seemed to be confirmed when the dog stopped for a long sniff around the base of a concrete light standard.

The boy pulled on the leash. "*Komm!*" he said to the dog.

The dog continued its examination. After a few minutes, there was another tug at the leash. "*Komm!*"

But the dog wasn't ready to *Komm*. It extended its examination further up the pole.

There was a far more insistent pull on the leash this time. "*Komm Lucky! Du Scheisshund!*" Reluctantly, but displaying what I thought could only be a victory wag of its tail, the dog moved off.

I followed the bank of the Neckar to the railway bridge, along the railway line as far as the cemetery, then over to *Weinheimer Strasse*, and finally into the old town along the *Hauptstrasse*. I found a pleasant young man in the town hall who dug out a sheaf of walking maps for me, then I walked past the public library, where I noted the opening hours, and along *Kirchenstrasse* into the *Marktplatz*. Since it was market day, I was able to mingle and eat the lunch Frau Rohde had prepared. Although I had practically memorized the street map of Ladenburg, I now felt I had a better sense of what the place actually looked and felt like. From a seat in the nearby coffee house, I was able to observe my surroundings carefully. Everyone was protecting themselves in various ways from the continuing drizzle, but I recognized nobody.

Next stop was the Lobdengau-Museum, and I spent most of the afternoon there, circling back through areas I had already seen, and peering out every window I came across. Although the Jupiter Column caught my eye for a few moments, I was really here to look like, but not to be, an out-of-season tourist. At the end of two hours—the museum staff must have begun wondering what could be engaging me this long—I had convinced myself that nobody was following or watching me.

From the museum it was a short hop to the Carl Benz House, and that provided another hour of considerable interest. It appeared that I was the only visitor.

Moving now along the southern end of the old town, I approached the car park next to the Evangelical Church. It was highly unlikely that the red Opel would be there, but taking five minutes to check was no hardship. It was raining more heavily now, and people were hurrying, sheltering from the rain under umbrellas or newspapers, to and from cars. There were few cars in the car park, perhaps twenty-five. No red Opels. Walking through the grounds of the Evangelical Church, I approached the St. Gallus Church. This was by far the oldest church in Ladenburg, and would be my centre of interest. I did one fairly quick circuit of it, concentrating furiously to take in everything and at the same time make note of anybody in the grounds. There was nobody around. I tried the main door to the church, it yielded, and I passed quickly inside. My internal tour of the church took a bit more than twenty minutes, longer than I had intended, but through all that time I was intensely examining the floors, the walls, the chapels, the nave, the choir. I descended into the crypt, pulling out my flashlight when I neared the bottom of the steps and they began to vanish in the gloom. Thinking of the map of the church in the village, I oriented myself and began looking at all areas of the floor and the walls. The crypt isn't large, but when I wasn't seeing anything promising, I took another five minutes to go over the whole area a second time. I went back to the foot of the stairs, switched off my flashlight, climbed silently upwards, and looked carefully into the main body of the church. An elderly man was seated about two-thirds of the way back on the left side as I faced the entrance to the church. There was also a man carrying a camera. He was walking slowly along the aisle furthest from me and examining the ceiling and windows. I moved slowly back down the steps and into the gloom.

Ten minutes passed. I heard the door to the church open and close. I climbed the steps again, and took another careful peek into the church. The older man was no longer there. Suddenly, the man carrying the camera came into view. He was less than ten feet from me. I almost jumped out of my skin, but managed to slide back down the steps without making a sound.

Fifteen more minutes passed. The door to the church opened and closed again. Once more, I crept up the steps. The church was empty, but even so, I waited another few minutes at the top of the steps. Moving slowly out from the top step, I confirmed that there was nobody in the main body of the church. There were no sounds typical of someone walking slowly: the occasional sound of a shoe rubbing over stone, the sound of pocket change, the sound of a camera clinking lightly against a jacket zipper or against buttons. I walked quickly to the main entrance, and opened it the smallest crack.

The rain was coming down even more heavily. There was nobody directly in front of the church. Neither the older man nor the man carrying the camera was anywhere to be seen. I ducked quickly out of the church, around the corner past the exposed foundations for the old basilica, then returned the long way to the *Marktplatz*. There were only three or four people about, plodding through the rain, heads down, and the few traders present looked like they wished they weren't there. I bought two apples and a piece of sausage, then made my way across to the restaurant *Backmulde* where I sat over another cup of coffee.

It was now time to move on, and after browsing the bookshop on *Kirchenstrasse*, facing the fountain in the *Marktplatz*, I found a shop where I could pick up a couple of compulsory purchases, which I tucked into my backpack. I then made my way to the southern part of the town, where I had a quick look at *Trajanstrasse*, *Vespasianstrasse*, *Lopodunumstrasse*, and *Jupiterplatz*. There was nothing Roman about them whatever, of course, but that direct knowledge might be useful later if Frau Rohde asked any questions that might need this information. Leaving the town, I made my way back to *Gasthaus im Wald* following a route quite different from the one that morning, past fields, nurseries, along farm tracks, and joining another stream, the Loosgraben, that ultimately led back past Rosenhof. At just past five thirty, I opened the door to *Gasthaus im Wald*. There was a repeat tut-tutting from the welcoming party, but I cut this short by saying that I had to dry off and change and would return immediately.

When I came back downstairs, Frau Rohde was again in the early stages of the schnapps routine, but I interrupted this proceeding by presenting her a bottle of good *kirsch*.

"I'm not sure how you guessed that I like *kirsch*, Herr Rowntree."

"I didn't. But I like it, and you are German, so it seemed a safe bet."

She had a good laugh over this, and said, "Well then, we must try it."

We gave it a thorough test. Which it passed handily.

The time was now past six thirty, and Frau Rohde suggested that we eat at seven. "I've made *tafelspitz*, and it is almost ready." I made noises of agreement, excused myself briefly, and went back upstairs. When I returned, I found the table set, and another bottle of wine opened, a *Grauburgunder*, so I placed my bottle of unopened *Schwarzriesling* on the sideboard. She returned carrying two plates of soup and slices of walnut bread on a tray, and gave a chirp of delight on seeing the *Schwarzriesling*. Her preference was to recork the *Grauburgunder* and have the Riesling instead, but I insisted that it could wait until tomorrow. The meal was every bit as competent as that of the previous day, and was also another relaxed social occasion. Dessert was *bienenstich*, and this was all held down by another round of *kirsch*.

At nine thirty, I pleaded a tiredness that was partly true, excused myself, and said goodnight. Although I had taken my tablet with me, carried in its case and strapped to my stomach by a modified moneybelt, I hadn't used it, and now I checked my email. Nothing new. There were a few notes I had to make based on the day's observations in Ladenburg. It took me about twenty minutes to prepare and send off to Stuart a summary of what I had done thus far and what the plan was for the next day. My summary was a story of both success and failure. There was nothing obvious (I hadn't expected there would be), but there were two possibilities. Fortunately, if these possibilities concealed anything, there was no easy access to either of them. In fact, any access at all would involve considerable dismantling of stonework, in areas where it was impossible to work unseen.

My communications completed, I decided that it really was time for an early night. Beneath the thick duvet in my room, all the familiar doubts and hesitations crowded in on me again the moment I switched off the light. *What are you doing here, Gould?* But then another voice in my head spoke forcefully in my defence: *He's doing the only thing he can, you stupid whiny little prick! He's exercising the only option that bastard Burns has left open for him!* The surge of anger that followed surprised me by its strength and heat. It took a long time to bring this under control, but eventually I drifted off into the silence surrounding *Gasthaus im Wald*. When I re-emerged at almost seven thirty the next day, a dam-burst of late autumn morning sunlight was spilling in through the windows.

Forty-two

Breakfast on such a morning was a meal not to be missed. The sheer wattage of sunlight was the concert master's signal to the dark beams and panelling in Frau Rohde's dining room and they seemed almost to be doing tuning exercises in preparation for the Saint-Saëns parade of bread rolls, scrambled eggs, sausages, butter, jams, and honey to the table. Frau Rohde jettisoned her apron, and we began another meal well greased by conversational variety.

Frau Rohde asked me in a general way how the day before had gone, while indicating she felt it must have been fairly unsatisfactory because of the weather. I replied that weather is something one simply must prepare for, and having done that it can be relegated from a serious obstacle to a minor nuisance. We talked a little about things Roman, and she said, almost by way of apologizing on behalf of Ladenburg, that there was precious little left as evidence of the serious Roman habitations here. I replied somewhat enigmatically, and probably a little pompously, that one needed simply to know where and how to look, and that one needed to be prepared.

"Would you like a small lunch for today?" asked Frau Rohde.

"Oh, no thank you. It's kind of you to offer. But I'll probably have something hot for lunch. But, if I may, I would be grateful if I could borrow a bicycle."

"Yes, by all means. When we finish here, I'll come out to the garden shed with you."

It was a brilliant day, although the expectation was that it would cloud over in the afternoon and begin to rain. As soon as we had finished breakfast, I helped Frau Rohde carry the things into her kitchen, over her objections. I went upstairs to collect my coat and backpack, and when I returned downstairs, Frau Rohde was waiting in the hallway wearing a heavy loden jacket.

Out in the garden, she unlocked the shed, pulled out a respectable bicycle, and gave me the combination to the bicycle lock. There was more fussing, but I assured her that this was just fine, more than fine in fact. She said she would leave the shed unlocked, and I said I would be back sometime that afternoon. I wheeled the bicycle out to the road, mounted, and rode off while Frau Rohde waved and wished me a good day. I took the most direct route into Ladenburg, made my way to the public library, locked the bicycle in the rack where already about fifteen bicycles were parked, and walked inside.

There was quite a lot of activity in the library, and I discovered that it was well stocked. There was a great deal on local history, something that would make my work easier, and I soon came across repeated references to a local worthy, one Klaus Kolb, who had died just recently and was universally admired. From the shelves, I pulled six or seven volumes on the Roman history of the area, took them over to a large table away from traffic where the screen of my tablet was not visible to anyone else, and spread them out, opened as though I were doing quite specific research.

It was crunch time. I planned to spend most of the day going over again the elaborate plan that Stuart and I had evolved, including all the variations to deal with potential scenarios and uncertainties that could arise. This plan occupied a single file in my tablet but it covered about twenty pages. Stuart had the identical file, and we took considerable care to make sure that both of us always were referring to the same version of it. We had evolved a number of important statements that formed the basis for all this, and I thought back to our final discussion and review of the plan before I left for the airport:

"We've gone through this many times", Stuart had said in preamble, "but we need to cover every aspect of it one last time. Last chance for any questions, niggling doubts, possible problems no matter how far-fetched." I had nodded.

"Okay. Burns. He's ruthless, utterly determined, wealthy, probably psychopathic. He's a collector of rare documents on Christianity, among other things. He knows, or at least is convinced, that there's an original copy of the *Heidelberg Catechism* out there, and he wants it. He suspects that there might be much more than this, and whatever there is, he wants it all. He believes that you are a central player in this, but we have cast enough disinformation about to leave him in quite a bit of doubt. We're fairly sure he doesn't know where any of this material is, so we expect that he needs to get that information out of you, by whatever means. But he isn't sure that even you know where all this stuff is, and he can't risk showing his hand until either he knows the scope of your knowledge, one way or another, or until he's sure you've located the material. Once he knows where the material is, you become a serious risk to him, so he will do whatever he can to kill you, but without anyone ever knowing that he was involved. Do you disagree with any of this Richard?"

"No."

"So far, he's left a trail too thin for any police to take action. They've caught some of his small fish, and they know that something's going on, but they don't know any details. Burns also has a particular problem. If he's successful in locating the material, he needs to remove it to the US without leaving any trail. Removing material from Canada is probably not that difficult depending on where it is and who else knows it's there, but removing material from Europe introduces challenges on another level. Anything in Europe will be hidden someplace, and he needs to get it out of that hiding place, or those hiding places, and smuggle it out, all without being detected. Depending on the hiding place, that might be difficult or even impossible. We also believe that he'll probably rely on you locating the material, but then he has to act very quickly before you're able to alert any local authorities on what you've found and where it is. Once people in authority are convinced that a culturally important find is involved, his task becomes extremely difficult, and likely impossible. Are we still agreed on this?"

"Yes, with one proviso." Stuart cocked his head, but I'm sure he knew what was coming. "Burns might just bring in someone local who has the right subject expertise and operate independently of us."

"He might", Stuart agreed, "but there are two difficulties. First, we believe we have unique information that Burns doesn't have. So even someone having independent expertise might do him no good. Second, if he did bring in independent expertise, then there would be another person or other people who would need to be told quite a bit. Burns is paranoid about secrecy, and this would be a huge problem for him, opening up in his mind the possibilities of double-cross, blackmail, leaks, possibly huge amounts of hush money, or the risky prospect of having to kill all those people, once he has what he wants, without leaving any trace that he was behind it. So, yes, Burns might bring in some local talent for the endgame but we've considered this unlikely every time we've thought about the possibility. Do you think anything has changed since the last time we went through all this?"

"No."

"Good. Well, not good, but you know what I mean. So now we look at what might actually happen. Here are the possibilities:

(1) It might be the case that none of this material exists. Either it never did exist, it's been found already by someone else, or it has degraded or been destroyed naturally over time.

(2) The material might exist, but we won't be successful in finding it.

(3) We find the material, we alert the relevant authorities, they take it all seriously, and they sequester the site.

(4) We find the material, but the relevant authorities don't believe us, don't take it seriously, or take too long to act.

(5) We find the material, Burns outflanks us, gets to it first, and spirits it off to the US.

(6) We manage somehow to give the game away, Burns finds the material first, and takes it back to the US.

(7) Burns manages to get to the material first, but is caught either removing it or trying to smuggle it out.

Are you still okay with all this? Any problems? Gaps?"

"Yes, still okay. No problems or gaps."

"On to our strategy. Try to locate the material while Burns is still in the dark and get it into the hands of the authorities. The first of the two difficult areas: our guess at what Burns will do.

In the event of possibilities one or two, we could expect Burns to persist, to believe that we were trying to hoodwink him, and the risks to us would continue or even increase. In the event of possibility three, we expect that Burns would give up. But even in that case, he could become irrational, and we couldn't count on zero risk. Possibility four is likely to lead to either five, six, or seven. In the event of possibility five, everything is likely to go quiet, because Burns will have what he wants. But on the other hand, he might want you to be permanently silenced, just so that there were no loose ends whatsoever. Possibility six is likely to be the worst, because this includes the situation where Burns extracts the information he needs from one of us. In the event of possibility seven, it's hard to say what might happen. He might want to try to implicate you, take you down with him. Depends on the circumstances."

This was all familiar, and I nodded agreement.

"The second difficult area", Stuart continued, "involves an assessment of our risk. The only possibility that might result in no threat from Burns is the third, perhaps also number six or seven. All the others present risks, some of them the worst possible sort."

I checked my watch. Almost eleven o'clock. Sitting in the Ladenburg public library, I was also glancing around every few minutes, carefully, surreptitiously, looking for new faces or anything suspicious. Nothing.

Stuart and I had gone through in detail the document we had produced, and it was very similar to the one on my screen now. We had found nothing to change. Stuart had dropped his pencil and looked at me steadily, "You know, Richard, that we will need to be ready to throw all this, or part of it, out the window. I'm a great follower of Eisenhower's logic here", and Eisenhower's phrase was in my mind even before Stuart quoted it. " 'Plans are worthless, but planning is everything.' It's all got to do with mental preparation", and as he continued, I recalled also the quote from Louis Pasteur (*"La chance ne sourit qu'aux esprits bien préparés"*) and its rather insipid English translation. We sat there with our private thoughts for a moment, thoughts of things coming unexpectedly from left field, and our hopes that if or when that happened we would be well enough prepared and sufficiently nimble.

A ping from my tablet brought me back to Ladenburg. It was an email from Stuart. He had written, *Something unexpected is going to occur in the next few minutes. It would be best if you didn't look surprised.* It wasn't like Stuart to deal in riddles, so I wasn't sure how to take this. Was something going to happen back home that he would inform me of shortly? Was there some news he had got wind of that would be fleshed out at any moment? Had he become aware of something here, in Germany, that I needed to know about? Whatever it was, he wanted me to be on my toes. What I was expecting was another email, one that would add more sense to his cryptic comment. After five minutes, no email had turned up.

While I waited, I checked another file in my tablet, then did one of my periodic unobtrusive sweeps around the reading room. The same people were sitting in the same places doing what appeared to be the same things. Two had left, since they and their notebooks and coats were gone. Three were either in the loo or getting something more from the shelves. But, over near a set of shelves about five metres from me, there was someone standing, his back to me, scanning titles. He was fairly tall, appeared solidly built, had close-cropped hair from what I could see that protruded from beneath his hat, and I was certain he had not been in the reading room ten minutes ago. Chances are it was nothing, but I kept a close but unobtrusive eye on him anyway. He had none of the characteristics of any of the people who I believed had been shadowing me at various times since I had arrived in Germany. But then, all at once, I became apprehensive. There was something familiar about him, but I couldn't place just what it was. If he was shadowing me, had I missed him earlier? The possibility concerned me. His clothing was nondescript autumn greys and browns. My basic strategy had to be to appear to ignore him, wait him out, see what he did, look for a chance to give him the slip.

Suddenly, he pulled a book from the shelf, turned until he was almost facing me, glanced at the wall clock, and walked to a free space two tables away.

He was cool and calm.

But then that was entirely typical of Stuart McLachlan.

Forty-three

I returned to my tablet, as though nothing had happened, but inside I was plunging down a wild white-knuckle ride of apprehension, anger, and curiosity. When Stuart pulled out his cellphone, I immediately sent him a text message.

"What's wrong?"

We were soon into a cryptic exchange. "Nothing specific. Burns in Europe somewhere."

"Change of plan?"

"No."

"Why no advance warning?"

"No point. What would you do differently, apart from worry?"

"We need to talk."

"Agreed. Meet me at *Zum Löwen*, one hour, Reception. I'm Anderson. You're Webster. Questions?"

"Not now. Later."

Stuart drew a notebook and pen from his pocket and spent about fifteen minutes appearing to make notes from the book he had taken off the shelf. Then he rose and left without looking around.

It was difficult to concentrate, but I continued on what I had intended to do: the last bits of checking and keeping as low a profile as I could. If our operation were to come off as intended, and we were both to survive, the next two days had to unfold very closely to plan. Otherwise, things would hinge on improvisation.

I did the best I could to brush all this aside and carry on in what I planned to do that morning. Documents already familiar were reviewed again. I went through, once more, a whole tree of plans and contingencies. Time dragged, but eventually I packed my stuff, left the library, and headed off to *Zum Löwen*.

In Reception, Stuart sat reading a copy of the *International New York Times* in apparent unconcern. I walked up to him.

"You must be Anderson."

"Ah! Mr. Webster. Good to meet you", Stuart said, folding his paper, rising, and extending his hand. "We can talk in my room."

We climbed to the first floor, Stuart unlocked his room and waved me inside. He closed the door, I took a seat at the chair in front of the small desk, while Stuart sank into a large armchair in one corner.

"What's going on, Stuart? We're not at the endgame yet."

"I decided to come a little early, and since I'm no longer sure just what the endgame will look like, I can't be sure we're not there."

"Fine. But why not follow the script and contact me from somewhere in Heidelberg?"

"There's something not right."

"What?" I asked, sounding impatient, petulant.

Stuart looked at me, then looked down at his hands.

"A feeling?" I asked.

"Yes. But don't knock it."

I just sat there like a spoiled brat.

At length, Stuart asked me, referring to the email I had sent the day before, what I had noticed specifically on my first quick tour of the St. Gallus Church.

"There are two possible spots where something might be concealed. One is under a floor stone. The other is in the wall."

"Nothing in the crypt?" Stuart asked.

"Just to be clear, it could be anywhere, including in the crypt. But there's no *obvious* location. Equally, it could be nowhere."

"Which one of the two spots do you think is most likely?"

"The wall. The floor stone is likely set on soil. It will be damp down there, regardless of what anyone might do to protect against that, and hundreds of years is a long time. Anything perishable would likely be gone by now. I think our guy would have known that his stuff might have to sit, safe and dry, for a very long time."

"So. In the wall."

"Yes", I said. "That has the best chance of being dry."

"What's the indicator that might make that location probable?" Stuart asked.

"Just beneath the eleventh Station of the Cross, the stonework in the wall is slightly irregular. It could be an old repair. It's the only spot on the walls where that kind of irregularity appears."

"And that's it?" Stuart asked, incredulous.

"Yes." Stuart looked at me steadily, evidently wondering if I had picked up some sort of debilitating fever. "Well", I continued, "you'd hardly expect the words *dig here* to be engraved in the stonework, would you?"

"What's the eleventh Station of the Cross?" Stuart asked.

"Jesus being nailed to the Cross."

"Ah! I see. You think this is a reference to Luther?"

"Yes. It's the only possibility that I can spot. But I could be drawing a spurious inference and it really is somewhere else. Or the indicator for the spot where it really was hidden has now disappeared. Or—"

"Or it's not there at all."

"Yes", I agreed. "Or it's not there at all."

We talked about this for another half-hour, about the work needed to gain access to whatever might be in the wall, about the time it would take to do that work and the tools needed, about noise, about whether it could be done at night, and most critically how many people would be needed to do it in a reasonably short time.

"As far as I'm concerned", I summarized, "there's really no way that anything concealed in the wall could be accessed by two people in less than an hour. Reducing the time a lot below an hour would need more specialized equipment, and that means unacceptable noise, and the problem of trying to bring into a church items that have no business being there and that just can't be hidden or disguised."

"What about a violent access from the outside. Blast, grab, and run?"

"Nice if you say it fast and don't think too hard", I said. "But you need to know exactly where to blast, you need to know quite a bit about the wall to decide what blast force you need, and you have to be concerned that you might pulverize the treasure as well as the wall. Also, you've got one chance at it. If you pick the wrong spot, you won't be able just to come back the next night and try again."

"So it seems like something having a low success probability."

"So it would seem", I agreed.

"Okay. I guess then that we just carry on with the plan. Spend tomorrow making a good record of everything. Whatever photos and measurements you can take. Agreed?"

I agreed.

There was a rumble outside. Thunder.

"That's the predicted bad weather closing in", I said. "I'm going back to the library to spend a bit more time, then I'll cycle back to *Gasthaus im Wald*." I must have sounded down.

"Cheer up, Richard. We're getting near the end. We knew from our planning that we might see a web squib outcome, that it would all just fizzle out. At least by this time tomorrow we'll know, we'll have documentation, and we can move on."

"Yes, I know. But an empty-handed result is hardly satisfying, and certainly not conclusive in any way. And Burns would still be out there. It's like leading the pack in a marathon, only to find that the last half kilometre is an impassable swamp."

Stuart smiled. "Come on. Off you go. Let's carry on so that we can bring this thing to whatever conclusion there is."

I walked back to the library, and the rain began in earnest just as I went in the door. I found the next several hours dispiriting, but I applied myself to the details of what I would have to do the next day. At about five o'clock, the already grey day began to become even greyer. I assembled my things, pulled on my rain jacket, went to the front doors and looked carefully around outside through the glass, saw nothing that looked suspicious, then carried on out to the bike racks, unlocked Frau Rohde's bike, and prepared to set off. Two other people were doing the same, and they nodded to me saying, "*Auf Wiedersehen*". I did one last check, to confirm I had my tablet, file of notes, but then fumbled for my keys to the *gasthaus*. They weren't in my jeans or rain jacket pockets. Odd. *Where are my keys?* A more systematic search finally located them in the outer zip pocket of the backpack.

There was heavy cloud cover, the rain was coming down steadily, thunder continued to raise the occasional querulous grumble in the far distance, and the gloomy afternoon was barely holding on under scudding low cloud as I cycled out of Ladenburg.

It was head down and just keep cycling, as I picked my way through the streets and onto the path along the Kandelbach. Gusts of wind whipped at my rain jacket, and I had to wipe rain from my eyes frequently. Not surprisingly, there was not a soul out. Shapes in varying shades of grey, depending on their distance from the path, drifted by. I had paid careful attention on the way into Ladenburg, I could visualize the map in my mind, and I knew what the shapes were and where I was. It took about twenty minutes to reach the lane leading in to *Gasthaus im Wald*, and I dismounted and wheeled the bicycle past the house toward the garden shed. By now, the rain had eased to a light drizzle. The enclosed back garden was even gloomier than expected, thanks to the mass of the house, the beech trees, the shed, and some hedging behind the shed. The house was in darkness. Perhaps Frau Rohde had gone off somewhere, although that seemed odd for this time of day. Dropping my backpack to one side of the shed, I opened the door and manoeuvred the bike inside. It was too dark inside to see to lock the bike, and rather than fiddle with my flashlight trying to do a three-handed job using only two hands, I decided to come back out later using a larger flashlight. Re-emerging from the shed, I bent to pick up my backpack.

"Good evening, Dr. Gould."

I was hazed and fuzzy from the wet and the chill, but it took only a second for me to realize that something was dreadfully wrong.

Raising my head, I found myself looking into the smiling face of Gale Burns.

Forty-four

I looked at him for some time without saying anything.

"Yes, it's a surprise, isn't it?" he said, and chuckled contentedly. "Please allow me to do the talking, at least for now. But I assure you that you will have your turn to talk a bit later."

Although the rain had eased, the cloud cover had deepened considerably, and it was much gloomier than it would have been normally for this time of day.

"You sure are a resourceful fellow, Dr. Gould", Burns said in a smiling, conversational tone. "My goodness, you did lead my hired German dunderheads on quite a chase, on more than one occasion. But now that we're here together, we can have a nice chat. Oh, and in case you aren't all that talkative, I've brought Karl along. His German is pretty good, too, so if you don't feel like speaking to me, you two should be able to get along fine."

Burns stepped to one side, and I could see Karl as he moved out of the shadow near the corner of the house. Karl had a pistol in his right hand and clearly meant business.

"Where is Alois?" Burns said curtly to Karl.

"Parking the car."

"Fine", Burns said. "We can wait."

"So, Dr. Gould. Did you find what you were looking for?"

"I wasn't looking for anything. I spent the day in the library."

"Hmm", Burns said. "Not a surprise that you would say something like that. Not that I believe you by any means. And it really would make more sense if you didn't play these silly tedious games."

"Believe what you like", I said evenly. "And it looks to me that it's you who's playing stupid games."

"Come now, Dr. Gould. You and I both know what's going on here. We're both here in Germany because we're looking for something."

"Really? Do you always talk in riddles like this?"

"I see you are going to play the dumb innocent. That's fine. It's a waste of time, though, and you will tell me the truth, eventually. Evidently though, that won't happen just here."

"Where is Alois, dammit?" Burns said to Karl impatiently.

"Don't know. I go and look."

"No you won't", Burns said sharply. "You'll stay right here."

"I assume you are aware, Dr. Gould, that I know at least as much about this little treasure lark as you do, and probably a good deal more." His smile, which appeared at first to be pleasant and friendly, was now reptilian.

"What you assume is up to you."

Burns made a mild tsk-tsk noise. "It really is not a good plan, Dr. Gould, to try to be a smartass with me."

"Thank you, Mr. Burns. I appreciate the advice."

I thought I saw a flash of anger in the contraction of Burns's jaw muscles.

"Where the fuck is Alois?" Burns hissed angrily.

"Forget Alois. And I suggest that you not make any sudden moves at all. Either of you."

Burns's face brightened. "Ah! Mr. McLachlan! I'm pleased that you were able to join us."

There was a metallic click.

"Now!" Burns began theatrically. "Unless I'm mistaken, that sound was Alois's pistol, and I believe that it's aimed at your head, Mr. McLachlan. So why don't you be a good boy and come out of the shadows? It really is best to be able to see someone when one is talking to them."

Stuart's face emerged into what light there was.

"And unarmed, too!" Burns said in feigned surprise. "I know it's much harder to get a handgun here than in the US, but you really should have taken the extra trouble, Mr. McLachlan. Oh, well, I guess that's just life."

We're finished, doomed, I thought to myself, but then Stuart's rules scrolled behind my eyes. When you sense real fear, try to override it using logic. Think of all aspects of the situation. Look for anything that could be used as a weapon.

I rewound the images of wheeling the bicycle down the lane, past the house, toward the shed, dropping my backpack, lifting the bicycle into the shed—

Spade. There was a spade leaning against the garden shed right behind me.

"Well", Burns said, as though about to summarize the conclusions of a symposium, "it looks as though we're all here. Dr. Gould appears to be in a defiant mood. Perhaps Mr. McLachlan is feeling more co-operative. Hmm? Do you know where it is, Mr. McLachlan?"

"Stuart!" I said almost in a shout. "Don't say—"

"Gould!" Stuart barked coldly. "Just shut up!"

"Well now!" Burns said softly, giving one gentle clap of his hands. "It would appear that there's a breach in the walls of Camelot! Do carry on, Mr. McLachlan."

"It's not here", Stuart said. "It's not in Ladenburg. In fact, there's serious doubt whether it exists at all."

"Ah! I see!" said Burns calmly. "This could mean that you are working some clever plan, or Dr. Gould has been made a patsy, or you, Mr. McLachlan, have decided that you and I can be partners in this. It could also mean that you have another partner or that you've decided to try for it all on your own. Good, in the sense that it shows initiative, enterprise. Bad, in the sense that you need to know your rivals, and as usual I'm way ahead of you. So, I fear, Mr. McLachlan, that you have no bargaining power at all. You would have been better to keep your hand in with Dr. Gould. Pity."

There was a rumble of thunder, not quite so distant as the last few Jovian whispers.

Stuart laughed coldly. "Dr. Gould, indeed! He's an innocent abroad, he's a", and here Stuart searched for words, "he seems to think he's some kind of superhuman Henry Hudson."

A thousand volts shot through me as I recognized the words, a blinding jolt of understanding, and a renewed feeling of determination and hope, an inner steely sense of sheer grit. Stuart was saying to me, in code, 'We're far from being dead yet.'

"I hate to say it, Mr. McLachlan", Burns intoned smugly, "if you wanted this prize, you would have been better advised—"

"What would I want with a bunch of mouldy old documents, Burns? They're rubbish!"

"Yes, I understand that it's just filthy lucre that drives you. But you can't have the lucre unless you've got the documents."

"You're sick, the whole lot of you", Stuart said, with venom.

There was a pale flicker of lightning, and a few seconds later a closer bark of thunder.

"This has been a stimulating exchange, gentlemen, but I think now we will all climb in the car, go for a little drive, and finish off our discussion."

The photoflash of the lightning left a printed image for me, an image clear in every detail, and I used that image next. I had a sharp 3-D picture of where everyone was standing. I could see where Karl's pistol hand was in space, and I used that to take aim. Possible circumstances that would give an opportunity flashed behind my eyes, as my right hand closed around the shaft of the spade.

The circumstance that turned up wasn't among the possibilities I had considered. Not even close.

It all happened in less that three seconds.

"*Was ist denn hier?*" a voice barked authoritatively through the gloom. I could see Karl's head turn toward the voice. Something in me recognized that the moment had arrived. Anger and deadly purpose flared to life within me. My spade sliced through the air, almost severing Karl's pistol hand at the wrist. He screamed in agony. At the same time, I saw from the corner of my eye a sudden flick of Stuart's right arm, and there was a sharp wail of surprise from Burns. A muzzle flash burst from Alois's gun, which roared angrily. Burns shouted in alarm, "No! No! Don't shoot them, you idiot!" Stuart stumbled back against the tree that was behind him, and I heard him grunt, then fall to the ground. There was a sharp crack, and Alois dropped like a sack of bricks. My too long pent-up need to avenge Buck powered the second blow from my spade, it came down again, driven by strength I didn't know I had, and the flat side struck Karl full in the face. There was an odd crackling sound, and he fell heavily, making disgusting gurgling noises.

Almost instantly, Burns had been stripped of his local advantage. It was payback time. I dropped the spade and ran at Burns, screaming "You son of a bitch! You son of a bitch!" The adrenalin concentration in my blood shot up. I could think only of Buck. I could see Buck sitting dead and peaceful in the chair in front of my house. I could see the grief-stricken faces of Peter and Andrea Filmore. I could feel Andrea Filmore's convulsive sobs as she leaned against me. I could see Burns's smug, self-satisfied, reptilian smile. And then all the intolerable intrusions into my life and the lives of my friends by this egotistical, entitled, lump of scum, were lined up before me. "You son of a bitch! You son of a bitch!" I grappled with Burns.

We fell and rolled on the wet ground. He was shrieking like a cowardly bully. Flailing wildly, he was trying to say something, but I had no interest anymore in anything he might say. A hand came toward my face, but I struck it away violently, heard bone thump dully against something solid, and there was another shriek from Burns. "You son of a bitch! You son of a bitch!" We rolled back and forth on the ground, and Burns squeaked, "You win!" *Not yet, you bastard*, I said to myself. I felt something solid high on the right side of Burns's chest, near the shoulder. The haft of a knife. Stuart had thrown a knife at him.

I grabbed the knife and pulled. Burns uttered high-pitched gasping screams, shouting "No! No!" but the knife wouldn't move. I heaved at it again, willing my muscles to complete one single Samsonian act, ignoring Burns's wild shrieking that was filling the dusk. The knife came out slowly, grating heavily against bone, and Burns was ululating a high-pitched keening. His legs thrashed wildly. I don't know what I planned to do with the knife. I tossed it aside.

My hands closed on Burns's throat, throttling all sound from him, but my hands were wet or muddy and they kept slipping. My grip tightened and I continued screaming, "You son of a bitch! You son of a bitch!" I was screaming and sobbing at the same time. Burns's eyes were bugging out. His face was horribly contorted, making him outwardly the harrowing goblin that he really was on the inside. Using his good left arm, he struck at me feverishly, in full panic. My hands tightened further around his throat. "You son of a bitch! You son of a bitch!" I wailed, in white hot anger. Long threads of saliva slid from my mouth, and trailed across Burns's face. Choking and gagging noises were all Burns could utter now. I leaned down so that my own upper body weight would add extra force.

My face was now two inches from his. "You son of a bitch! You son of a bitch!" I looked into his treacherous, psychopathic eyes, and I understood unadulterated evil, I knew the fearful grip of pure hatred, I knew anger, anger so hot, so highly distilled, that it became serene, it became blinding Luciferian white light streaming from the eye sockets of a death's head, I understood temporary insanity. "You son of a bitch! You son of a bitch! You evil son of a bitch! Die, you son of a bitch! Die! Die! Die! Die!"

In the distance, there was a siren. Burns continued to thrash. I continued to scream. My hands were as tight around his throat as I could make them, but they continued to slip, and fire was now rising into my forearms. But then there was an explosion of pain in my abdomen. My hands left Burns's neck and went reflexively to my groin, where one of his flailing legs had struck a glancing blow off my thigh and grazed my testicles. It was light contact, but it was enough. Pain joined the anger that already filled my entire being. Then everything went to a muffled black.

Flashing lights. An emergency services attendant was holding me in a sitting position, asking me in German if I could move. A woman's head was next to mine. She was weeping freely.

"Stuart!" I panicked. "Where is Stuart?" The emergency services man looked at me and asked me, in broken English, who Stuart was. I managed to switch to German and say that Stuart had been shot. The attendant said that the man who had been shot in the chest was just being placed in the ambulance and would be rushed to hospital. I tried to rise, groaned at the shooting pain in my groin, but continued struggling, and pulled myself toward the ambulance that was now idling behind us, its doors just beginning to close. The attendant helped me into the ambulance, while I repeated again and again that the injured man was a friend. My friend. My oldest friend. My best friend. Stuart was fine. Stuart was all right. I had to be with Stuart, make sure that he was all right. Stuart would be all right. Stuart was hurt, but he would be up and about in no time.

From there, it was mostly a blank, peppered by half-remembered fractured images.

I learned later that Karl, whose full name was Karl Wassermann, had almost died. I had pulverized his nose, crushed one of his cheekbones, and driven bone fragments deep into his face and sinus cavities. But he would live and was in a hospital under police guard.

Alois, who was Alois Kirchschläger, had died instantly from the blow Frau Rohde had delivered to the back of his head, when she saw his pistol fire, using the mallet she had brought with her from the house in the event that her challenge needed to be backed by some real authority.

But the bitterest news, the information that brought bile into my throat and mouth, was that Burns was gone. He had slipped away, had disappeared, had vanished. Burns, that evil bastard Burns, had escaped. The police said, I heard later, that he could not remain free for long, that he would be found and brought in as someone the police would like to question. But I knew that they were wrong. Burns had indeed escaped. He had deep pockets, he was very cunning, he had an acute sixth sense, and within days he would be back in Philadelphia. He didn't need to rely on commercial airlines. He could make his way to a coast and organize passage on any one of a number of dubious freighters. He could slip out of Germany and arrange to be whisked away by a private jet. Worse still, as far as the police were concerned, he was not known to be present at the site where any crime had been committed. Allegedly, I had seen him at the scene at *Gasthaus im Wald*, but nobody else who had also been there, and knew who he was,

was still either alive or conscious, and there was no record of a Gale Burns having entered Germany at any time within the previous month.

As far as the officials were concerned, Burns was a ghost.

I was also told later that from the ambulance I had texted Werner, saying that I needed help, and giving the name of the hospital we were heading toward. How I was cogent enough to get that information from the ambulance attendant, and relay it to Werner, I don't know.

Werner and Heinz were there when I limped unsteadily back into the emergency room waiting area, after the doctors had determined that there was nothing physically wrong with me, apart from a lot of bruising. Werner and Heinz both said later that I had looked a mess. The right side of my face was bruised from temple to chin, and my eye was swollen almost shut. The jacket I was carrying was torn and covered in mud. Part of one shirt sleeve was missing.

The police were there as well. They spoke to the doctors. They also spoke to Werner. Apparently, they spoke to me, but I was not able to give any coherent answers. The emergency room staff wanted me to stay another day or two under observation, but I knew that I was losing my grip, that I was slowly falling off a black cliff, and would soon be engulfed in an unfathomable abyss.

I needed to be with somebody I knew.

I needed to be with Werner.

And that is what was arranged.

Forty-five

The week following these events was a blur. Things slipped in and out of focus. When they were out of focus, I really didn't care about anything. I think I answered a lot of questions using the single word *whatever*. But when they were in focus, they were painfully, searingly, so.

I relived the sounds. Over, and over, and over again.

The roar of Kirchschläger's handgun, the grunt of surprise as the bullet lodged in Stuart's chest, the sharp crack as the mallet and the back of Kirchschläger's head connected fatally, Burns's shriek as I pulled the serrated knife roughly from his right shoulder, and felt it grind past a rib or collarbone, my own animal sounds as I fell onto Burns and tried to choke him, the harsh discordant dual tones of the siren as we sped to the hospital.

At the time, I didn't know how the emergency services were notified; maybe I called them, but if so I don't remember when. Maybe Frau Rohde called them. It was a short ride to the hospital in the ambulance, and during this trip jangled images, cascades of shattered memory, tumbled through my consciousness. One of these images I had been able to grasp and hold in view for a few seconds.

Frau Rohde. I had brought this horror into her life. The contagion of serious violence had splashed onto her and she would need comfort and support. How was I going to provide that? Could I perhaps rely on Werner? But then the continuing avalanche of images swept all that away, and I was lost again in the confused kaleidoscopic flow.

One of these images, that of Stuart lying inert and unconscious in the ambulance, is something that will never leave me. Vivid mental pictures of my recent time with him rose up before me. Stuart working, focused and determined. Stuart and I sharing meals, bottles of wine, glasses of scotch and brandy, in great gusto and in intimate friendship. Stuart explaining to me his memorable jobs, with a twinkle. Stuart uttering his big open laugh on my patio.

The verdict that this was all my fault fell upon me as a heavy cross. In the ambulance, I half remember taking Stuart's hand in mine and talking to him the entire trip to the hospital, assuring him that he was going to be okay. At the hospital, he was rushed off immediately to an operating theatre. Stuart died about an hour later, but I'm not sure how I came to know that. Somebody (a doctor? a nurse?) had checked me over in the emergency department and properly patched my scratches and cuts.

I don't remember any details of the emergency room or meeting Werner and Heinz there. I don't remember where we went. I do remember sitting with Werner, at a place I found out later was Heinz's home.

The next thing I remember must have been a day or two later, and we were at Werner's place. Werner kept talking to me in his calm voice. Among the things he said to me were two that I needed to know. One of them was a question about Stuart that arose in my mind as soon as I realized where I was, realized that I was not back at *Gasthaus im Wald*, and that only Werner and I were in the room. The other was about Frau Rohde.

The police had determined later, because of a complaint of a bicycle theft in broad daylight, that Stuart had snatched a bicycle from a youth in front of the Ladenburg library, and had sped off into the rain. That was how he had made it to *Gasthaus im Wald* as quickly as he had done. What must have happened eventually became clear to me. True to form, and the consummate professional always, Stuart had watched from a distance as I had unlocked Frau Rohde's bicycle, and he must have seen one of them, Karl or Alois. When I realized all this, when I knew what must have happened, I was hollowed out inside, all over again. It was that dreadful agony of no longer being able to feel the pain.

Then there was Frau Rohde. Werner learned later from the police that she said she had been lying down inside the house, heard voices, peeked out through a window, and saw someone holding a pistol. The rest was evident. What was also evident was that I owed her everything, and somehow I needed to try to even the balance. But the efforts I might have made then to acknowledge and deal with that debt would have been no match for the blackness that had already begun to pull me down. It was a personal debt that weighed on me, but one that would have to wait. In this, as well, Werner was tireless on my behalf and spent a lot of time with Frau Rohde, made sure she had help and support, both legal and psychological.

It was much later that I learned something else. Werner said that Frau Rohde knew from the first day I was there that probably I was not English, and that therefore my name probably was not Rowntree. It was my engineering ring, my iron ring. She had told Werner that her husband, Herr Rohde, spoke quite good English, something that had helped him land the job at the Benz museum. In that job he met all kinds of engineers who came to the museum, many of them to behave like young boys let off the lead for a day, and he talked to almost all the museum's visitors. Herr Rohde was a bit of an anglophile, and was fond of Kipling. A group of Canadian engineers had come into the museum one day, he was asked to show them around, and he conducted their tour in English. But he also noticed that each of them wore a ring on his little finger. He was tickled pink when he learned that, through the ceremony for conferring these rings, there was a connection to Kipling, and apparently he never tired of recounting that information to Frau Rohde. Werner had learned this from talking to Frau Rohde directly, since he had contacted her once he knew the central role she had played in getting me out of that situation alive. Werner had asked her whether she was afraid or apprehensive when she knew I was passing myself off as someone else, and she had answered that no, it was only a name, and that she had no trouble reading "Herr Rowntree" as a straight arrow.

I quickly lost all track of time. One day, the police questioned me for several hours. Werner and Heinz were there, and I had someone to represent me. I'm not sure how I was able to give any coherent answers, and perhaps I wasn't able. Maybe there was enough information available otherwise to satisfy the police. I don't know. There had been a lot of discussion of my tablet, which Werner had found and handed over to the police. It must have been several days, perhaps a week later, in Königstein, when the flow of time became relatively unbroken again, and things started to make sense. And then Werner and Gudrun explained to me that it was over, but to me it didn't really matter. I was numb. I didn't feel anything. And I didn't care. Werner had found contact information for Greg, and had called him to explain the situation and give an update on me. Greg, in turn, had updated those people in Greenvale who he felt should be in the picture. All this I learned much later.

I remember a long farewell with Gudrun and Werner at Frankfurt Airport, landing in Toronto and being met by Greg, and then I was back in Greenvale, being looked after by Jill and Greg at their place, and under a doctor's care. The general word about me had got round. Everyone knew that something terrible had occurred in Germany. There had been dozens of expressions of concern, relayed to me through Jill or Greg, from people in Greenvale I knew well, and from some I knew only in passing. Jill and Greg had actively gone out to inform, in person, the people closest to me, to give them the latest information, to say that I was still brittle, and would be in no shape to see anyone for some time, but that Jill would keep them as up to date as possible. During that time, I avoided all public contact. I couldn't have faced concerned friends, and I hoped that they understood. Greg went to my place every day to feed Max.

I went through a time, probably only a few days, but I don't recall just how long, of intense anger, and I tried to abate this through long walks in the hills around Greenvale. I was able to take these walks early in the morning, since in general sleep evaded me day and night except for short, troubled snatches. I wanted to avoid running into local people. Seen from the hills, the mill in the valley below stood out like a beacon, but it seemed somehow odd and irrelevant, as though it had nothing to do with me, as if it were someone I had once known but who was now long dead. I learned later that during all this time Greg took over the job of managing the mill. Much later I also learned that, after discussions with Monty, Henry Newhouse had taken the initiative to contact the appropriate German cultural authorities, and to ensure that information was passed between them and their Dutch counterparts.

In the first week of November, I was back in Germany. The police wanted to wrap things up, and for reasons that I can no longer put my finger on I insisted on doing it in person. Greg and Jill objected strenuously, Jill tearfully, but when they saw it was hopeless they arranged for Werner to meet me at the airport, see the whole thing through, and make sure I got back on the plane home. It took surprisingly little time. I made a deposition, although the German police called it something else. I had to sign a lot of sheets of paper, under the watchful eye of the *Anwalt* who had been brought by Werner to look after my interests. And then the official part of it was over. I was back at Werner's place for a few days, and it was only then that I felt as though my life had begun coming back to something like normal, however slowly. Under Gudrun's hawk eye, which seemed to be on me all the time, I felt that things were beginning to have meaning once more. The three of us made bread one evening, and that was the first time I smiled since *Gasthaus im Wald.* But it was all still an emotional roller coaster ride. Some days I was almost normal. Other days I felt unable to do or say anything. There were still spells of spontaneous weeping, but they diminished. Most nights, though, I wished I would just go to sleep and not wake up.

After I had returned again to Greenvale, and on one of the better days while I was still with Jill and Greg, I sent Frau Rohde a long email. I related what had happened after I left Germany, I said that I, and probably neither of us, was in a condition to have back-and-forth exchanges by email, but that Werner was being kept up to date, through Greg, on how things were going, and that I was also getting word on her through Werner. I ended in a long statement of gratitude for everything she had done for me, and an apology for having dragged her into the whole sordid mess, hoping that she was well, and said that as soon as possible, she and I would get together again.

By the end of the third week of November, I had started doing things at the mill again. But Greg had declared to my three young staff that it would be a firing offence for any of them to ask me about what had happened in Germany, or even to allow anyone else to do that. As a result, my companions were the milling machines, I was kept from entering the coffee shop, and my exchanges with Karen, Michael, and Graham were limited pretty much to "Hello". I made telephone contact with a few of the local people I was closest to—Mrs. Williamson, who was evidently very shaken by the whole business, Monty, Lonny, Jasper, Henry, and a few others—but I found that after just a few sentences I was completely stressed out. It was touch and go whether I would break down during any of these brief exchanges, which would have been to the embarrassment of everyone. But they had all been so good to me that I felt I owed them some attempts at an explanation, no matter how poor or brief.

There was a very bad patch when the woman who had worked as Stuart's part-time office administrator contacted me to say that she was wrapping up Stuart's business affairs, and she had organized the files on my project so that I could come and look at them and take away with me whatever I wanted. I asked her just to package everything, ship it to Greenvale, and send me an invoice for the shipping costs. Three days later, a box arrived along with a letter from her. The letter itemized what was in the files, but advised me that she had not looked in a sealed file labelled "Richard Gould – Private", could not comment on its contents, and left the matter in my hands. It took me more than a week to gather the strength to open that file.

The file consisted of three separate sections.

The first section was evidently printed out from an Excel sheet, and was a detailed, annotated accounting of the time that Stuart and his operatives had spent on the "Greenvale Mill" project.

The second section was Stuart's project notes. They were in his fine and elegant handwriting, and they ran to more than sixty pages. The notes were in sections by date, up to the day he left for his final trip to Germany. I avoided going through them.

The third section was something I didn't expect.

It was a detailed itemization of investments, accounts, holdings. The various items were spread across the US—New York, California, Texas, Pennsylvania—and indicated a net worth of more than forty-five million dollars. In my normal condition, I would have worked it out right away, but it took me a while to realize just what I was examining. Stuart had assembled a financial profile of Burns, by means that were without doubt illegal. This section was all in Stuart's neat hand. I was certain that this was the only hard copy and that no electronic copy of it existed. At the bottom Stuart had entered a short annotation: *Might be something here we could use to get this clown off our backs.*

The last of this third section, also in Stuart's neat hand, consisted of a single page, headed *In The Event*, which I glanced at, and then I closed the file.

Early in December, once again over strenuous objections from Jill and Greg, I made another quick trip to Germany, to *Gasthaus im Wald*, for a very emotional two days with Frau Rohde. I made it only partway through my grateful thank you to her before choking up and being unable to continue. When I had regained some control, I carried on with difficulty but determination, and stepped through in detail the time I had spent at *Gasthaus im Wald*, explaining the background, why I had done what I had done, and apologizing again for not being straight with her. We wept together several times. We had another wonderful meal of *hirschgulasch*, and then we sat late into the night and drank almost an entire bottle of *Himbeergeist*. She thanked me for putting her and Werner in contact. I promised to come back again soon, in a few months. There was another few days spent with Gudrun and Werner, to whom I now owed a towering debt.

Some time later, back in Toronto, where I had spent the previous night in my condo, I called Steve Angeli, Stuart's "hacker", on a cloudy, blustery, Wednesday morning. It had been clear to me by the way Stuart had talked about him, that he and Steve had had a long-term working relationship and had become friends. Steve as well had been hit badly by Stuart's death, and he didn't know what to say to me any more than I knew what to say to him. I told him that I wanted to meet, he was hesitant, and I said it was nothing to do with events, it was just an item of business I wanted to discuss, which was both true and not true. Finally, he agreed with great reluctance.

We met that afternoon, at a fairly grim but ironically well-chosen pub, *The Taxman*, on College Street. It had a rooftop patio, and the radiant heaters made the patio reasonably comfortable despite the wind and the chill, so we sat up there, surrounded by half-dead potted plants. We were The Taxman's only patio customers, but the unswept floor and dusty, crumb-laden tables probably had at least as much to do with that as did the season.

We sipped our beer in silence for an uncomfortably long time.

"I'm sorry, Steve", I said slowly, but then could only look at my beer.

"We're all sorry. You don't lose a guy like Stuart without having a big hole left behind."

"No. I don't mean that. I mean I'm sorry because it was my fault."

Steve's face clouded over. "You're not doing anyone any favours by blaming yourself. And you know damn well that if Stuart were here now he'd beat the living shit right out of you. So, stop talking like that, man. Stuart knew the risks, probably better than any of us. He knew what he was getting into."

"I can't help it, Steve. I feel enormous guilt and it's not going away."

There was no answer to that, we sipped our beer some more, and the silence began to feel like a creeping shadow.

At Steve's hesitant and oblique question, I described at some length what had happened in Germany. Steve's face was set grimly, and when I finished there was another long silence.

I reached into my jacket pocket and pulled out several folded typewritten sheets of paper. Handing them over to Steve, I said, "Take a look at those. Don't say anything until you've spent some time thinking about it."

Steve read for two or three minutes, then looked at me wearing a blank expression. He returned to the sheets for a few minutes more, then leaned back and gazed up at the sky. Turning to me about five minutes later, he asked, "Where did you get this?"

"Does it matter?"

Steve shrugged, then looked at the sheets again.

Eventually, he asked, very carefully, "You know what this means?"

I looked straight at Steve. "I am absolutely crystal clear on what this means, Steve, right down to all the personal impacts." Then after a long pause, I asked, "Are you interested?"

"Can I think about it?"

"You really ought to take quite a long time to think about it", I replied evenly.

"Okay. Do you want to know what I decide?"

"No. I don't need to know."

He and I both knew that if he decided to go ahead with it, we would be forming a most secret pact, that it would be the crowning achievement in Steve's career as a hacker, but also the end of his current persona. And it would be a pact that would exist only in our two heads.

We finished our beer, shook hands, and I left.

Forty-six

By the end of the second week in December, I had felt steady enough to call Karen, Michael, and Graham together, along with Greg, for a staff meeting. We met in the mill kitchen early one morning. I did all the talking.

I asked them not to interrupt, and then told them just what had happened in Germany, what had happened after I returned, said that they had a right to know, that it was unfair for them to have to pretend that it had all been business as usual over the past couple of months when it was clearly nothing of the sort. On the events in Germany, I spared nothing, apart from toning down the gruesome bits, and said simply that it all had taken its toll on me. I thanked them for their patience and their understanding and their willingness to carry on over the past weeks. I handed each of them an unmarked envelope, and asked them to open them later. Greg knew about this in advance and told me beforehand that he thought $2500 each as a year-end "thank you" was too much, but I waved him down since the money was all coming from what would be my dividend from the mill, had I taken one.

"Any questions?" I asked.

Karen's eyes were brimming, and she walked over to me and gave me a long, forceful hug.

I looked at Greg and said, "Maybe I should ask 'Any questions?' more often", and that broke the ice. Graham, who is the least demonstrative of the three, subjected me to a bone-cruncher handshake, while Michael gave me a light hug, blinked quickly several times, and said, "I can't tell you how good it is to have you back."

"Well", I said, looking from one to the other of them, "I need to tell you all that I am the lucky one here." There were exclamations of "No!" and hand motions of protest, but I gave the "down beasts" gesture, moved back to the fridge, and pulled out a litre bottle of Prosecco.

"Karen! Five glasses, please! Graham! There's a box of Baci on the counter behind you! Michael! Open this and pour!" We drank, talked, laughed even. Graham told me about customer comments, Michael proudly described his successes with new menu items, Karen took turns wiping her eyes, bubbling unashamedly, and saying how the coffee shop had become a local institution. Greg said simply that the place practically manages itself. We talked for about an hour, and would have gone on longer, but a group of customers came in and it was as though someone had shouted "Action Stations!"

Although I was falling back into a Greenvale routine, and it was a great relief to feel that happening, I knew that there were black clouds elsewhere, unresolved problems that I would have to settle ultimately. I knew also that it was obvious what was needed to deal with those problems, but at the same time, the thought of having to do it filled me with an immense dread.

Also in December, I met the people in Greenvale I felt closest to, one at a time, in The Fox. Their explicit statements of support, but even more their unspoken concern and love, were deeply moving. During these meetings, Jasper made it clear to everyone else that nobody was to approach me unless I asked them to, and when Jasper is adamant, nobody breaks his rules. But by now, I was much more stable, and it appeared to me that these one-on-one meetings were often harder on the other party.

We had a long autumn. Light frosts had come and gone all through November and well into December. Then we had another mild spell. December 18 was warm enough for shirtsleeves only, and it carried on like that well past Christmas. My mood and general condition were on a strong upward curve, and I got back to regular kibitzing with Graham, Karen, and Michael, and spent more time in the coffee shop. We were closing down the mill and the restaurant for Christmas Day and Boxing Day, but were staging a New Year's Eve party, for which Karen, Michael, and Graham had done an enormous amount of planning. Graham and I worked twelve-hour days on December 23 and 24, and we produced and delivered literally tons of flour. On Christmas Eve, I shut everything down, did a last inspection of the kitchens, set the alarm, locked up at eight thirty, and headed home, thinking of quiet, some music, a bit of reading, and a lot of sleeping. I shed my shoes and coat, dropped my keys on the kitchen counter, put some food down for Max, and poured myself a brandy. Max had followed me around ever since I had come back from Germany and resumed living in my own home. He slept on the bed at my feet every night, something he hadn't done before, except the one or two occasions when I was not well. And he stuck his whiskers in my face every morning, also something he had never done before.

I guess Max was just concerned.

Holding my brandy, I collapsed into my favourite leather armchair. Max walked to a spot in front of me and sat down to wash. We looked at each other for a few minutes.

"Well, Max", I said, "I think things are coming right at long last. You'll be pleased to hear that, no doubt. Too bad you don't like brandy. It's better to drink with somebody."

Just at that moment, there was a knock at the door, which then opened before I could get to it. It was Greg.

"Jill asked me to come over to see if you're all right."

"Why wouldn't I be all right?"

"I don't know. But we were expecting you an hour ago."

"Shit!" I had forgotten completely. I was supposed to be spending the next two days with Greg and Jill. "Shit! I'm sorry Greg. Give me five minutes to pack a few things. Shit!"

"Take your time. There's no agenda tonight."

I could feel the cold, free-floating anger coming back, and I sat down again and took another sip of the brandy. The best remedy against that dreadful, alien anger, I had found, was to think general thoughts about the mill and the people who work in it. By the time I had finished my brandy, equilibrium was being restored.

The two days with Jill and Greg were like an emotional whirlpool bath. By the end of Christmas Day, I felt more relaxed than I had since all this crap started. I came back home each of the two days, fed Max, and spent an hour or so fussing him. I thought it would be a letdown to return home on Boxing Day evening, but Jill had closed that off by insisting that I stay over and go home on the morning of December 27. I didn't even try to object. The warm weather continued to hold, and we had the last soak of the year on Boxing Day evening in their hot tub.

Then, it was back to a regular routine at the mill, although this was overlain by the run-up to our New Year's Eve bash.

On the morning of December 28, I went to get the mail, at about eleven thirty, as usual. There wasn't much mail, all advertising by the look of it. I had expected none at all. I carried home the small bundle of flyers, since there was work to be done responding to items on the mill's website and it was easiest to do that from home. When I finally turned to the little pile of junk mail that afternoon I found, among the five or six items of advertising, one plain white envelope, postmarked Montreal, addressed to me in typescript, and bearing no return address. Inside, there was a small clipping, taken from *The Philadelphia Inquirer*, judging from the byline. The page header giving the date hadn't been included, there were no annotations on the clipping, and no accompanying letter or note. The clipping read:

> *Police revealed today that the body of a local businessman was found yesterday in his home. Mr. Gale Burns, a noted collector of antiquities and a dealer in real estate, had been shot once in the head. No note was found and there was no weapon at the scene. Police are treating it as a homicide. When pressed, the police spokesman, Sergeant James Christie, said that police had no suspects at present. Another police spokesman, who wished not to be identified, stated later that it looked like a professional hit.*
>
> *Mr. Burns was fifty-three years old. He was divorced with no children. His name has been in and out of the news the past years because of real estate deals which many people criticized and were the subject of political discussion and some police interest, but no charges were ever brought against him.*

Immediately, I was in turmoil. I knew what had happened, and I should have felt relief, but my hands were shaking. I was neither glad nor sorry that he was dead, but this had made it all come rushing back, in all its inky, suffocating blackness. Max leaned against my leg and looked up at me. I picked him up and we walked around the room while he started a soft purr. I began to feel better. *Just hold on*, I told myself. *It will go away. Well, most of it will go away.*

That afternoon, I was back at the mill. Graham and I had a lot of work to do, and the sacks of flour were piling up satisfactorily. Six customers came in to pick up their orders, the coffee shop hummed, and Michael was busy in the kitchen getting ready for a party of sixteen people that evening in the restaurant, an event that had been booked weeks previously by a local family. By five thirty, Graham and I had finished for the day, and

I went to check whether Michael needed any help with the meals for the dinner party. Michael had everything in hand. He showed me the menu, indicated where he was with everything, then kicked me out of his kitchen.

That night, the rabbit nightmare returned:

I was in a field. The hay had been cut and was lying in rows. I was anxious, looking for my keys. I had a pitchfork, and I shifted small piles of hay around, saying repeatedly, as though it were a mantra, "Where are my keys? Where are my keys?" Then I saw the young rabbit. It had the charming but distorted characteristics of baby animals, in this case huge eyes, large feet, short ears, and a head that was disproportionately large compared to its body. I knew I should be thinking how appealing it was, but I just asked it, "Where are my keys?"

I realized that it was terrified, frozen, afraid to move, but I became irritated, then enraged that it wouldn't tell me where my keys were. I stuck it with the pitchfork, the prongs going through it and deep into the soil. It didn't move, and then I was instantly aware that the rabbit wasn't afraid. It had come to help me. One of its hind legs began to twitch. I asked it again, "Where are my keys?"

The fur began to disappear from its face. The ears receded. The eyes moved slowly around until they were both at the front of its head. The face widened and flattened. The pitchfork began to vibrate. The rabbit was struggling and it was strong. For some reason, I suddenly realized that I was wearing my rain gear, including my rain hat. It began to rain, light at first, then heavier, and then coming down in streams, gobs, surges. The rain ran into my eyes, and I had to wipe them continually to be able to see. It ran down my neck and into the front of my shirt. I looked again at the rabbit. It now had a chin and there was hair. I thought I recognized it, then suddenly I did recognize it. It was Stuart. I looked at my hands. Water was running off them in streams, but the rain wasn't falling. It wasn't coming down. It was coming up at me. I knew at once that it wasn't rain, wasn't water.

It was blood. And it was coming from the ra-, Stu-, "Where are my—"

Forty-seven

I awoke bathed in sweat. Max was crouched on the bed uttering a low growl. I jumped up, ran to the bathroom, and was painfully sick.

As happened the two previous times when I had been visited by the rabbit nightmare, I paced, trying to settle down. I drank a lot of water. I took several sleeping tablets. Eventually I fell into a deep sleep. When I awoke early the next morning, I was very refreshed. Max was sitting on the pillow next to my head, looking at me. I remembered the dream, but the recollection didn't raise fear, or anxiety.

There was nobody else at the mill when I arrived, and I set to work immediately. What needed to be done was clear, Graham arrived a bit later, and the day passed quickly. I was neither depressed nor elated, just rather flat, but things gradually began looking better, in some way, in the afternoon.

Graham and I finished bagging a large amount of flour, and we were able to wrap up early. The way Graham kept looking at me, he seemed convinced I was working like someone obsessed, and when we completed the day's milling, he said he was going to clean the equipment thoroughly and do some maintenance, but declined my offer of assistance with a smile.

I joined Michael and Karen, who were working on the arrangements for New Year's Eve, and my mood improved increasingly. Michael was fired up about his menu, and when he offered me trial portions of his dishes, I was impressed at how good they were. Michael was becoming an increasingly competent chef, and he now had a good feel for which gastronomic risks had promise and were worth running, and which he should avoid.

Karen was looking after the physical arrangements for the New Year's Eve romp. On the face of it, this wasn't a serious logistical challenge, because apart from the four of us there would be only twelve guests in all, but she had brought a lot of imagination to the task, if the custom napkins and lighting decorations were anything to go by, and I knew that this and her attention to detail would pay off handsomely. Greg had promised to handle the music, and past experience indicated that he would come up with something special.

Work was winding down in the mill. Graham and I finished the last of the milling for the year by noon on December 29. The next day and a half we spent cleaning and maintaining all the equipment. By the morning of December 31, the spirit of the day was upon everyone. Greg came by to do a last test of the music, and I treated them all to a lunch I had prepared surreptitiously. My mood and feeling of well-being had improved greatly over the past few days.

By late afternoon, the decorations were finished, and Karen had completed her checklist of preparations. What she had done was nothing short of fantastic. There were balloons and streamers. There were groups of assorted candles. On each table there were large, elaborate, and attractive bracelets woven from wavy strips of various colours of light construction paper, and mock wigs made from ringlets of crepe paper tied to crowns of braided coloured string in which were embedded tiny flashing lights, the crowns to be set on the guests' heads.

Four of the dishes Michael had chosen were prepared in advance, giving them time to blend and infuse, and he was now putting together the elements of the remaining dishes. Michael and I had collaborated on the breads and the wines. The breads were on their first rising and would be baked late in the afternoon. The white wines and dessert wines sat moodily in their cooler; the reds huddled impatiently in racks in a cool corner of the restaurant.

Greg put on his afternoon playlist. I walked around, listening to the sounds of competent people doing their jobs. I drifted through the kitchen. It was spotless. Michael smiled and winked at me, as if to say "we'll knock their socks off". From elsewhere in the mill, there were faint sounds of Graham doing some final clean-up work. I ran my hand over the exposed oak beams, cool limestone walls, and softly glowing inlaid bricks. The mill and I were reconnecting.

The afternoon held one surprise, which was delivered by Karen and Graham, who approached me in what was clearly delegation mode.

"I hope you won't mind", Karen began, "but Graham and I plan to spend the night here in the mill after the party finishes."

My look must have signalled what had flashed across my mind, because Karen flushed and said, "That came out completely wrong! What I mean is, we both drive in and we'd prefer not to be teetotal so we've set up camp beds at opposite ends of the meeting room upstairs. We should have asked you first. Actually, this is linked to a business idea we've had."

"Karen, I have no problem at all with you spending the night here. Very sensible, in fact."

Before I could respond to the second part of her statement, Karen said, "Good. Thank you. Now isn't the time to discuss new business ideas, so we've worked it out in some detail and want you to take a look at it. Whenever you have time." And she handed me a folder containing about eight typewritten pages stapled together. Opening the folder, I read on the title page *Proposal for Greenvale Mill Bed and Breakfast*. Flipping quickly through the pages, I noticed that it was all neatly broken down in elements of cost and income.

I looked at them both. "I'm intrigued. Can I wait until tomorrow to look it over?"

They smiled in what seemed relief, probably because I hadn't frowned, or hesitated, or otherwise signalled that the thing looked doubtful.

"That's fine", they said, and went back to what they had been doing.

Just before five o'clock, Michael and I pulled the breads from the ovens, and set them on racks to cool. We had prepared sticks of French bread on a different schedule so that they would be coming out of the ovens at seven, in order that the place would be filled by the intoxicating smell of freshly baked bread just as the guests were arriving. At five o'clock, we all left to get dressed for the evening, except Michael who carried on in the kitchen and had brought a change of clothes with him that morning. We would be back by six thirty, in time to receive the guests who were due at about seven. I returned at six, and began setting out the wine we would drink with our appetizers, which Michael was busy laying out on the counter and on two tables at one side of the room.

That evening was a balm for any troubled soul.

The entertainment was entirely self-generated, tapping into a well-primed spring of social creativity, and without any of the dreadful forced jollity that is too often the uninvited guest who takes over on New Year's Eve.

The party attire that adorned the guests that evening was, by turns and in some cases all at once, colourful, arresting, elegant, dramatic, and insouciant. Monty and his wife, Marjorie, arrived first, and they had chosen the usual relaxed but slightly unorthodox garments that were by now their trademark. Mrs. Williamson entered in a blaze of red, white, and blue: navy pants suit, white tailored blouse, and matching silk neck scarf, hair ribbon, handbag, and low-heeled shoes, all vibrant red. Jill and Greg sported complementary but unapologetically brilliant primary colours. Henry Newhouse had booked himself into a local motel for the night, and arrived from there by taxi wearing a stylishly severe suit of Delft blues and creams that every woman in the place had to touch and admire. Inspector Raymond apologized at not being able to spend more than an hour, but turned up in an elegant grey suit. Even before the full complement of guests had appeared, discussion and laughter was filling the room.

Karen and Michael steered me firmly away from the role of purveyor of wine, appetizers, and first round of breads, saying they had it all under control and that my job was to mingle. So, I worked my way around the room. Inspector Raymond and I had a brief conversation that avoided everything to do with the law and its breaking and enforcement. There was a companionable few minutes standing next to Jasper, but we didn't do much talking since that wasn't Jasper's thing. Monty spent twenty minutes talking excitedly about his most recent enthusiasm. Lonny was in top form and gabbed away happily. I conversed with several local residents, who had retired here within the past six months and wondered why they hadn't done so years ago, and two genuine locals who seemed to have an unquenchable thirst for lore about the mill. I probably shared more time that evening with Mrs. Williamson than with anyone else, and I started off by asking her how things were going in the library. She gave me a thumbnail summary, but then said she wanted to talk about how things were going in the mill. I began to answer, but she held up a hand.

Through a half-smile she said, "Richard. Do you think you could bring yourself to call me Janet? I've had that name quite a while, and I assure you that it works." I assented in surprise and pleasure, and our conversation then resumed on a relaxed plane.

Greg's music was perfect, as usual. There was almost every type, apart from hurtin' country music and heavy metal. At one point, the tone of the general conversation changed suddenly, and when I looked around to see why, I noticed that Jill and Greg, both accomplished ballroom dancers, were gliding flamboyantly to *The Skater's Waltz*. There was a ripple of applause. They broke off well before the music finished, both to retrieve wine glasses, and Greg plucked his glass from the counter near where I stood talking to Karen, who was flushed and animated by the many compliments she had received on the staging for this bash. Before Greg had even finished his first sip, Karen put down her glass, took Greg by the arm, and asked in a forthright way that clearly was not interested in refusal, "Can you teach me that?"

Greg quickly put down his glass, led Karen out onto the clear space of floor, and as he talked continuously into her ear, they began first a stylized walk, then some careful but rather stilted stepping, then a bit of bounce and glide was added, and within a few minutes the two of them were swooping across the floor. It was a delight to watch. Karen glowed, and it needed far more than just alcohol to account for the brilliant sparkle in her eyes. Not to be outdone, Jill set off like a torpedo in search of a target, and she homed in on Henry Newhouse. He demurred initially, but then agreed, and to Jill's evident pleasure they immediately moved into a graceful circuit of the room.

The strains of *The Skater's Waltz* concluded, but before the next piece of music began, a loud gong sounded, and Graham and Michael were wheeling the main courses out of the kitchen on trolleys, and placing the half-dozen large casserole dishes and trays of vegetables into warming pans on the counter. Michael clapped his hands, told everyone it was self-serve, described each of the dishes, and asked Janet and me to start things off. Seating was pre-arranged, names having been written on cards in a calligraphic hand, and the buzz of conversation was soon accompanied by the sounds of cutlery on plates. A trolley of fresh wine glasses had been wheeled in from a corner of the room, and Michael and Karen made the rounds doing initial pours, after which a bottle each of red and white was left on every table. While Janet went back for seconds, having been too stingy with herself the first time round, I took the opportunity to scan the room. The only thought that came to mind, and it popped in unbidden, was that I had changed my life completely compared to just a few years ago when I was still working full time and had no conscious intention of living in the country. But I had moved from a large city to a small village, where I had a new home, one that I loved greatly. I had acquired a new set of friends and acquaintances. And since retiring (less than six months ago!), I had a new business that consumed me but handed back far more. And this mill was the icon that reflected all those changes. That transformation, and its positive impact on my life, was beyond anything I could have imagined. My scan brought me to where Greg was sitting, we made eye contact, and he mouthed a silent "*Perfetto!*"

Janet leaned over to me at one point and said, "This reminds me so much of the big opening night." I must have stopped whatever I had been doing or saying rather abruptly, because she looked at me and asked, a hint of concern showing, "Did I say something wrong?"

"No. No. It just, I just, well, it seems so long ago now but it was only a few weeks, and I...I...I find it hard to take in."

There was a barrier, between now and then. *Now* was recovery, but I realized, suddenly and again, that my 'now' still floated on heaving troubled waters, home to monsters. I was still clinging to a small raft of sanity, and the mill itself was a Janus image at the centre of it all. I brushed these thoughts away as best I could.

This had caused something of a social hiccough, and I wasn't sure how to get past it, but just at that point, Michael stuck his head between us, clearly euphoric that the whole gastronomic thing had gone well, and asked "Everything all right? Enough food? More wine?"

"Michael", I said, "this is utterly fantastic", to which Janet added "Sublime, Michael. Sublime. I think we both could use another good chug of red wine", and without missing a beat, Michael filled our glasses.

I raised my glass to Janet, "Here's to competent young people!"

She responded, "Here's to competent young people of all ages!"

The momentum of the evening showed no signs of dissipating, and before anyone knew it the pop of a champagne cork had everyone glancing at their watches.

We had the champagne poured approximately on time, but nobody was worried about a few seconds or even a few minutes. When we were all ready, Happy-New-Year wishes were exchanged round the room. I had the feeling of being singled out for particular attention by Henry, Monty, Greg, and then by Jill and Janet, each of whom spent more time than was really warranted for Happy-New-Year wishes. It was bittersweet for me, and I wanted to wish Happy New Year to absent friends, but that made no sense really, and would have cast a dreadful pall over everything. Besides, even though we all knew this would wrap up within the next hour or so, the gathering had acquired a second wind, something to be savoured, and Greg's after-midnight playlist was a catalyst that helped power that particular reaction.

Several slightly tipsy chirps of surprise turned all heads toward the entrance to the kitchen. Michael had just emerged bearing a large tray of goodies that he and I had prepared. I had asked him just to place them on the counter and wait. We hadn't long to wait.

"Oh my God!"

The expression was so vehement, so unforced, and so full of surprise, that the conversation all but stopped.

"It's *poffertjes*! You've made *poffertjes*!" Henry turned to Jill, who was standing beside him at that point, and repeated, "They've made *poffertjes*!"

Michael handed Janet, Jill, Greg, and me a napkin each, and the intention was that we would lead the way, but I passed my napkin to Henry and asked him if he would try the first one. He did, and at the first bite, he closed his eyes and beamed. I nodded to Jill and Janet, indicating they should go next. Within a minute, Henry was gesticulating and trying to explain to three women, past a mouthful of sugared delicacy, what it was they were eating.

Janet joined me as the crowd had followed Henry who was now in a deep discussion with Michael. "Did Michael know how to make these?"

"He did after I showed him", I answered, also past a half-mouthful.

"Nice touch", she said, placing her hand momentarily on my arm, "moving Henry from being something of an outsider to the centre of attention."

"Not really. Henry drew attention the moment he walked in, and I haven't seen him spending a lot of time being a wallflower."

"Hmm", she said, and tilted her head doubtfully.

At quarter to one, Monty announced that he and Marjorie were leaving, and at that point the fourth movement of our New Year symphony began drawing to its close. Michael, who had drunk very little during the evening, and had brought his car, insisted on dropping Henry at his motel. There were lots of warm thank yous, and by ten past one, there were just six of us left. Janet had found her handbag and gone off to the loo; Jill and Greg had pulled on jackets and I accompanied them to the door. Graham and Karen were finishing cleanup in the kitchen, and would then no doubt head upstairs and collapse onto their camp beds. When Janet returned, I was the only one in the room.

"Well! You look like the victor, standing alone in the field."

"I'd say that we all won. Can I walk you home?" I asked, and the offer was accepted without hesitation.

We pulled on our jackets and stepped out into a still night. The temperature was dropping, and would drop further, a sky generously laced by stars being a good indication of that. But it was not yet below freezing, and was, in fact, a beautiful evening.

Somewhere in the distance, two cats wailed. I stopped.

"What is it?" Janet asked.

"I just realized that I didn't feed Max before I came out. Do you mind if we drop in at my place so I can do that now?" The words were scarcely out of my mouth when I realized how this might be interpreted as a ridiculously transparent move. But I just gritted my teeth inwardly and decided to ignore it.

"No, I don't mind at all. Let's go and feed Max."

I never know what to expect of Max when his usual routine is interrupted. He might have been waiting accusingly at the door. He might have been off sulking in another room. He might have been lying on the kitchen counter, where he knows he is never to be, in protest. But, there he was, sitting in patrician splendour, the picture of feline tidiness, on the back of the sofa, and his tail rose in greeting as I came through the door.

"Hello, Max!" Janet said, walking directly over to him. The shameless little bugger rubbed his cheek against her hand—the hand of a complete stranger—and he started to purr. I went over to the kitchen to get his food.

"Why Max? Is he named after somebody?"

"It's really Maxwell", and by now Max was rubbing against my legs as I prepared his food.

"Is that Maxwell as in James Clerk?" Janet asked.

"Yes", I said in some surprise. "It's definitely not Maxwell as in silver hammer. You're well informed!"

"I run a library. I have to be."

I put Max's food down, moved to put the knife into the sink, and asked, "Can I offer you coffee? Brandy? Something else?" I turned to see what her answer would be and noted that she had taken off her jacket and was looking around the room with great interest. She opted for brandy, I shed my jacket as well, and moved to the cabinet to pour us two. When I turned back holding the two snifters, Janet was looking at the floor-to-ceiling bookcases next to my desk.

"Heavy on technical books", she observed.

"Yes, a collection that goes back through a career of thirty years."

"Doesn't retirement make a difference?" Janet asked, continuing to peruse.

"Intellectually, no. I loved my work. I've always enjoyed physics, chemistry, math, and engineering. And I do still do some real work. Did quite a bit as part of the job of getting the mill up and running. Those books are a real part of me. The rest of them, the non-technical books, are in the library."

I had said the magic word.

"Library?"

"Yes. I'll show you."

"Could I have the full tour?" Janet asked showing a level of enthusiasm that I hadn't expected. My surprise at her interest must have shown.

She walked over toward me, accepted her brandy, we raised glasses, and sipped. She looked at the glass appraisingly. "Very nice." And then, after a short pause, she said, "I guess you don't know."

"Don't know what?"

Janet's smile was one of amusement at what she was evidently about to share. "Practically everyone in this village is dying to know what the inside of your house looks like. The only people who reportedly have seen it are Monty and Greg, and they're not talking."

My puzzlement only increased Janet's amusement. "But, if they want to see it", I said, "all they need to do is ask."

"Ah, yes. But there's another logic at work here: the logic of idle chatter. Nothing kills gossip faster than facts, and if you gave some of the people in Greenvale the facts, they'd feel permanently cheated out of a staple of daily gossip. It's harmless. But you, Dr. Gould, are the object of intense curiosity, whether you know it or not."

I just stood there speechless for a moment. "I'm stunned!" was all I could manage.

"You shouldn't be, Richard. Just look at what they see. Here you are, an educated and successful urbanite, who blows into a little hick town without warning, history, or connections, converts a ruin into one of the two most desirable homes in the village, retrieves a tumbledown old mill from the trash heap and turns it into a village centrepiece and meeting ground, starts a new and successful business, and charms just about every bird out of every tree in the process."

Here, I could only laugh. "You make it sound as though I walk on water for morning exercise. What's the other one?"

"The other what?"

"The other most desirable home."

"Oh! Greg Blackett's."

Another sip of brandy, and as I moved to sit down on the sofa Janet slid into place beside me.

"But your place is nice, I assume", I said, although it came out sounding like an objection.

"Yes, it's okay, and it is nice. But it's not like this, Richard", she said, looking around the room. "For Heaven's sake! This place is fantastic, even more so since everyone assumed that its only future was the bulldozer. How about a tour?"

"Certainly", I said rising, "but it's getting late. Shouldn't I be taking you home?"

Janet looked at me evenly for a moment. "Well, it's either your place or my place."

This one stopped me. I realized again that I had been spending all my effort trying to stay on my small raft of sanity, without seeing that there was someone else who wanted to help. All I had to do was to take the offered hand. So, it wasn't a penny that dropped, but a ten-ton I-beam. Finally, I had grasped where all this could go, and in my single-minded focus I had drifted past a number of clear signals.

I ran a hand through my hair in mixed embarrassment and exasperation at myself.

"You can see, quite clearly", I began, "that whatever expertise I might have had at one time in this area, is now just a solid block of rust."

Janet laughed in genuine amusement. "I can hardly claim that my own walking stick is notched beyond recognition. A tour?"

"Just so that we know where we—" I began.

"Indeed. Just so that we know where we stand, I don't need a meal ticket or a husband. Been there, done that. I just want to get to know an intriguing guy a little better."

I stood, took a large gulp of brandy, and began.

"Mrs. Williamson. Welcome to my home. It was walking dead when I obtained it, a true handyman's dream, but now, as you see, a two-storey heritage house, boasting a basement containing sauna and workshop, main floor that includes living, slash dining, slash study area, library, full bathroom and small guest room, and a second floor having two bedrooms, full bathroom, and second study, slash workroom. Large outdoor back patio and barbecue, slash herb garden, area all rendered private by an earthen berm and red currant hedge. Vegetable garden able to feed six people for a full season. Delightful front patio with rock garden. Carport and rainwater collection area. This way please to the library."

In contrast to my adolescent fumbling to that point, the tour was relaxed and leisurely. There was a good deal of critical examination and approving nods. Janet asked many questions, about the history of the place, about the internal layout of the house before I started, about where I got the ideas I incorporated into the renovation, about the colour scheme, about the woods I had used. I switched on the outdoor lighting so that we could tour the back patio, despite the chill. The library underwent a close professional inspection, and did not come up wanting, the sections on history, philosophy, and ancient Greek literature causing noticeable eyebrow activity. The kitchen layout, and the cooking utensils and capacious storage received particular mention. The oak stairway and bannister drew a long appreciative silence.

The tour ended in the bedroom at two thirty. By then, speech had become an irrelevant encumbrance. We undressed each other in something resembling a silent, gentle, slow-motion dream, slipped into bed, and became intimate friends.

Just before the endorphins arrived, I muttered, "and so we begin a new year", but Janet was already on the way to Morningtown.

I awoke early, and the thought that sat already in my mind had to do with beginnings. Looking out through the window, there was nothing that could possibly be mistaken for a sultan's turret, and the early dawn was hardly a noose of light, but the first streaks of pink and purple nevertheless had set the night's grey clouds into full retreat.

I climbed out of bed quietly, pulled on my robe, and went downstairs. Max was waiting to be greeted and fed, and I did both those, before pulling bread, eggs, bacon, and a few other items from the fridge. I measured out the coffee and got it going. Walking through to the mud room, I grabbed a bag of seed, stepped outside into a cold and exhilarating day, and filled the bird feeder sitting at the top of a squirrel-proof pole that was sunk into the ground at the edge of the back patio. Already, the morning was getting into its stride, and everything was bejewelled by frost. Back in the living room, a quick check on my laptop revealed one email, from Monty, thanking me for another great party. I closed the laptop just as a creak indicated my guest was moving upstairs.

All I could think of was that the world felt different.

Back in the kitchen, I looked up from pouring orange juice in time to see Janet coming down the stairs. She had donned the guest robe, and it looked a lot better on her than on St-, but I stopped that thought short.

"I hope you slept well", I said. "The coffee's almost ready. I can offer everything from just toast to a full blowout wmfff—." My list was cut short by a firmly planted, moist kiss.

"Good morning", Janet said. "Yes, I slept very well, and I'm ready for a substantial breakfast despite having pigged out last night. Shower first. May I use the bathroom on this floor?"

"Please! The door on the left over there."

Janet retrieved her handbag, disappeared into the bathroom, and I headed upstairs to have my shower.

Twenty minutes later I was back downstairs wearing my usual fatigues of jeans and cotton shirt. Five minutes after that, Janet emerged, also in jeans and a cream cotton top. *The largish handbag—of course! Successful urbanite, indeed! More like slow, backwards yokel!*

Breakfast took two hours. I drove Janet home, and returned to sit and think about what had just happened. Certainly, things had changed. Equally certainly, no abrupt personal adjustments were required. But the notions "platonic" and "bedroom" weren't a natural pairing for me. *Just take it one step at a time.* There were two people's outlooks to account for, and we would just have to see where this might lead.

Forty-eight

Winter, the real winter, arrived at the end of the first week in January, when we acquired half a metre of snow in four days. I quite welcomed the outward and visible change of season.

Things moved forward in the mill. The demand for our flour was flourishing, and I guessed that if things continued on the present trend we would be close to our maximum production capability by summer, by which point a decision would need to be taken on whether to turn away new business or install additional capacity. It all had to be worked out in detail, but we were in good financial shape, and I suspected which way it would end up going.

I had several meetings with Karen and Graham on their proposal. It was mature, innovative, and exciting, and we set a schedule for them to go ahead with it, because it would be their project.

Janet and I had continued to see each other, and our friendship deepened. She learned of my four-year marriage to Alice that was ended by a drunk driver. I learned about her fifteen-year stormy marriage to Eugene that was ended by abuse. I had a strong sense that Janet had divined my state of no-man's land residence since Alice's death, that there had been other potential partners—Michelle, Amanda, Teresa, and particularly Sarah— who I ultimately had turned away, but it was some time before I was able to discuss with her my relatively recent final farewell to Alice, the image of her as the eternal thirty-two-year-old that had appeared before me within the past three months, then shimmered and vanished one last time.

The two earth-shakers arrived within two weeks of each other in early March.

I took a call on a Thursday morning from Ivan Filmore, Buck's brother. He had been for a tour of the mill in January, but then he had slipped from my mind.

"Ivan! Good morning! Nice to hear from you. What can I do for you?"

Without much preamble, Ivan asked if I had ever heard of something called The New Start Foundation. I said no, and asked why.

"I've been contacted by them. They want me to act as administrator of a fund for vocational training to be named for Buck. It will be a million dollars, the tax already paid if the offer is accepted. I've done what checking I can. They appear to be based in the Cayman Islands, they have a website, and look legitimate, but I wanted to see whether you knew anything about this."

"No, I don't", I said, controlling my voice carefully. "What do you think? Are you going to accept? And are there any conditions applied?"

"There are conditions, at least according to the letter I received, but they look pretty standard. I've found a lawyer who has experience in these things, and if he says go ahead, I'll go ahead."

"How about your parents? Do they know about this yet?"

"No. Not yet. I won't tell them until it's clear that this is on the level and we have a path forward. But I wanted to speak to you first."

"Can you keep me up to date?" I asked.

"Certainly."

We talked about unimportant things, and Ivan said he would get back to me as soon as he knew something more definite.

I hung up and pondered for a long time what I had just heard.

A little more than a week later, Janet called and asked if I could drop by the library at lunchtime. I did, and she handed me a letter without comment. The letterhead was *The New Start Foundation*, and it took everything in me to act normally. A quarter million dollars was being offered on a one-time tax-paid basis to support the Greenvale Library, on the conditions that the capital and interest were to be used exclusively by the Greenvale Library, that none of the money was to be used for capital expenditures (excluding purchases of books, CDs, DVDs, and other items listed, and of computers intended for public or administrative use in the library), and specifically that the fund was to be managed by an administrator independent of the Greenvale municipality and of any other municipality.

"Wow!" I said softly.

"Yes", Janet agreed. "Double wow! Do you have any idea what I could accomplish using the interest from a quarter million dollars? But is this legitimate?"

"I know a lawyer in Toronto who deals with foundations. I could ask her."

"Please do."

I went immediately back home to think. There was no doubt in my mind just what had happened here, what was going on. Burns was dead, and I was all but certain that it was his own money that had paid for the hit on him. There should have been a sense of justice in this, that the world was somehow a better place, but all I had was an unpleasant metallic taste in my mouth and an odd sense of letdown, of deflation, of strange emptiness. On the other hand, I wanted to feel that, somehow, some good would come out of the whole mindless tragedy of the deaths of Buck and Stuart. There were two pieces of good that I could see here, and I could only hope that there were many more that I was unaware of. There was also no doubt in my mind that investigation would determine The New Start Foundation to be solid and above reproach, and that the offers would end up being accepted by Ivan Filmore and by the Greenvale Library. My personal knowledge of things that might be related was purely anecdotal and impossible to prove, but that would all remain an absolute secret. Up to now I had been burdened by a frightful albatross. Steve had lifted that burden, and now I could move on.

The month of March advanced. The sun moved up higher in the sky. The snow melted, slowly at first, then picking up speed. The first signs of spring appeared.

At the end of March, I had visited Stuart's gravesite for the first time since his ashes had been scattered there, but I had not been present at that earlier occasion—another potent source of guilt for me. I was a mess within five minutes. But the grief was the first real release, the first stage of a genuine if reluctant farewell.

April brought the indisputable true signs of spring: tufts of grass greening between patches of snow, the tips of crocuses and daffodils harnessing life's silent power to thrust aside a senescent winter, the orange-green tint creeping outward over willow branches, the robin's familiar warble.

As soon as we were able, and before it really made much sense, we sat out on Jasper's patio at The Fox. It was a brilliant sunny Saturday, the temperature was just a cool fourteen degrees Celsius, there were still remnants of snowbanks at the edges of the patio, but rich sunlight flooded the moist, blue-tinged air in the valley below, the river was in flood and winked and leapt in delight at the return of spring, and I sat over lunch with Monty and Henry. Although outwardly I was what one might call "healed", I knew that my experience in Germany had marked me permanently, but more importantly that the unfinished business lying behind recent events was casting a pall over everything. A mint condition copy of a book, previously believed not to exist, had fired Burns's avarice, and his unscrupulous moves to acquire it had cost me my best friend. The possibility of a deeper mystery behind that book, and perhaps the thing that had really driven Burns, remained locked away, and I knew, even though I was unprepared to admit it, that I needed to come to terms with all that. Just a few short months ago, that mystery was intriguing, exciting. Now it was oppressive, suffocating, but still demanding, imperiously, to be resolved. As my mental stability improved, the more I tried to deny, to suppress, the need to resolve this mystery, to move it permanently out of my life, the more implacable it became.

But what I was really recovering from, I realized slowly over a period of weeks, what would leave wounds that could never really close, make me a different person, was the moral dimension of what had happened. I had had a choice to make: trust in the mechanics of the police and the courts to deal with Burns, or go rogue and do the job myself. My choice had been the latter, and it was clear that I had done this mostly subconsciously. But the path I had selected meant that I had become a shadowy murderer, and the financial largesse that Steve had scooped out of the shell remaining of Burns's life was blood money. I had to live with this. I also had to trust my own judgment that following the other path, while more virtuous, would have left the future strewn in mortal hazard. There was no clear win in either direction. And I had to come to terms with this on my own. None of it could be discussed with anybody. Not with anybody. Ever.

An Uncompromising Place

Two days earlier, I had visited Henry in Belleville, ostensibly to help him prepare his vegetable garden, which we actually did do, and that in itself was an exercise in precision. But the real purpose of the visit, as I soon discovered, was to hear his proposal.

"Richard, I want you to come to Holland with me next month. I think you and I need to wrap up this catechism business."

Even the word chilled me to the core, but this was a sign that Henry was right, that I had to put it all definitively behind me.

"It's not something I look forward to, Henry."

"No", he replied, "but it's a loose end that will eventually entangle you again if you don't deal with it. It was chance that brought you into contact with that unspeakable asshole Burns, and events then forced you to be an active participant, but you won't be free of this business until you drive an olive stake through its heart."

He was right. I knew he was right. But still I had sat in indecision.

"I have good contacts, Richard. I know we can do this."

"I have no proof that what Burns was looking for even exists", I said by way of objection. "In fact, in hindsight I think that I was a gullible mug to fall for the idea at all. Imagine! A full collection of the original documents from all the editions of the *Heidelberg Catechism*! As ridiculous as it is improbable! I'm pretty sure now it's just wishful thinking that passed through rumour and became presumed and accepted fact. It's a pipe dream!"

Henry was shaking his head. "It's natural to try to bypass it all, to take the easy denial route." I made to object, but Henry raised a hand to forestall me. "In those times, and in those places, religion was the only solid refuge in people's lives. They took it seriously. To them, the idea of someone spending his life actually assembling such a collection would not be far-fetched at all. Okay, there is a chance that either it never did exist, or that now it never will be found. Perhaps there is nothing squirrelled away in Ladenburg, and although Heidelberg is indeed, or was, an academic city of many people's dreams, so is, and was, Leyden. After all, that man on the *James Goodwill* would be described now as a Dutchman, so if the speculation is true, the prize is at least as likely to be somewhere in Holland as it is to be somewhere in Germany. I don't doubt that you would shudder, just as I would, to think that a cultural treasure like that might disappear into a private collection. All the more reason why we, you and I, should set up a project to try to get to the bottom of all this, using the knowledge, quite probably unique, that you have acquired."

"What's the point, Henry? It's over. Burns is dead."

"No Richard! It's not over! Do you think that Burns was the last of his type out there? Do you think that others won't be drawn by the lure of something like this, speculative though it might be, that a possible prize of almost inestimable value won't fire their rapacious, pathological avarice? Do you think that there are not others who are possibly even less principled, even more determined, than Burns was? And surely you don't think that anyone, who might be able to stop it, should just stand by while one of the worst fucking scourges of civilization…"

Henry's vehemence shocked me, and I realized when he left his tirade unfinished that his mouth and chin were quivering in anger and outrage. I was about to try to bring the temperature down, but Henry abruptly carried on, once more under control.

"Besides, there are other, different but equally important matters to tackle."

"Such as?" I asked in some surprise.

"Have you been to Spinoza's house? Have you seen where Huygens and Erasmus and Leeuwenhoek lived? Have you been to Delft? To Leyden? Have you visited Nijmegen? And I must show you around my city, Utrecht."

"This sounds like it's going to be a month-long stint."

"Yes. And?"

"Surely your flat isn't that big—"

"Richard. I have many Dutch friends and colleagues. At any given time a handful of them are away, and I have standing offers to use a number of flats. Finding a place to stay is the smallest of the problems we would face."

"And what would be the biggest?" I asked, still trying to find some credible dodge.

"Fitting it all in. Look", he said, passing me a single sheet of paper. "Here's a reading list. The book by Arblaster is a good place to start. Most people know little or nothing about Dutch history. But you ought to. I guarantee that you will be hooked by page twenty."

I hesitated still.

"You're worried that you won't ever be able to bring things back to what they were. Am I right?"

"No. I'm not worried", I said. "I'm convinced of it. I used to derive great enjoyment just from the anticipation of visiting Germany, seeing Werner and Gudrun, doing all the things there that I've done now during visits that span more than twenty-five years. That's all gone."

"No, Richard, that's all still there. Those people and those places are still there. They haven't changed. You have. What you've got to do now is get to know all those things over again. If you don't do that, the only loser will be you, and being aware of your European knowledge, and your inherent ability to savour it, I can say that you would lose big time."

I had agreed to think about it.

Henry looked at me for a moment. "What prompted you to put so much weight on Ladenburg, I mean as a possible location for this collection? That matter of the modified Hölderlin poem was really a bit thin, as a solid clue."

"Ah, yes. Friedrich Hölderlin!" I said, more than a tinge of bitterness coming through. "My message from Friedrich! That's partly my point, Henry. I was blinded by, caught up by, the whole romantic notion. I didn't have the background, the historical and cultural context, to make a level-headed judgment, I let myself be played by circumstances. Stupid. Puerile. Infantile."

I hesitated for a long time; Henry waited patiently for me to go on.

"Christoph Sauer was born in Ladenburg. And it appears that the man who became known as Mason was born and lived somewhere near Ladenburg. The enticing proximity of these things, remote connections that all this invited, the possible real connections, the presumed connections—the connections that I myself made, too willingly, too uncritically—well, they were just, just, too good to be true." I shook my head, and let my arm fall onto the table in frustration and regret. I really was not telling Henry the full story, although deep down I think he himself had the same inkling that I did. Robert Bine was probably Robert Bein originally, and his education had provided him access to German culture and literature. He would certainly have been well-versed in Goethe and Schiller, probably knew of Novalis and at least might have been aware of Hölderlin as a major romantic German poet, might have known that Hölderlin was the starting point for other German thinkers. Bine was a friend to the last to Carl Mason, and I had come to suspect that from Mason's confidences Bine knew that two books were in the altar in the little Belleville church, that he had been entreated by Mason to see that they were safeguarded into the future, that it was Bine who had placed the doctored poem with them, that Bine had tarred the box against damage over an unknown time, and that his hints about Ladenburg were a deliberate false scent. Mason had most likely confided in Bine near the end, had made him aware of all that Mason had known, that if the "big prize" existed at all, it was concealed elsewhere.

Henry also asked me about the whole confusing Boersma-Ambrose business. I explained to him what I thought had happened, even though much of it was speculative.

"I think that Burns came across some document that alerted him to the Boersma connection that existed back in 1727. When the business of the Ambroses and the books became clear to him, I think he deliberately clouded things by planting the seed with the Ambroses that someone called Boersma was a major but shadowy player, and he let them make the assumption that this Boersma was some sort of modern-day descendent of the guy from 1727. Burns had a very subtle mind, and he played Ambrose as though he were a gypsy fiddle. But, Burns wasn't any sort of contemplative intellectual. He was well aware of the value of information, but information was interesting to him only if it was of use in one of his projects. I think that masquerading as "Smith", or more likely having someone in Holland do that for him, he played up the historical connection, the value of rarity, in the minds of the Ambroses. He might even have gone as far as nudging them to accept a link back to Rodolphus Agricola, pandering to whatever historical vanity they might have had. In any case, I'm pretty sure that the fact of the names Ambrose and Boersma coincidentally having the same letters was not lost on Burns. He just spun a nice little web."

Henry was nodding. I could sense from his expression that he was detecting interesting historical threads, but also that he was evaluating things here and now.

"I can see how it would hang together as an enticing little tale for some people, like the Ambroses, even if I wouldn't buy it. I have to say, Richard, that you have a historian's mind."

There wasn't really a reply to that, and we just looked at each other, appraisingly. I knew that, at some point, soon, I would also discuss with him this Robert Bine business as well as the whole German connection. But in the present moment, it was clear to me that in his big-hearted empathy, Henry sensed my loss, disappointment, and disillusionment, understood that the basic thirst for knowledge had not been extinguished, and felt that the underlying hope and wonder were struggling to re-emerge.

After a long pause, Henry considered my judgment that I had made hopeless and amateurish miscalculations of the significance of the Hölderlin and Ladenburg connections. "You're being too hard on yourself, Richard. You've been through one hell of an ordeal."

Henry then added a final comment that I think probably tipped the scales for me, that ultimately was to set Henry and me off on a Dutch venture of personal rediscovery and renewal. He put an arm across my shoulders and said, "Historical detail can be very brutal, and the people who study it need to have a fine sense of realism, a solid feeling for time and place, an active empathy, a beady-eyed focus on evidence, and sometimes a compensating strong stomach. But the day that historians stop having at least some stars in their eyes, will be the day the lights go out."

A puff of breeze rolling up from the river brought me back to our lunch.

"I'm talking to you, you stone-deaf old adder!" Monty said to Henry.

"Look, you misguided old Falstaffian schemer. There's a priority for dealing with these matters, and I'm afraid that yours is at the very bottom of the proverbial Chestertonian Mendip mine."

I couldn't help it. I broke out laughing, and I kept on laughing uncontrollably. Wiping the tears from my eyes, I was able to say eventually, "Gentlemen! How good it is to be among sensitive and restrained friends! We're talking about who's going to drink what for the next round, for God's sake! I'll just go and buy us something." And I broke out laughing again as I rose to head for the bar.

When I returned carrying a tray and three pints, they were, once again, close and respectful colleagues, making notes on the draft outline of a paper they had decided an hour ago that they were going to write.

We chinked glasses. There were smiles all round.

After the beer was gone, we sat and looked at the scene in the valley. It looked much as it had the first time I saw it seven years earlier.

At length, Henry brought the palms of his hands down heavily on the table. "Time to go", he pronounced.

"Go where? To do what?" Monty asked querulously.

"First, just to walk and celebrate being alive on such a day as today."

"And then?" Monty prompted, a half-hearted but now good-humoured challenge still lurking in his voice.

"Second, Monty, to talk a bit more about history, something you and I know from a great height, but that Richard here has seen from the sharp end, at the level of a Jan Hus, or a Giordano Bruno. You and I can learn a lot from Richard. He knows far better than we do that history is a dangerous place, an uncompromising place."

"Second. Is there a third, Henry?" I asked.

"Most certainly", Henry said, stepping between us, and putting an arm over each of our shoulders.

"Third, let's go and make some bread, while the sun shines."